Appearances

Appearances

A Novel

by

Sondra Helene

SHE WRITES PRESS

Published 2019
Printed in the United States of America
ISBN: 978-1-63152-499-8 pbk.
ISBN: 978-1-63152-500-1 ebk.
Library of Congress Control Number: 2018961556

For information, address:
She Writes Press
1569 Solano Ave #546
Berkeley, CA 94707

She Writes Press is a division of SparkPoint Studio, LLC.

Book design by Stacey Aaronson

For my sister, with love.

Chapter One

_____

$\mathscr{B}$efore I receive the phone call that separates my life into before and after, I am out with my husband, Richard A. Freeman, at a fund-raiser in a swank suburb of Boston. It's for Pine Cliff College, where Richard is on the board: a small private school in the affluent suburb of Chestnut Hill, named for a stretch of trees that once ran from Dunster Street to Reservoir Lane. Richard, a Harvard Business School graduate with a career in private equity—which I google whenever I have to explain it—thrives on boards like this. It's in his blood to give back, especially to those without the financial means that my husband has worked his whole life to achieve.

Richard is six foot one and lean, with a full head of wavy hair the color of smoke. Tonight my husband's late-summer tan and the jade pocket square accenting his deep-set green eyes make him look ten years younger than fifty-nine. I am thirteen years his junior, five foot eight, with highlighted auburn hair that grazes my shoulders when I use a flatiron. Richard stands with perfect posture. Were we to embrace, his lips would meet the slope of my hairline. From all outside appearances, people say we belong together.

It's a warm and humid early September evening, the last month the trees are lush and green before setting off their autumn fireworks. The air is thick, and, even though I'm fresh from the shower, my thighs stick to the mint leather interior of Richard's Aston Martin. Richard pondered for years whether to buy this car. He considers himself a value guy. Even though he can afford it, for example, Richard would never think to charter a private plane. But he held a torch for this car for five years, driving thirty minutes to the dealership every few months to talk the salesman's ear off and take the Aston for a test-drive. Finally, our preteen daughter, Alexandra, convinced him to buy it. Using a cliché she must have heard somewhere but, at eleven, couldn't fully understand, Alexandra said, "Daddy, you're not getting any younger," and giggled.

Richard lowers the top, puts the AC on high, and fiddles with the radio until he finds WEEI 850 AM sports talk. We pull out of the garage and drive a few miles on Route 9 to the fund-raiser. Richard has been on Pine Cliff's board for the past four years and has helped this annual event to become a huge success. He likes to invite people he enjoys, who possess a sense of humor, with whom he can have what he calls a "solid conversation" about politics, sports, cigars, and world events. Richard doesn't waste time on gossip, on whoever is selling their home, filing for bankruptcy, or getting divorced—like some people we know.

During the ride, I'm quiet. I can't stop thinking about my sister, Elizabeth. She's been complaining about a pain in her hip from a pulled muscle during our workout weeks ago. When we met for coffee yesterday, she had trouble scaling the few steps into the café. Her pain worries me. But I haven't expressed my concern to Richard. He and I don't talk about Elizabeth anymore.

Tonight is Pine Cliff's largest fund-raiser of the year. The students from the culinary school will prepare and serve dinner; silent and live auctions will span the evening. The superstar hired auctioneer is a genius entertainer, jumping on chairs, using comedy to charm and disarm attendees out of their money, and all for a good cause. Last year, in 2002, the fund-raiser grossed half a million dollars. The goal this year is even greater. The proceeds will fund a new Student Success Center, a sorely needed campus hub.

In the Aston we follow an elegant, topiaried, figure-eight drive to park at the college's VIP entrance, where a valet takes our keys. "Cool car, sir," the student says, as other eighteen-year-olds clad in red valet jackets swarm.

"Careful, please," Richard says, and laughs, but I know he is serious.

Richard opens my door. With a gentleman's flair, he takes my hand. I gracefully step out in my Manolo heels and a black cocktail dress. Richard is wearing a charcoal Brioni suit with a crisp white shirt. We lock eyes before my husband kisses me on the lips and says, "Still beautiful." This is Richard with his most contagious confidence: about to perform his ideal self and our ideal marriage in public.

Our friends—Jeffrey and Jordana, Bob and Carol—arrive after us. Richard and I await them at the curb.

"Hey, Rich!" Jeffrey says, walking toward us with his model-thin, thirtysomething wife Jordana on his arm as the valet drives away in their Porsche. She's very sweet.

"Richie, baby!" Bob says from a couple of paces behind Jeff, waving frantically.

"Hi, Samantha," Carol says when they reach us, bathing me in the scent of her apricot perfume. Carol slopes her shoulders to give my arm a squeeze, towering above me in her four-inch platform stilettos embossed with rhinestones, like disco balls.

"Thanks so much for coming," Richard says, "I really appreciate it." He shakes the men's hands, hoping his friends will bid high once they go inside. Richard kisses each of the women chastely on the cheek, before saying, "This way," and leading us to the cocktails. With a smile fixed on my face, I follow the others, my heart sinking like the sun on the horizon. Years ago, I would have invited my sister and her husband, Jake, to join us at the event, but now the hostility between them and Richard makes it impossible. I brace myself for a night of trophy wives and garish perfume.

"Tasteful decorations," I say inside, to no one in particular. The gala committee has dimmed the lights and set elegant tables, transforming the drab college auditorium with floor-length tablecloths, fuchsia napkins, and dense centerpieces of French roses. As at any respectable fund-raiser, there must be at least five hundred people here.

Hors d'oeuvres are passed. Servers squeeze invisibly between us with silver trays of mouthwatering crab cakes, spicy shrimp on skewers, and adorable mini–lamb chops. Everything smells yummy, but I'm going to save my calories for dinner. My sister canceled our workout this morning so she could rest her sore hip. I decided it wouldn't kill me to miss a day. But no cardio this morning means I have to watch what I eat even more carefully tonight.

Richard and I stroll to the bar, where he orders two glasses of pinot grigio. Thank God they have pinot grigio, because I don't drink oaky Chardonnay, and I take pleasure in a couple of glasses of wine at these events. Richard stands tall, relaxing his shoulders down his back to swell his chest. Since we met, he's had a presence, a confidence like a force field that I imagine extends to me. My husband is powerful and smart, one of my definitions of sexy. While Richard and I stand coupled at the bar, a different sort of man approaches, short and wearing a red bow tie.

"Nice to see you, Mr. Freeman, *and* your lovely wife." The college president bows to me, then addresses my husband. "Pine Cliff certainly appreciates—relies—on your generosity. Let's hope we gross the most money yet."

"Our friends will bid high," Richard says. "I'll lean on them. This is the best fund-raiser in town," he says excitedly, adjusting his tie knot. "I only invited people who want to support the school."

"Mr. President," I say, "we look forward to this every year. Last year we won the ski trip to Aspen." The Pine Cliff president smiles and shakes our hands before moving on to greet more patrons. He's perfect for this job, affable and not overbearing.

Richard and I mingle, finding our guests at the silent-auction tables before a bay window overlooking the soccer field. Carol and I make small talk about our kids, dance classes, and gymnastics. Jordana, who has a nine-month-old, gushes about being a new mom. They are superficial friends whose company I enjoy, but I would never think of confiding my real troubles in them.

"Richard, what's new in the empire?" I overhear Bob, a real estate developer, ask.

"I closed on Boylston. Going to move my offices. Just have to file with the BRA now for the build-out."

"Location, location," Bob says, slapping Richard on the back. "You really know how to catch the market."

"I know my business," Richard replies. "And a bit of yours." They both laugh, and my husband beams, completely in his element.

Dinner is served. In the perfect performance, Richard takes my hand; we glide to our table, and he pulls out my chair. I observe where our guests are seated. Even though I like them well enough, I consider them all acquaintances, *Richard's* friends. I have actually begun to like it better this way. Because if the company we keep is not my own family or friends, at least I don't have to worry about what anyone says or how they treat each other.

"Who wants to play golf tomorrow?" Richard asks, as he cuts into his grilled chicken. "We can make it a threesome." Both Bob and Jeff instantaneously free up their schedules for a coveted round of golf at the exclusive Rose Wood Country Club, where Richard and I are members.

"Yeah, baby," Richard says, as the server asks if we want red or white. Richard's arms soar into the air. "I'll bring cigars!"

These men are high achievers, hedge fund and real estate guys at the peak of their careers, who own their businesses. But not only that: Bob and Jeff are family men, and they are charitable.

"Remind me where your kids are in school?" I lean over to ask Carol.

"I switched them out of public to Rivers last year," she says, using a broad "a" in "last" with a Kennedy-esque accent. "They get much more attention." Rivers is a private school with a well-paid faculty in Weston, another upscale suburb. Richard would not be pleased, because, unlike many of our friends and neighbors in Wellesley, he believes in public education unless a child has a learning or behavior problem.

"You made the right decision," I say to Carol. If she wants her kids in private school, why not?

After dinner, the president steps to the podium.

"Good evening. Tonight we are raising money for our new student center." For 2003, this is the cutting edge of campus life. He ends his speech, thanking everyone for their support. "Bid high and bid often," the president says, pinching his bow tie.

Richard leans over and whispers loudly in Carol's ear, "Make Bob bid. About time he takes you on a nice trip."

This comment sets off belly laughs between Bob, Carol, and Richard. I sip my wine. A thousand memories and resentments come to mind, of Richard's feuds with Elizabeth and Jake, my family, and none of them makes me laugh.

Paul, the auctioneer, takes the stage. "Shh! Shh! Shh!" he blows, testing the microphone before his voice fills the room. "Good evening, ladies and gentlemen. Let's start with a bang! This first item is just the tip of the iceberg." He details a four-night stay at the Georges V Hotel in Paris. I know Paris well and this landmark is mere steps from the Champs-Élysées, walking distance to the Arc de Triomphe, the Eiffel Tower, and nearly every designer store I can think of. "The City of Lights, people! Go deep in your pockets for this one." Paul quits the stage and walks between tables, sharing perks of the luxury package: a king-size bed, a marble bathroom, breakfast included. "Four nights and five days. Starts at two thousand. Do I hear three? Four?"

Richard's number stirs on the tablecloth. Before lifting it, he seeks my permission with a raised brow. I nod, reluctantly, and Richard raises his number. Only we know that our marriage is crumbling. A loudmouth at the next table, wearing a poorly tailored coat, initially beats our offer, but Richard's friends, rowdy from the wine, spur him on. When Richard wants something, he's nothing but persistent.

"Sold for seven thousand!" Paul declares when Richard wears the other guy out, $250 at a time. The auctioneer races over to congratulate us, recognizing Richard as a trustee. "They say a happy wife is a happy life—Mr. and Mrs. Freeman are going to Paris!" Paul cheers and the crowd claps. It's not his job to understand that no trip to Paris will make this wife happy.

I lean over and kiss Richard drily on the cheek. "Thank you," I say. But a sinking feeling overcomes me, dread settling like the humidity outside, a suffocating feeling. I hate myself as Richard takes my hand, strokes my sweating fingers. How will I explain to Elizabeth that we're going to Paris?

Our friends applaud and congratulate us. As the evening passes, with Richard's encouragement, they bid on various items. Some prevail and others are outbid, but returns are high for Pine Cliff. The more people drink, the more they spend. The school raises $750,000, outdoing last year, and Richard is on cloud nine.

As we share goodbyes, hugging friends, my smile again fades. The valet brings us the Aston. I plop onto the seat, worn out from the evening, and can't help but land on the issue that has been at the top of my mind for years: Will I ever reconcile the animosity between my husband and my sister, or is my only solution divorce? I notice the pride that Richard exudes from the event's success, and it irks me. He seems unaware of my grief—of who, what extension of me, is always missing from these happy moments. He fondles my knee while starting the car, but I turn away toward the window.

I'm a bit tipsy from three glasses of wine, pining for my sister, whom I know as well as I do myself. But no matter how much I drink, it doesn't change the facts. At family dinners, Richard sits off by himself, staring at the cubes in his drink. And when Elizabeth's husband, Jake, comes to our home, my brother-in-law sits across from Richard but obscures his face with a stiff newspaper. The tension has settled on our children now, an unmelting snow. They tiptoe around both fathers, on eggshells.

At a stoplight on our way home, I am watching the gypsy moths beat themselves insensibly against the red, rounded eye of glass, and Richard blurts, "Can't you just be happy—once?" He seals his lips on a moody silence that lasts the rest of the night.

Being Richard's wife is a full-time job. If only I could get it right.

Chapter Two

———

*F*rom a young age, I was confident that I knew how I wanted to live my life: surrounded by a loving family—grandparents, aunts, uncles, and cousins. Maybe I was foolish not to realize that my husband might find my family connections stifling when he didn't have the luxury of the same attachments. When there was a whole world out there of fascinating people yet to meet.

I didn't grow up thinking there might be a rift, a feud, in my own adult family. The tense, long-standing conflict that my life has become was never on my radar. When I heard that two brothers didn't talk because of a clash in a family business, I couldn't imagine it being something they couldn't fix. When a friend told me she hated her sister because her sister had deep-seated jealousy of her, I couldn't relate. Sisters share. My sister has always been a part of me.

The Charles River Park complex was a perfect place in the 1980s for singles and young professionals to live; its apartments were full of lawyers, stockbrokers, and medical interns and residents. The courtyards were impeccably land-scaped: impatiens for the summer, yellow and orange mums in the fall. Gardeners strewed white lights on trees for the winter and cultivated tulips and daffodils to usher in spring. Each building had a doorman, and up-to-date apartments featured the newest GE Profile appliances. Though I did not consider Charles River Park *home*, because my heart still lodged with my parents and siblings, it was the perfect middle ground between graduate school for speech pathology and starting my so-called real life.

Although I loved having roommates in college, I quickly eased into living alone at Charles River Park. I framed posters from *Vogue* for my walls and stacked back issues of *Cosmopolitan* on my coffee table. Living alone entailed certain freedoms: to come and go as I pleased, to leave breakfast dishes in the sink if I didn't feel like tidying, and to litter my makeup and shampoo in the bathroom without worrying about being in someone's way. I wasn't lonely, either. Friends from high school and college also lived at CRP. We were the epitome of trendy. On weekends we'd eat at Friday's on Newbury Street, jump in a cab to hit the disco at Fan Club, and always end up at Jason's, the "it" nightclub. Behind all this frivolity, however, was a serious purpose: as I brushed on my makeup, ordered glasses of wine, or danced until closing to *Saturday Night Fever*, my singular goal was to meet someone.

My sister, Elizabeth, who was three years younger and worked as a paralegal at a fancy firm, had already found that love. Her boyfriend, Jake Gordon, grew up on Atlantic Road, our family's street in Gloucester, a waterfront city on Massachusetts's North Shore known for beautiful beaches and a strong fishing industry. Elizabeth, Jake, and I spent years together as kids, but neither Elizabeth nor Jake maintained contact until they ran into each other as students at Northeastern University. I remembered Jake as charming and flirtatious, a bit of a troublemaker. Elizabeth was petite, thin, and lovable, always trying to make people feel comfortable. Her big blue eyes drew the attention of plenty of male suitors.

Jake had matured into a striking presence at six feet, with dark hair and angular brows. One evening, out of the blue, Elizabeth and Jake sat side by side on a Green Line subway train, and they soon became inseparable. They kept separate apartments after graduating from college, of course, but they were already a single unit in every other way. My family valued this type of bond, and I knew Elizabeth was lucky to have found someone like Jake. There I was, turning twenty-six, then twenty-seven, and, despite the men circling, starting to doubt I'd ever find the one.

One night when I was still at Charles River Park, I had the flu and Elizabeth and Jake stopped by with chicken soup. Elizabeth had already checked in on me during the day, taking quick breaks from work. When the lovebirds entered that evening, I was sitting on my bed cross-legged, four pillows propping my head, with a runny nose.

"Thanks," I said, accepting the soup but waving them away. "Don't get too close."

"Hope it makes you feel a little better," Elizabeth said, curling her lower lip onto her teeth in the funny way that she did. She wore black leather pants with a white cashmere sweater. Night makeup announced her eyes.

"Smells yummy," I said, then covered my mouth to cough.

"I'll call you tomorrow," Elizabeth said. "We're going for a bite." She took Jake's hand to lead him out, but Jake pulled my sister back and turned her to face me.

"Today's our anniversary!" Jake said with a toothy smile. "That makes exactly four years." They embraced. I tried to smile, but my lips wouldn't turn up at the corners.

"That's great," I said flatly, not even attempting to muster any excitement. I hoped they mistook my listlessness for flu symptoms. I knew I was being petty, but every little touch or glance between Elizabeth and Jake that night seemed amplified and made me want to squeeze my eyes shut. Once they left, I could barely touch the soup.

The next morning, I called my grandmother, who took an active interest in my love life. I admitted that I felt jealous that Elizabeth had a serious boyfriend and I didn't.

"*Mamala*," my *bubbe* said. "Don't worry, you're a catch. You'll find someone who's right for you. Don't think so much."

Bubbe, originally from Lithuania, always listened openly before she doled out advice. She eternally wore a pair of fourteen-karat gold hoops and three solid-gold chains. She was fifty pounds overweight, wise, and compassionate. Aside from my girlfriends, with whom I gushed about superficial things, Bubbe was my confidante.

I would say to her, "I don't like the way that guy dresses. He didn't open the car door for me." Or, "He didn't care about my feelings when I told him I was upset."

"He's not for you, *mamala*," Bubbe would say. "Who needs someone like that?"

I often fretted to Bubbe that I should have married my college boyfriend Stuart, worrying that no one would ever love me as much. I tried to explain my regret, but words fell short. "He brushed the snow off my car," I said to Bubbe. "He bought me NyQuil when I was sick." What I didn't describe to my grandmother was how gently Stuart had toweled the water from every part of my body after we showered.

Now I wished I had given Stuart a chance when we graduated from college. But I had been too immature, grasping for someone to fulfill a dream.

⫸⫸⫸

I MET RICHARD at the bar at St. Cloud, a restaurant in Boston's brick-lined South End. He had just turned forty and held his vodka with a financier's confidence and well-manicured hands. His clothes were tailored, French cuffs secured with RAF-monogrammed links. He was eloquent despite a slight Boston accent, dropping his r's at the end of some words. I figured out only later what made Richard so damn handsome in the evenings, with that irresistible glow: he had always just come from playing squash.

Throughout our courtship, Richard took a gentleman's pains. He pulled out my chair and, as he became acquainted with my tastes, suggested food and wine if he knew the restaurant well. When I play it all back in my mind, I remember how his eyes sought me when he spoke, fringed with the eyelashes women dream of. Although he seemed a little old for me, the chemistry was there, and something more: beckoning from under Richard's polish and shine, some secret intrigued me and kept me interested. Even after Richard confessed that he was divorced and had a six-year-old son, Harrison, what I saw in him was someone who I could trust and rely on.

I never hid my closeness with my family from Richard. I never thought I had to. Until the first night he accompanied me back to my apartment at Charles River Park. We had just walked through the door, and the phone rang, eleven at night. Richard looked at me, eyes narrowing. "Aren't you going to get that?" he asked.

"Of course." I picked up the phone. It was my sister calling to say a cheery late-night hello. She and I had gotten in the habit of talking whenever I got home late. If I didn't call, she called me. With Richard looking on, I said quietly, "I have a date."

"Who's calling you at this hour?" Richard asked, standing so close that he himself could have heard what Elizabeth said.

"My sister," I said. I didn't bother to cover the receiver with my hand. I knew that Elizabeth, too, could hear every word.

"Your *sister*?" Richard asked. " Cut it out. I don't like teasing."

"Here, say hi to Richard," I said, with a nervous giggle. "He thinks you're a guy."

"Put him on," Elizabeth said, laughing, unaware of the tension at my end.

I passed Richard the phone. "Hello?" he said tentatively.

"Samantha told me so much about you," I heard Elizabeth say through the receiver. I took a deep breath and shook out the hand I'd used to grip the phone, not realizing how tense I'd become. I rubbed my ear.

For a couple of minutes, I tried to relax while I listened to Richard and my sister make small talk about how he had once been to the beach in our North Shore neighborhood and the proximity of their offices in the financial district.

When Richard hung up, he asked, "Does she always call you this late?"

"Yes, we talk like this all the time. We're sisters," I said, thinking that one statement explained it all.

I came to know Richard as a tenacious and worldly man whose aptitude for risk taking allowed his private equity business to thrive. Savvy, charming, and willful, he exuded my favorite qualities, some of which I believed I could improve in myself through mere proximity to him.

"Is there anything else I should know about you?" I asked my future husband one night over our hundredth glass of wine.

"I'm very stubborn," he said to me, the future Mrs. Freeman.

We dated for three years.

Richard was resourceful and persistent, the type of man who stopped at nothing to get what he wanted. His power and success excited me. I felt confident steering the waters of my own family, but here was a man who exerted force over people in the world.

By the time Richard and I got serious, in my late twenties, my friends were already years into their marriages, and I had the rack of satin, pouf-sleeved bridesmaid gowns to prove it.

⋘

AFTER GRADUATING WITH my master's degree and moving to Charles River Park, I landed one of five speech-language pathology positions at Beth Israel Hospital. I loved my job. It felt special and rare to have made a career out of nurturing others, which came naturally to me. My small therapy office had a wooden desk, a window, a filing cabinet, and room enough for a wheelchair. I hung my college diploma and, above that, my newest accreditation credential, which together covered the available wall.

My first patient most mornings was Barbara, seventy-four, whose stroke had affected her right side. Barbara's right arm and leg were weak, inhibiting her ability to walk or grasp a fork. Her speech was slow and halting. She had difficulty finding the words she wanted to say, as if they were on the tip of her tongue but she couldn't get them out. I knew she wanted to show off her six grandchildren to me, four boys and two girls ranging in age from nine to three, whose pictures she slid into and out of her bathrobe's left pocket. She cried in frustration. I explained that it was all normal, that with practice she would improve. My goal was to help Barbara recover, from deep inside the speech center of her brain, the words that seemed lost. Barbara's husband visited her every day after work. I wanted him to see her progress.

Feeling professional in my white coat, one morning I wheeled Barbara into my office and set the brake. A beige thermal hospital blanket covered her bedpost legs. My patient's hair was so thin that I could see through to parts of her scalp; my big '80s hair, wavy and thick, cut a ridiculous contrast. I noticed Barbara's wedding band sliding from her finger, and, with her permission, I moved the band onto the gold necklace she wore, feeling the foolishness of my youthful abundance. Barbara would possibly never stand from her wheelchair, never again speak fluently. We had work to do.

"Did you have breakfast this morning?" I asked Barbara, taking her cold hands in mine. Whenever she smiled, I could see the weakness on the right side of her face. We began with word associations. I pointed to a picture of breakfast pastries, including doughnuts, croissants, and muffins and, slowly, enunciating each word, I said, "I am going to eat a blueberry..."

"Muffin," Barbara said, finishing my sentence with a hint of pride.

"I am going to eat a blueberry muffin," I repeated, beaming at her.

"Blueberry muffin," she repeated.

"Bread and..."

"Butter," Barbara said.

"Yes! Excellent." Then I tried to work on opposite meanings with her.

"Black," I said.

"White," Barbara replied.

"Yes! White is black's opposite. Now, try *happy*."

"Sad." That was an easy one. As we worked, Barbara's face evoked defiance, not depression. She seemed determined to recover the living she wanted to do and had already made improvement since her initial evaluation. I had every hope that, with enough cues and practice, we could break through and Barbara's speech would improve.

"Stop," I said, working down my list.

"Go," Barbara said.

"Young."

"Old."

"Married," I said.

This one stumped her. "Not married," she tried.

"What word means *not married?*"

"Divorced?"

"Yes, and"—I felt unusually impatient—"what word means *never married?*" I perched on the edge of my seat.

Barbara shook her head.

"Single," I said, and leaned back in my chair.

"Single," Barbara repeated. Then, pointing her index finger at me, her voice rising to a question, she asked, "Single?"

I nodded.

My patient grasped my hand and squeezed.

THE WEATHER WAS remarkable for early March, sunny and seventy-five, the day in 1987 when I became Mrs. Freeman in a ceremony at the Ritz. I was only thirty, but I felt old. Elizabeth and Jake were already celebrating three years of marriage.

The ceremony and reception would take place in the grand ballroom at seven, and the Presidential Suite would be ours after Richard and I kissed the last guests goodbye. At three o'clock, my sister arrived with the hairdresser and makeup artist. My eyes widened like a princess in a fairy tale as we entered the penthouse, overlooking the Boston Common and Public Garden, where Richard and I would spend our wedding night.

I savored that private afternoon—drinking pink champagne, dressing in my lace-and-taffeta gown—with that view of the manicured shrubbery and colonial statuary, my mother Rachel and my Auntie Gloria, her sister, making bubbly, nervous visits, Elizabeth at my side.

Our chuppah was adorned lushly with orchids, roses, and simple greens. A harpist strummed. Richard, dashing in black tie, walked the aisle, smiling ear to ear. My father, debonair in his tuxedo, held my arm, and I held a single white rose, with pure, unadulterated joy in my heart, a thin cloud of netting over my face.

When we reached the chuppah, my father placed my hand in Richard's and moved aside. In accordance with Jewish tradition, the cantor chanted a prayer and we sipped red wine from a goblet that had been my great-grandfather's. Richard and I exchanged vows promising to love and cherish each other till death. He stepped on the glass, and when it shattered, the rabbi pronounced us man and wife. When Richard and I kissed, everyone applauded and shouted, "Mazel tov!" I felt warmth rise from deep inside me, as if the sun had replaced my heart, and thought naively that all the worries I had would disappear now that I was Mrs. Richard A. Freeman.

After months lived in details—from the floor-length, pearl organza tablecloths to the orchid centerpieces that mimicked the chuppah to the pounds of votive candles on display—our wedding was a dream. We dined on rack of lamb with grilled asparagus and roasted potatoes and danced tenderly as husband and wife.

"If I knew I could be this happy, I would have skipped my first wedding altogether," Richard whispered in my ear.

I waltzed with my father. Richard danced with my mother, then his sisters. I danced with the best man and the ushers. The celebratory energy of Auntie Gloria in her red beaded gown and exquisite diamond necklace, along with at least one hundred other relatives and friends, surged the dance floor. My joy overflowed.

On a whim, Richard invited thirty or so spontaneous guests to our wedding suite for an after-party. A case of Yellow Label appeared, and the champagne flowed. We hadn't discussed any such gathering, and I was surprised to have the intrusion on our wedding night, but I could see that Richard was proud of the suite and wanted to show it off. Shrugging off my annoyance, I indulged in the emotional high of my fairy-tale evening, placing an order for extra crystal flutes with the concierge.

Champagne in hand—watching the twinkle of the Boston skyline through the penthouse window, and making small talk with someone I hardly knew—I suddenly realized who was missing. My sister. I straightened my spine and peered into the crowd. I didn't see Elizabeth anywhere, or my brother, David. Richard's two sisters were also absent. Why hadn't he invited our siblings? My sister was my maid of honor. My brother was an usher. Richard's brother-in-law was his best man. I excused myself.

Richard was mid-conversation when I tapped him on the shoulder and handed him my glass. "Where are Elizabeth and David?" I asked, gathering my train and hurrying to the hallway, not even waiting for an answer. I needed to set this right. My family would be so hurt to know that Richard and I had extended our celebration without them.

The elevator opened right away, but when I arrived in the ballroom, it no longer resembled a fairy tale. The lights were on, and the hotel staff were striking the room. I took the elevator back to my marital suite alone, avoiding my image in the mirrored doors.

Our guests finally departed at two thirty. I paced, interrogating Richard, discarding pins from my updo. "How could you forget to invite Elizabeth and Jake? David and his girlfriend, Jill? Your sisters? They're our family."

"Relax. I just didn't think of it," Richard said dismissively. "Let's go to bed."

"But you thought of all those *other* people?"

"Please. Now I'm only thinking of you."

The last thing I wanted was to argue on my wedding night. On the pretense of brushing my teeth, I escaped to the bathroom. I wanted to be that couple holding each other and whispering in the candlelight.

When I emerged from the bathroom, I had taken off my dress.

Chapter Three

———

*T*he night after the Pine Cliff fund-raiser, Richard and I go out for dinner alone. If there's any spot in Boston where we can discuss our marital problems, it's Abe & Louie's, one of *our* places, a pillar in the life we've built together. Its mahogany-paneled dining room with deep leather booths represents a comfort and luxury that put us both at ease.

Richard greets the maître d' with a rehearsed handshake. "Good to see you, Romeo," he says, slipping him a twenty. My husband wants to ensure that we'll be seated near the windows at the front of the dining room, away from the kitchen and the commotion of its two-way doors.

Romeo selects two menus and gestures for us to follow him to our favorite table, perfect for people-watching. "You're looking well," Romeo says to me as we walk, concealing the $20 bill in his cuff. "Have not seen you for a while, Madame Samantha," he adds tentatively.

"I've been well," I say, and smile, though I feel myself wince. As Romeo seats us and engages Richard in small talk, I fidget with my wedding ring, taking it off, sliding it on. It stays on my finger this time. The scent of drawn butter, fresh black pepper, and roasted thyme in the restaurant has a pacifying effect.

Romeo leaves us with leather-backed menus, and I look into the eyes of the man I've loved for twenty years, allowing myself to trace the soft folds of his jowl and the chiseled crease above his lips. He doesn't believe that I appreciate him and all his success affords us, and I don't feel valued by him as a mother and wife. Richard sits erect with his perfect posture, wearing his Nantucket tan, these unspoken accusations between us.

"I like that blouse," Richard says, alternating his eyes between the menu and me. "New?"

"Yes, I just bought it at Saks." I sit straighter—it's easy to feel slouchy next to Richard. For this evening, I've worn a black lace top with dark skinny jeans and a pair of gold, backless heels. In my mid-forties, I know that how old we look depends on how well we take care of ourselves, and I keep myself in good shape.

I take Richard's hand on the tablecloth and draw his eyes from the menu because he already knows what he will order. We reach into the basket of warm bread that Romeo has placed without instruction, and, for a brief time, the conversation flows.

We talk about the Red Sox, how this might be the year they really win the World Series, careful not to hope too hard. The fact that I'm a Sox fan bonded me early on to Richard, a season-ticket holder for thirty years, and it's one of the passions we still share. When we first met, I impressed him by knowing the starting lineup of the 1967 dream team. "You know Joe Foy played third base?" he said incredulously, palming his forehead. Now we take our daughter, Alexandra, to Sox games at Fenway. Richard is intensely proud of her fandom. "My daughter takes the Sox–Yankees rivalry to a new level," he boasts to his friends, meaning that Alexandra, eleven and whip-thin, will berate anyone wearing a Yankees hat.

The server brings our cocktails: pinot grigio for me, Ketel One on the rocks, with a splash of cranberry and a lime, for Richard. I take my first sip and unfold the pressed cloth napkin on my lap. Richard rearranges the water glasses and shifts the salt and pepper shakers, as if to assert complete control over his surroundings, the same way he shuffles the deeds of buildings in the Back Bay.

"We may as well talk about why we came," he says.

I take a gulp of wine to ease the sudden tightness in my chest.

"What's your decision?" Richard asks, dropping his voice to the center of the table, out of range of any eavesdroppers. "Are you going to change or not?"

I bow my head but feel the fury of Richard's anger through my curtain of hair. We have been through this so many times that it's a song on repeat. What Richard is really asking is for me to distance myself from my family, especially my sister, Elizabeth.

"We both have to change," I say, trying to keep my voice measured, but I can feel it wavering. Richard thinks that Elizabeth and I communicate and see each other too constantly—she lives ten minutes away—and that I take on my sister's problems as my own. In childhood photographs, I always stood behind Elizabeth, my hands on her shoulders. I peek at my husband's face through my hair, hoping for a shred of understanding. If I ever go along with Richard's request to marginalize Elizabeth in my life, it means I won't be the same person.

"All I ask for is some privacy," Richard says, "in my own house, with my own family. Or is that too much for you? Look, our family—you, me, Alex and Harrison—does not include your sister. Just the way you feel and think about her takes time away from me." This diatribe against Elizabeth has made Richard breathless. He inhales deeply. "You know what your problem is? In a nutshell?" He rushes. "You don't know how to be a good wife *and* a good sister at the same time."

I begrudge my husband his somewhat valid point but his resentment over the years has persuaded me to conceal more and more of my relationship with Elizabeth from him. All this sneaking around, you could accuse me of carrying on an emotional affair. Richard's blunt thinking has taken over. I can see that he believes diminishing Elizabeth from my life will save our marriage.

Mercifully, our first courses arrive: salad and oysters, followed by glazed vegetables and juice-drenched steaks. I slice into my steak and place the first morsel in my mouth. "Eat," I say, with my mouth full. "It's good." Richard gives me a tepid smile. We have always loved going to dinner, and for a few minutes we're quiet, tasting, chewing, and swallowing. The server brings more wine, another cocktail.

Richard wipes the corner of his mouth with the linen napkin and starts again. "Let's try to talk calmly."

Feeling fed and less tense from the wine, I still find myself taking a deep breath and bracing myself.

"You say you've changed. You really haven't," Richard says. "Maybe you've modified some of your habits, but you haven't changed your core feelings."

"So you're not satisfied with changing my behavior. You want to change my heart," I say, a little too loudly. A woman from the next table actually turns her head.

"You don't get it," I continue. "She's my *sister*, not some faucet I can turn on and off!" So much for a calm discussion.

Richard rubs his forehead, as if I exhaust him. "You can still love her; just don't take every call." The server replenishes our water as we cease fire. Richard lifts his ice-melted vodka and downs it in three gulps.

In moments like these, when I feel frustrated and out of control, I turn my attention inward and focus on strengths and the things I am grateful for. I remind myself that I am a devoted, responsible woman who thrives on solid family connections. My desire to make things right for everyone I love tugs at my heart, even when my own best interests are at stake.

"I've jumped through hoops to please you," I say. My stomach turns over on itself, and I become a bit breathless. Lately I wait on Richard at family dinners, sit by his side at Hanukkah, focus all of my attention on stoking his ego and his accomplishments, much less so on Elizabeth and the rest of my family.

"You don't even know what I do at the office," Richard sneers. "Do you? The money you spent on that blouse? You know what your sister does every hour!"

"I know you just raised capital to buy out the Gilman Company. You're renovating on Boylston to move your offices there. Watch yourself." But what I think Richard is saying is that I don't know how he ticks, and on that score he might be right. Perhaps I am guilty of discounting his needs and feelings.

"We talk about our kids," I say, to explain why I cherish Elizabeth. "We vent." I would assume that such attention would only smother and annoy a person as independent and self-made as Richard, but in fact he craves attention. It's not enough for him to succeed—he wants to bask in my pride of his success.

I slump in my seat. As with so many similar conversations, we've reached a stalemate. The deep booths and mahogany walls that I've long associated with glamour and ease now only make me feel trapped. The wineglass sweats in my hand, my second already, and I can't wait for my third. This conversation is so old, it has grown a beard.

"Ever hear of moderation?" Richard blurts, as I order another glass of pinot grigio. I don't dignify that question with a response.

I try to take interest again in food, eyeing my bloody, half-eaten steak without much of an appetite, but, despite myself, I kick the wheel.

"I've stopped inviting her to our home," I say. "I've stopped taking her calls in front of you. I know it upsets you. But why can't I talk to my own sister when you're not around?" I lean back onto the tufted banquette, my shoulders shaking.

"You're welcome to talk to her, just not every day," Richard says, then shakes his head in disgust. "You don't need to know about every problem her kids have, how they do on tests, what their teachers say and every goddamn time Elizabeth goes to the bathroom."

"I don't like where this is going," I say, and drop my napkin on the tablecloth.

Richard brings his fist to the table. Water sloshes from my glass. My eyes dart around the dining room, wondering who might have seen. The woman at our neighboring table looks over again.

"Is this even a conversation?" I say, lowering my voice. "You just want me to agree with you."

"Let's go," Richard says. "All you do is piss me off."

My husband flings his napkin, flags the server, then stands and pushes himself from the booth. "I deserve to feel like number one in my marriage," he says. "How hard is that to understand?"

⋘

THE NEXT DAY. I do the only thing that ever makes me feel better after a fight with Richard: I go for a walk with Elizabeth. Despite Richard's hope otherwise, Elizabeth and I are closer than ever. His ultimatums about creating distance from my sister have made me run to her even faster.

As I pull up to the Brookline Reservoir, the early sunlight stabs at my eyes. I lean against the weathered fence, and when I see Elizabeth's car, I try to put on a good face. But she can tell something is wrong. "You've been crying," she says.

If I open my mouth, it'll come out garbled, so I press my lips together and nod.

Elizabeth knows all about my problems with Richard. Actually, I tell her too much, and confiding in her ends up making Richard seem like a villain. She hugs me, and we squeeze our hands together—the secret code of comfort we've had since we were young.

A primitive trail of dirt and gravel surrounds the reservoir. Maple and birch trees offer shade, and teak benches a place to relax. Every time we meet, Elizabeth and I circle the water at least three times, walking and breathing through constant conversation. Today we begin our walk briskly, with the sun warming our faces, as if it's giving us strength for what's soon to come.

"Spill," Elizabeth says. "Tell me everything." But as we finish the first lap, she begins to lag. I'm so wrapped up in my story that I don't notice when Elizabeth falls back a few paces. I turn and run to her. She's limping, her face twisted in pain.

"Seems worse than yesterday," I say.

"The doctor thinks it's sciatica. But the pain keeps getting worse." She grimaces.

"Should we stop?" I ask.

"No, no, I'm fine." Elizabeth takes a few steps that would have been easy before, trying to straighten out her walk. She always puts on a brave face.

We continue at a slower pace. Cars rumble faintly behind

us on Route 9. The wind picks up as we round the corner, forcing us to put more energy into our steps. The path gradually crowds with people speed-walking and jogging. Just ahead, two women barricade the lane with their strollers, carrying cups of steaming coffee. They're talking loudly, laughing, and I want to interrupt, to scold them harshly for acting like the path is theirs, to insist they be considerate of other people. I'm not sure from where this sudden anger surges, but it startles me. Instead of berating the stroller moms, Elizabeth and I detour onto the grass, wetting our shoes with dew.

"I have to get out of this mess," I say.

"Maybe it's the last straw."

The last thing Elizabeth wants me to do is leave my husband, but she loves me and knows that I'm suffering.

We finally circle back to the parking lot and drink from the water bottles in our cars. I see Elizabeth wince again. "Go home and call your doctor," I instruct, snapping out of my self-absorption, happy to inhabit the older-sister role.

"I already have an MRI scheduled for later today," Elizabeth says.

"Oh, okay. Please let me know how it goes."

"God, don't let it be surgery," Elizabeth says, reaching for the Aleve she's been keeping in her glove box. She rarely takes any medication, so I know it must be bad.

❦

THAT MORNING, WHEN I get home after my walk, Richard and I barely speak. He races out of the house to his office, grunting goodbye. I stand alone at the kitchen counter, eating a bowl of Special K.

After dropping Alexandra off at middle school, I take a

cardio-and-strength-training class at my gym. Then I treat myself to a blueberry muffin from my favorite coffee shop, Rosie's. Later, I drive to Winston Flowers to buy sunflowers and orchids to brighten my home, hoping to elevate my mood. At Winston's, lulled by the murmur of polite voices and the faint snipping of stems, I feel as if I'm in the South of France. I studied the language and joined the French Library in my twenties and still speak French fluently.

I pull out of Winston's onto Route 9, and on my right I notice a fit, dark-haired man on the sidewalk. His elbows are loose, hands placed casually in his pockets, but he walks with a certain air of confidence. There *are* other men out there, I begin to think.

In fifteen minutes, I'm pulling into my garage and getting out of the car, juggling a few books I've bought: *How to Have a Good Divorce*, *The Woman's Guide to Divorce*, *A Spiritual Divorce*, and others. Maybe what I'm feeling is clarity, an acceptance that Richard and I will never resolve our conflicts. It might be a relief simply to move on. At the same time, I worry about how it will affect Alexandra and Harrison and I obsess about what it will be like to be on the other side of Richard in a nasty divorce. Even if I get alimony, I worry about my financial security.

I hear the kitchen phone ring and rush in from the garage to grab it. It's Elizabeth, but I barely recognize her voice, whispering and crying at the same time—I've never heard her sound like this.

"The MRI," she says. "Something's really wrong."

I freeze, as if caught outdoors below zero without a coat.

"The radiologist just called and explained the results," Elizabeth says, her voice cracking. "I don't want to die."

"I'll be right over," I say. My body springs into action. I

scoop up the divorce books and shove them into the back of my closet. I rap knuckles on my daughter's door.

"Get your things," I say, barging in. "We're going to Auntie Elizabeth's. Now."

"Can't. I have homework," Alexandra says, but looks up from her notebook, curious. Going to Auntie Elizabeth's right now is not how Alexandra's weeknight schedule goes. My daughter is sprawled on her bed, surrounded by pink faux-fur pillows. When I dropped her off at school this morning, I promised to make her favorite meal for dinner tonight, pasta with olive oil, just us. Richard will be out somewhere, eating at a bar, chatting with whomever is next to him.

"Bring your homework," I say. "Let's go. Shoes."

With Alexandra in the car, I pull back onto Route 9 in full traffic. I'm impatient, switching lanes to coast through the lights. I whip out my cell and call my parents, who live nearby in Newton. "Mom, meet me at Elizabeth's," I say to her voice mail. "Something is seriously wrong."

When I turn into my sister's driveway, I see the front door framing Elizabeth; her husband, Jake, still wearing his sport coat from the office; my two nieces, Brooke and Lauren. For the first time in my life, the sight of them makes my heart sink. Elizabeth, at five foot five, looks shrunken and small. Jake is holding a paper report in his hand, his dark eyes squinting to make sense of it. Brooke, fourteen, is quiet and still, hiding her hands in her sweatshirt. Lauren, just eleven, looks down at the new red sneakers Elizabeth told me she had bought her yesterday. "Cancer," Elizabeth gasps when Alexandra and I are finally in front of her, naming the thing.

Where I would expect tears in my sister's eyes, instead I see bewilderment and dry curiosity.

Chapter Four

$\mathcal{L}$ike almost every moment of our wedding, our honey-moon on St. Barts was a dream. Richard and I lunched on *salade du marché* and *pommes frites* and sipped chilled rosé. Afternoons, we amused ourselves like teens, singing invented, silly songs as we strained our mini-moke up steep slopes and coasted to far-flung, deserted beaches.

At dusk we could skinny-dip in the turquoise water that warmed us like a bath. Often we made love right there in the salt water or outside on our secluded balcony. The best part of St. Barts as newlyweds was being alone, of having each other completely to ourselves. I wasn't a mother yet and couldn't fully understand the sacrifice, but in two weeks away Richard phoned his son, Harrison, only twice. He had worked long hours right up until the night of our wedding, and our honey-moon was a vacation he truly deserved. He slept a lot. I toyed with the idea of reaching out to my sister, brother, or mother on those quiet afternoons when Richard sprawled heavily on the bed, but I never did, content to watch my new husband enjoy his sleep, and to dream of our happy married life.

Once Richard and I returned to work in Boston that spring, I missed our being alone. In June, Richard's son moved in with us and I became a full-fledged stepmother. My extended family now included Richard's ex-wife *and* her new husband. While Richard's ex seemed nice enough, someone I might even have been friendly with under different circumstances, I didn't have a choice about having a relationship with her. She and Richard argued whenever they tried to work anything out. I wanted what was best for Harrison, of course, and, above all, I wanted peace in my house. I took over coordinating with Harrison's mother my stepson's comings and goings. After a while, it all worked pleasantly.

Weekday mornings, Richard woke Harrison for school.

"I'll turn on the shower for you," he said, as Harrison sat up and rubbed his eyes. Richard read the *Boston Globe* in Harrison's room while he got dressed. "Hurry. If we leave by seven forty-five, I can give you a ride on my way to the office," Richard said. Otherwise, Harrison would take the bus that stopped directly across the street from our house.

It was complicated being a stepmother and simultaneously a new wife. Over breakfast, father and son told stories about a ski weekend they'd had in Colorado before they knew me, or talked about looking forward to the Celtics game they were attending over the weekend. After a testosterone-drenched conversation like that, Richard would give me a quick kiss goodbye. I knew he was thrilled to have his son in the house with us, but I struggled with feeling left out. I had spent quality time with Harrison before our marriage and becoming a strong blended family was what I wanted. I understood it would take time, and I began to pick Harrison up from school and help him with homework. We bonded over shared feelings and experiences. Soon we developed a close and loving relationship.

Within a year, we had other problems: the economy. Richard spent his waking hours in 1988 trying to save sizable investments. I cut back on spending—no flowers, no trips—and we loaned Richard's firm our personal funds. At night, Richard lay next to me with his eyes closed, as if his body still craved the deep sleep of our honeymoon but his mind had another plan.

-≺≺≺≺-

A YEAR LATER, Elizabeth was pregnant. As soon as she went into labor, I called Richard at work. "I'm going to the hospital," I said.

"Wait until the baby is born," he said. "Could be all day."

"I'm too excited. I don't care how long it takes." I hung up and sped to my sister.

I was the first to arrive, besides Jake, of course. Throughout the day, more and more family members streamed into the waiting room—first my parents, Rachel and Joseph, then Jake's parents, then my brother and Jake's brothers, Auntie Gloria and Uncle Irving, and finally Jake's uncle, carrying food to feed us all: corned beef, pastrami, and turkey sandwiches with mustard, on light rye.

"Now taking bets," Jake's brother announced. "I say the baby will be a boy and he'll be born at seven eighteen."

I looked at my watch. It was already six o'clock. Eyeing the pastrami, I opted for the healthier turkey instead and prayed that Jake's brother would be right. My nerves were already shot.

Richard arrived at six thirty, forlorn and tired. Outside the maternity ward, he plopped onto a beige leather sofa. His expression made it clear that he was there for one reason and one reason only: out of obligation.

"You'll love this, Richard. We're taking bets," I said. "One, when do you think the baby will be born, and two, what sex will it be? I say nine p.m., girl. Your turn."

"Earlier than that," Jake's uncle interrupted from an adjacent couch. "Quarter after eight, boy."

"I don't like any of this," my father said. "Just let the baby be healthy."

Richard leaned over to me and said, "This is absurd. What if it takes all night? I have to work tomorrow, you know." But day in, day out, there would always be work. I wanted my husband to share in our family's excitement.

"You really want to go? Now?" I asked him, my heart thumping.

"No reason to be here yet," he said. "Come home with me. Come back in the morning."

"I'm staying until at least nine," I said loudly, trying to draw the others in. "What about my bet?" I giggled and smiled at Jake's uncle, inviting him into this impossible conversation, trying to turn Richard's rudeness into a joke. Everyone had a chuckle over my quip—everyone except for Richard, who folded his Burberry trench coat over his arm and left.

In the end, I lost the bet, narrowly, on one count—timing— and returned home just three hours after Richard. Brooke was born at eight pounds and healthy, my parents' first grandchild, marking the new generation of our family. Richard was asleep when I entered the bedroom.

"Hey," I whispered loudly, "it's a girl! We have a niece named Brooke!"

My husband barely stirred. I shook his arm, wanting him to wake and acknowledge this new person in our family. I shook so hard that there can be only one explanation for his lack of response: Richard was feigning sleep.

The next day was our anniversary. When Richard came home with flowers and surprised me with a dinner reservation at our favorite restaurant, I told him I was too tired to go out.

Of course, when it was our own child, it was a different story. A year later, during my own pregnancy, Richard was completely attentive to my needs. And even though he already had a child, he never undermined my excitement to be a mother for the first time. My husband accompanied me on my first prenatal appointment and, to my surprise, bought all the pregnancy books he could find. When he handed them over, however, there was a catch. "No crowd at the hospital," Richard said, a new ultimatum.

"What do you mean? No family? I want my family there. Your sisters, too."

"No—nothing like when Brooke was born."

"It's not like we interrupted anything sitting on the couches, eating turkey and pastrami. Elizabeth was busy giving birth."

"Those sandwiches were awful."

"Look, Elizabeth loved having us there, supporting her. I want that."

"And I want my privacy."

"And I want my family," I insisted.

"*I'm* your family," Richard said. He had a point.

At the hospital when Alexandra was born, Richard greeted my parents and sister warmly enough—nothing could have kept them away—but he was fiercely protective of me and of our new daughter. At first he wouldn't let anyone enter our room, holding them off for a full hour until I had showered, applied makeup, and pulled on the silky reception robe that I had bought for the occasion. I relished having everyone there. I needed to share my joy with Elizabeth. I wanted my parents to hold and cradle their new granddaughter, whom we named Alexandra, the brave protector of man, a future daddy's girl.

My brother, David, flew in from New York, and Richard's sisters visited, brimming with pride over the Freeman family's first baby in fourteen years. When Auntie Gloria arrived, she was thrilled that I had given birth to a healthy baby girl. Harrison was away at his mother's in Pennsylvania, but he would be home again soon and we would begin our new phase together as a blended family, in which I intended to have more power.

I loved being a mom and felt more purpose than I ever had. Caring for a baby made intuitive sense to me. My parents visited us at home to cuddle and fawn over Alexandra. Elizabeth and Jake came frequently with Brooke, now two; they soon shared the news that Elizabeth was pregnant. David, then childless, flew up from New York on some weekends to spoil his new niece. After exchanging the briefest of greetings with our family guests, Richard would seclude himself in the master bedroom to pore over the Sunday *Globe* while I entertained everyone downstairs.

"Why don't you join us?" I asked when I went up to check on him during one such visit. "What's wrong?"

"You'll just ignore me. I'm staying right here, where what I want counts."

"I didn't realize I was ignoring you," I said. "When I try to bring you into the conversation, you barely speak."

"I'm not interested in what your mother had for dinner last night."

Elizabeth began to remark that she felt more comfortable coming over if Richard wasn't there. "Look, he doesn't like me," she said. "We ran into each other at the Dunkie's in Newton Center, and it was like we were strangers. He barely said hello. What'd I ever do to *him?*" At the time, I had tried to talk Elizabeth out of her opinion that Richard didn't like her or our family, but I was actually beginning to believe it.

"Your sister doesn't care about me; she only cares about you," Richard said matter-of-factly when I confronted him about not greeting Elizabeth. My parents and siblings eventually only visited on days when Richard played eighteen holes of golf. After the initial shock of the conflict wore off, I began to resent my husband's feelings, and I admit I took Richard's rejection of my sister personally. Elizabeth was part of me. I resented having to choose between my sister and my husband. I resented Richard for making me.

With Alexandra to care for, I cut back on my hours at Beth Israel to work part-time with patients in home care. And when the last of those clients no longer needed my therapy, I didn't seek others. I spent most days with Elizabeth and Brooke and Elizabeth's new daughter, Lauren, or with other friends who had toddlers.

A few years later, when Harrison left for college and Richard missed having the camaraderie of his son at home, he began to verbalize his strong distaste for my family and my allegiance to Elizabeth. He also began limiting his participation in my extended family to large gatherings, and that weighted every holiday, birthday party, and social event with expectation. Getting together became stressful; resentment took root on both sides. Small hurts and snubs between my family and Richard had officially started a cold war.

Chapter Five

_A_s soon as Elizabeth's MRI shows cancer, we waste no time in scheduling an oncology consult at Beth Israel, consistently ranked as one of the best hospitals in the United States. Luckily, I know whom to call to get in with Dr. Berg, the oncology director. All these years later, I still volunteer at Beth Israel after that first job treating stroke patients like Barbara. Now I'm involved with the Beth Israel Deaconess Medical Center Friends, a fund-raising arm of the hospital; I just finished a two-year term as president.

Within two days, Elizabeth, Jake, and I step from the elevator onto the hospital's eleventh floor. Elizabeth and I wear matching pale blue cashmere sweaters that we bought separately at Bloomingdale's. We didn't plan to wear the same sweater today, but it doesn't surprise me. Already we are twinned in this crisis.

The coded medical language of the faxed report—"right lower-extremity paresthesia, multiple T1 hypointense and T2 hyperintense bone marrow lesions"—becomes only more real when we stand before the large sign that reads SHAPIRO CANCER CENTER. The nurse takes Elizabeth for a CT scan, leaving Jake and me in the waiting room, where I can't concentrate enough to read even a celebrity magazine. I cross and uncross my legs.

I consider that someone else's report was mixed up with Elizabeth's. I begin making bargains with God. Even doctors make mistakes, I hope. Elizabeth never smoked, and she exercises five times a week. She buys organic groceries, eats her five fruits and vegetables. For Pete's sake, she broils, rather than fries! How could someone like my sister be diagnosed with cancer at forty-three?

Jake, a real estate guy, takes out his BlackBerry, pretending that there could be more important things to do. He's built relationships with national chains over the years and locates them to New England, scouting out a decrepit gas station on a corner lot, making an offer on the property, and leasing to a corporate chain. The franchisees like Jake because he's fast at numbers, decisions, and getting the job done. Although locals will try to stop his projects, Jake convinces the community that they will benefit from a big-box store or national supermarket chain, even if the trade-off is traffic. "Think of your property values," he tells them. "Through the roof!" Jake knows how to scale his projects but still turn a profit for the deal to make sense. He's tough, aggressive, and charming.

Jake turns his wrist to look at his watch. "Ten thirty," he says. "What the *fuck* has happened to us?"

I ignore my brother-in-law's question and grab *Vogue*, flipping pages. Sitting at Shapiro already feels like an eternity. I have always tried to protect my sister, and now I imagine her, alone, in the cavern of a hulking piece of CT machinery. I am at an utter loss.

When Elizabeth was born, I was three. My mother came home from the hospital and handed me her warm bundle while I was seated on the couch. Everyone who crowded the house in those days—my two sets of grandparents (Bubbee and Zadi, Nana and Papa), Auntie Gloria, Auntie Hannah, uncles, and neighbors from up and down the street—emphasized my responsibility as the big sister. Now that I'm grown, I realize it was just something to say to make the firstborn child feel special when the new baby was getting all the attention. But at the age of three, I took it very seriously and watched over Baby Elizabeth. That early impulse—and an awful knot in my stomach—only deepened as my sister grew into a toddler who suffered a bump on her elbow or a scraped knee, then into a little kid with a cold or the flu or a fever. Not that Elizabeth was ever a sickly kid, but when we both had the chicken pox, I was the one not able to sleep, listening to the rhythm of her breath on the other side of our nightstand.

The nurse calls, "Gordon," and Jake and I practically sprint into the scan room. No windows, dark except for a white-blue light in the corner.

Elizabeth sits on a metal table, wearing a light blue johnny. The whites of her eyes are large and liquid. The interpreting oncologist, reported to be one of the best at Beth Israel, closes the door, scratching his trim white beard. I actually know this particular doctor from my fund-raising work, and I remember him as a brilliant, down-to-earth gentleman who is easy to talk to. I can't ignore the irony that I've raised money for this very center. Although I knew it was important at the time, I realize only now that I did it pityingly and without empathy, naively not thinking that cancer could touch me.

Dr. Berg squints behind his glasses. The skin on his cheeks tightens and pulls. I take shallow breaths like a panting dog, waiting to hear the verdict. I want Dr. Berg to tell my sister and me that we can continue our lives, carpooling our children, walking at the reservoir, sharing our hopes and secrets, supporting each other in hard times. We're supposed to do this through all of life's changes, keep each other company as our children leave for college, interview for their first jobs, and get married, like we have. Despite the struggles I have in my marriage, it's how we are and how we want our children to be.

The doctor speaks softly, as if he doesn't want us to hear the bad news. He studies the film, and the words that come out of his mouth sound strange, like those on the fax.

"I'm sorry," Dr. Berg says. "Tumors have metastasized to the sacrum and hip area. A questionable spot on the liver."

I grab Elizabeth's hand and squeeze, squeeze, squeeze. From her mouth comes the high-pitched, frantic screaming of a wounded animal: "No! No! No!" Only when a nurse appears and places her hands on my sister's shoulders does Elizabeth calm down to a daze.

"My kids," she says, shaking her head back and forth.

Holding Elizabeth's hand, I feel a tremor travel through her body, like a zipper opening. Jake's face is drawn, pained. He paces the room before crouching in the corner to stare at his BlackBerry, unable to figure out how to use the force of his personality to fix this situation.

"We'll need more tests," the doctor says. He places a hand on Elizabeth's back, her complexion now flushed with what appears to be a combination of panic and sorrow.

The doctor prescribes Decadron, a powerful steroid. He says that it will begin shrinking the tumors in her hip and lessen her pain. He tells us to see a radiology oncologist, Nathan Gold. "He's who I'd see if it were for my own family," Dr. Berg says, and offers to set up the appointment himself.

I'm having trouble breathing. I feel as if I must leave the room, that it's too small for my rage. But I stay and see Elizabeth's mind racing, sizing up the situation. My energetic younger sister, who's fiercely private, must be collapsing inside. I guide her off the table and hug her, trying to absorb her sobs.

I shepherd Elizabeth out of the room to get her clothes and see Jake approach Dr. Berg. I know Jake—he always wants the bottom line. He likes his bad news the way he likes his vodka: straight up. I hear him whisper, "She'll be lucky to have five years, right?"

I glance at Elizabeth, whose attention seems focused on putting one foot in front of the other. When I'm sure she doesn't hear Jake's questions, I'm relieved. At least I can protect her from that. In five years, Elizabeth won't even be fifty. Brooke will be in college and Lauren about to graduate high school.

Dressed, Elizabeth walks ahead of me toward the elevator, holding a tissue to her nose. I wait for the doctor, who has followed us outside, wanting an answer to Jake's awful question, despite my fears. Dr. Berg closes his eyes, but not before I see the look he tries to hide. He's seen other fortysomething women with metastatic cancer; he must know what all of this means. He nods his head, slowly. "Yes," he says to Jake's question, by which he must mean *lucky to have five years.*

I stop short. That didn't sound like a five-year yes. I wonder what that yes really meant. Two years? Five months?

Walking the hospital corridors to the garage, I keep my arms around Elizabeth, her shoulders slumped, her head down. People hooked to IVs are wheeling by, and doctors pass us in white coats.

"You're going to be okay," I say to Elizabeth, trying to believe it myself. "We don't even know what type of cancer it is. They have so many different treatments now," I say, speaking as if mere wishes can come true. I hug my sister and kiss her forehead like I did when she was a little girl.

Elizabeth looks as if she wants to believe me, scanning my face for the hope I'm desperately trying to inject into my words. "What does this all mean?" she asks.

"We have to find out what type of cancer it is," I say, fixing our next step.

Elizabeth stands taller, back straightening, her shoulders squaring. "Sis, one thing's for sure: it don't sound good."

I study Elizabeth, considering all she stands to lose in the prime of her life as a young wife and mother. If she dies, her children's and our parents' lives will never be the same. I will lose my only sister and best friend—over forty years of us. We've been each other's maids of honor. She's the first person I call with good news. No one but Elizabeth notices when my hair gets trimmed a quarter inch, not even Richard. My first reaction to this tragedy is to feel desperately lonely.

We trudge to the car and return to the Gordons'. I sit in the back of Jake's Range Rover as he maneuvers through traffic on Beacon Street. No one speaks. We are spent.

"Thank God you're here," Jake says unexpectedly, meeting my eye in the rearview. He has said curiously little to Elizabeth. But just as I was the first person to know he was going to propose, I am the one with them now. Looking out the Range Rover's window, I notice men and women walking together, laughing with friends. What used to seem normal already feels foreign.

We pull up beside the Gordons' colonial in Weston. When they bought this house on a corner lot, just like one of Jake's franchises, he loved the idea that they could live in the leafy suburbs but be downtown in minutes via the Mass Pike. Elizabeth loves making her surroundings beautiful, so when it came to decor, she chose a designer with talent and a solid reputation. Elizabeth's home has always been her sanctuary, full of comfort, nurturing, and love. Entertaining enlivens her. She serves homemade food from our grandmother's recipes on her fine bone china, with authentically elegant style.

As Jake's business grew, he encouraged Elizabeth to enjoy spending. Slowly they redid the entire house. Carrara marble replaced worn tiles to make the bathrooms look like they belong in a luxury hotel. Elizabeth had the oak floors stained black. Her master bedroom sports an off-white carpet with a hand-cut crystal chandelier, showcasing a curvaceous headboard, and a built-in armoire—not for clothes, but for a widescreen TV. For the bed: three-hundred-thread-count, champagne-colored linens and a bedspread heavy against the floor with extra material. Last month, Elizabeth finally finished the kitchen with shiny white cabinets, black granite counters, and a mirrored backsplash. In her marriage and mine, luxury means love, and Elizabeth's new home represents the love-filled life she has made for herself and her family. Before, I wished only for Richard to see her in that light. Now, all of that has changed. All I want is for Elizabeth's cancer to disappear.

At the Gordons', Elizabeth and I collapse onto sofas in the den. Above us hang two framed, twenty-by-thirty-inch, black-and-white photographic prints of Brooke and Lauren, cross-legged at Breakwater Beach on Cape Cod. Two summers ago, they were twelve and nine, their smiles wide with innocence and privilege.

"They're all I ever cared about," Elizabeth says, pointing to her children's portraits. "I don't even care about myself."

I can't help but feel a twinge of hurt that she doesn't add Alexandra and me to this declaration, but I don't dwell on the slight. I know that there is reciprocity in my sister's feelings, even without her saying it.

"Why did this happen to me?" Elizabeth asks.

"I don't understand it," I said. Why her and not me? I am older, after all.

My cell phone buzzes in my pocket, and I check it. When I

see that it's Richard, I press DECLINE. I didn't tell him where I was going this morning. This isn't something that I feel like sharing with him.

"Richard?" Elizabeth asks.

"I hung up," I say. Even so, I can see her anger rise, the way she sets her shoulders.

"Listen, I don't want that man to know anything about this, about me," she says. Her voice is soft but stern. "That man cursed me. This is all happening because of him!"

Upon hearing this accusation, I go numb. Although I know cancer is not a curse, I actually understand how Elizabeth feels. For years, Richard has been trying to render her invisible.

Elizabeth's diagnosis also causes a truth to pulse forth in me: I no longer wonder what to do about my marriage or where my priorities lie. I will spend the days with my sister and her family. I will cook her dinners, drive her kids where they need to go, and navigate her through this illness. I will take Elizabeth to chemo and radiation, laugh, weep, console, and hope to heal her.

⫸⫷

THE TEST RESULTS return within days. A bone marrow biopsy confirms lung cancer, Stage IV. Too late for surgery. The cancerous tumors that spot both lungs have spread into my sister's bones. After dinner that night, I sit at my marble desk with a glass of red wine, googling *metastatic* and *chemotherapy* and *survival*. The more I learn, the more I drink, searching in vain for something positive or hopeful to read.

I learn, to my surprise, that lung cancer is the number-one cancer killer of men and women in the United States. It kills more people than breast, colon, prostate, and pancreatic cancer combined. Only 15 percent of people live more than five years postdiagnosis.

How did my sister get lung cancer? I used to assume that smoking caused lung cancer, but Elizabeth has never smoked a cigarette in her life. In fact, nobody in my family ever smoked cigarettes, so we can also rule out secondhand smoke. The mystery—what feels more like an injustice—compels more research. I discover that there is an epidemic of lung cancer among American nonsmoking women in their forties.

I find a lung cancer chat room that supports family members. I instantly create a profile and explain my situation. The first question anyone asks is, "How long since your sister's diagnosis?"

"Five days," I type back.

"I felt the ground give way," someone types back. As soon as I read that, I feel understood. The ground is indeed giving way, and I am trying not to fall in.

When I drag myself to bed, it's 2:00 a.m. Alexandra has fallen asleep with her television on. I slip into her room, turn it off, and kiss her on the forehead. She knows that her auntie has cancer but still doesn't comprehend the gravity of the situation.

In our room, Richard is fast asleep. Not that it would matter if he were awake. These days, we barely speak. I know he must sense that something is terribly wrong, but he hasn't expressed the slightest curiosity or concern. He's been busy at the office. I can't bring myself to tell him about the diagnosis, and Elizabeth doesn't want me to anyway. I crawl onto my side of the bed, careful not to touch Richard.

My head hits the pillow, and I'm out.

I have always been an early riser, a lover of the morning hours, but now when I wake before dawn I am on high alert, with a cortisol rush: tense, on my back, my arms at my sides.

The room is still dark; the bedside clock ticks loudly. Around Elizabeth and Jake, I have tried not to acknowledge how miserable I feel, but my grief runs as deep as the cancer in my sister's bones. I pull myself from the bed and to the bathroom.

My face is drawn and pale. I splash water on it, rub in moisturizer with the tips of my fingers, and pull on spandex pants and sneakers in the half-light. I find my car keys and slip out of the house.

I drive to the reservoir. I run once, twice, around the expanse of gray-blue water. Cold air slaps my skin and draws tears. I run harder and faster, until I'm near collapse. But no matter how hard and fast I run, I can't overtake the terror.

None of us had any reason to doubt a diagnosis of sciatica. People injure nerves, pull discs, rip muscles, and break bones all the time, especially in their forties and beyond. You live with it. You buy a bottle of Aleve and give yourself time to heal. But this isn't sciatica. It's worse than a spot on the lung. I buckle over on the side of the path.

A filmy mist covers the reservoir today. I feel bitter about Richard's feelings toward Elizabeth. I'm angry to have wasted precious time allowing my marital problems to be top of mind for so many years, the now-embarrassing frequency with which I compared my marital problems to a cancer spreading.

I remember a particular argument I had with Richard one morning before he left for the office. "I can't stand this focus on your family," he said, as he yanked the knot in his tie and slipped on a sport jacket. "You work too hard at those relationships."

"I don't work—they come naturally," I said.

"You want Alexandra and Brooke to be like sisters. They aren't sisters; they're cousins."

"Yeah, you sure took care of that." I knew Alexandra was afraid to mention the Gordons in front of Richard. "Brooke and Lauren don't even feel comfortable in our home," I said. "You ignore them, you criticize. You even accused Lauren of eating too many pickles one Passover."

"You're always on their side," Richard said.

"And you're always testing whose side I'm on. Come on—they're children."

Richard wanted loyalty—and, as my husband, he deserved it—but it was difficult to be compassionate when he showed so little concern for me. If I shared my feelings, he dismissed them, or he put me on trial like a prosecutor, questioning every word I said. I could not work through my indignation to compromise.

"I can't stand how important they are to you," Richard said for the umpteenth time. "You don't have to see your brother *every* time he's in from New York."

"He visits six times a year."

"And it's like the king has arrived, every time," Richard said. "Your mother? She calls too damn much. When you're all together, everyone ignores me. They don't ask me questions about myself. I wish I could just put them all on a plane to California and say 'see you later.'" For so long, these conversations had felt like a spreading disease.

At the reservoir, I glance at my watch. I've run for an hour. I stand and take a deep breath, drawing strength from this quiet place. The leaves on birches across the water are autumn yellow; they dance in the breeze. I will drive home and make breakfast for my daughter. I will be there for my sister, her husband, and her family. Richard won't like it, but I'll do what I have to do. Anything less is inconceivable.

When I arrive home, Richard is in the kitchen, briefcase in hand. "Where were you out so early?" he asks.

"The reservoir." I blurt, "My sister has cancer," and burst into tears.

"I knew something was wrong," Richard says, moving toward me.

"I'm so upset," I say, backing away.

"What kind of cancer?" he asks softly. But his tenderness does not comfort me.

"We're not sure yet," I lie, and wonder if he can already see the gravity on my face.

"Well, don't overreact," he says, turning chipper. "Hopefully, she can beat it. She needs to have a good attitude." Although another person might take that as encouragement, Richard's comment makes me feel belittled and blamed. So if Elizabeth doesn't make it, she didn't have a good enough *attitude*?

I immediately regret having told Richard about Elizabeth's cancer. If he couldn't be kind to her in health, I don't want his kindness for her now, and neither does Elizabeth.

I can count on one hand those who know the real diagnosis: my parents, my brother and sister-in-law, and Jake. Elizabeth realizes that people will find out she's sick, but she doesn't want anyone to know that it's metastasized, or that it started in her lungs—the cancer of blame. Even Jake's extended family is still in the dark. The last thing my proud and private sister wants is for anyone to know that she might die.

Chapter Six

*E*ight thirty on a Tuesday morning, and Elizabeth, Jake, and I are tense but hopeful, en route to a string of oncologist appointments. As we file into Beth Israel, it still feels surreal—it will every time—to have crossed the point of no return.

I now identify with my sister's diagnosis to the extent that, when we walk into the morning's first appointment, the radiation oncologist asks, "Who's the patient?"

Elizabeth says, "I am" and raises her hand with a nervous giggle.

The oncologist, Dr. Gold, is surprisingly young: braces on his teeth, thick brown hair over his ears, and nerdy—until he speaks and his wonderful personality emerges. His office is painted in warm golds and creams that complement his name and persona.

"Nice to meet you," Dr. Gold says, and reaches out to shake Elizabeth's petite hand. I sit on one side of her, Jake on the other. The doctor takes a seat behind his desk and speaks in a soothing voice. "You need radiation treatments right away."

Elizabeth bites her lip, placing her hand on Jake's knee. I take out my pen and legal pad, knowing he will give us a lot of information.

Dr. Gold tells us that Elizabeth will receive twenty treatments over a three-to-four-week period. They will be short and concentrated—no more than fifteen minutes each—but frequent, five days a week. There will be side effects: fatigue, skin irritation, diarrhea, nausea. Elizabeth will be tattooed light green in order to undergo repeat radiation in exactly the same area.

Having a doctor speak so candidly is more comforting than I'd have thought. We listen intently. Dr. Gold is giving us a plan, a trail to follow out of this chaos. I take fervent notes on my yellow pad. Elizabeth and Jake huddle together, his hand in her lap.

"I know all of this is very difficult," Dr. Gold says. "What are your questions?"

"What can I focus on that's positive?" Elizabeth asks.

The doctor pauses and smiles. "You have youth on your side. No other significant medical problems, no lymph node involvement. Your liver and adrenal glands are okay."

"What if Elizabeth had had the MRI at the beginning of summer?" I ask. "Would that have made a difference?" I can't rid myself of seeing my sister at the Cape, limping after our walk on the beach. At that point, Aleve still helped.

Dr. Gold tents his fingers and shakes his head. "No difference. At that time, the cancer had already spread."

"Why no other warnings?" I ask, amazed at such devastation without a trace.

"Patients are often asymptomatic," the doctor tries to explain. "No shortness of breath, no coughing up blood, no chest pain." He says this like it's a good thing. What he doesn't say is that *asymptomatic* really means there was nothing to alert us to Elizabeth's condition before the cancer progressed to Stage IV. The mutation was stealthy; it took over before we had any chance of stopping it. I feel so helpless.

Dr. Gold has already asked if Elizabeth has ever smoked, and whether there was any radon in the house in Gloucester where we grew up—also no. I'm afraid he'll say that the cancer was stress induced, that Elizabeth and I will forever blame Richard, but the doctor doesn't say anything like that, and I don't dare ask. According to that logic, I'd be the one with cancer.

"Elizabeth," Dr. Gold says, "you belong to a group called Nonsmoking Women in their Forties with Lung Cancer."

"Why? How did I get this way?"

"We don't know," he says apologetically.

"What's the radiation like?" Elizabeth asks.

"You'll feel tired. The effects are cumulative, so the beginning will be a bit easier."

"Can I drive?" Elizabeth asks.

"Yes, depending on your energy."

"Will I feel like exercising?"

"Some of my patients do," he says. "You look fit."

"Will the side effects last a long time?"

"The skin over your hip that is radiated will turn red." He describes how Elizabeth should apply aloe to it every day, right from the beginning, to ease what will feel like a sunburn. I make a note to buy an aloe plant, and circle it.

"What can we hope for?" Jake asks. I notice how carefully he monitors his question, damming up the words that might otherwise spill.

"I'd say that we can be . . . cautiously optimistic," Dr. Gold says.

My eyes widen. Does *cautiously optimistic* mean that Elizabeth could live a normal life, or that she could survive a year? I don't press the doctor because I don't really want to know. For now, I like how his phrase sounds without the qualifiers.

Dr. Gold's kindness is brilliant and unending. He stays

with us for an hour, answering all of our questions, giving us hope. Then he sends us upstairs to a thoracic oncologist, whom he calls a rock star.

We take the elevator from the first to the ninth floor. When we check in with the receptionist, she says the doctor is ready and escorts us to a small corner office.

Dr. Blaz Varghas, five foot ten, with light brown hair, shakes our hands. Even his grip is reassuring. He speaks with a faint Eastern European accent. The doctor's gaze is direct and steady, and his face is open and kind, not yet hardened by the toll of his profession. I remove my beige linen jacket—the room is warm—and take out my notepad.

Dr. Varghas treats Elizabeth as if she were his only patient in the world, and all of us as if we were the most important people he knows. He seems a bit younger than we are, and he is patient and tolerant of our questions. I find myself mesmerized. Dr. Varghas spends nearly three hours explaining Elizabeth's options for treatment and giving us a picture of the near future, taking question after question, no matter how redundant they seem to be.

"Elizabeth's cancer is indolent," Dr. Varghas says, "slow-growing. But she needs chemotherapy as soon as possible." He recommends that Elizabeth receive a combination of carboplatinum and Taxol every three weeks for four to six cycles. Two weeks into chemo, she will begin losing her hair. There will also be a monthly infusion of Zometa, a bone-strengthening drug that prevents fractures. Taxol will make her joints feel achy and/or tingly. Seven to ten days after the infusion, she will feel most tired, when all of her blood levels will be at their lowest. "Elizabeth, if your temperature ever spikes to 101.5," Dr. Varghas warns, "call me immediately. I will give you my cell phone number."

As we leave, the doctor's eyes hold mine for a beat. He seems to understand that even though I am not the patient, I, too, am suffering. I can't help but glance at his left hand. No ring, but, then again, not all married doctors wear wedding bands. I catch myself, vowing not to fall for this kind man whose voice could melt ice.

Exhausted with information, Elizabeth, Jake, and I sprawl on the hospital steps and soak in the seventy-degree day. Brookline Avenue is choked with traffic. Medical buildings line both sides of the street, like the campus of a large university. Cars and taxis stop and start, and buses drop off nearby, all those tailpipes polluting the air.

"I always sort of wanted a tattoo," Elizabeth says.

"I'm glad we're getting started," I say.

"We'll have to make arrangements for the kids," she then says, turning serious. "Mom and Dad will have to pick them up from school."

Even two feet away on the steps, I can feel the adrenaline behind my sister's plans. Elizabeth's entire life is her children. She will protect and support their healthy development through this challenging time. She'll help them cope, putting their needs ahead of her own healing—if I don't stop her.

"Only the two of you should come to chemo and radiation," Elizabeth says to Jake and me. "No friends ever. If David's in town, he can come. Once in a while, maybe Mom and Dad."

Jake stands. "Let's grab a sandwich."

Our next appointment is with a doctor who I know Jake hopes will enroll Elizabeth in a medical trial, but I already feel attached to Dr. Varghas.

After a couple of soggy food-court sandwiches, we drive to Dana Farber, a cancer center of national repute that we're lucky to have nearby. An affiliate of Harvard Medical School, the Dana Farber Cancer Institute is known for its cutting-edge research and up-to-the-minute treatments. If there is a medical trial that could save my sister, it will be here.

As we walk inside, I get an eerie feeling. It's different entering Dana Farber. Unlike at Beth Israel, a general hospital, everyone treated in this building has cancer.

We navigate our way to Thoracic Oncology for the proverbial second opinion, from someone named Dr. Stern. He's tall, about our age, with caterpillar eyebrows like Governor Dukakis. Jake heard that Dr. Stern lives in the Gordons' neighborhood and coaches a soccer team.

We sit in Stern's office and hand over the results of Elizabeth's MRI, bone marrow biopsy, and CT scan. This newest oncologist reviews the reports at his spotless steel desk, never making eye contact. I try to read him as a defendant might read the faces of jurors filing into the courtroom one last time with their verdict already etched in stone.

The matter-of-factness Dr. Stern uses to present our treatment options gives me the sense that Elizabeth will need a miracle to stay alive. This doctor's attitude toward her prognosis is very different than Varghas's and Gold's, and I begin to question their optimism.

"We would use a combination of two drugs, carboplatinum and Taxol," he says. At least this much is the same. "Standard protocol for advanced lung cancer." I can't help but be stung by his use of *advanced*, which somehow sounds worse than *Stage IV*.

"How often would we come for treatments?" I ask, leaning forward.

"Every three weeks," Dr. Stern says. "And she—you," he says, now addressing Elizabeth, "should pack a lunch. Plan to spend the entire day."

"Will any of this make me better?" Elizabeth whispers.

"That remains to be seen," the doctor says. "Frankly, some patients respond better than others. It's idiosyncratic, just like people. There's no way to predict whose treatment will be successful." He pauses. "I'll take questions."

"What about clinical trials?" Jake asks. From his tone, I can tell that he's steamed; why didn't the doctor raise the possibility of a trial himself? "What can Dana Farber offer us that Beth Israel won't?" Jake demands. I smile despite myself upon hearing him adapt a line that he has probably used in business.

"There is a new drug, Iressa," the doctor stammers. "But I don't advise it. Elizabeth will have better success with the standard protocol."

"Why?" Jake asks.

"Iressa is designed for those with the EGFR mutation." Because it's 2003 and genetic testing is not mainstream, Dr. Stern believes that the long wait for genetic testing will compromise Elizabeth's treatment. Like Dr. Varghas, he urges immediate chemo. "If she responds well and the tests later show EGFR, Iressa can be Elizabeth's second-line drug."

Elizabeth tucks her hair behind her ears, and I detect that her hands are shaking. I write *EGFR mutation* and *Iressa* in my notebook so I can look them up when we get home.

"Chemotherapy is much easier to tolerate than it used to be," Dr. Stern says, for the hard sell. "We have far better anti-nausea medications."

When we leave this last office, I am startled to find that we've been inside for only thirty minutes. I take a long, steadying breath. The looks on Elizabeth and Jake's faces suggests that their hopes are dashed. I can't believe that doctor's icy demeanor.

Back at the car, Jake jiggles the keys in his pocket and asks the obvious question. "Who do you like better, Varghas or this asshole?"

"I like Varghas much better," I say.

"No question," Jake says, turning to Elizabeth. "What about you?"

"Varghas. Definitely Varghas."

We climb into the Range Rover. Elizabeth slides into the passenger seat, and I buckle up in the back. "But do you think it's okay to go to Beth Israel when Dana Farber is supposed to be, you know, *Dana Farber?*" I ask, even though I know that both hospitals are affiliated with Harvard Medical School and have fine reputations.

"Both doctors gave us the same treatment plan," Jake says, "and Varghas is more compassionate, willing to explain everything. We need someone like that."

"He gave me hope," Elizabeth says.

"That's true," I say.

"Now I've got a question for you, Samantha," Jake says. The edge in his voice takes me by surprise. I look up to see him glaring intently in the rearview mirror, key poised before the ignition. "Are you going to be there for us? For our family?"

"What? Of course I'll be there."

"Okay," Jake says, starting the engine, but he doesn't seem satisfied.

"Why are you even asking me this? I'm here now, aren't I?" I try to catch Elizabeth's eye in the rearview mirror, but she has put on her sunglasses and turned away.

Jake cranks the wheel, and the Rover jolts out of the parking space. Then Jake stops us short with the emergency brake and turns to me in the backseat.

"I don't want Richard within a *mile* of this," he hisses. "Do you understand? He should never be involved or know anything. No access. Whatever he finds out, it can be through the grapevine."

Elizabeth adds nothing, signaling her assent.

For a few seconds, there is silence in the car. I can hear my heart pounding and Elizabeth breathing. Even in this dire circumstance, it is Richard who tops their minds.

"Why would you bring up Richard now?" I ask.

"He wished this on Elizabeth," Jake says.

"That's unfair," I say. Jake is twisting things.

My body feels rashy, as if my clothes have suddenly turned to sandpaper. These words squeeze my heart like a vise. Having to promise Jake and Elizabeth not to tell Richard anything more keeps me where I've been all these years, in the middle, alone. In another moment I might have pushed back against their demand, but I'm exhausted from the doctors' visits and dread, now shocked by Jake's petty priorities.

"I just need ten years," Elizabeth says, as if part of an altogether different conversation. "I just need to see my kids grow up."

Chapter Seven

————

*A*s businessmen, Richard and Jake had both managed seasons of scarcity and plenty, but it did little to increase their mutual understanding.

In the late '80s, just after we married, Richard's business went through a rough patch. Interest rates were at historic highs; it was a tough climate for private equity. Richard's investors demanded higher returns, but the margins didn't allow it. "Having money doesn't mean having sense," he was quick to say of others, complaining that his clients called only to "cry me the blues."

It was around then that Jake called in a favor to Richard, his new brother-in-law. At Elizabeth's suggestion, Jake asked Richard if he had any office space that Richard could spare, that Jake might occupy—for free—to get back on his feet.

As grueling as business had become for Richard, for Jake things were worse. He had earned steady commissions as a real estate broker, but then the company he worked for went bankrupt. Jake and Elizabeth found themselves forced to sell their house in Weston and rent a modest apartment in Watertown. Brooke was a baby, and the apartment was too small for a home office. Jake couldn't afford to have an infant crying in the background, to be distracted while trying to woo potential investors for his new venture. To Richard, Jake framed the favor of the office as a convenience, but I knew it came from desperation. He had already borrowed money from his parents just to keep him, Elizabeth, and Brooke afloat.

"Anything is fine," Jake assured Richard. "A closet, a storeroom. It's temporary." But as soon as Richard agreed to give Jake the office, I knew we were in for trouble.

Resentments already simmered between the two men, and, on top of that, their personalities clashed. Richard's coldness and indifference toward Elizabeth were snowballing and beginning to make even me uncomfortable. My gut warned me that doing Jake a favor was not a good idea, but it was almost impossible for Richard to say no. Here, Richard had a chance to live up to our family code, and, to his credit, he did, sort of: he told Jake that he could occupy one of Richard's office suites rent-free. In exchange, Jake had to give Richard the right of first refusal to fund Jake's projects.

According to Richard, that was when the problems began. In that simple transaction—one man asking a favor, the other granting it with conditions—a grave misunderstanding occurred. As Richard told it, Jake quickly started to take advantage. In addition to having the office and using Richard's receptionist and secretary, Jake went on the market, leveraging Richard's name and reputation for his own profit.

"Without me," Richard complained, "Jake couldn't get financing from a bail bondsman. He might have a head for deals, but he has no capital."

While Jake did give Richard first rights on some of his early closings—a strip mall, a forty-unit apartment building at a T stop—in a skittish, cash-scarce economy, those deals fell through.

Jake's "temporary" situation continued for a few years. Richard worked long days and nights in his penthouse office, watching accounts dwindle, trying to balance the payouts he owed banks and other lenders against cash on hand, contemplating the real possibility that he could lose everything he had worked for. Jake, meanwhile, worked sixty hours a week from Richard's third floor and borrowed living expenses from his parents. He canvassed New England in a used car, casing the region for real estate.

Slowly, breakthroughs came. Jake's contacts eventually flooded Judy, Richard's receptionist, with calls. This was in the '90s, before some offices had digital voice mail, when receptionists spent a considerable amount of time dictating and delivering messages.

Jake's cash deals were numerous but small fry, well below Richard's interest and his fund's threshold. When Richard didn't stand to benefit from Jake's profits—and when Jake, according to Richard, began to abuse his staff by treating them as if they were incompetent—Richard pressured me to broker a deal between them.

"He's *your* brother-in-law," Richard said. "Call him and tell him to pay me."

The next day, I did just that. After allowing Jake to fill me in on several of his latest closings, I saw my chance. "Now that you're making real money, why don't you offer Richard some rent?"

"I knew it," Jake said. "He put you up to this, didn't he? Why doesn't Richard call me himself?" I had the same question.

Jake and Richard did manage to work out a reasonable rate for Jake's tenancy: $400 per month. *Good*, I thought. Of course, I wanted them both to succeed—our families depended on it. I was heartbroken when Elizabeth had to sell their house. It hurt me to see her struggling and was strange for us to be on unequal footing; I felt guilty and awkward whenever I even bought a new blouse.

Then Jake got a lucky break. He became involved with Stars, a national discount retailer looking to make inroads in New England—what would become his specialty. He scouted suburban sites where Stars might want to bulldoze and locate; he invited franchisees on real estate tours in a leased Audi. Because he was now paying Richard rent, Jake didn't think he owed him anything anymore. In the ultimate rebuff, Jake used an outside partner to finance Stars' relocations because he would be able to control the majority of the deal.

When I visited Richard's office, if the two men crossed paths in the stairwell, they avoided eye contact. Soon Jake was making deal after deal and didn't need Richard anymore. He had a new luster and with it came the intensity of a hard-nosed businessman. Eventually, Jake rented his own suite of penthouse offices in the financial district and left Richard without expressing gratitude. Richard felt like a used dishrag.

The tension in my family came from two places: Richard and Jake's business issue on top of Richard's allergy to my family's closeness. Richard and I had opposite goals involving the people I loved, which caused a deep wedge in our marriage.

I remembered two incidents. The first was when my mother invited us to my father's birthday brunch at their two-bedroom condo. The slick high-rise overlooked a pond, part of Boston's historic string of treescapes and waterways called the Emerald Necklace, everything bursting in autumn colors. Alexandra, Richard, and I were the last to arrive, which embarrassed me. Richard had awoken late that morning and, oddly, before he would leave had insisted on reading the entire *New York Times*.

"My allergies are bothering me," he explained, sneezing twice in quick succession to prove the point.

I observed his reddened face and suspected he was allergic to my family.

When we arrived at my parents' building, we took the elevator to the fifth floor. My clammy hands stuck to the knob as I turned it. The first people we saw were Elizabeth and Jake, sitting around the glass dining room table, immersed in conversation. I leaned over to kiss each of them hello while Richard rushed his greeting and disappeared into the kitchen. Jake, following Richard with his eyes, smirked. Alexandra ran past the adults and took her place on the sofa in the den, with her cousins.

Richard then appeared in the doorway and, with a jerk of his head, motioned me to the kitchen. We loaded our plates with bagels, lox and kugel, a scrumptious noodle pudding that was my mother's specialty. When we were ready to sit, Richard scanned the dining room, but the only open seats were near Jake. We hesitated. Elizabeth; my father; my brother, David; and his wife, Jill, were also seated at the glass-top dining table, and Richard felt less resentful, at the time, toward them. We sat. But as soon as Richard lifted a forkful of kugel, Jake stood, picked up his plate, and moved to the den on the pretense of supervising the kids. My mother came out of the kitchen and we locked eyes. *Here we go again.*

"Jake?" my father said. "Were we finished talking?"

"I'm in here, with the kids," Jake shouted back, a bit too harshly.

After Jake's antics, Richard gave Elizabeth his back. He turned to David. "Skiing this winter?"

"No plans yet," David said, chuckling. "But I can see you're planning ahead. Will your house be done?"

"I'm leaning on the contractor to make it happen. I can't wait. It's going to be our own little slice of Aspen in Vermont—right, Samantha?" Richard asked, as I forked food around on my plate.

"Love log homes," David said.

Elizabeth squirmed. "Richard," she said, trying to engage him, leaning forward and torqueing her neck. "We're actually going to Aspen at the end of February."

Richard narrowed his eyes and gave her a quick turn of his head. "Okay," he said. Then he turned his back and continued talking to David. "We're skiing next weekend. Mount Snow got a foot for our annual Thanksgiving run!"

"Richard, once you build, will you still ski out West?" Elizabeth tried again.

Richard deliberately finished chewing his bagel. "This is the second time you've interrupted me." He took a gulp of orange juice and banged his glass on the table. "I'm leaving," he announced, standing.

Elizabeth's face reddened. "I just wanted to be included," she said, stunned.

The rest of my family was shocked into speechlessness. My gut instinct was to protect my sister, not my husband. I could see that the party was excruciating for him, but I couldn't get past his bad behavior. I followed Richard as he ran out.

"Wait," I pleaded. "She just wanted to talk to you."

"I'm out of here," he growled. He pushed past me and slammed the door.

There was silence in the room, except for Alexandra, now weeping. Jake jumped off the sofa and walked toward me.

"After all Richard did for you? How could you be so childish?" I asked.

"Get used to it. We don't like each other," Jake said.

"What is wrong with this family?" my father shouted from the table, his birthday brunch ruined. "You're telling me we can't enjoy a meal together?"

ONE YOM KIPPUR I hosted Richard's family for break the fast. Yom Kippur is the holiest and most sober of high holidays, when Jews fast to atone for their sins. For those of us who are observant, once we reach the age of thirteen, we consume no food or drink.

I consider myself a spiritual Jew. I don't derive much meaning from hearing and reciting Hebrew itself, but I love the rich, rabbinical debates captured in the midrash. Was there really a God who recorded each of our names in the Book of Life, listing who would live and who would die? I doubt it. Although I know most prayers in Hebrew by heart, it is always the rabbi's sermon at temple that I most enjoy, the practical wisdom he imparts. Of course, the topic of any sermon on Yom Kippur is forgiveness. Yearly, as we acknowledge and atone for our sins, we make space in our hearts to forgive others, who in turn forgive us. At least, that's the way it's supposed to go.

Since we'd gotten married, Richard and I had been members of the synagogue where his deceased parents had belonged, where he attended Hebrew school in short pants as a child. I would have preferred to have joined a new synagogue together as newlyweds—a fresh start, claiming an area of our lives as our own—but Richard wanted to extend his family's tradition, and I acquiesced, hoping to nurture a rare connection to his past.

Every Yom Kippur, Richard had the honor of holding the Torah while the rabbi and cantor recited prayers; the three of them circled the congregation. These holidays were almost as important to Richard as his business. When Richard entered the synagogue, men shook his hand, and a profound peace settled on my husband's face when he chanted in Hebrew.

After Richard returned the Torah to the ark, he walked

back to me, Harrison and Alexandra in our seats, nodding and saying, "Good *yontiff*" (meaning *good holiday*) to those he passed.

"I had the heaviest one," Richard whispered in my ear as he sat.

"I noticed," I said, and we shared a laugh appropriate for temple. Torahs could weigh as much as thirty pounds.

That year, Rabbi Bromberg ended his sermon with a quote from the scholar Hillel: "Do not do unto others what you would not want done unto you." I tried to live my life like that but at times I knew I had failed.

After the service, Richard's extended family came to our house for break the fast. By the time we got home from temple, it was seven o'clock. I knew everyone would be ravenous for that first bite of food. I had prepared a traditional meal of bagels, whitefish salad, sablefish, lox, and herring. Richard's sisters, brother-in-law, nieces, and nephews swarmed the house, arming themselves with salads, fruits, and desserts.

"You made it to the finish line," Richard said, as he leaned down to kiss his thirteen-year-old niece, Chloe.

"I'm starving! This was the first year I fasted, Uncle Rich."

"I'm proud of you," Richard said. "Eat, eat—there's plenty."

As I observed this interaction, my smile froze. I immediately dropped the lesson of Yom Kippur, forgetting the rabbi's admonition to forgive, indignant that Richard could enjoy himself with *his* family but be a part of so much friction with mine. Half in annoyance, half in shame, I fled to the kitchen.

I opened the refrigerator to take out the platters when Richard's sister Patty, upbeat and skinny, with two inches on me, came in and asked, "Can I help you with anything?"

"Sure," I said. "Put out some more of that lox?"

"You okay?" Patty asked.

"Just tired," I said. I wouldn't dare confide in her my problems about her brother. I handed Patty the fresh platters, and we quickly set up a buffet at the kitchen counter.

"Help yourselves. You guys must be famished," I said when it was all set.

In the dining room, Richard sat at the head of the table, his two sisters on either side. I sat at the opposite end and watched everyone eat, waiting for the satisfaction of feeding our family to hit, but it never did.

"Look at the kids loading up on those pickles," Richard said, his smile as wide as the pickle jar. "True Freemans."

While this beautiful scene should have made me happy and proud, a knot tightened in my stomach. My husband was such a different man with his own relatives. Chatting casually with those around the table, I realized I may never be as close to them as my own family. It should have made me feel empathy for Richard, who might similarly never penetrate my family's inner circle. Instead, I decided that my closeness to them was the root of the problem.

"Richie, remember Irving's? The toy store?" Claudia, Richard's other sister, said. She was five years younger than Richard and dressed even younger than her age, wearing a short skirt and suede, thigh-high boots I thought more appropriate for a night on the town.

Richard chuckled. "Of course, I remember. We walked by it today."

"That same woman still owns it," Claudia said.

"She must be a hundred years old," Patty chimed in.

"I used to load my pockets with candy as a kid. There, I've confessed," Richard said, and he and his sisters exploded in laughter and shared nostalgia.

I tuned out, watching Richard's nieces and nephews gorge

themselves on pickles and bagels. When they finished eating, Harrison led them to the den, where he had a PlayStation.

Seeing all of this effortless cheer made me begrudge the lack of cohesiveness between Richard and my family. The message of Yom Kippur, the holiest and most transformative day of the year, was lost on me. I felt like I was hit in the stomach, a gut-wrenching combination of anxiety and loneliness.

I started to sense that I might be wasting my time trying to make my family and my marriage into something they were not.

Chapter Eight

————

*W*e arrive from Beth Israel and Dana Farber to our mother and her nervous tension, pacing the marble foyer at the Gordons.

"Daddy's waiting in the kitchen," she says, opening the door before we reach it. "Another delivery person just called." Bouquets of flowers are everywhere.

My mother—blue-eyed, size 8 in her seventies, with blond, salon-styled hair—raised us on good manners, social grace, and the ability to balance a checkbook. She has always been enterprising. The second we kids no longer demanded so much of her time, she opened a candy store, and when Elizabeth was diagnosed, my mother was enjoying a successful third act playing partners' tournament bridge.

Tonight everything about our mom's appearance reads heartbreak. Although she still looks ten years younger than her age, her posture has slackened. Her facial muscles seem paralyzed, as if she might never smile again. For the first time, I notice her long, elegant fingers tremor.

"It's never the things you worry about that knock you on your ass," she later confides in me. We have no family history of cancer.

We find my father with his elbows planted on the Gordons' granite breakfast bar, hands clasped. He's five foot eleven and square-faced, an ex-Marine and retired pharmacist dating back to when most pharmacists owned their own stores, in the 1950s. After all those years of dispensing confident advice and nursing others back to health, my father will surprise me with his timidity, now that it's one of us.

We stagger with exhaustion into the kitchen. Jake disappears into his home office off the hallway, needing a break.

"Daddy, I'm so sick," Elizabeth says, her shoulders sagging.

"What? What did the doctors say?" my father asks.

"I need chemo and radiation. No guarantees," she says, and breaks down.

My father's eyes brim with tears, and he wipes them away. I've never seen him cry before.

"Please, tell us everything," he says.

Until now, we have known only the big picture—lung cancer—but we haven't known what the treatments will entail. I stand with my legal pad and relate all of the information, appointment by appointment, flipping pages, surprised at how calm I am. I explain about the radiation and chemotherapy, repeat Dr. Gold's phrase "cautiously optimistic," and reiterate that Elizabeth has youth on her side. I concentrate on comforting my parents the way in which I, too, crave comfort.

They listen, speechless, and when I finish, my parents cling to Elizabeth and me in a hug. The timeless scent of my mother's Chanel lingers on her clothes, and I wish we could transport ourselves back to decades earlier, to our childhood home in Gloucester—an innocent time. I wish the hug would make me feel better. It does not.

"I'll research the side effects," my father says. "We'll get through this," he chokes out.

I excuse myself to the bathroom to be alone. The counter

is teeming with flowers, as if my mother has stashed extra deliveries here as they came. The combination of different aromas turns my stomach, especially the pungent stargazer lilies, which smell like pee. Elizabeth has begun telling close friends that she has a treatable form of cancer, not Stage IV, and those friends have told friends. I have never seen so many different arrangements outside of a florist. Orchids, roses, mixed flowers, aloe plants, and topiaries, all a little too much like a funeral. I want these offerings to look as if they belong in a home of the living, not of the dead.

I pull pots from the bathroom, begin tucking them onto sills and end tables. Any ordinary day, a single vase of pink tulips would sit alone on Elizabeth's coffee table.

"People must know I'm really sick," Elizabeth says as I leave the bathroom. "It doesn't matter what we say." The phone rings, and she looks at the caller ID. "I don't feel like talking to anyone."

We listen to the voice that projects out of the answering machine, one of Elizabeth's best friends. "Hi, it's Jane. Please call. I've been trying to reach you for days."

Elizabeth punches STOP on the machine and crosses her arms. "I'll call her later," she says, leaning against the wall.

Lauren sprints into the kitchen in shorts and a sweaty T-shirt. A friend trails behind, holding a bottle of Poland Spring.

"Mom, can you take us for ice cream?" To be eleven is to be oblivious.

Elizabeth looks at me as if to say, *How will I ever tell her?* Lauren doesn't know the extent of Elizabeth's illness, nor can she imagine what lies ahead. This is not the time.

"Later," she says about the ice cream. "After dinner."

"How was the doctor?" Lauren asks.

"I'm going to have some treatments, but I'll be okay. It wasn't too bad."

Lauren squints and fiddles with her Red Sox cap. "When? What kind of treatments?"

"We'll talk later, honey bunch," Elizabeth says, which seems to satisfy her daughter. Lauren and her friend run back outside to ride their bikes. "I want you showered in thirty minutes," Elizabeth calls after her.

"I dread that conversation," Elizabeth says when Lauren is out of earshot. "I'm failing her as a mother," she says, choking up.

"Don't you ever say that," I say, holding my sister. I rest my chin on her head.

"So many people care," she says, peeking at the flowers I've just placed. "I'm surprised how nice that feels."

"I'm not surprised—people always tell me how caring you are."

"But, honestly?" Elizabeth pauses. "So many flowers kinda creeps me out. Like having the funeral while I'm still alive."

I gasp and get ready to scold her—*Don't talk like that!*—but when Elizabeth turns, I see that she is smiling.

"I'll check on Brooke," I say. "Be right back." Little scamp.

I climb the carpeted stairs and find Brooke sitting at her computer in a red hoodie. She's sucking on her sweatshirt laces, which has become a habit, but I don't say anything. Brooke notices me in the doorway, turns, and gives me a quick "Hi," then retreats to her computer screen. She's not ready to accept this.

At the foot of the stairs, I peek in on Jake in the office. He's got his Sox cap pulled low, brim below his brow, nose nearly touching the computer screen.

"What could possibly be so important," I ask, "that you have to do it *now?*" But we both know that Jake's work is just a pretense today, a way to cope.

"There are too many people here," he says. "I can't stand

the phone ringing every two minutes." He yanks off his cap and throws it at the computer screen. "I wish you'd all just get out of my house."

I am stung, but I do not take any of Jake's comments personally. What he really means is that we are living a fucking nightmare. I inhale and approach him, placing a hand on his shoulder; he shrugs it off. The doorbell rings. Maybe Jake has a point.

It's another delivery. A young, twenty-something Latino holds out the most enormous floral arrangement yet. I wonder how many times he's been here.

"Thank you," I say, and take the flowers, pulling a $5 bill from my pocket. "We're celebrating," I shout, as he walks the brick path to his truck, and I am shaken by my lie. The delivery guy turns and smiles pityingly.

I return to the kitchen, cradling peach French tulips leaning gracefully from a substantial, urn-like vase. Clearly, whoever sent these has given it a lot of thought and expense.

"Room for one more?" I say to Elizabeth, placing the urn on the counter, and I laugh. It feels better than crying.

"A secret admirer? These must have cost a fortune," she says, excited.

She casually opens the little white envelope. Then she says, "Oh my God." Her eyes dart as she reads the message silently. Then she reads it out loud. "Thinking of you. Feel better soon. Richard.'"

I take the card and read it for myself, in shock. Where would Richard get such an idea? He, Elizabeth, and Jake have barely spoken all year. My mind races to consider ulterior motives.

To my surprise, Elizabeth's face brightens. "Look," she says, "even Richard cares," and I'm not sure whether I detect sarcasm. I allow myself a moment of relief and pride.

"*Richard* sent those?" my mother says, returning to the kitchen. "They're gorgeous. So thoughtful of him."

"He obviously feels guilty," Elizabeth says. "For causing my cancer." She smirks and, to my relief, seems to be at least half-joking.

"Come on," I say. "He honestly feels bad that you're sick." I wish she could try to accept his gesture.

Elizabeth rolls her eyes.

"He *does*," I say.

"Makes no difference to me," she says. "I have bigger problems than Richard will ever have—like, oh, telling my kids I have cancer. Breast cancer, okay. But *lung cancer*? How am I going to explain this?"

"Tell them the truth: you have cancer, and you're going to fight it," I say.

"I can't just act like I'll make it," Elizabeth says, "and deny the very real chance that I'm going to die."

"You *will* make it," I say, knowing that this is what she needs to hear. "You're going to need Brooke and Lauren's support to do it. Tell them that."

"I hope I won't cry," Elizabeth says, tearing up.

"And say that you'll feel tired from the treatments. Jake can help you talk to them," I say.

In the adjacent office, the clicking of Jake's keyboard stops. He appears in the doorway. From the state of his seething, I know that he has heard every word. He glares at Richard's flowers as if they're infectious.

"We couldn't even get an easy cancer," he says. "I told you, keep that prick away!"

I don't want to deal with Jake's anger or hear him malign Richard.

"I guess I'll be going," I say, and nobody protests or responds. Not even Elizabeth or my mother sticks up for me. The silence is surprising, painful.

When I'm at the door, Jake taps me on the shoulder and hands me the beautiful urn that held Richard's tulips. Their French tips now peek out of the kitchen trash.

"Here, have a vase," Jake says, and dumps the container in my hands.

⨯⨯⨯⨯

THE NEXT DAY, I drive to the reservoir and ruminate on Jake's behavior. I circle twice, grounded and calmed by the metronome of my feet. At the bottom of this chaos and my own hurt feelings, I recommit myself to being there for Elizabeth, no matter what she and Jake say or feel about Richard.

When Richard and I were dating, he took me on my first trip to Nantucket island, thirty miles off Cape Cod. Richard had summered on Nantucket since his twenties, when he came into some money, partying and meeting girls. It was the island he fell in love with: its dune-backed beaches, upscale restaurants, boutiques, and cobblestone streets.

After we'd known each other just a few months, Richard invited me to the shingled house he'd rented for the season on Madaket Beach. One night, having cocktails on the deck in rocking chairs, Richard confided in me about losing his mother when he was a child. He rocked while he spoke, puffing his cigar at the dusky sky, his hand resting on my knee. I listened, watching the curtains billow in the humid breeze, then pull close to the screen. I realized that the shock of Richard's mother's death was very much still with him, that it had molded him like a piece of clay.

"I couldn't be like other kids after she died," Richard said, sipping his third vodka. "I couldn't *feel* like other kids." His expression had changed from that of the confident man I knew to the tense, quivering face of a vulnerable boy.

I took Richard's hand and looked into his eyes, but he turned away.

"How did she die?" I asked.

"Cancer. She got sick while I was at sleep-away camp, this same time of year. No one thought to tell me. By the time I got home, she was almost gone. But I still had a mother. For weeks I slept near her bed in a sleeping bag on the floor. Then, when she died, I was the boy without a mother."

I imagined Richard as a short, skinny twelve-year-old with a bowl cut. His confession touched me. I wondered if as a boy, Richard had reasoned that he could protect his mother by sleeping near her bed, or if he had thought it would be impossible that way for her to leave.

"What happened when she died?" I asked, and for a few seconds took my stare above the dunes and to the horizon, completely absorbed in Richard's tragedy.

"My father finally took her to the hospital for treatment. I wasn't allowed. It was 1956. People didn't talk about cancer the way they do now, and not to children. She died in some other bed."

"I'm so sorry," I said. I was born in 1956; Richard was barely thirteen then.

"At school, everything revolved around mothers," Richard continued, his eyes filling. "Whose mother made the best tuna fish, whose mother packed peanut butter and Fluff, whose mother put chocolate kisses in your lunch bag . . ."

I squeezed Richard's hand, and he took another drink.

"I had to cope."

"I can't even imagine."

"My aunts were around."

"Did that help?"

"All I wanted to do was spend time with my father," he said.

Richard told me that he loved going to his father's law office in Cambridge—which he credited for his work ethic. But Richard's father remarried a year later, and his stepmother favored her biological children.

"That *woman*—I don't even call her my stepmother; that's got the word *mother* in it—resented any bit of time that I spent with my dad," Richard said. "She didn't give a shit about me and my sisters. She would have been happy if we'd disappeared." He explained that she cooked lavish, affectionate meals for her children, made a fuss out of hugging and kissing. When it was just his sisters and he, she was distant and cold. Dinners were silent and rushed.

It would take time to draw connections between Richard's earliest family experiences and the friction between him and my family of origin. My own generous affections for my family might have first attracted Richard, then amplified his old wounds, raising his anxieties about being an outsider, first as a stepchild, now as an in-law. But when I first heard Richard's sad story, we weren't family yet. As the conflict intensified between us, my heart closed to that understanding.

"Every Saturday in high school, I went to work with my father. That's why I didn't play football," Richard continued. "Then things really became a mess."

"Why? What happened?" I asked.

"He died, too."

I sighed. I knew Richard had lost both of his parents, but not the details.

"I was supposed to go to Florida during spring break," he continued. "It was midnight, and I was booked on an early-morning flight. I pulled up and noticed every light on in the house." He had just spoken to his father a few hours before. He thought his aunts must have come over to wish Richard a good trip. When he walked in, his aunt Emma was at the kitchen table, crying.

I shook my head and rubbed his outstretched arm.

"I had just missed the ambulance. My father died of a massive heart attack."

"How horrible," I said, and climbed out of my chair onto his lap to embrace him. "Any father would be proud of you and all you've accomplished."

"Yeah. But I was a bit of a fuckup for a while."

"You went to Harvard. You're such a hard worker," I said.

"Never to accumulate wealth—none of it. Do you understand? I worked hard in order to survive. I had no choice. I had to support my sisters."

"You could have stayed a fuckup," I said, and we laughed. "What a huge responsibility at a young age." I thought of myself at twenty-one, a senior in college. I spent my time studying and going to parties, having long conversations with my parents once a week from the phone booth at the end of the hall.

"My father taught me that the most important thing is to have a good name. I don't know. My whole life has been one adversity after another, even in my marriage."

I sipped my wine at the mention of his ex. To say that my life had been uncomplicated compared with his at that point was an understatement. I'd survived grandparents, sure, but they'd all lived long, full lives. While their deaths were sad, they were not tragic.

Richard dropped his head and held the bridge of his nose. I wanted to take that lonely boy in my arms and rock him to sleep, telling him that everything would be all right. Richard hadn't experienced the unconditional love of a mother since age thirteen.

After another lap, I retreat to my car, exhausted, and finish a bottle of Poland Spring. I have always considered myself an empathetic person, but only amid Elizabeth's illness, and after all this conflict, have I begun to reconnect with Richard's pain.

Richard's parents were robbed—like Elizabeth might be. Neither lived long enough to see their children become adults, let alone experience the joy of becoming grandparents; Elizabeth might not, either. Richard too, was robbed. Robbed of the unconditional love that he still seeks consciously or unconsciously. Will the same thing happen to my nieces if Elizabeth dies? Will the tragedy of Elizabeth's death compromise their adult lives?

Just before I start the engine, my cell phone rings. It's Richard.

"You okay?" he asks.

"Okay," I say. "Just went for a run." I keep my sentences short and to the point. I still don't trust him with my emotions.

"People keep calling me about Elizabeth. I don't know what to tell them."

My mind jolts. Why would anyone ask Richard about Elizabeth?

"My sister wants to keep things private," I say, hand tightening around my phone. I'm irritated because I don't want all of Wellesley discussing Elizabeth's health, least of all Richard.

"What kind of cancer does she have? What's the prognosis?" he asks, as if he can sense what I'm hiding.

I switch to hands-free and start the car. I step on the gas and lurch over the gravel parking lot.

"I told you," I say, "Elizabeth wants her privacy. Trust me, it's very serious."

"Serious how?"

"Jesus Christ, Richard, it's in her bones."

Richard is silent on the line. "I get it," he says.

My husband finally knows that Elizabeth's illness is not an exaggeration and that I am not a drama queen. For a couple of beats, Richard and I hang on like that, listening to each other's breath.

Then he says, "Elizabeth is the same age as my mother when she died."

Chapter Nine

─────

*T*he point of no return between Richard and the Gordons was Brooke's bat mitzvah, and I'm ashamed to admit that I played a major part. This joyous occasion, one that I should remember now only for my niece's bright smile and her parents' beaming pride, is tarnished. It has remained a thorn in my side all these years, for reasons much more significant than a snowstorm or an issue with the caterer.

Two years before the word *cancer* crossed our lips, Elizabeth and I were having lunch at Aquitaine Bis, one of our favorite restaurants in Wellesley. We'd spent the morning together at the gym, lifting weights and walking on the treadmill. Our next stop was the hair salon, where Megan, our stylist, had outdone herself cutting, coloring, and highlighting. At Aquitaine, we sat in a burgundy leather booth, feeling chic about our workout and up-to-the-minute hairstyles.

The waiter, who resembled a Brazilian soccer player, took our order.

"We'll both have the salade Niçoise," Elizabeth said.

"No anchovies for me," I added.

"I'll take hers," Elizabeth said. "Dressing on the side for both, please."

Brooke had just turned twelve and was beginning to study

for her bat mitzvah. "I think she'll do really well," Elizabeth said. "She thrives in front of an audience."

"She sure loves the spotlight," I said, with similar enthusiasm.

Halfway through our salads, Elizabeth raved about Moshe, the rabbinical student tutoring Brooke on her Torah and haftorah. Apparently, once you got past his nervousness and acne, he was a wise and considerate young man.

"Listen, I'd love to have the party at Rose Wood," Elizabeth said, placing her hand over mine. "There's a history—Jake and I had our engagement party there."

I knew what she was getting at. Since she and Jake weren't members, the only way they could hold Brooke's bat mitzvah at the private club would be to get sponsorship from first-degree relatives—namely, Richard and me. Before I was married, Jake's uncle sponsored their engagement party.

"The dining room has just been redecorated," I said, looking at my salad and clearing my throat. Richard didn't like for me even to take Elizabeth to Rose Wood as a guest for lunch on what he called "*his* membership."

"I could have it at a hotel, I guess," Elizabeth said. "Oh, but Rose Wood brings back such good memories." My sister suspended her fork in midair. "You'll sponsor me?"

"Of course," I said, but as soon as the words popped from my mouth, I wished I could swallow them. I could have said, "I'll have to check with Richard," but I didn't want to admit to Elizabeth that I had to discuss something like this with him first.

When I had suggested to Richard that we sponsor my parents' thirty-fifth anniversary brunch at Rose Wood, it had been his pleasure. Same for David and Jill's engagement party. Neither event had cost us any money because the people who throw the party are responsible for the costs—unless, of course, they don't pay, and then you have bigger problems. We had sponsored these other family events when Richard and I were newlyweds, well before he and my family were at odds. Not to mention that Richard's particular resentment toward Elizabeth and Jake was in a league of its own.

As far as Elizabeth could tell, smiling at me over her salade Niçoise, it was decided. But I knew that Richard would never sponsor Elizabeth's family. I didn't want to ask him because I didn't want hear no. Thing is, Jake's brother also belonged to Rose Wood. When we ran into a problem with Richard, I reasoned, Brooke's bat mitzvah could simply be transferred to a Gordon account. More than just a financial arrangement, I actually wanted the honor of sponsoring my niece's bat mitzvah. I didn't know how I would manage to convince Richard, but with or without his blessing, under our account or a Gordon's, I knew that this bat mitzvah would be the next Rose Wood family event.

For as long as I could remember, I'd been trying to protect Elizabeth from Richard's slights. If she called to say they had tickets to the Red Sox, asking if they could park near Kenmore Square in one of Richard's paid spots, I lied. "You know, game day is such a nightmare," I said. "The spots are all rented. Sorry." I never told her the truth, which was that Richard thought that Elizabeth and Jake took advantage of him. My passivity, avoidance, and half-truths only made the problem worse.

Like most people, Richard wanted to be appreciated in the form of thanks. "I don't *have* to give them anything, you know," he said. "They thank you, not me." Maybe I didn't always do a good job of conveying to Richard Elizabeth's gratitude, which I took for granted.

When it came to my family, Richard was thin-skinned. It

was hard for me to be sensitive because I felt he held a double standard for his relatives, versus mine. He didn't expect excessive thank-yous for every favor he paid his own family. If he gifted his sisters our Red Sox tickets, did I care if they thanked *me?* I just wanted them to enjoy the game. All of this tit for tat was exhausting—it caused tension—but whenever I confronted Richard, our conversations went nowhere. He decided to stick up for himself by being rude to my family and creating distance. Even when I told them to thank him, it never seemed to be quite enough.

Sitting at Aquitaine, I felt like a hypocrite, a fraud. I hated lying to Elizabeth. Fierce arguments with Richard repeated in my brain as I rehearsed my next confrontation: *I am Brooke's godmother and aunt. Even though you don't like my sister, you love me. Do this for me.* Or, as a last resort, *I already said yes. The bat mitzvah is booked. It's too late.* That day, my stomach clenched and didn't relax for six months.

I concealed the bat mitzvah from Richard over the summer, hoping for a positive interaction between him and Elizabeth that would thaw the ice and change Richard's mind. But as the fall date approached, it invaded my thoughts: at the gym, when I drove Alexandra to school, when I ran at the reservoir, even during dinner with friends. At the end of the summer, Elizabeth told me she wanted to have Richard and me over for a barbecue, to thank us for hosting Brooke's bat mitzvah and to talk over the details. The jig was up. I would have to tell Richard everything and admit I'd been deceitful.

First, I summoned the courage to convince Richard to come to the barbecue. "Sweetie," I said, my mouth dry, "the Gordons invited us to a barbecue on Labor Day. It's going to be special. They want us to be their guests."

My husband turned to me, his face visibly drained of the

lightness and ease he had when enjoying distance from my relatives. It broke my heart.

"Thanks, but no thanks. You know I can't stand Jake. He's so phony with me. That fake smile and handshake." Richard imitated Jake in a way that infuriated me, that made me want to defend my brother-in-law. At least Jake could fake it when he wanted to.

"Well, my parents will be there as a buffer," I countered.

"Oh, I see," Richard snarled. "So it really wasn't for us after all."

"Elizabeth and Jake want to be friendly. They're family."

"Those are two different things," he said.

I cringe to recall my sheer naïveté in thinking that peace could be possible.

"They treat me like shit," Richard continued. "They only care about you anyway. You go with Alexandra."

Three days before the party, the Friday night of Labor Day weekend, Richard and I had plans with other friends. To my dismay, the other couple insisted on going to Rose Wood.

I could no longer keep my silence, not because I'd been struck with sudden courage or strength but because I was petrified that the subject of the bat mitzvah would come up while we were at the club. I sat on the edge of our bed, where Richard catnapped before we dressed for dinner. The pillows were tousled, two propped under his legs to ease pressure on his lower back.

"Listen, Elizabeth is having Brooke's bat mitzvah at Rose Wood," I said to him.

"Why are you telling me this?" he asked, with his eyes closed.

"I said we'd sponsor them."

"What?" Richard's eyes popped open. "Are you nuts?"

Caught, I was terrified at what Richard would say or do after digesting the news. Muscles tensed in his chin. He sat up, pulling his legs into his chest.

"How could you agree to that, knowing my feelings?" he asked me slowly.

"I couldn't say no," I whispered, and I understand that Richard must have felt betrayed. In that moment, I so desperately wanted him to know where I was coming from, to feel understood.

Richard rolled off the bed and, wide awake, began to dress. "I'm not sponsoring," he said, fixing the top button of his dress shirt below his Adam's apple, meeting my gaze in the mirror. "I'm done with being used."

"They'll pay every penny. What does it even matter to you?" I shouted, my eyes burning with anger. How could I ever face Elizabeth?

"You should have asked me," Richard said with finality.

"Is there a chance in hell you would have said yes?"

"It's the principle. This is about loyalty—yours. Jake bad-mouths me to everyone. It gets back to me, you know. The last thing I want is to look like a jackass."

"What do you mean, he badmouths you?" I asked, even though I knew it was true.

"Next they'll ask me to sponsor their membership to the club. Your whole family, members at Rose Wood, *my* place. No fucking way."

"That's not true," I said. "I'm sorry, Richard. I know I should have discussed this with you first." But this was not about Rose Wood. It was about who belonged to whom.

"Damn right you should have."

I took my husband's hand—one last try. "Please," I said, whining like a child. "For me, Richard—do it for me. Please. I love you."

"I said *no*." He shook off my hand. "'I love yous' aren't going to change my mind." Richard had warned me about his stubbornness when we were dating, but it still made me want to explode.

I plopped onto the bed, crying.

"You've changed," Richard said. "For the worse."

"What do you mean?"

"You're not a Freeman," he said, turning around. "You're a Gordon," he sneered.

Gordon, he had said, instead of my maiden name, Kaplan. That put Jake, Elizabeth, and me on the same team, against him.

Fifteen minutes elapsed, and I remembered that we had been on our way to meet friends. I got up reluctantly, with half-closed, swollen eyes, and slipped on jeans. I resolved to try again that night to get Richard to change his mind.

"Time to go," Richard announced, fetching me from the bedroom.

During dinner, Richard was distant and didn't care who saw what. I placed my hand on his arm, hoping to warm things up between us. He didn't conceal shrugging it off. My face burned. I barely made conversation with our friends. In retrospect, we should have canceled. If Richard's sister had asked me to sponsor her at Rose Wood, I would have agreed, no matter what my feelings were, because she was family. But I was adrift, flailing even with the conviction of my values. I couldn't yet access the empathy that would strengthen my marriage, that would allow me to see my own values as subjective, not universal, and give Richard the space to approach my family in a way all his own.

Over breakfast the next morning, we started up again. Richard pointed across the table and narrowed his eyes.

"No more avoiding. You tell Elizabeth that she can't have the bat mitzvah under my membership."

"Impossible. She has everything planned," I said, lips quivering.

"Make something up. Say anything; say it's about money."

"You know Jake will pay!"

"I said make it up," Richard growled.

"Come *on*." I was so frustrated, my fingers were vibrating. "Think of the staff—Jake will tip bigger than anyone."

"No. End of discussion. And by the way, this marriage sucks."

"Fuck you," I said—I couldn't help myself—and left the room. The words hung in the air behind me like exhaled smoke. I knew I should have been straightforward from the beginning. I had been candid and direct when we'd first married, but, after being shot down time after time, I became afraid to express myself. When I tried to be intimate, Richard discounted my feelings. I was never right. I was a drama queen. I got defensive. Eventually, I gave up to protect myself and my loved ones.

My heart throbbed in my chest, matching my shallow breathing. I grabbed my phone from the night table and drove to Rosie's for a cup of coffee. With deep breaths, I calmed myself before dialing my sister.

"We have to talk," I said. "Let's meet at the reservoir."

The entire ride, I rehearsed how I would break the news gently, but, facing my sister in person, I came up short. With the water on our right, I focused on the twigs on the path, the white pom-pom bouncing at the back of Elizabeth's sock.

"I just hired a planner," Elizabeth said, bubbly with excitement. "Next we have to decide the menu."

"You need to ask Jake's brother if he'll sponsor you," I said flatly, losing my gentle way in.

Elizabeth shot me a look of genuine confusion. "What?" she says, shoulders shrugging, arms wide open. She stopped on the path and placed her hands on either side of her head. "What are you talking about?"

"Last night I finally told Richard about Brooke's bat mitzvah—"

"*Told* him? You hadn't told him?"

"And he said because of the Jake situation—you know, the office—he says no, he won't sponsor you."

"I didn't think you needed his permission."

"I know," I said, my heart thumping. "But you can still have it there! Don't worry. Just ask Jake's brother to sponsor you. I don't want any more bad blood between Richard and Jake."

"We've been planning this for months. Why didn't you say something before?"

"I was afraid," I admitted.

"Afraid of who? Richard? *Me?*"

I didn't have a response to that.

"What's the worst that could happen?" Elizabeth continued, in full rant. "People have bat mitzvahs at Rose Wood all the time. If anything breaks, we'll pay for it." She was missing the point that Richard didn't want to sponsor them because of how Jake had taken advantage of the office, and how Richard felt they still took advantage of him.

An elderly married couple passed by, their elbows swinging. Elizabeth and I started walking again, slowly now. My feet felt nailed to the ground. We rounded the reservoir in silence, and I couldn't even look at her. Being the bearer of Richard's ultimatum made me feel cruel, and I was ashamed that my lack of courage had complicated things. That pom-pom on Elizabeth's right foot was hanging by a thread, about to come loose. Up and down. The twigs and gravel crunched under our running shoes. I heard Elizabeth breathe in. I didn't hear her breathe out.

"He just wants to ruin it—is that it? What the hell is wrong with him? Poor Brooke . . ." Elizabeth trailed off. Her arms were moving wildly, out of control. "Is he going to prevent us from having it there?" she demanded.

"Of course not. Why say such a thing? If Jake's brother sponsors you, Richard won't get in your way."

"Will I need a policeman to protect us?" she asked, her voice rising.

This took me by surprise and seemed uncalled for. "Richard's not going to hurt you, Elizabeth. Don't make the situation worse—"

"He hates us," Elizabeth said, clipping the end of my sentence. "Jake's going to have a fit! He told me to have his brother sponsor us in the first place. I didn't want to hurt your feelings by asking him. No good deed goes unpunished."

The wind picked up. My sister had just confirmed that her invitation for me to host Brooke's bat mitzvah had been an honor. Now, just as quickly, she was insulting me. I began to feel betrayed, a little like Richard must have felt.

"Forget the barbecue. You're not invited under these circumstances," Elizabeth said, as we were about to drive off.

From that point, our family injuries festered into deep, infected wounds. Things between my sister and Richard became even worse. Elizabeth's cancer diagnosis two years later was the fatal blow.

Between my lie and Richard's snub, the tear between Richard, Jake, and Elizabeth was complete.

Chapter Ten

———

After an exhausting first round of doctor's appointments, and Richard's so-called misfire with the flowers, my sister, parents, and I gather days later at Elizabeth's kitchen table, trying to cope. My sister rakes her fingers through her shiny, chestnut-highlighted hair. Now that she knows it will soon be gone, she can't keep her hands out of it. "How's this for a goal?" she asks. "See my kids graduate high school. Let's shoot for that."

After we've turned over all the options, after we've read and reread all the literature from doctors and whatever we can find on the Internet, my parents turn to religion. My father begins to unbutton his shirt. On his speckled chest, a golden *chai* gleams on a thin chain. He ducks his head and pulls off the necklace, dangling it before us.

Chai is a Hebrew word and symbol meaning *life*. Wearing a *chai* is supposed to bring you luck; I have no memory of my father without his. His grandfather gave it to him as a gift for his bar mitzvah. As a kid, when I skinned my knee or if I was scared during a movie, burying my head in my father's chest, I felt the *chai*'s cool metal on my cheek. My father shines it once a year, on Rosh Hashanah, before attending temple services for the High Holy Days.

"Life," my father says now, his lips quivering. He pushes

out of his chair and shuffles around the table to lean over Elizabeth, kissing her forehead and fastening the talisman around her neck. At that moment, it doesn't matter what our religious beliefs are—we all believe in my father's humble, homemade Jewish magic.

"Thank you, Daddy. I'll never take it off," Elizabeth says, and holds the *chai* over her heart, squeezing the metal in her fist as if summoning God to pay attention.

Unlike in the early days of our marriage, when I pined for Richard to belong to such moments as these, I find myself relieved now that he isn't here to disrupt our intimacy.

"You'll get better, I know it," my father says to Elizabeth, and nods.

The possibility of divine intervention flashes in my mind. My family is Jewish, but not religious in the traditional sense. And although I have always attended services on Rosh Hashanah and Yom Kippur, now that Elizabeth is sick, I need more. We all do. My family and I grasp for something bigger to make meaning of our suffering and rescue us. We dust off an old faith, pleading with God for Elizabeth to be healed.

Later that week, I make an appointment with my rabbi, hoping he'll have some answers. I meet him at his office in Brookline on the first floor of the synagogue.

"Shalom. Come in," he says. "Sit." He motions to a leather couch against the wall. His bookshelves are stuffed with scriptures. Rabbi Bromberg is a pious and learned man with the build of a tennis player, all ankles and wrists. He wears a yarmulke on his short brown hair. Bromberg has been our rabbi for a long time. He officiated my marriage to Richard and our grandparents' funeral services.

"I heard the news about your beloved sister," the rabbi says. "I'm very sorry."

I explain the particulars of the diagnosis, ten days now since the ground gave way, very much still trying to find my footing. "I'm devastated," I say.

"I understand," Rabbi Bromberg says. "My heart goes out to you and Richard. And to your sister, her family, and your parents."

"Do you believe in curses?" I ask bluntly. "Like, if someone is envious of my sister, could it eventually cause her harm? Or if someone is under constant negative energy and stress, do you think it's possible for them to get cancer?" I am a bit wary of confiding in the rabbi about this kind of thinking, because Richard has been on the board of his congregation, but today I have no choice.

Around my wrist I am wearing one of those red strings that are supposed to keep away the evil eye. Elizabeth does these days, too. I bought one for each of us last week at the Kabbalah store in Newton Centre. I wear the red string all the time now, even in the shower. I can't stop fiddling with it.

Rabbi Bromberg leans back in his chair, crossing his ankles in front of him. "I don't believe in things like that," he says calmly. "Nobody knows God's plan."

"Well, what does the Torah say about why young people get sick?" I ask, frustrated with his elusiveness.

"There is no definitive answer. I'm sorry."

I try to hold back my emotion, but tears dribble down my face. I'm actually a bit relieved. I had been half-worried that Rabbi Bromberg might cite lines from the Torah proving how negative energy impacts people's health, to terrible ends. Although I don't believe in curses, I understand that Elizabeth is searching for someone or something to blame for her disease, and so am I.

Rabbi hands me a tissue. "People depend on prayer, of

course, to commune with God. Some feel comforted by charms and talismans, like that bracelet you're wearing. For thousands of years, Jewish people have fastened mezuzahs to their doorposts to ward off evil, and more recently they've begun wearing the *chai* symbol for luck. Ritual objects are a way of drawing on God's power even when God doesn't want to talk to us. However," Rabbi Bromberg says, raising a finger, "there *is* something I deem helpful." He explains the prayer *Mi Sheberach*, chanted during Saturday-morning services. "At this time, any congregant can say aloud the name of a loved one who is ill, and the community as a whole says a prayer on the sick person's behalf." The rabbi nods his head, as if agreeing with himself. "It's a powerful moment."

"I remember that prayer," I say, comforted, if only slightly. I love the community aspect of Judaism. Saying Elizabeth's name to the entire congregation and having them pray for her healing is encouraging.

"Samantha, I will say Elizabeth's name every Shabbat morning, even if you aren't in the synagogue," he says, and places his palms together.

I know he is trying to be helpful, but I want to believe that prayer is capable of changing more than just people's thoughts. I want to believe that it can cure cancer. "Thank you," I say. Then, because one sorrow begets another, I tell Rabbi Bromberg how troubling it is that I cannot bring together the people I love most. There is a rift between Richard and Jake, Richard and Elizabeth, and even Richard and me.

"My husband really doesn't like my sister, her husband, or her kids. He won't admit it but I feel that he's jealous of my closeness to them. And to top it off, years ago, Richard and Jake became enemies over a business misunderstanding. I can appreciate why my husband doesn't want to be best friends with my sister and my brother-in-law, but I can't comprehend his extreme dislike." I confide in the rabbi because I'm wondering if he can speak to Richard and present our family issues differently, more persuasively, than I have. As with Elizabeth's illness, it feels like I need help from a higher source if I plan to stay married.

"Have you seen a marriage counselor?" he asks.

"A few," I say, and laugh.

"Is there any good in your marriage?"

I think about what I like about my marriage, if there's something worth saving. We have a home, a daughter, and mutual friends. Our similar interests bond us. When we travel, our relationship is easy. Neither of us could spend more than a couple of hours at the Louvre. And both of us work the room at a cocktail party like pros.

I admire Richard and his business acumen. I admire his resilience and fortitude, another kind of stubbornness. He has qualities I still aspire to, like always having a plan B. He leads his life the way he navigates from the driver's seat: fast lane, no one slowing him down. If the car in front doesn't move over, or if there's traffic, he negotiates the obstacle to reach his destination.

Richard can be especially generous when he feels loved and admired. "You know, when we first got married," I say tearfully to Rabbi Bromberg, "I was so proud to be his wife. He was romantic and made me smile, took care of me, always kissed me hello and goodbye."

"Were Richard and your family ever on good terms?" the rabbi asks. He's sitting on a frayed cloth seat and listening patiently while I pour out the whole story.

"Yes," I say, and explain the rest: how, a few years after we married, Richard began excusing himself from time with my family. He wanted us to have our own life as spouses, compartmentalized from the rest of my relatives, when my idea of the border between marriage and family of origin was a spillover. Richard didn't understand this about me, and I had trouble understanding him, too. We tried to change each other, instead of appreciate and value our differences. Now, I ask myself, is it possible that Richard's behavior, which seemed callous at the time, was motivated by something other than selfishness or ill will, as I interpreted it? Was he merely, understandably, protecting his own heart, guarding it with a vigilance he learned as a child?

"My family has always given me enormous love," I say. "So when things got difficult with Richard, even though my family was half of the conflict, that's still where I turned. That only isolated Richard further."

Because the rabbi nods sympathetically, I tell him more. How I obsess about the idea that Richard, Elizabeth, and Jake should become friends. How I want our children to be closer. How I push for Richard to be in the relationships that come so naturally to me, how he pulls back under pressure, standoffish to everyone. I want closeness, and Richard wants distance. Even if he doesn't fully enjoy the time he spends with my relatives, I can't figure out why he won't sacrifice his own comfort occasionally for my sake. It's as if he fears that any compromise now puts his independence at stake. I don't know what to do to change the situation.

"Rabbi, for years, this problem has taken up most of my head. Right before Elizabeth got sick, I was afraid even to mention her name in my house." All these invisible threads connect me to my parents and my sister, and them to me. Over many years, we have woven the threads together to form a multilayered, shimmering tapestry. I could offer Richard a role as the centerpiece of the design, but I can't have him obliterate the whole thing with his attitude.

The rabbi raises his gaze and considers me with warmth and compassion. "What is it that you would like me to do?" He's fifty-five reputed to be wise and skilled in untangling complex Talmudic arguments. Surely he can help untangle the mess I'm in.

"It's not just me," I rant. "Until my sister's cancer took over, Elizabeth was obsessed with the problem, too. She didn't understand why Richard disliked her. She's tried for years to have a relationship with him, but he's standoffish and uninterested. He's an expert at pushing her away, so she gave up. He refused to sponsor my niece's bat mitzvah at Rose Wood. And now my sister has lung cancer. I know it seems crazy, but part of me feels like the animosity between my sister and my husband may have something to do with it. The cancer, that is."

"Samantha," Rabbi Bromberg says, leaning forward and placing a calming hand on my knee, "your sister's illness is a lot for you to digest right now. Be there for her. Your husband will have to understand. And you must know that Richard doesn't have the power to cause your sister's cancer."

"I know, but it's creepy," I say.

He's right, though. If Richard had the power to cause her cancer, he could use that same power to cure her cancer. Being supportive of Elizabeth is all I can manage now.

⪻⪻⪻

THE NEXT MORNING. Richard and I sit on opposite ends of the couch in our sunroom, with its exposed-brick fireplace—our favorite room in the house. Richard is immersed in one of his crime novels. I'm reading the newspaper with the dogs curled at my feet. They don't leave my side. Animals sense anxiety.

Richard closes his book and looks up. "You know what our problem is?"

Here we go again.

"Guess what? I don't care anymore," I say.

"Our problem," Richard continues, uncrossing his legs. His shoes smack the floor. "Our problem is that you want your sister and her family in the back seat of our car, and I want them five cars back."

He's right. I never want that much space between my sister and me.

"Why are we still discussing this?" I jump up angrily, rousing our poodles, Bella and Bentley. I leave for the kitchen, deciding I need a glass of water. In all of our married life, even the early years, I have never left an argument feeling satisfied—because I usually chicken out.

Just as I turn off the water at the sink, Richard appears.

"I'm taking the dogs for a walk," I announce. The trees still sport their autumn foliage. I could use the air.

I leash the dogs and lead them out the front door.

"I'm coming with you," Richard says, grabbing his keys. He locks the door behind us.

We plod halfway around the block in silence, until a squirrel runs across the street and activates Bentley's prey drive. She begins pursuing the squirrel with a sudden force that pulls me and her sister, Bella, along. Bella joins the pursuit, and both dogs halt, barking, at the trunk where the fat autumn squirrel has managed to scurry up and out of sight.

"Did your sister get the flowers?" Richard finally asks. His tone is soft, conciliatory.

"Yes, thank you," I say matter-of-factly. "That was nice.

What made you send them?" I've prepared for this moment.

"I suggested it to Catherine, and she said it would be a good idea." Catherine is our therapist, which means that Richard is trying to work things out, in his own way.

We continue walking, the dogs trotting alongside, and I draw into myself. We reach the bulb of our street's cul-de-sac and circle back to our house.

"Do you need any help getting a good doctor?" Richard asks. "Someone on the board at the temple has a connection to Beth Israel."

"Thanks," I say. "She's all set. We met some great doctors."

"Things could turn out better than you think, you know," Richard says, straightening into the posture he uses for a sell. "The way I look at it, if the odds are against me—only a slim, ten or five percent chance that things will go my way—that's still hope."

Richard has experienced so much adversity in his life, and he's still an optimist. Just hearing him say this with such conviction does makes me feel a tiny bit better.

But as our dogs bound across the threshold and we collect our reading in the sunroom, I realize that Richard's sliver of hope equally describes both the outside odds of Elizabeth's surviving her cancer and those of our remaining married.

Chapter Eleven

*O*n the years following Richard's ultimatum about Brooke's bat mitzvah, I initiated several conversations with my therapist, Catherine, about the conflicts in my marriage. When Richard hurt Elizabeth, I felt like he was hurting me. Catherine and I explored the possibility of divorce.

Soon after Elizabeth disinvited us from the Labor Day barbecue, I made an appointment with one of the best divorce lawyers in Boston, Jonathan Mann; I wanted to retain him before Richard did.

Mann's office was on the thirtieth floor of a prestigious office building on Berkeley Street, with views of the Charles River and the Back Bay. I entered the high-ceilinged marble lobby, showed my license to the young security guard, and took the elevator.

I checked in with a middle-aged receptionist. She wore a simple, elegant navy dress with three gold bangles that tinkled when she hung up the phone.

"Jonathan will be right with you," she said. "Please have a seat." She motioned to a pair of tufted gray club chairs with silver studs.

I tried to make myself comfortable. The discipline and self-control I displayed on the outside matched my inner anxiety and insecurity. No one in my family had ever been divorced. I was beginning to feel like a failure.

A distinguished-looking man in a tailored suit and starched white shirt entered the waiting area. "Good morning," he said, with a solid handshake. "I'm Jon Mann." He was wearing the monogrammed cuff links to prove it.

I followed Mr. Mann into his office. My eyes widened at the beauty of the view and the cloudless sky. What a place to house such disaster, to negotiate all the problems between husbands and wives.

Jonathan sat comfortably at a stately walnut desk, his walls lined with law-school diplomas, honorary degrees, and framed photos of a wife, son, and daughter. The lawyer listened intently as I detailed my grievances. I told him of my early years with Richard, filled joyfully with travel: London, France, Italy, Hong Kong, Thailand, and China. How we had strong roots in the community, our synagogue, and our daughter's school. How we maintained an extensive social network with friends across Wellesley, Mount Snow, and Nantucket. We were charitable; we complemented each other socially. "As long as my family isn't around, we actually get along very well," I said.

Then I highlighted the recent years of hostility and emotional distance, especially the conflict with Elizabeth and Jake, and the bitterest twist: the bat mitzvah.

Mr. Mann's professional demeanor was comforting, even more comforting than my therapist had been. His depth of understanding human relationships reassured me. I blinked back tears as I told him how Richard didn't want me to be close to my sister and her family, how he refused to be in their company anymore. For two hours, we sifted these facts and emotions.

"It's essential for me to know your expenses, how much money you spend each month," Mann said, changing gears. He produced a blank budget ledger resembling today's spreadsheets. "Don't leave anything out—no manicure or cut and color. I need to know absolutely everything you spend on Alexandra. Please be thorough." Then he explained each step of proceeding officially with a divorce. The first task would be to request quarterly statements for Richard's business, and our joint tax returns.

As calm as I had been within those four walls, when I left the lawyer's office, I panicked. Thinking through the actual process of getting a divorce made my stomach churn. Aside from finances, Richard and I would have to negotiate visitation schedules for Alexandra. Would I move out, or would he? My life was unraveling into sums of alimony and child support. I didn't want to be a divorced person, but I couldn't imagine being married to Richard anymore. When we were together, there was a palpable tension. It strained our voices and filled the space between us.

Back when I raised the possibility of divorce with Catherine, she sat on a black leather chair and took notes. Her office was in the lower level of her home in Newton, with a large picture window that overlooked Crystal Lake. Books about marriage counseling, healing relationships, and divorce lined her shelves. A tin of hard candy sat on the client side of her desk. I habitually placed a peppermint on my tongue before reclining on her upholstered couch, a box of tissues within reach.

"I'm dreading Brooke's bat mitzvah," I said. "Now that Richard has refused to sponsor, I'm embarrassed to show my face. Can this just be over? The bat mitzvah *and* the marriage?"

"I understand how you feel, but maybe you can work through this," Catherine counseled. "View this as a setback in your relationship, not the end of it. He's not an evil person, trust me," she said with a laugh. "I've seen many men in this office over the years."

"I'm so angry, I can't even be in the same room with him! But divorced?" I closed my eyes.

"You don't have to decide now. I've seen women who divorce and remarry. Some have the same issues with their new husband, except worse. They enter the marriage with baggage, which causes a new set of problems."

"He's always trying to change me," I say. "It's exhausting, like I'll never be good enough. Love him more, love my family less. I'm always on trial."

"Do you ever try to change him?"

Catherine's question caught me off-guard, but I now know it shouldn't have.

"I do," I said. "I scrutinize every word he says to my family." I started to consider how tough it must be for Richard to relate to my family under those conditions. I always found fault with him, too, I admitted to Catherine, nursing grudges that he didn't do the right thing, or enough. Richard must have felt criticized every time he was with my family.

Catherine shifted in her chair and put her pen down. "You have such a good life, Samantha. Friends, a great reputation. It's not that easy to be divorced. I've seen men who hide their money from their wives, have affairs and give their wives herpes, or worse. Richard's not one of those. Let's work on getting you a thicker skin."

"This situation is killing me from the inside out," I said. "I'll do anything. If I can't change Richard, maybe I can change myself or my expectations."

"Let's work on changing your reactions. Even if you do get divorced, you'll still have to deal with each other as co-parents."

She was right. I thought about how Richard related to his ex. They had to remain in relationship because of Harrison, but I witnessed every pained conversation they used to have.

"I know that marriage is a compromise," I said. "But I don't want to compromise who I am. Where's the line? Any amount of time I spend with my family is too much for him."

"Take a moment and hold Richard in your mind as a twelve-year-old," Catherine said. "See him there without a mother, no one to protect him. He's still trying to keep that boy safe."

I recalled Richard, curled into a ball, sleeping on the floor next to his mother's cancer bed. It made me feel some tenderness and sympathy toward him, but I didn't think it excused him from being disruptive.

"I read that we're attracted to people who trigger our childhood wounds," I said, "so that we can realize them and heal them."

"Yes, that is often true," Catherine said.

"Well, neither of us is doing a good job of healing. Richard doesn't invite me in."

"Before any change occurs," Catherine said, "there has to be quite a bit of self-awareness."

WHEN THE DAY of Brooke's bat mitzvah finally arrived, my sister and Jake didn't want Richard there, and Richard didn't want to go. He sped off to enjoy the weekend alone on Nantucket.

Before he left, I asked him what I should say when people at the bat mitzvah asked why he wasn't there.

"Tell them the truth," he said. "Tell them how rude and greedy the Gordons are. That you planned an entire bat mitzvah in my name without my permission. That you never stick up for me."

"You've been rude, too, Richard. This whole situation has gotten out of control, like the Arab-Israeli crisis."

"That's your side," Richard said, and pushed past me on his way out the door.

Alexandra and I arrived at Brooke's bat mitzvah arm in arm. Harrison, who had just graduated from college, flew in for the morning service to join us, which I deeply appreciated. Now in his twenties and living in New York, Harrison somehow managed to engage with my family *and* stay out of a feud with his dad. His loyalty was a testament to what I thought was possible.

I kept busy the whole morning, trying to distract myself from Richard's absence, helping Alexandra with her hair and makeup. We dressed in new suits. I wore classic navy Chanel with the skirt right above the knee; Alexandra's was a peach, teenage version. "Brooke must be really nervous!" Alexandra said. "I know I'll be."

"Auntie Elizabeth said she really knows her stuff," I replied, smoothing my daughter's hair. At the service, Brooke would recite her haftorah and portion of the Torah in Hebrew, then give remarks in English on the meaning of this day.

When we arrived at temple, the Gordons were seated in the front row, on the sanctuary's elegant suede benches. Alexandra and I walked down the aisle to join them, and guests who were seated swiveled to watch. Richard's absence already felt like the elephant in the room.

Elizabeth's friend Jane and her family arrived next, also taking front seats; Jane rushed over, giving us all hugs, kisses, and "mazel tovs." Elizabeth and Brooke excused themselves to get prepped, to make sure Brooke's tallit draped evenly across her shoulders, and to rehearse her haftorah one last time.

Jane's gaze landed on me. "Don't you look beautiful! Where's Richard?" she asked, turning as if to find him. She might as well have said his name through a megaphone; *Richard* reverberated in the room. My face flushed, and Alexandra looked at me to account for what I couldn't possibly explain. Just as I opened my mouth to give some version of what Richard had told me to say, I felt a relieving hand on my shoulder. I jumped at the sight of my parents, and we excused ourselves from Jane, embracing my mom and dad.

Brooke's service went off without a hitch. She was poised, rehearsed, and radiant on the bimah, or sanctuary stage. I devoted my full attention to her for forty-five minutes, but when it was done, I couldn't shake the feeling that people were talking about Richard. A three-hour service allowed for lots of gossip. At least five women had given me polite smiles and whispered something into their husband's ears. In this community that placed so much importance on the nuclear family and maintaining reputations, I felt my status as Mrs. Richard A. Freeman being stripped.

I could tell that no one believed the paltry excuses I had offered to explain Richard's absence: that he was away on business. People planned vacations and business trips around family bar and bat mitzvahs; the dates were set two years in advance. Besides, everyone knew how close Elizabeth and I were. The only acceptable excuse for missing this kind of event would have been severe illness or death. Richard's absence felt like a social death, and it only stoked my rage to realize he must have known that.

After the Torah service, at the kiddush reception that traditionally follows, Jane approached me in her Armani suit and stilettos. "Where's Richard?" she asked again, as if for the first time. Her eyes held concern, but her voice was overly cheerful.

"On a business trip. A meeting out of town," I said carefully.

"Today? Couldn't he cancel?"

"It was last-minute."

"Oh." Jane hesitated, clearly attempting to read my face. My dread about attending the bat mitzvah had been realized, and we weren't even at Rose Wood yet! I had never felt so embarrassed. I smiled and smiled and gulped sweet kiddush wine.

At the black-tie reception, for which the men donned tuxedos and the women dressed in Oscar-worthy gowns, I heard the same refrain, as if the residents of my community were all reading the same cue card: "Where's Richard? Where's Richard?" The repetition finally wore me down. When a group of Elizabeth's friends descended and began to badger me about his whereabouts, I finally snapped. "None of your business." They walked away, holding their martinis, shocked by my change of character.

I managed to pull it together. When the band played the hora, I jumped from my chair and grabbed Elizabeth's hand, leading the dance. Jake, Brooke, Lauren, my parents, Alexandra, Jill, and David joined in. "Everyone up," the emcee said, and within seconds, two hundred guests had risen from their seats. We grasped hands and circled the room, dancing and singing the old-as-time song "Hava Nagila."

According to tradition, Alexandra led Brooke to the middle of the hora. The dancers broke the circle to accept a gold ballroom chair, and the lead singer crescendoed his voice into the microphone. Jake, David, and a few others led Brooke to the chair and lifted it, soaring. My niece beamed, waving to guests, who sang and clapped along with the band. The glow on her face at that moment rivaled the sparkle of the chandeliers.

When she was lowered, Alexandra, Elizabeth, Lauren and I joined hands with Brooke, twirling like ballroom partners in the center of the circle. Even in the midst of such pain, I felt complete, not hiding, in that moment. I didn't have to check to see if my husband disapproved of the love and attention that I was bestowing on my family, because he wasn't there. I had been freed.

The guests took their seats, and the caterers wheeled out Brooke's cake. Each one of its five tiers was a splendid confection, with thirteen candles on top that would be lit ceremoniously. The first candle was for my parents. Brooke called their names, and as they approached, the music of "Sunrise, Sunset" played. Next were Jake's parents. I had forgotten about the candle ceremony, and with Richard missing, I began to feel alarm. When Brooke next called Uncle David and Aunt Jill and their kids, cousins Brittany and Justin, she included Alexandra and me.

Heat rushed up my neck. Everyone saw the mistake in the choreography, how Alexandra and I had been lumped in with my brother's family. I wanted to disappear under one of the tulle-covered, lit-from-below cocktail tables. But it was Brooke's day, after all. I didn't want my situation with Richard to divert any more focus from the ceremony of this ritual than it had already. What I did instead of shrinking away was grab Alexandra's hand. Joining the New York Kaplans, we lit the candle.

Chapter Twelve

------

*A*s teenagers, Elizabeth and I had naturally curly hair that frizzed at the slightest humidity, mine a darker shade of brown. It was the '70s, and straight hair was in. To achieve it, my sister and I limited our shampooing to twice a week, helping each other to section and wrap our wet hair around Velcro rollers secured with silver clips. Then we sat under portable hair dryers at home, just like the women we saw in salons sitting under plastic bubbles like space-age Jetsons. Under the dryers, Elizabeth and I considered ourselves sophisticated, important adults with appointments, leafing through magazines.

On cold winter days, especially, I loved to bask in the heat and read. The snowbanks might have grown six feet high, but under the hair dryer I indulged in steamy page-turners by Danielle Steel and Sidney Sheldon. I loved the slow, luxurious pace of those afternoons with Elizabeth, the ritual of reading interrupted with chatter about boys. It made us feel pretty, especially when we combed out our hair before the mirror and saw the smooth, straight results. Elizabeth and I wore our hair identically throughout high school: a blunt inch below the shoulders, middle part. There was never any mistaking us for anything but sisters.

Now, in our forties, on a sticky morning in Indian summer, it's already October, weeks since Elizabeth's diagnosis. My sister, my mother, and I are in the car, thirty miles west of Boston. Elizabeth needs a wig. She wants to keep this trip private, so instead of soliciting the Parisian wig boutique in Boston's Back Bay, through research I've found a modest but reputable wig specialist, named Terry, who sells wigs from her suburban home.

We pull up to what looks like a dollhouse, orange and yellow mums bordering the lawn, a family of statues in the garden. I am trying to decide what Terry will look like, when the door opens and a petite woman in her early sixties says, "I've been expecting you. Come in, come in." She's barely five feet tall, with highlighted blond hair. Her voice is warm and nourishing. "Follow me," she says.

Towering behind Terry, the three of us tag along through her spotless kitchen and down a short flight of stairs. The comfort that the neatness of her home brings me leads me to recognize how much I feel like a grief-stricken mess.

Elizabeth has chemo again tomorrow, but at the moment, she still has her hair. We're here because the doctor recommended she purchase a wig *before* losing her hair, to make the transition easier. But buying a wig cements her diagnosis in a way I didn't anticipate. We're slowly but surely entering the world of the ill. Cancer invades our every thought, takes over every conversation. It has waged daily combat on Elizabeth and my family, and all I can do is stand by her side.

"Here we are," Terry says when we reach her finished, yellow basement with views of her garden. It's a cheery place, one that could host family gatherings, but the extensive wig display—rows and rows of mannequin heads—reminds us why we're here.

"Wow, look at these," I say, as if this were some ordinary

shopping trip and we've come upon a cache of purses or shoes. I maintain external positivity even though I suffer deep sorrow inside. Dozens of wigs on Styrofoam heads greet us in every shade (auburn, brown, black, blond) and various styles (short, wavy, straight, with and without bangs). My sister touches an auburn-colored flip, then leans toward a mirror and runs her fingers through her own hair. Lately, she wears it layered above her shoulders. My own hair is longer and still a bit darker. She and I frequent the same salon, and we often schedule our blowouts at the same time with different hairdressers, side by side, as if once again teenagers under our bedroom hair dryers.

"Please sit down," Terry says to Elizabeth, gesturing to a salon chair and mirror.

"How could this happen?" my mother yelps out of nowhere and covers her mouth.

I give my mom a hug, but she breaks free, pacing. "I would trade places with you," she says, walking toward Elizabeth. "It should be *me* who has the cancer," she says, pointing at her chest.

"I wish it were nobody," Elizabeth says. She sits.

"You will get better, dear," Terry says, addressing Elizabeth in the mirror. She explains that many of her clients wear wigs for only a few months, through chemo.

For all Terry knows, Elizabeth's cancer is temporary. No one mentions that Elizabeth has Stage IV and will undergo both radiation *and* chemotherapy to control the disease. That, outside of a miracle, there is no expectation of a cure. As close as I am to my sister, I haven't fully faced how I'd feel if it were I. Would I blame myself? I know I would worry about Alexandra. Whom would she be close to? How would she choose a college major? Who would plan her wedding?

"How long have you had this business?" I ask Terry, to quiet my mind.

"I used to be a hairdresser," she says, placing her hands on Elizabeth's shoulders. "I got into the wig business when my niece developed alopecia."

Elizabeth looks in the mirror, smoothing her hair. "Alopecia?" she asks.

"It's a disease where you lose your hair. Not cancer, but it's still very difficult," Terry says. She ponytails Elizabeth's hair. "But most of my clients are cancer patients. My way of helping."

"You have a wonderful selection," I say.

Terry fits Elizabeth with a nylon hair cover. "This is to flatten your hair so we can size the wig. Now, why don't we try a few on to see what you like?"

Elizabeth gives Terry a slight nod, but her eyes line with tears.

"That one?" Elizabeth points to a wig similar to her current length and color.

For the next half hour or so, we bask in Terry's kindness as her manicured hands place various wigs on Elizabeth's head, then whisk them off. I keep my eyes on my sister in the nylon hair cover between wigs, trying to picture her without hair.

The wigs on display are only samples, it turns out. Terry opens several drawers to show us the retail stock, all neatly organized. She explains that some are made from genuine hair and some are synthetic. The synthetic wigs are easier to wash and dry, but the hair doesn't look as real. "Whatever you want, I have," she assures us. "And what I don't have, I can order."

"I like the first one you tried," I say to Elizabeth. "It looks natural."

"I don't want to look any different," she says.

My mother rubs the back of Elizabeth's neck. "You're going to beat this."

"This one?" I plop on a curly red wig to lighten the mood,

peeking in the mirror. "Think I could pass for Barbra Streisand? If only I could sing," I say, and laugh. Elizabeth doesn't smile.

We leave Terry's with two human-hair wigs, each nestled in its own white box like a cake from a bakery. In the car Elizabeth says, "I'm going to bring these to Megan and ask her to style and highlight them so they're as good as my own hair."

"Great idea. I'll go with you," I say.

"It was a perfect place to go. Private. Thank you," Elizabeth says, and bows her head. "If I just knew I had a chance to beat it . . ." She starts crying. "I'm sorry. It'd be so much easier to deal."

"The doctor says you're still young," my mother says from the backseat. "Don't forget, you have that on your side!" I can tell from her deliberate manner that this is the same mantra she repeats to relatives and friends.

As we drive, Elizabeth opens one of the boxes and fingers her new wig. "God, I hope it won't frizz. That would make it all worth it." For a brief moment, the three of us laugh, a small relief.

"We'll get through this," my mother says, wiping her face.

Elizabeth closes her eyes, and we ride in silence. The only voice is the newscaster's at the top of the hour, and the only noise the sounds of cars swishing by.

⋘⋘

THE NEXT MORNING, Elizabeth has her first radiation appointment, scheduled before her regular chemo at Beth Israel. First she'll burn, and then she'll be poisoned.

At 8:30 a.m., the radiation room is bright. Light, windows, upholstery, and plants—the semblance of vitality and life. Still I fixate on a display of pamphlets in the corner detailing various cancers: lung, breast, ovary, pancreas, kidney, colon. What a world apart from the pamphlets I scanned through just last month at the dermatologist's, reading about Botox, Restylane, and Fraxel treatments, back when I had the luxury of frivolity.

We sign in with the receptionist and wait. Elizabeth drinks green tea that she brewed at home and carries in a thermos. Regis and Kelly are on TV, with their perky smiles. Kelly wears pink Spandex that shows off her sculpted body. She's lifting a leg, crunching her abs, and flexing her arms. I steal a glance at Elizabeth, who smiled that same way a few weeks ago when we took an exercise class, upbeat and youthful, her whole life ahead of her. I survey the room. It seems as if everyone but us has gray hair and wrinkled skin.

"Everyone here is old," Elizabeth whispers, confirming my own observation. Gone is my sparkly-eyed, chatty sister. She seems irritated, and I don't blame her. "Samantha, if something happens to me, I know Jake will get married again. He's young. He'll need someone to take care of him."

"Where is this coming from?" I ask. "Not now." I repeat my own mantra: "Dr. Gold said we could be cautiously optimistic."

"I'm up all night thinking about what's going to happen to Brooke and Lauren."

"You're just starting treatments. Try to relax. Let's see how things go."

"What if you're still married to Richard? Can my kids even *be* with you then?" Elizabeth asks worriedly.

"No matter what," I assure her. I know Richard doesn't accept my relationship with Elizabeth and Jake, but he's not evil. I wish she didn't have to mention it.

"Mrs. Gordon," calls the nurse at the perfect moment.

"Good luck," I say, and kiss my sister on the cheek. Time to burn. She leaves the waiting room to have the treatment, alone.

Although it's not my own life at stake, I, too, feel alone, unable to share these day-to-day struggles with my husband. He's not there to hold me and tell me how strong I am being for Elizabeth. Lately, I can't lean on anyone but myself. But my alone life began long before Elizabeth got sick. Tiny words and gestures of caring have all but disappeared between Richard and me.

Despite myself, once Elizabeth is in radiation, I am drawn back to those cancer pamphlets like a moth. In the lung cancer brochure, I stare at blackened lungs. I scan the medical jargon: *non-small-cell adenocarcinoma, clinical trials, Stage IV, incurable*. Most people die within a year of Elizabeth's particular diagnosis, but this isn't news to me; I read it on the Internet. But these clinical papers here in my hands sadden me more, even though Elizabeth's lungs are not blackened. Dizzy, I head back to my chair and hear a robotic voice, the sound of a man with no vocal cords.

I reach my seat and place my head between my legs, taking slow, deep breaths, forcing myself steady. Elizabeth needs to come here for radiation five days a week. I will be here with her every time.

Fifteen minutes later, she reappears.

"How was it?" I ask, and put my arm around her.

"I didn't feel a thing."

I look closely and can now see the dark splotches under her eyes, the tight clench of her jaw. I imagine her lying on the table, obsessing about the future she might not have.

"Jake should be upstairs already," I say. "Let's go. I need a cup of coffee."

After leaving the café down the hall, we board the elevator, and in a moment the doors open onto the ninth floor: Shapiro Cancer Center, where Elizabeth gets chemo. As if drawn by something beautiful, we bypass the waiting area and rest on a cushioned bench near a ten-foot fish tank, or what have become our good-luck seats. The water filter hums soothingly. Watching red and yellow fish weave lazily through the coral, indifferent and oblivious to the anxiety in the room, is a kind of therapy. For a moment, I allow myself the whimsy of shrinking down to a swimming fish, making my slow figure-eights around miniature castles and treasure chests.

Jake finds us. He's already checked Elizabeth in. I admire their symbiosis.

Elizabeth continues sipping her green tea from her steel travel mug. She read an article about the powers of antioxidants last week, so that's her new thing: green tea. I'm double-fisting Starbucks coffee, one for me and one for Jake. I set Jake's on the table, pushing back old issues of tabloid magazines. We sip and gaze through a glass partition into the hallway, expecting Dr. Varghas. We always see Elizabeth's beloved oncologist before chemo. His warmth relieves some of the sting.

In solidarity with my sister, when chemo started I stopped taking pleasure in what I wear. For the past few weeks, I have applied very little makeup and for coming to the hospital rarely choose my leather pants, designer jackets, or any jewelry, except for a watch. Dr. Varghas has seen me mostly in the same clothes as Elizabeth. Craving comfort, we reach for fleece jackets, workout pants, and exercise tops.

Today, though, I have dressed in a new outfit: gray cashmere sweater, black jeans, and black ankle boots. This morning I took care applying my cognac lip liner and Beige de Chanel lipstick. I want Dr. Varghas to see that we haven't always been worried and subdued, that Elizabeth and I are women who take pride in appearances, that we value how we look because it shapes the way we feel. I feel naked without mascara and bronzer; I think a little polish makes me look like myself. When Elizabeth and I were teenagers, our mother always said, "Don't leave the house without your lipstick." We were raised to indulge our vanity, and we had the privilege to do so. I can still see Elizabeth sitting on her bedroom floor as a teen, applying eye shadow with a beauty magazine to guide her, how she loved a smoky eye. Soon she will approach the mirror with a very different goal: fixing her wig to appear like the woman she used to be.

Elizabeth has also dressed well, if comfortably, for her appointment with Dr. Varghas: in a beige cashmere sweat suit. The sleeves roll up easily now, for her blood test and, soon, for chemotherapy.

"Thanks for the coffee," Jake says, kissing me hello. His stubble stings my cheek, unusual for Jake, who is usually meticulous about a clean shave.

"Drop off the kids okay? How'd it go at the school?" Elizabeth asks.

"I went in to speak to the headmistress and told her," he says.

"And?"

"She thanked me for letting her know the kids will be having some tough days."

Elizabeth's eyes fill. "Poor babies," she says. I reach out and squeeze her hand.

When the phlebotomist calls Elizabeth's name, I follow her in and Jake stays at the fish tank.

"Have a seat and roll up your sleeve, my dear." Our phlebotomist is a Jamaican woman with a lilting voice and a face full of compassion.

I sit beside Elizabeth with my folder full of medical notes.

"I'm her sister," I say, to explain why I'm here. The technician acknowledges my statement with a smile.

"Date of birth?" she asks Elizabeth.

"November first, 1959."

"Make a fist, dear," she says. She gets the vein easily—I can tell because Elizabeth doesn't jump but I do—then draws four vials to ensure that Elizabeth's white blood cell count is high enough, her body strong enough, to withstand chemo's shock.

Watching Elizabeth, I wince. No matter how often I let hope rise in my heart, I don't actually believe that Elizabeth will beat this cancer. There is no Stage V.

After the blood draw, the nurse deposits us in the doctor's office. Elizabeth and Jake sit next to each other in armchairs. I take my seat on a swivel stool.

"How's your appetite?" the nurse asks.

"Not bad," Elizabeth says, though she's been eating less than she used to.

"On the scale, please."

At five foot five, Elizabeth weighs 125, the same she has for years. The nurse measures her oxygen level by clipping a clothespin-type device on her finger. "Ninety-eight percent," she reads. "Very good."

Dr. Varghas walks in, and it's like the lights have come on. We all snap to attention, including the nurse. "Good morning, everyone," he says. I take out my pen and hold it poised.

"And how are you feeling, Elizabeth?" he asks, with legitimate concern.

"Still some lower-back pain, and I've been pretty tired," she says. Elizabeth loses the irritation that has generally accompanied her diagnosis. Dr. Varghas nods and listens.

Elizabeth continues, reporting on her pain. "I have stinging in my shoulder socket. It seems like the left side is stiffer, more swollen, than my right." She rolls up her sleeve and displays her arm. "Some numbness in my feet, too."

"The PET scan you had last week specifically looked at the shoulders. There's no cancer there," Dr. Varghas says reassuringly.

He always anticipates what we want to hear, which in this case is that the cancer has not spread to other bones.

"It seems like the new symptoms you're experiencing are side effects from the steroids and medications," the doctor speculates.

Elizabeth sighs with relief. "Do you think I'm getting better?"

Dr. Varghas now turns his attention to the computer. He doesn't answer right away, scanning the screen to consult today's blood tests. "Everything looks good," he says, without gazing up. "Your body is strong enough for chemo."

"Will I ever get better?" Elizabeth asks again.

I lift my head from my note taking. I, too, want to know if she'll get better.

"Your age and relative health are a definite advantage," Dr. Varghas repeats, as if for the first time. I scan the oncologist's eyes for any sadness or pain that may belie his words but find nothing conclusive. I want to believe that for Elizabeth, he *would* feel pain.

Elizabeth persists, "But do you think I'll—"

"We'll know much more after the chemo."

Dr. Varghas stands. I feel bad Elizabeth keeps asking if she's going to get better, as if the foggy shock of her diagnosis were still brand new.

"Thank you, Doctor," I say. "We always feel stronger after speaking with you."

"My pleasure," he says, and shakes my hand.

-⧸⧸⧸⧸-

THE INFUSION ROOM is bright and smells strongly of antiseptic. Every chair is occupied by a patient in treatment. Some are bald, some wear wigs, and others, like Elizabeth, are at the very beginning. You can tell by their unsure steps and nervous eyes.

We keep the curtain closed halfway around Elizabeth's chair, enough for privacy, short of feeling claustrophobic. Jake and I flank Elizabeth, alternately sitting and hovering. Sounds of chatting patients reach us—it is clear that some of these families have become friends—but we keep to ourselves, at least for now. Elizabeth wants to quarantine cancer from the rest of her life.

The IV nurse inserts a thin needle into a pumped-up vein on Elizabeth's right hand, securing it with white adhesive. A clear liquid begins dripping down the narrow tube and into Elizabeth's body. She winces. "It's burning," she says, opening and closing her fist.

"Only for a few minutes," the nurse says, soothing the port with a warm, damp cloth. Elizabeth shivers. The nurse adds a heated blanket to her shoulders and dispenses an Ativan. "Take it with some water." Then she adds, "I've seen patients live a long time on this chemo."

"I don't want to die," Elizabeth says.

"I know," the nurse says. A loud beeping interrupts her. "Just an air bubble," she explains, massaging the tube. The solution drips without disturbance for a few minutes.

"My kids need me," Elizabeth says, pained and exhausted.

The nurse rubs Elizabeth's arm. "I'll be back to check on you."

Elizabeth turns her head toward me. "I hope this is worth it," she says.

"If not, new treatments come out all the time," I say. "I'm researching everything." She knows my point of view. My attitude is that her cancer can be managed with medication as a chronic illness. It's optimistic *and* realistic. Elizabeth turns away because this isn't what she wants to hear.

"You're doing great," I say, scrutinizing the IV.

Elizabeth scrunches her nose. "Jake?"

"You're a champ," Jake says, and gets up to kiss her on the cheek. When he sits, he lowers his eyes to his BlackBerry, working his thumbs. He would never think of not being here, but he can't afford to get caught in a web of sadness and despair.

"A friend told me I should try acupuncture," Elizabeth says.

Jake rises again and tucks his shirt into his jeans. He's wearing a pressed button-down shirt, size large, even though he only needs a medium, never wanting to feel constricted. He keeps his hair short, cropped close to his head every Thursday, with a little scalp showing through. Jake's toned body is the result of his five-mile-a-day runs and four-times-per-week weight training. That's Jake. He believes in discipline. Salmon for dinner, turkey for lunch.

An elderly volunteer with a purple rinse walks by and glances in between the curtains. A large button on her shoulder says SURVIVOR. "Would you like any lunch today?" she asks, and her face folds into a hundred smile lines.

Elizabeth and I order the usual: tuna on whole wheat with lettuce and tomato, a bag of chips, a bottle of water. Jake orders turkey on wheat, no mayo. We begin to flip through magazines—W, *Self, Vogue*—while the IV does its wicked work.

"Look at these." My sister points to Christian Louboutin black patent leather pumps. "I'm going to buy them," she announces with a half-smile. I can see her in those shoes, wearing an ivory pantsuit at an event for the Asthma and Allergy Foundation, where she fund-raises, the spring restored to her high-heeled step as she takes charge, raising awareness of peanut allergies, which affect her daughter, Brooke.

Elizabeth suddenly puts the magazine down and lies back. "Never mind. I can't do this right now." That's my cue to pull the curtain.

With our privacy restored, I rub Elizabeth's feet and begin a meditation that I learned while studying Herbert Benson's Relaxation Response from Joan Borysenko at Beth Israel Hospital in the '80s. I've used it with my speech pathology patients, and I use it on Elizabeth now to relieve her anxiety and frustration.

"Sit back. Breathe deeply. Relax," I say. "In, out. Relax. From the top of your head to the tips of your toes, you feel calm, comfortable, and warm. Breathe. Relax."

Jake raises his eyebrows. He has no use for hocus-pocus. Before she was diagnosed, Elizabeth never went for this kind of thing, either, but now she's open to anything, desperate to heal.

"Your whole body feels calm and strong," I continue. "The chemo is entering, your ally. This therapy heals. Your body regenerates. All of your strength battles the cancer that has invaded your body." I begin to improvise as I continue rubbing Elizabeth's feet. "Breathe in all that strengthens you. Breathe out everything that weakens you. May you feel happy and healthy. May you be free from suffering. May you find peace." The foot massage is something tangible I can do, skin to skin; it feels good for both of us. I watch Elizabeth, her eyes closed, breathing deeply. She dozes, partly from the meditation, partly from the IV bags, labeled TAXOL and CARBOPLATINUM. I think about the poison coursing through her body, hoping it hits its target and little else.

Now that Elizabeth is asleep, I am suddenly aware of my own exhaustion. We've already been at the hospital for hours. I glance at Jake, his business documents scattered on the floor around his chair.

"I have a lot going on," he says, catching my gaze. "Hey, Don," he says into his BlackBerry. "Yeah, I need that done yesterday." Don is Jake's lawyer. Jake makes demands. "Increase the offer. Keep up the pressure. We close by Friday." I know Jake: whatever it takes, he will close that deal. It's what my brother-in-law can't promise that scares him, and me.

Chapter Thirteen

——————

$\mathcal{S}$ix weeks after her diagnosis, my sister turns forty-four. It feels as if the hourglass of her life has widened at the middle, her sand falling faster than the rest of ours.

The day before Elizabeth's birthday, she, Jake, and I arrive at the hospital as unwitting members of a family portrait, each wearing midnight denim, lightweight leather jackets, and sunglasses. It has become natural to want to restrict our senses, to limit the onslaught of uncertainty. We three on the front lines have become even closer, in a way I never would have expected, veterans of chemo's burn.

Elizabeth has completed a month of the combined chemo-and-radiation regimen, and now it's time to hear the results of her newest scans. We'll learn if any of this has been working, if Elizabeth's hair loss, nausea, and fatigue from the chemo have been worth it.

Dr. Varghas enters the room on soft-soled shoes, holding the folder with Elizabeth's scans, and the three of us straighten our slouches. I don't breathe until he nods his head and smiles.

"No disease progression," Dr. Varghas reports. "Even slight shrinkage of the number of cancer cells. Absence of progression is a victory here. At the moment, Elizabeth, your life is not in jeopardy."

This is the best news we could have hoped for. I shriek and hug my sister while Jake takes her hand. We share a collective sigh, having cleared a major hurdle. Elizabeth allows herself a smile. Dr. Varghas hasn't said that the cancer has disappeared; rather, he's explained that it hasn't made any progress. I watch my sister's body relax in stages, like a fist opening.

"Only fifteen percent of patients respond as well as you have—hence our earlier caution," Dr. Varghas says, almost proudly. He displays a scan of Elizabeth's lungs on the computer and points to small black dots, explaining that the lesions themselves haven't gotten any bigger and the number of them has actually decreased.

"Amazing," I say. It's an exaggeration, but I was so nervous about the results that I now feel euphoric. Maybe Richard was right about difficult odds.

"Congratulations," the doctor says with a nod. "The best we could hope for."

"Dr. Varghas, why this epidemic among young, nonsmoking women?" I ask.

"Could be many things. Secondhand smoke is a culprit. Women have been found to be more susceptible to its effects than men. Estrogen is also believed to contribute."

We nod.

"Then there is the possibility of an inherent genetic susceptibility. We have identified a gene thought to be linked to lung cancer in nonsmokers. With the proper drug development, Stage IV lung cancer might be looked upon one day the way diabetes is: as a chronic disease that can be managed with treatment. We have a new drug in trials that is quite promising."

"Chemo for life?" Elizabeth asks, and frowns. "That's what you call promising?"

"A pill with fewer side effects," Dr. Varghas says. "When we have all of the data, I promise I will tell you more."

The news makes me light-headed. I was preparing for the worst and didn't sleep well last night. Having now received the best outcome possible, I can barely make sense of my relief.

"A pill sounds good," Jake says.

"I don't mean to raise false hopes," the doctor says, "but in the trial, I have a patient who has survived on this drug for four years."

We exit Dr. Varghas's office and shake hands. It's a lot to take in. What if that pill could prolong Elizabeth's life until the next drug is discovered?

"See you in a couple of weeks," he says.

Leaving the office, I mention to Jake that this pill sounds like the drug Dr. Stern told us about at Dana Farber.

"Maybe it will be my miracle drug," Elizabeth says.

The next day, David takes an Acela train up from New York. My family celebrates Elizabeth's birthday and the excellent news of her scans at Mastro's. Richard opts to have dinner with a friend. He's been making his own plans over the last few weeks, and I don't blame him—I've been spending all my time with Elizabeth.

Alexandra accompanies me for this celebratory night. Even though my sister-in-law, Jill, can't make the trip, I know she feels the warmth of our family, as does Jake, who is seated at Elizabeth's side. Besides, Richard doesn't even like Mastro's. He favors Abe & Louie's—calling Mastro's filet mignon "a piece of shoe leather"—but I think the real reason Richard dislikes Mastro's is that it's my family's restaurant: Kaplan-Gordon celebrations are always there.

The night of Elizabeth's birthday, I have the strange experience of imagining the man who shares my bed at a separate table down the street, where he'll converse about business, sports, and politics. He'll treat his dinner partner with respect and excuse any of his friend's bad qualities in order to feel revered.

Meanwhile, I cherish the members of my family gathered around the table at Mastro's, a comfortable, loving circle. Together, we savor Elizabeth's good news. Jake orders bottles of California pinot noir for the table. Ever since he and Elizabeth traveled to Napa a few years ago, he's displayed the expertise of a domestic sommelier.

Jake leads with a toast. "Happy birthday to the best wife I could ever hope for," he says. We raise our glasses and look at Elizabeth, whose eyes sparkle for the first time in weeks. "May there be many, *many* more birthdays," Jake says riskily. We all want to believe him.

"I'll drink to that," my father says. *"L'chaim."*

"L'chaim," David says.

We reach across the table to make sure that each person's glass gently clinks against the rim of everyone else's, that briefest sonorous contact that says, *Family, hope, and love.*

After we toast, Elizabeth stands. She's wearing a gray wrap dress made of silk jersey, black suede ankle boots, and, to an outsider, what looks like her own hair. She peers around the table, making eye contact with each of us.

"Thank you so much for being here for me, tonight and all these weeks. I couldn't do this without you," she says, choking. She sits and places her hand over her mouth.

The server takes our orders, then our menus. The wine is silky, making you want just a little more. My father falls quiet, looking from Elizabeth to David to me, obvious with the pleasure of having his three adult children at the same table. I wonder if my parents lament Richard's absence tonight, and the struggles that I still have.

David clears his throat. "And we just closed another deal!" We toast again. David has become the New York regional representative for Stars. Elizabeth sits between our brother and her husband, now business partners. David affectionately places his arm around Elizabeth's shoulder as they speak, obvious that he wishes he could spend more time with her.

Kissing David on the cheek, I hear Elizabeth say, "Just amazing. Jake says that everyone at Stars loves you. What a great fit. It takes a special kind of person to combine business and family." My parents beam. Here, we replenish and celebrate each other.

Alexandra and I share a New York strip with sautéed spinach and a salad. Next to Alexandra is Brooke, then, following the table clockwise, Lauren. The teen cousins begin a conversation at a level I can't possibly overhear, probably about school and mutual friends. I take comfort in the closeness Alexandra shares with her cousins, breaking bread with extended family, all of the security that this table represents.

"How was bridge today?" I ask my mother, on my right.

"I came in third," she says halfheartedly.

A few weeks ago, she told me that bridge is just a distraction, the only time she doesn't dwell on The Problem, meaning Elizabeth's cancer.

When we get home that night, Richard is still out. An hour later, when he arrives, the dogs bark and wake me. I whisper good night, not knowing whether he hears, and fall back to sleep.

⚜

NOT LONG AFTER Mastro's, there's more chemo, which is always a moody day. Returning to the Gordons' from the hospital, Jake, Elizabeth, and I fit ourselves into our family's new pattern. My mother cooks dinner. The kids hunch over homework. Elizabeth dashes upstairs without saying a word—after six hours of chemo, she barely speaks—and puts on a pajama set, beyond the reach of our comfort.

Alexandra and I have taken to spending afternoons at the Gordons' between radiation and chemo. I scoop her after school and get my mother whatever she needs to make dinner. My parents lurk in the house with nothing to do, trying to keep their spirits up. A month after Elizabeth's birthday, their weariness again sets in. The creases on my father's forehead deepen, and my mother's eyes sink.

Elizabeth and her family used to dine casually at the kitchen counter, but now there are so many of us that we eat formally in the dining room. I set the table as Elizabeth rests upstairs, draping a bleached linen tablecloth on the oval, setting out plates, napkins, forks, knives, and spoons. The very first time, I set it impeccably, but now, after so many weeks of sordid routine, I find myself slacking, forgiving the flaws.

"Grey Goose?" Jake asks from the sideboard, making himself a drink.

"Yes," I say without hesitation.

He hands me a vodka on the rocks the way I like it, with lime.

"Elizabeth tells me to marry someone who's good to the kids," Jake says. "I don't want to have that conversation." As if I do.

I shift in my chair. "Remind her about the new pills coming out," I say.

I wander into the kitchen with my glass, ice clinking. "Smells good," I say. My mother looks up from ladling a red sauce over the chicken, comfort food from when Elizabeth, David, and I were children. Jewish chicken, we called it. I recognize the aroma of the simple mixture: ketchup thinned with water, paprika, and salt. "Mmm, my favorite," I say, inhaling deeply. Richard and Alexandra love it, too, when I make it at home, but I don't dwell on its being my mother's own recipe, fearing that Richard will decide he doesn't like it anymore. I notice how relaxed I am without him here.

When I first said that I planned on accompanying my sister to all her appointments, he couldn't understand why Jake would want me around so much.

"If you were in Elizabeth's position, God forbid," Richard said, "I wouldn't want your sister at every appointment."

"It's not about what Jake wants; it's what Elizabeth wants," I said, although I knew Jake appreciated having me as much as Elizabeth did. "If I were sick, it would be what *I* want, Richard, not you."

The three of us had grown up together without Richard; even Jake's taste buds had developed alongside Elizabeth's and mine. When Jake sees his mother-in-law upending the ketchup bottle, he implicitly understands that her meal evokes the safety and happiness of Gloucester. Jewish chicken brings back the times we tore down the street on our bikes, the years we drank beer in each other's finished basements, able to read and forgive each other's moods as well as our own.

I sip the vodka and let it heat my chest. Then again, Jake has always had another side. He dropped out of Gloucester High, acting out after his parents' divorce. Eventually he went back for his GED and diploma and was accepted to Northeastern University, where he reconnected with Elizabeth. On his own Jake could wreak havoc, but their love was a blessing that stabilized him and smoothed his rough edges. Elizabeth integrated with Jake's family, becoming a sister to his two brothers and, according to Jake's mother, the daughter she never had.

With a keen mind for numbers and articulate communication, Jake graduated summa cum laude with a 3.8 GPA, the highest in our extended family. Elizabeth had rescued him.

When Alexandra and I arrive home from eating Jewish chicken, our own house feels cold and empty, and I cringe at the contrast. Elizabeth's home, a battleground, is filled lately with friends bringing lunch and homemade dinners, well wishes and love. Richard is out tonight again with friends, a pattern I recognize from what he has told me of his marriage just before he and Harrison's mother divorced. Crisis has made Elizabeth's house feel even more like a home, whereas mine has become a cold container, a place to rest my heavy head.

As I'm settling into bed with Alexandra—she sleeps next to me for now—Jake texts. "Elizabeth is depressed. Call."

"You okay?" I ask when she picks up the phone. Alexandra puts down her journal and listens.

"Can you read me the notes from our last appointment?" she asks. "I need to remember the good things Varghas said."

For a good hour, I read and reread the entries from my pad. By the end of the conversation, Elizabeth feels more at ease. Alexandra has drifted off on the pillow beside me, and I'm ready to join her.

The next morning, freezing and blustery, I stop at Elizabeth's after dropping Alexandra off at school. It's December, and I rush from my car to the Gordons' front door, the air slapping my face, my eyes watering. Even for December, I don't remember winter ever having been this bitter. But Elizabeth needn't be outside too much. She's chauffeured garage to garage, from home to Beth Israel—a silver lining. I enter the Gordons' with a gift bag from Bloomingdale's for Elizabeth: peach La Prairie moisturizer, a long-sleeved cotton nightgown, and fuzzy socks.

I find her propped up in bed, eating scrambled eggs and toast. I take off my coat, give her a kiss, and notice she looks sullen.

"Your nose is cold," Elizabeth says when I kiss her.

"My thermostat read fifty-five when we woke up. I need to call the gas company," I say. "I brushed my teeth wearing my mink coat."

"Oh, no," she says, and laughs. "Want to sleep over?"

"Fun!" I say, permitting myself to indulge in the experience of sleeping at Elizabeth's, instead of at home. When she finishes her eggs, I say, "Let's go downstairs."

Grasping the railing, her breath rapid and shallow, Elizabeth makes her way down. She's wearing a thick bathrobe and slippers the color of pink ballet shoes. No wig. Her head is wrapped in a patterned Pucci scarf instead. We sit at the kitchen counter.

"I want to try acupuncture," Elizabeth says. "Someone in Chinatown."

"Give me the name. I'll check it out and make an appointment," I say.

Elizabeth adjusts her scarf. A few strands feather the nape of her neck.

"Have you been listening to the tape I made?" I ask. Last week I recorded Elizabeth an hour-long guided-imagery meditation. On the recording I lead her through a series of exercises in which she visualizes her body's cancer cells being eaten by her healthy cells, which are still abundant.

"I am strong and healthy," Elizabeth repeats back to me. "Thank you. I listen to it every night. And then I obsess about the new pills."

"Me, too."

"Samantha, there's something else," Elizabeth says.

"What?" I ask, worried.

"Wheatgrass," she says. "I read it helps with some cancers."

I sigh with relief. "Sure, we'll get some. I know a café in the Highlands that sells shots of it." I squeeze her hand.

Elizabeth smiles, a look lined with innocence, and I see that she honestly believes the acupuncture and wheatgrass will help. I believe it, too. I have to. Faith to the point of obstinacy is our only hope. Purple crystals upstairs on her night table. The *chai* around her neck. A friend traveling to Israel just placed a note in the Western Wall, God's mailbox.

Soon we are in Tom Tam's office on Kneeland Street. He's a licensed acupuncturist who has treated people with cancer and other chronic diseases for twenty-five years. At first, the run-down office dismays us. Then a pretty Chinese lady with bright red lipstick, Tom Tam's wife, greets us. "Fill out the forms completely," she says with a smile. "He'll be with you soon."

A shelf overflows with stacks of books on Chinese medicine. Charts show pressure points. Above Mrs. Tam's desk is a bulletin board with notices about healing and energy services written in Chinese and English. The waiting room is full, every chair taken by people of all ages and races.

"I will see Mrs. Gordon," Tom Tam says to the waiting room. Elizabeth and I rise, and then I sit. "You, too," Mr. Tam says, motioning to include me. "Follow me."

We enter a small exam room that hasn't been updated in decades. Elizabeth sits on what looks like a massage table, and I take a wooden chair. Tom Tam extends a doll stuck with small pins and explains the different meridians in the body: heart, lung, stomach, and kidney. Elizabeth and I steal a glance at each other, eyebrows raised, as if we are going to see voodoo.

"You have lung cancer. I will help you," the acupuncturist

says confidently. I notice a book on the side table entitled *The Tom Tam Healing System* and can't help but be impressed.

"I have two basic approaches," Mr. Tam says. "Acupuncture and *tui na* medical massage. We have to remove the blockage in the body." I can follow what he's saying, but Tom Tam's accent is thicker than his wife's.

"What blockage?" Elizabeth asks.

"The energy is blocked. Blockage interferes with proper functioning. You come every week for one hour. I do acupuncture, stick needles in your skin, and end with *tui na* massage."

Elizabeth looks plainly skeptical. Tom Tam laughs.

"It won't hurt. Please lie down. We restore the body's natural ability to heal." He turns to me and says, "See you when we finish."

I return to the waiting room and strike up a conversation with a man who I learn is fifty-four and a dentist. When I find myself revealing Elizabeth's diagnosis to him, the dentist confides that he has had Stage IV colon cancer for six years. At the beginning of his treatment, he went to Dana Farber and had surgery and traditional chemo, but, of course, those weren't a cure. Since surgery, he has been seeing Tom Tam for acupuncture and feels that it's kept his cancer under control. He still sees his oncologist for checkups, but as long as the cancer doesn't get worse, he's sticking with Mr. Tam. The dentist is extremely positive and has every reason to be: he has already outlived his prognosis. He retired early, exercises, and travels. He looks radiant and healthy.

I realize that I am nervous about the treatment only when Elizabeth comes out.

"How was it?" I ask.

"Very relaxing. Tiny needles in my legs, feet, face, and

chest," she says, pointing to these parts of her body. "It didn't hurt at all."

"What did he say?"

"That my energy got a little better by the end. He was reading my pulses. Who knows if it will help?"

"Do you feel any different?"

"It's only one treatment," she says.

On the ride home, I relay my conversation with the dentist to Elizabeth.

Chapter Fourteen

———

*A*fter Elizabeth's first treatment with Tom Tam, I pick up a rotisserie chicken for dinner with Richard and Alexandra.

"It's time to make the list," I say to them when I walk into the house.

Richard is reading the *Wall Street Journal* at the kitchen table, and Alexandra is seated next to him with her legs crossed, doing math. My heart expands tentatively.

"Eat first, list later," Richard says. We kiss hello, and I inhale his familiar freshness. "That chicken smells good," he says. How does he not ask me where I was?

Now, two years since Brooke's bat mitzvah, it's Alexandra's turn. It's true what they say about your past self having no imagination for your future. I am still married to Richard, and my sister has cancer, neither of which I could have foreseen.

We eat as a family, and then Richard, Alexandra, and I put together a guest list for her own bat mitzvah.

"Only people who matter—no one extraneous," Richard says. "It's going to cost a fortune no matter what. We have to cut back where we can."

"I agree," I say, but our total still comes in at 250 guests.

Tomorrow I will hire Carol Stickman, the party planner at

Rose Wood, and a DJ and a photographer. My main contribution, besides overseeing everything, will be a video montage of Alexandra's life, birth to *bat*. By the time we hold the reception on May 15, Elizabeth will have completed chemotherapy. A nice finish to have these two milestones coincide. Knowing Elizabeth won't be scheduled for more treatments after Alexandra's big day makes it easier. I feel less guilty, and I decide to enjoy the planning.

By February, it's time to say yes to a dress. Naturally, Alexandra and I shop at Pink Domino, where all the girls from Newton, Brookline, Weston, and Wellesley find their dream dresses for a special occasion. An entire wall of the store is covered with photographs of bat mitzvah girls posing in dresses purchased there, complete with professional hairstyles, makeup, and manicures, the Jewish equivalent of a *quinceañera* or debutante ball. Alexandra rushes over to see if she recognizes anyone on the wall. Sure enough, there in her peach A-line gown with a full tulle skirt is her own cousin Brooke.

After only three dresses, Alexandra settles on one from the trunk show: a pale blue strapless gown, its hem embroidered with tiny white flowers. The dress is appropriate for a black-tie bat mitzvah and transforms my thirteen-year-old into a young woman. "I can't wait until my picture is on the wall," she says, twirling in tulle.

THE REST OF the winter passes like whiplash: chemo and acupuncture for Elizabeth, weekly bat mitzvah lessons for Alexandra, oscillating between maternal pride and desperate hope. As we get closer to spring, my spirit lifts. Fifty-degree temperatures and longer days cheer me. I'm impressed by

Richard, who sacrifices an afternoon a week to assist with Alexandra's haftorah lesson.

After chemo with Elizabeth, one day I arrive home around four to find Alexandra, Richard, and Moshe, the bat mitzvah tutor, in our library. Alexandra chants a portion of her haftorah in Hebrew, and Richard follows her, word for word. At a pause, I enter.

"Not one mistake," Richard says. Our shared parental bond makes our marital crisis both more complicated and more painful. Day after day, I ask myself, *When Richard does so much, am I wrong for wanting more?*

⸙

JUST A MONTH before Alexandra's bat mitzvah, in April, Elizabeth finishes her fifth chemo cycle. Today we meet again with Dr. Varghas for the results.

Elizabeth still verges on weepiness, but her overall mood has improved. She and Jake have begun socializing again with other couples. Lately, Elizabeth even ventures out for dinner and shopping with friends. When she finds the energy, we have continued our workout walks around the reservoir. Over the winter, we started practicing yoga to stay flexible and centered. To celebrate this last cycle, Elizabeth even hired a personal trainer; she begins private weight and interval training next week at the gym. Her spirit is fierce.

For our moment of truth with Dr. Varghas, I'm wearing my favorite jeans and a clingy boatneck sweater. Elizabeth looks elegant in ballet flats and tight black jeans.

"I like that color blush," Elizabeth says when we meet at our good-luck seats before the fish tank in Dr. Varghas's waiting room.

"Thanks. It's new," I say, and touch my cheek, then pull out my compact. Because I've forgotten the name of the color, Elizabeth and I try to pinpoint the exact shade. Paprika? Orchid? Risqué? This is the old Elizabeth, who had the luxury of being lighthearted.

When we are called into Dr. Varghas's office, as always, I receive his warmth at first sight. We take our usual seats like a family at a dinner table.

"It's really remarkable," he begins, looking down at the chart once more to make sure there's no mistake. "Your cancer markers show absolutely no disease progression."

"What a relief," I say, and let out the breath I've been holding.

"You're very lucky," Dr. Varghas continues. "As I've said, only a small percentage of patients respond as well as you have."

Elizabeth doesn't make a sound. She looks at her lap with a tight smile. She wants the doctor to tell her she's cured, not to report on her "disease progression," or lack of it.

Jake takes her hand. "That's good news, honey," he says, and looks at Varghas. "Does that mean we're done with chemo?"

"Yes, for the present." The doctor hesitates.

"What do I do next?" Elizabeth asks. "I still have cancer, right?"

"I'd like to start you on a new drug, Elizabeth. It's called Iressa, and it just came out of clinical trials. It couldn't be easier to administer—one pill a day. Your test for the EGFR mutation, fortunately, came back positive. That qualifies you for the drug. As I've said, a few of my patients in the trial survived on Iressa for years."

"Years?" Elizabeth asks, a lift in her voice.

A small poster on the wall distracts me. *How much pain are you experiencing?* it asks. On a scale of one to five, it ranks pain with human expressions, from smiles to frowns. This time, I relate to the smiles. I write *Iressa* in my notebook, circle it, and make an asterisk. The drug sounds lovely and feminine, a girl with long tresses in a white cotton dress. Later, Internet research will also raise my hopes; Iressa has just recently been FDA approved for advanced-stage lung cancer, with major success in its trials. Something nags at me in the exam room, and I flip back to my medical notebook's earliest entries. There, on the third page—I wrote *Iressa* during our appointment with Dr. Stern. It's the same drug we heard about at Dana Farber.

"Iressa's side effects are minimal," Dr. Varghas continues. "Elizabeth, your quality of life will be close to normal. It's a much less brutal treatment than chemo."

"What a huge difference," I say. "This is great!"

Dr. Varghas nods his head. "This medicine is targeted—it attacks only cancerous cells—and works well with people like you, who have the EGFR mutation. Your hair will grow back. You'll have more energy for your children. Just one pill a day, and you can go on with your life. We'll monitor your progress at a monthly appointment."

"It arrived just in time," Elizabeth says, absorbing the drug's significance. "Thank God I'm done with chemo. I can't wait to chuck this wig."

Dr. Varghas smiles. "See you in three weeks," he says. "That's when we'll start the pill." He stands as we pack up and head for the door.

"I'm actually a little excited," Elizabeth says to Jake and me in the elevator.

"It sounds like Iressa could keep your cancer under control for a long time," I say.

My sister could actually live with cancer. For how long, we don't know, but I am desperately grateful for this gift of extended time. I set my mind on enjoying Alexandra's bat mitzvah, the last weeks of planning. Maybe I can even begin to enjoy Richard, too.

-᪲᪲᪲-

UP TO THE last minute, Alexandra practices her speech and her haftorah, "Behar-Bechukotai," or "Blessings and Curses."

The section comes from the end of Leviticus, the book in the Torah that itemizes the laws of the Jewish people. There are laws that mandate taking care of the elderly, the poor, and the sick; laws that prohibit incest and bestiality; laws that spell out in no uncertain terms that it is forbidden to cheat another when selling land; laws about keeping the Sabbath; even laws about leprosy and mildew. At the end of Leviticus is a series of admonitions, the blessings that shall rain down upon those who live by the laws of Moses and the curses that shall be delivered to those who disobey.

In the synagogue with its stained-glass windows, the same place where my husband was bar mitzvahed and where we now attend High Holiday services, Rabbi Bromberg calls Alexandra to the bimah.

"We are all very proud of you," he says. "Congregation, please turn to page 353."

Alexandra stands in front of more than two hundred friends and relatives and chants the blessings and curses. Even though I can't follow the Hebrew, I listen for the blessing that will cure an illness that has taken root in a good person. I find myself listening for the curse I fear must also be there in Leviticus: that one's sister shall become deathly ill if one marries a man with whom her sister does not get along.

I listen intently, as I have all the months Alexandra has

been practicing, but now something is transformed, and it's as if my daughter is teaching me. Listening to her pure sweet voice, Richard and I look at each other timidly. He squeezes my hand. I squeeze back.

There is a moment in the service when five of us—Richard, Alexandra, and I, joined by Elizabeth and Jake—stand on the bimah to say a prayer. It appears that a net of happiness has fallen on us, and I'm grateful for appearances. No one looking at us would ever see the wounds.

After Alexandra finishes, the rabbi calls upon me to speak. I stand in front of the congregation and share my pride in the caring and compassionate young woman my child has become. I talk about her kind nature, how she excels in skiing and waterskiing, and how lucky I am to have her as my daughter.

We have a few hours between the service and the reception, but Alexandra and I spend most of it getting our hair and makeup done, before slipping into our evening attire. Richard and Harrison, too, wear matching tuxedos. When the time comes, the four of us arrive early at Rose Wood to take pictures with extended family. My parents arrive before we do. When we get there, my parents make a point of shaking Richard's hand.

"Congratulations," my father says. "Alexandra did wonderfully. We're proud."

"Thank you," Richard says. Uncharacteristically, he lets the handshakes linger, cupping my parents' hands with his.

When the Gordons arrive, my stomach twists, and I'm on guard. Elizabeth's black strapless gown hugs her body. She is breathtaking. Although I know her hair has begun to grow back, she still wears a wig for this occasion; it falls gracefully to her shoulders. Jake and the kids arrive behind her with tense smiles. The Gordons are cordial with Richard but don't congratulate him like my parents did. Nevertheless, I don't let them break this spell.

Once we've all exchanged greetings, the photographer poses our nuclear family for a portrait. Alexandra looks beautiful, flawless in her pale blue strapless gown. Our girl is glowing, the belle of the ball, the princess, the bat mitzvah girl.

Next, we take pictures with Richard's family: his two sisters, their husbands, and their children. They're all close but not in constant contact like I am with my family. When I'm pulled into the middle of a Freeman family photo, I am struck with a thought: *Maybe a little distance isn't so bad. It certainly reduces the drama.*

The photographer then poses the four Gordons. You'd never know that Elizabeth has cancer. Her eyes are sparkling sapphires. She leans into Jake, who warms at the contact and holds my sister loosely around the waist. Brooke and Lauren pose, squatting, in the foreground.

Finally, there's a shot of David, Jill, Brittany, and Justin, just six and eight years old. As David's family disperses, the photographer gestures to Elizabeth and me.

"You two?" he says. "Sisters?"

He raises the lens to his eye, and we grin and pose.

"Now let's have a picture of the entire family," I say, the original Kaplans and their extended clan. "Mom, Dad, come over." We're positioned with Alexandra in the middle, and although I'm a little on edge in my gold sparkly gown, I smile. The show must go on.

I watch Richard, hoping that he will approach Elizabeth and ask her how she's feeling or tell her she looks great. It would mean so much to me. But it's his daughter's bat mitzvah, and I'm sure he thinks that guests should be approaching him.

Or maybe he thinks it's inappropriate to remind Elizabeth of her illness at a celebratory event.

Elizabeth and Jake still haven't congratulated Richard. As they head to their seats, it doesn't appear that they will—an obvious snub. Under different circumstances, they would have been sitting at our table as guests of honor. I wonder if the silence on their part might also be calculated, since Richard didn't attend Brooke's bat mitzvah, after all.

Last fall, after her diagnosis, Richard wrote Elizabeth a letter. He wanted to explain the behavior that had made him resent her all these years, and he hoped that Elizabeth would hear him out. He wanted to meet. Maybe then she could understand why he shunned her in the parking lot at our kids' Hebrew school, or why, when they passed each other in Wellesley Center, Richard saw only air.

Elizabeth refused. She had just completed the second of her five rounds of chemo. "That's not where I want to focus my energy right now. I'll let bygones be bygones, but hell if I'm going to sit and listen to every little thing I've ever done to piss Richard off."

Richard felt he'd offered an olive branch, and when Elizabeth declined their meeting through me, he again felt snubbed. I felt differently. I thought the letter was a good start, a gesture that might get them in the same room for holidays and family events, minus the stress.

After Richard sent the letter, one night over a home-cooked meal of grilled swordfish and vegetables, he said, "I wrote your sister a letter apologizing for my part. Where's her apology?"

"I understand your feelings," I said, as I served myself and sat with my plate. "She's scared, you know. She has cancer."

"What a waste of time to write that letter," he said. "Cancer can't be her excuse for everything."

"I appreciate that you wrote it. It meant a lot to me," I said. And it had softened Elizabeth's hard feelings, a bit.

I wished that they could both be less self-absorbed about this situation, although Elizabeth's illness was certainly a valid excuse to create a boundary. Richard hadn't observed the fear in Elizabeth's eyes when she saw the company logo on the envelope, how she had dropped it on the table where she stood, as if it contained anthrax. "Should I open it? What if it says something bad? I can't take any more." Richard didn't know that only after two days did Elizabeth summon the courage to open his letter.

In full-blown hostess mode at the bat mitzvah, I mingle with friends and family. "Alexandra did a fantastic job," my friend Lynne says. "So poised. Great party," she adds. We have transformed the Rose Wood ballroom into a South Beach–style nightclub, with floor-length white tablecloths, orchid centerpieces, and clusters of pastel balloons. The DJ plays Top 40 music by Usher, Alicia Keys, Maroon 5, Jay-Z, and early Beyoncé. Our guests dance and socialize, drinking mojitos and champagne.

It's 2004, and the recession we faced in the early '90s is long over. Rose Wood members are radiant with prosperity—no amount of cosmetic work can match a financial face-lift. Investments are up, especially in finance and real estate, Richard and Jake's fortes. The stock market rises steadily. Some in Wellesley are benefiting more obviously than others—it's at Alexandra's bat mitzvah that I first hear someone say they invested with Madoff. Those whose profits are less visible snipe about a bubble.

But no amount of celebratory music, cocktails, and cheer will change the fact that Elizabeth has cancer. Iressa or not, cancer management or not, I'm coming to terms with the fact that my sister won't live a full lifetime. I stand, smiling and gracious, taking in my friends' compliments, but I actually feel shaky. My legs wobble on my high heels. Champagne in hand, I walk to Elizabeth's table. My beaded gown makes a light swishing.

I stand behind my sister, with my hands on her shoulders, and beckon for the photographer.

"Let's hope the big guy doesn't see," she says with a quick laugh, self-conscious.

After the first portrait, Elizabeth stands. We put our arms around each other, tilt our heads, and smile as the light flashes in our eyes.

"I'm so proud of her," Elizabeth says, turning to me. "I love watching Alexandra with all her friends. She's got her whole life ahead of her."

"Everyone played a part in how she turned out," I say. "She sure loves her auntie."

"She spoke so beautifully. So did you. She really takes after you."

"Thanks." I pause. "How are you holding up?" This is Elizabeth's first big event since her diagnosis. I regret the question as soon as she tugs at her wig.

"I'm definitely tired, but overall pretty good." We embrace.

I move along to speak to other guests and notice Richard chatting with friends, his eyes detouring from mine after they make contact.

When the music breaks into "Hava Nagila," our guests leap from their chairs, form a circle, and put their arms on each other's shoulders. Dancing the hora, they kick. I always pictured Elizabeth leading the charge, but other friends step into the void. Jake returns from the bar with a vodka on the rocks; he and my sister remain seated.

David and my male cousins raise Alexandra on a ballroom chair while Richard and I clap and circle. We join hands with friends, embracing the joy of this ritual. I spot Brooke and Lauren dancing with their little cousins Justin and Brittany. When the hora is over, they join Alexandra and her friends on the dance floor, spicing it up with teenage energy.

Elizabeth remains at her table, poised and lovely in her dark sequined gown with a plunging back. She chats with anyone who approaches her. Elizabeth's skin is as vibrant as ever, nothing gaunt or hanging about her limbs. A blessing of sorts. Jake doesn't ever leave her side, his hand steadfast on her chair.

Guests take their seats for the candle lighting. All eyes are on Alexandra beside a three-tiered cake. Like a miniature adult, she takes the microphone and addresses the crowd. Harrison stands beside her, holding a lit taper candle. If not for Richard's earlier marriage, Alexandra would have been an only child, but in this moment a brother supports her.

"Good evening, everyone. For my good deed, I will be donating my bat mitzvah money to the charities designated by those I call to light the candles," Alexandra says. "The first candle is in memory of my father's parents, Harry and Faye Freeman, my grandparents who are no longer with us. My donation will go to the American Cancer Society." Harrison hands Alexandra the taper to light the first of thirteen candles, and everyone applauds.

"The next candle is for Grandma Rachel and Grandpa Joseph. Please come up and light candle number two, supporting a donation to the American Heart Association." The DJ plays "If I Were a Rich Man," from *Fiddler on the Roof*, as my parents walk hand in hand and greet their granddaughter with simultaneous kisses on the cheek. Cameras flash.

The Gordons take the stage to "Italian Restaurant," by Billy

Joel. Alexandra announces a donation to the Beth Israel Deaconess Medical Center Cancer Fund when Elizabeth lights the candle. Our guests stand in ovation, and my heart swells.

David, Jill, and the kids approach to "New York, New York," by Frank Sinatra. Alexandra will donate to the Susie Stein Fund in memory of Jill's mother, who died of breast cancer last year. Finally, Alexandra's best friends rush the stage at the sound of "Uptown Girl," and a donation to the Boys & Girls Clubs of Boston is announced.

With all thirteen candles lit, Alexandra passes her father the microphone, and I join Richard for the toast. He speaks about Alexandra's caring nature and personality. "I am so proud of the young lady she's become," Richard says. When his eyes well up with tears, I put a hand on his shoulder and swallow, refusing to cry.

We pose for a final family photo near the cake. There's another standing ovation from our friends. Richard and I hold hands as we return to our seats for the meal.

The music slows during dinner. When the plates are cleared, Jake leads Elizabeth to the dance floor. He holds her gingerly, as if she might break, but close, afraid to let go. This tender dance recalls Elizabeth's voice on the phone over twenty years ago:

"Guess who I ran into on the T? Jake Gordon!"

"Such a troublemaker," I said. "But fun. And *cute*."

"He's changed. Just wait until you see."

As Alexandra's party hits the home stretch, the memories swarm. I see Jake waving goodbye in our front yard in Gloucester when he dropped out of high school, saying, "Ciao, princesses." I see weddings, births, Brooke's and now Alexandra's bat mitzvahs, all celebrated with loved ones bonded by blood, commitment, and history. Elizabeth, Jake, and I attended the same schools, the same teenage parties. We knew how each other's homes smelled, the number of steps at the back door, where our pets were buried, and the story behind each of our scars.

For a second, I have a glimmer of how impossible it must feel for Richard to penetrate this closed circle. Even in celebration, my family stands behind their own lines. I wish that Jake would shake Richard's hand for the sake of family and in the spirit of kindness. I wish that Richard could release his grudges and approach my sister's table.

But in this moment, I have an epiphany: I can't change other people. I can only change myself.

I begin to honor my own role in this family's demise.

Chapter Fifteen

———

 *T*he high from Alexandra's bat mitzvah lasts for a week before life settles into a new normal, made grim by Elizabeth's prognosis and everything that's unresolved between Richard and me. I try to remember that you can't fake good kids. At least we've been successful at that.

One afternoon in May, I step out my front door for a walk. My garden bursts with red tulips and clusters of yellow daffodils. Unlike my reservoir walks with Elizabeth, this stroll is solitary and serene. I have found myself venturing out alone more and more, late in the day, a kind of therapy. I consider the pros and cons of my marriage and realize that my expectations of marriage were particular, not universal, that not everyone seeks the same things I do. I begin to appreciate that Richard might have sought something different from our marriage, just as we clearly crave different ways of being loved. I didn't fully understand these things about myself before I got married; maybe no one does at such a young age or before intense conflicts. I never realized that I was so enmeshed with my family that if my husband didn't love them, I would equate it with his not loving me.

Today, seeking variety, I find my feet taking me to a quaint cluster of stores about a mile from my house in Wellesley Center. The days have become milder, and joggers have again taken to the streets. Crossing a parking lot, a tall man passes in front of me just a few yards away, working his knees high, breathing hard. My gaze lingers on his loose-fitting shorts and then his terry-cloth headband. "Dr. Varghas?" I say, with a shot of recognition and adrenaline.

The oncologist turns to me midstride. Slowing his jog, he gives in to a walk. I stand there for a moment, drinking in this tiny miracle. Rather than causing me to regret the imposition on my solitude, seeing Dr. Varghas energizes me. He takes a few steps in my direction, waves a hand. "Samantha, nice to see you. You live around here?"

I gesture behind me to the Tudor houses and leafy lawns. "This is my neighborhood."

"Really?" He smiles. "Me, too. I'm around the corner." He points. "Renting a place in Hulbert Village until I know where to plant roots." Without his white lab coat, my sister's oncologist resembles someone I could meet at the gym. He clears his throat, shifts his weight from foot to foot. Is it possible that he's at a loss for words?

On sudden inspiration, I say, "Are you finished with your run? You wouldn't have time for coffee?"

He looks at his wristwatch.

"Sure. That would be nice, actually. I have a little time."

We head to the Starbucks at the end of the lot and take a table in the back, before ordering at the register.

"How are you holding up?" he asks when we return from the counter with our cardboard-sleeved cups. "Elizabeth's lucky to have you."

"Thanks. I'll be lucky to keep her," I say.

Dr. Varghas sips his latte. The café is crowded with people talking, reading, and tapping on laptops. I pull my chair closer.

I realize how this must seem, especially if Richard or Elizabeth were to walk in. But our encounter feels serendipitous and cathartic, comforting to me in a way I didn't realize I needed.

"Dr. Gold said you came to Boston on a fellowship," I say.

"That's right, in thoracic oncology."

"Why oncology?" Dr. Gold had called him a rock star. The way he explains things to us during Elizabeth's appointments shows that he combines his expertise with deep emotional intelligence.

Dr. Varghas considers my question about his specialty by looking down at the table the way he refers to a chart on his desk. "In oncology the research possibilities are fascinating and endless. But I couldn't do only research. My patients—people like your sister—it's quite meaningful work."

"I don't know what we would do without you," I say, and place my hand on his arm. I allow it to linger perhaps a bit too long before returning it to my coffee.

Dr. Varghas pushes his chair away from the table and crosses his knees.

"Your sister is strong," he says, "and much too young for this."

"You have so much patience. We ask the same questions over and over."

"I work with the whole person, not just the disease," the doctor says, meeting my eyes. My face flushes with his attention. I worry that I may be crossing a line, but I have a nagging question about Elizabeth's treatment that I haven't had the courage to ask. Alone with Dr. Varghas, I find my nerve.

"Elizabeth's terrified, you know. We all are. Um, if the cancer progresses while she's on Iressa, is there anything else?" Elizabeth has given me permission to discuss the details of her condition. That's not what makes me nervous.

"We can double the dose on Iressa, if we have to," Dr.

Varghas says. "And there's a new drug in trials, Tarceva, Iressa's cousin, which is even more potent." He tells me that, as far as he is concerned, Elizabeth is finished with traditional chemo. He'd recommend a clinical trial for her only if first Iressa, then Tarceva, fails her. Above all, he doesn't want to interfere with Elizabeth's energy and quality of life, the time she has left with her children. He explains that each round of traditional chemo becomes harsher and harsher because the cancer cells toughen up. "They're smart," he says. "Cancer can actually learn to fool the chemo." I'm disheartened to hear that the disease can evolve to beat back such miraculous feats, but comforted that Dr. Varghas prioritizes Elizabeth's quality of life. I'm relieved that he has her on a different path.

Tears flow freely against my will, from a mixture of hope, grief, and Dr. Varghas's kind validation of my suffering. I never wanted to be a public crier—just like I never wanted to be a public fighter. My conflicts with Richard and Elizabeth's cancer have put an end to all that. I use a brown napkin to blot my eyes and decide to unleash my scariest question: "Will Elizabeth be sick the rest of her life?"

"I have every hope that medicine will keep Elizabeth's cancer under control for some time."

"We never talk about how much time she has left. We can't. She can't," I say.

"Cancer changes everyone's life, not least the patient's." The doctor covers my hand with his smooth palm. For a moment, he's not just a rising-star oncologist but both less and more: Dr. Varghas is another human, one who can see what I'm going through. I am grateful for this moment, even if I have overstepped my boundaries.

"I'm sorry, I have to go," he says. "My wife will think I ran back to New York."

Hearing Dr. Varghas say *wife* makes me cringe, but I control my face. He has never mentioned a wife in his office, nor has he had any reason to.

"I didn't know you were married," I say. I hope that my intimacy doesn't scare him away or somehow compromise Elizabeth's care.

"My wife's a dermatologist. We have a baby on the way," he says, beaming.

"What a lucky woman," I say. "I appreciate your time."

"You're very welcome," the doctor says professionally.

I walk the long way home, absorbing what Dr. Varghas has shared about Elizabeth and the prospects of Tarceva. I always felt guilty about our financial differences when Jake and Richard were on unequal footing, before Jake became successful. Now, my being healthy and Elizabeth's being sick introduces a new guilt. I have always felt that my sister and I are nearly the same person. Life likes to remind me we're not.

Richard still doesn't know the full extent of Elizabeth's illness; he thinks it's a limited type of bone cancer. Harboring this secret creates even more distance in my marriage. For now, at least, Richard has lost me to my family—Elizabeth's illness takes up all I have. David, Jill, my parents, and I speak every day on a desperate hotline. From one another we draw strength, further dividing our world into "us" and everyone else. Just as Richard has always feared, he's solidly in the second category.

⋘

THE NEXT DAY, I'm anxious. I can't rid the meeting with Dr. Varghas from my mind. I need to be with Elizabeth. Just seeing her looking healthy and feeling good will calm me. When I arrive at noon with my third coffee, the Gordon house is quiet.

"You hungry?" Elizabeth asks. "We just had lunch. There's plenty of salad left."

"I'm all set," I say. "Honestly, I just wanted to give you a hug."

I follow Elizabeth into the den. She tells me she just finished reading an article about acupuncture. Brooke and Lauren are at school, and Elizabeth and I sit on the sofa beneath their portraits.

In a club chair, Jake frowns into his computer. It's unusual for the three of us to be here alone, no feet moving on the stairs, no kitchen cabinets slamming, no friends of Brooke's and Lauren's stopping by. Elizabeth excuses herself midchat to use the bathroom, and Jake waits a beat before whispering, "Samantha, I want to get Elizabeth a present."

"How lovely. What are you thinking?" I ask. He always consults me when buying my sister gifts.

"I saw a beautiful diamond necklace yesterday at Shreve's. Will you check it out for me? Don't you dare tell Elizabeth! I want it to be a surprise."

"I'll go right now," I say. I love this job, reminiscent of happier times. I call to Elizabeth from the foot of the stairs. "Sorry, sweetie, I have to let the dogs out. Call you later." I bound out the door.

Soon I am whizzing down Boylston Street to Shreve, Crump & Low. When I arrive and ring the buzzer, Cindy smiles as she spots me through the security glass. I've known her for a long time—this store is where Richard bought me my first pair of diamond earrings, fifteen years ago.

"How's your sister?" Cindy asks, before I'm even inside. I hear a trace of her Canadian accent, even though she's lived in Boston for thirty years. We kiss twice, both cheeks, the French way.

"Better," I say, my head cocked to one side, nodding slowly— my canned response whenever anyone asks about Elizabeth.

"Is she in remission?"

Oh God. They mean well, but people are so nosy around here. Elizabeth will never be in total remission.

"Yes," I say.

Cindy takes the hint and moves on. "Jake was here yesterday and put aside a few pieces for you to evaluate. He wants your approval, of course." Cindy walks behind the brightly lit case filled with diamond necklaces, bracelets, earrings, and rings—some trendy, some traditional, all high-quality, elegant pieces.

While Jake appreciates my input, Richard would never need to ask Elizabeth for advice about a gift for me. Richard knows my preferences and has exquisite taste himself. He would want the gift, from inspiration to execution, to belong entirely to him. I can't complain. Every birthday and anniversary, he presents me with a meticulously wrapped gold gift box. For our fifteenth it was a diamond heart, and for my forty-fifth an antique-cut diamond bracelet I could easily have selected myself. Richard's knowing me is a kind of love that stops short at the wall of my family. How might I feel to have a husband who loved my family but never gave me thoughtful gifts?

Cindy lays out a necklace with centerpiece diamonds decreasing to smaller stones where it clasps. "This is Jake's favorite," Cindy says, "but he wants only large diamonds, to make them the same size all around."

That definitely sounds like Jake. Bigger is always better.

I place the necklace against my décolletage and look in the mirror. It's absolutely stunning, but I wonder how many occasions Elizabeth would have to wear it. It's not an out-to-dinner necklace or even a cocktail-party necklace; it's all-out black-tie. She'll be able to wear it to a wedding or a bar mitzvah, but how many of those does she have coming up? I can see why Jake selected it, but I know this necklace is all wrong. Elizabeth has been telling me what she really wants for years.

"It's gorgeous, but Elizabeth has always wanted diamond studs. Do you have any in the store?"

"None that are substantial enough, but I can get a pair by tomorrow. You know diamonds shrink over time," Cindy says, and we laugh.

She's right, of course. When I first got engaged, I used to hide my hand under the table when I met new people. I worried that my three-carat oval was too showy. I loved it but didn't want to flaunt it. That diamond engagement ring that Richard bought me in 1987 looks much smaller to me now.

Back in the car, I call Jake and tell him about the diamond studs. He's skeptical.

"I don't know," he says. "I wanted to spend more. You think that's all she wants?"

Because the earrings are smaller than the necklace, Jake thinks they aren't significant, but I assure him that Elizabeth will get much more enjoyment from the earrings than she will from the showstopper he chose. "She can wear them every day," I say. "And trust me, they'll be plenty expensive."

The next morning, Jake and I meet at the boutique. He judges the studs shrewdly against the light, then asks me to try them on. I'm two inches taller than my sister, and my face is fuller, but he wants to know what they might look like on her.

I fasten the studs behind my ears. The diamonds are brilliant and make me look regal. They're light and comfortable, not a burden to wear, despite their impressive size. I keep glancing at myself in the mirror, feeling like a treasured woman.

Jake admires the sparkle, and I know he's picturing Elizabeth. The look on his face, joy laced with a slight shyness—it's the way every woman wants to be seen.

"But are they big enough?" Jake says. "Elizabeth's ears are bigger than yours."

"Here, look," I say, placing the studs in his palm. "They're huge."

Jake stares at the studs intensely, rolling them in his palms. Cindy produces a magnifying glass to demonstrate the quality of the stones. "These earrings could be two engagement rings," she says.

"Tell me about the color," Jake says. Even though I doubt he knows much about the language of diamonds, he wants to learn. Cindy places a chart on the glass, speaking of inclusions and color grades. Jake passes the magnifying glass over the earrings on a black velvet tray. He'd never put regular gas in his Range Rover—high test or nothing!

Cindy remarks that these are exquisite, nearly colorless diamonds. No inclusions under the magnifying glass. Finally, Jake agrees.

"Want to come home with me and give her the earrings now?" Jake asks. I glance at my watch. It's almost one o'clock, and Alexandra's in school.

"Sure," I say, thrilled to share in the excitement.

I follow Jake home and reach their house to find Elizabeth also pulling into the driveway. Lila, her housekeeper, takes bags of Whole Foods groceries out of Elizabeth's car. Even though Elizabeth is strong enough to carry groceries, no one lets her. Even Elizabeth agrees that her cancer is heavy enough.

In the kitchen, Jake announces that he has a surprise. He takes the gold-wrapped box out of his pocket, says, "Catch," and tosses it lightly to Elizabeth. I've never seen him so cavalier. Usually he creates a ceremony around gifts—a glass of champagne, a dinner out.

Elizabeth is surprised when the box hits her hands. "What's this?"

"We're done with chemo. We have to celebrate!" Jake says.

"Thank you," she says quietly, appearing deeply grateful. "I hope I never have to go through that again."

I smile, seeing Elizabeth happy. She shakes the wrapped box, holding it up to her ear. "Shouldn't we wait for the kids?"

"No," Jake says. "I can't wait that long. And I want Samantha to be here."

I can see that Elizabeth really wants to wait for Brooke and Lauren, but she defers to Jake. She unwraps the gold paper and opens the velvet box, gasping when she sees the glint of the diamonds. "Oh my God, they're magnificent. I've always wanted diamond studs. These are huge—and so sparkly!" Elizabeth fastens the earrings and goes straight for the bathroom mirror. I follow, seeing her face shine in the reflection. She's wearing a cotton shirt and jeans, but these earrings give her polish.

"I'm never going to take them off," Elizabeth says, heading back to the kitchen. She kisses Jake, and they embrace. "I love you," she says.

"Wait until your mother sees," Jake says.

Elizabeth wears the earrings every day. Her friends admire them, and Jake beams whenever someone pays her a compliment. These diamonds are their bright lights—the first of many lavish gifts. A week later, when Elizabeth meets me at the reservoir, she leaps out of her silver Range Rover with another announcement.

"Jake bought me a car," she says, wide-eyed.

"What about your Range Rover?" I say, pointing to her car. "It's only a year old."

"A white Mercedes sports car. I've always loved that car. I'm getting it next week."

"And the Rover?"

"I'm keeping them both," she says.

"Wow! Not bad. That Mercedes is sexy," I say. I can picture Elizabeth driving a sporty two-door with the sunroof open, wearing her oversize sunglasses and her diamond studs.

"If I knew I'd be well," Elizabeth says, dropping her eyes to the gravel, "I'd enjoy it more." But her dimple reveals a bit of excitement.

"Use it well," I say, a family expression uttered whenever someone gets a new car or anything of significance.

"Jake has started spending money like crazy," Elizabeth says, growing quiet.

We begin our walk. I imagine her playing out consequences in a future she might not see.

Chapter Sixteen

---

*O*n Iressa, Elizabeth has more energy than she ever had on chemo. She swallows a pill each morning and makes the pilgrimage to Beth Israel once a month for a blood test with Dr. Varghas to assess the drug's efficacy. Otherwise, she's back to life as usual, managing cancer as a chronic disease. Sitting near the fish tanks for her first monthly appointment, however, she simmers with anxiety.

"I don't look like her, right?" she asks, gesturing discreetly to a pale woman with no eyebrows, wearing a scarf.

"Of course not," I say. Amazing how the inside of the body doesn't translate to the outside. Today Elizabeth wears tight jeans, a pale pink sweater, and navy Chanel flats. She has fringed her blue eyes with strokes of mascara. Although her natural hair is still thin and wispy, she looks chic. "You don't even look sick," I say.

Elizabeth smiles. "Let's go to London, see a show." We were scheduled to go with our mother, but we canceled after 9/11, and we never rescheduled when she got sick.

Scanning the waiting room, my habit, I can't help but fixate on a wheelchair cradling an emaciated old man. I look away and land on a young white woman with ashen skin and hollow eyes, chemo's signature, sitting with her "chemo club" support group. Her friends wear false smiles and muster up overzealous laughter in their efforts to deny her certain death. I understand how they feel. Because I am a chemo club of one. Today, however, my sister is the image of health: glowing skin, bright eyes, and regained weight—very much at odds with her surroundings.

I can tell from our first moments with Dr. Varghas that he will be discreet about our encounter at Starbucks. I watch my sister's oncologist more closely than usual as he scans his computer and examines the scans, mentally replacing his dress slacks and white coat with red running shorts.

"Looks good, looks good," the doctor assures us. "There is very little cancer now in your lungs. Iressa is doing its job. You could run a marathon if you wanted."

Elizabeth and I look at each other and smile.

"Guess we should start training," I say, which makes Elizabeth laugh. As much as we both like to exercise, a marathon has never appealed to either of us.

"This is fabulous news," I say more soberly, catching Dr. Varghas's eyes. "As for the marathon, we'll leave that to David, our brother." He's run two marathons, competed in a dozen triathlons and, until Elizabeth got sick, was training for an Ironman.

"How long do you think Iressa will keep working?" Elizabeth asks. "Will a pill cure the cancer in my lungs?"

Dr. Varghas touches the tips of his fingers, considering Elizabeth's question. Answering carefully, he says, "It would be highly unusual for a complete remission. But you're stable, which is excellent news. Let's take it month by month."

After a long, uncomfortable pause, my sister relents with a quiet "okay."

Leaving the hospital, I realize that neither Elizabeth nor I wants to accept less than perfection. Elizabeth won't accept less-than-perfect health, and I won't accept a less-than-perfect marriage. These high standards do not serve either of us right now.

In the car, I say to her, "London is a great idea. It's time to enjoy your life. Summer is here."

Iressa's results feel like a miracle on the order of Moses's parting the Red Sea. God nourished the wandering Israelites in the desert, sending manna from heaven. Let's see what He can do for us.

⧽⧽⧽⧽

THE GORDONS RENT a house for the season in New Seabury, right on the water, a beautiful and accessible part of Cape Cod. Now that Elizabeth has only one oncology appointment per month, why stay in Weston?

In June, a moving van pulls up and two twentysomething men, one with bulging biceps and a sleeve of tattoos, jump out of the truck. The driver holds a yellow cargo slip in his hand; Elizabeth and I walk outside to meet them on the brick walkway. Inside, Jake decides what they need to take: bedding, clothing, a television, staples from the pantry, golf clubs, and bicycles. It's already eighty degrees, and the sun glows on my face, reminding me of my own happy place, Nantucket.

The sky is blue and cloudless when we part. "I'm going to keep my body in good shape," Elizabeth says, "really take good care of myself. Now or never. I'm going to try a raw diet and swim in the ocean every morning."

"Best summer of your life," I say.

"I'll get to spend every day with the kids. Lauren is taking tennis lessons at the club," she adds. Lauren has become protective of Elizabeth during her illness, offering to help cook dinners, and lying on the sofa next to her watching TV at night. "Also, I have the name of a healer," Elizabeth continues. "She does Reiki and acupuncture. Tom Tam said it would be fine if I kept my treatments going with her, instead of shlepping back to Boston once a week."

I laugh. "You're sure on top of things."

We hug goodbye, but it won't be for long. Over the next week, I'll get Alexandra ready for summer camp in Maine. The week after, I'll head to Nantucket. All summer, my sister will be on the Cape and I'll be just a fifteen-minute flight away.

Driving to the Hyannis airport, I have my poodles in the passenger seat and the sunroof open, feeling freer than I have in months. I'm even excited to see Richard. Nantucket has been our place ever since Richard first let me in on the secret. I picture us as migrating seagulls that meet in a particular spot before returning to the ocean.

❦

ON NANTUCKET. Richard greets me at the airport with the warmest hug and kiss I've felt in a long time. "Sweetie!" he says, lifting me off my feet. "Girls!" he says, as the dogs jump on him affectionately. Richard's been on Nantucket for a week, and he's well into his tan, decked out in full island regalia: shorts, a beach-permit T-shirt, and Wayfarer sunglasses with a float strap.

"You look so handsome," I say, trying to control my surprise.

"It's really good to see you," he says.

I begin to relax. Even before Elizabeth got sick, Nantucket was my place to unwind. I didn't have to worry about running into her and Jake at a restaurant with Richard. I could let go of anticipating how the endless feud might ruin my day.

"It's so good to be back," I say. Richard grabs my bag, and

we walk arm in arm to our yellow Wrangler with bumper stickers on the back and front: ACK, Nantucket's airport code, and SKY'S THE LIMIT.

We plan to wake early tomorrow for a beach walk. Afterward, we'll take a leisurely drive into town, stroll the cobblestone, and buy coffee and newspapers at the Hub, not needing to rush anywhere. We might perch ourselves on a wooden bench to people-watch, allowing the day to take its own course. I look forward to worrying less about Elizabeth, but I still plan to call her every day.

When I open the door, our sheer curtains billow in the ocean breeze. I have designed the house to be bright and happy, a bit bohemian. I sink into my flowered, shabby-chic couch and finally feel the universe supporting me.

"Ready?" Richard asks the second I sit. Earlier, we'd RSVP'd to attend a friend's party down the beach.

"Sort of," I say. "It feels so good to be home. Let's skip the party." Everyone has been instructed to wear white. There will be a bonfire, steamers and lobsters, tequila, and dancing until the fog rolls in, or until it gets too dark to see.

"Give it an hour," Richard says reasonably.

Later, as I'm pulling on my white skinny jeans for the first time this season, along with my favorite linen shirt, my phone rings. It's Elizabeth.

"What're you doing?" she asks.

"Putting on our whites. What about you?"

"David's family just got here. We're going out with the kids. Just wanted to check in. It never feels right spending time with David and Jill without you."

For a moment, I wish I were there. Even though Elizabeth and I are together all the time, the history with Richard has given me the anxiety of an outsider. David and Elizabeth's families have no friction. How nice it would be to experience that. I crave how that used to feel.

Richard appears next to me with crossed arms. He can hear Elizabeth's voice on the line. "Hurry up," he says.

I put my hand over the phone and say, "Just a minute." I turn my back. However frivolous these calls seem to Richard, every conversation with Elizabeth is important.

"Where are you having dinner?" I ask.

"A new restaurant in Osterville."

"Have a blast. I'm getting ready for the party, so I'll speak to you in the morning. Love you," I say, and hang up.

"You still haven't done your makeup?" Richard says.

Instead of answering, I walk downstairs and pour myself a glass of Domaines Ott, my favorite summer rosé. A dressing drink. Richard paces the bedroom, which annoys me.

"Don't ever rush me off the phone," I say.

"You just got here. What could you two possibly have to talk about?"

I take a sip of wine to calm myself.

Richard peers out the bedroom window, down-beach, toward the party. We hear music. "I'll wait for you," he says. "Just hurry."

"Are the wine and vodka ready? Want to go down and make sure we didn't forget anything?" I ask, irked that Richard would micromanage my makeup without taking care of other logistics.

After the last coat of mascara, I meet Richard downstairs, grab the bottle of chilled pinot grigio and two long-stemmed glasses. Richard takes a thermos of cold, sour-apple martinis to share. We cross the dirt road and take the path between the dunes, leaving our shoes in the beach grass. Our friends are in full party mode as we approach, dancing to Billy Joel and drinking around the bonfire. "Welcome!" Chelsea, who planned the event, says. "Glad you guys came."

I drink one glass of wine, then another, trying to regain my earlier ease and enjoy myself with island friends. Richard wraps his arms around me, pulls me a bit too close. As the sun drops into the water and hues of orange, yellow, and magenta light the sky, we dance, my head on his shoulder. I yield to my husband's warmth near the crackle of a fire.

"It's good to have you here," Richard says, smiling with his eyes. And, for the moment, I'm comfortable in my own skin.

At home I undress and run a warm shower to wash the sand off my body and feet. *Keep clean sheets clean,* my mother always said. I'm behind the glass door when Richard comes in —to brush his teeth, I imagine—and I close my eyes, wetting my face and hair under the spray.

Before I know it, I feel Richard's body behind me. I turn in surprise. Within seconds, his tongue is in my mouth and we are unabashedly making out like we did during those first days of desire. Richard lifts me up against the blue starfish tiles and lowers me onto him. We make love with a passion I thought we had lost. Before he comes, Richard's face grows red and panicked; then he relaxes. He strokes my wet hair, kissing me tenderly and thoughtfully, as if kisses could be sentences.

"I love you," he says, pulling from my mouth just enough to say the words.

"I love you, too," I say, burrowing my face in his chest. I feel like I might cry. We've been distant from each other for so long. Gaps so wide can't always be bridged. I revel in the rapture of our new connection, and relief.

BEFORE RICHARD AND I are even out of bed the next morning, Elizabeth calls.

"I went to the bathroom this morning, and the toilet was full of blood."

My heart races, zero to eighty. "Did you call Dr. Varghas?"

"He set up an appointment for me at Falmouth Hospital with the doctor on call."

"I'll meet you there," I say, without giving it a second thought.

"Oh, thank you. I'm really nervous," she says, and hangs up.

Richard stirs sleepily on the pillow. Our dogs, Bella and Bentley, have joined us in the night. All three of them take up space without care or worry.

"What time is it?" Richard asks drowsily. When I explain about Elizabeth and the blood, he props himself up on his elbows and shakes his head, more frustrated than concerned. "Seriously? You have to be at every appointment?"

"Yes, I do," I say. I must be there to hear what the doctor says, and it's my job to write it down. I'm out of bed, pulling on clothes in high gear, making excuses. What if the Iressa has stopped working?

"It's a fifteen-minute flight," I say. "My car is at Hyannis airport. I'll be back for dinner. You're playing golf anyway."

"What about the book festival?" Richard asks. "That's why I'm playing golf," he says, with hurt in his voice.

"Elizabeth is more important." I have been looking forward to the book festival, and I can't help but be touched that Richard remembered. Alice Hoffman is scheduled to speak, and I'm curious about writing. But I wouldn't be able to concentrate anyway.

The day boasts full sunshine—perfect weather for flying on one of Cape Air's eight-passenger planes. We touch down in Hyannis, and I speed to the hospital in Falmouth. As soon as I see Elizabeth and Jake in the lobby, my heart knows it was right to come. Elizabeth's face is pale and drawn. I steel myself for what might be a bad turn.

"How's the big guy?" Jake asks, before greeting me. His tone takes me aback.

I have just left my husband, flown to meet them here, and this is the thanks I get? Jake doesn't hesitate to rely on me for gift advice, or to sit through chemo, or to cheer up Elizabeth with an evening call. I feel like a used Kleenex. I stand there, gaping.

Elizabeth takes my hand, and we check in. The exam room is painted, like everything on the Cape, ocean blue with white trim. Dr. Varghas has already briefed this doctor on Elizabeth's medical history, so we don't get into the details.

"Please, sit down," he says. This doctor wears Cape casual: khakis and a polo shirt, more of a vacation look than a medical one. When Elizabeth reports the red urine, to our surprise, rather than inquiring after pain or injury, the doctor asks first what she ate for dinner.

"I'm trying to eat healthy—I mean, healthier. I had a salad with beets and kale."

"Beets?" The doctor raises an eyebrow. "Beets can cause urine to change color. But let's do an ultrasound of your bladder to make sure there's nothing else going on. We may also do a CT scan. The nurse will call you when the room is ready."

Elizabeth, Jake, and I exchange looks. Could it be beets?

We hang out in a waiting room decorated like someone's yacht. Sail fabric hangs from the ceiling, and the lamps are miniature lighthouses. I look at my watch for the first time: 10:00 a.m. I'm dying for a cup of coffee.

"Coffee? Tea?" I ask, stirring, feeling the need to move.

"No, thanks, "Elizabeth said. "We had some already."

I dash to the cafeteria, afraid they'll call Elizabeth before I return. As I follow the signs, I think about Elizabeth's having seen the pool of blood in her toilet this morning. How frightening to wake to that. In ten minutes when I return, Jake and Elizabeth are still waiting.

An hour later, a technician says, "Mrs. Gordon, please follow me." I accompany Elizabeth down the hallway and turn the corner to a darkened ultrasound room.

"Please lie down," the technician says, and points to the padded exam table. "I'm going to lift your shirt so I can get at your abdomen."

My fingers intertwine with Elizabeth's while the technician works a small transducer and gel over her abdomen, as if she were pregnant again. My eyes barely leave my sister's face the entire fifteen minutes of the procedure.

When we return to the doctor's office, he hands Elizabeth a discharge slip. "The ultrasound shows a normal bladder. No evidence of metastasis. I'm positive it was the beets."

He tells us that he'll send the report to Dr. Varghas. "Go enjoy yourselves at the beach," the doctor says, to himself as much as to us.

"Thank you, Doctor," Jake says, and we leave the room.

Outside, in the bright glare of the parking lot at high noon, Elizabeth is sheepish. "Well, I guess it's good that we checked." I'm not going to tell my sister that she overreacted. I was onboard with all of it. If only we'd been more aggressive about the original pain in her hip.

"Of course," I say. "It's always better to know."

"Yup," Jake says, and takes Elizabeth's hand. "Let's get back to David, Jill, and the kids. We don't want to inconvenience them any more than we have." He doesn't mention inconveniencing me.

"Thanks for coming," Elizabeth says, and gives me a hug.

"How could I not? Talk to you guys later," I say, unlocking my car.

"Spend the day here with us," Jake says suddenly. "Don't you want to see your brother?" His so-called invitation only fans my anger.

"I have to get back," I say, irate to hear him use David as leverage. It couldn't be more obvious. Jake is coaxing me to stay in order to exclude Richard. Have I missed this before?

Jake dismisses me with a shake of his head. He and Elizabeth walk to their car, and I speed back to Hyannis to catch the next flight.

An hour later, I land and call Lynne for a report on the book festival, which she says was great. I set an intention to attend next year.

At home, I find Richard reading on the front deck. "What's the prognosis?" he asks.

"Beets," I say.

"Are you kidding?" Richard rolls his eyes.

"Elizabeth ate beets for dinner, and it turned her pee red. That's it. What a relief." I don't think to feel guilty or embarrassed. I'm satisfied that we took the precaution.

"You'd never drop everything like that for me."

"That's not true," I say. "Of course I would."

"Give me an example. When have you ever done something like that?"

"We've been through this a thousand times," I say.

I give Richard a quick kiss on the head, climb the stairs, and I plop onto the rattan chair at the window in our bedroom. Kids toss Frisbees on the sand, and teenagers surf to shore, inspiring memories of Elizabeth and me bodysurfing on boogie boards and building sand castles on the beach. Then I remember that Richard and I have dinner plans and realize that I need to get ready. I swallow the lump in my throat and dress.

That night, we dine at Lola 41 with Nantucket friends, Debbie and Max. "I miss you," Debbie tells me, her hair pulled back in a sleek black ponytail. Her husband, Max, whose hair has turned more salt than pepper over the last year, asks kindly about Elizabeth.

I don't go into the beets. "She's better," I say.

Their son is the same age as Alexandra, and our conversation revolves at first around sleepaway camp. Then Debbie, a staunch Democrat, starts bashing George W. Bush. "We need a woman in the White House. Someday, Hillary Clinton should run."

"Then our country would *really* be in trouble," Richard says, and it's not clear if he means because she's a Democrat or because she's a woman.

"Let's change the subject," I say. "I've had a rough day." When Max looks at me with concern in his eyes and exchanges a glance with Debbie, I wish I hadn't said anything. But before either of them speaks, Richard starts in on Mayor Menino, how he's delayed waterfront development and hurt his bottom line—something we can all agree on. Between the four of us, we polish off three bottles of wine.

Rain catches us by surprise as we leave the restaurant, pelting us in the dark night. Fortunately, Richard thought to put the cover on the Jeep. It's not until we're driving home, the windows streaked with water, that my mood takes over. I allow myself one of my silent sulks that Richard says is louder than any accusation I could make.

"What's wrong now?" Richard asks.

"Just thinking about Elizabeth. And Jake and the kids," I say.

"They hate me," he says.

"They don't hate you."

"You're here physically, Samantha, but your mind is elsewhere, with your sister." At first, I don't dignify that with a response. My silence speaks for itself. Then my mood takes over.

"As if Elizabeth didn't have enough to deal with," I say, "she has to have *you* as a brother-in-law."

"That's it," Richard says. "I'm done."

"Richard—"

"No excuses. I don't care how good it was last night. It always ends the same way. You put me down and your family first." His voice whipsaws on my skin. I've heard it all, hundreds of times. He doesn't know that I am beginning to take responsibility for our conflict, rethinking my role in our marriage, yet I want to punish him for what I haven't even told him.

Richard's face twists with anger; his voice is tinged with new vulnerability and a hint of desperation. "Am I not your family?" he asks.

We plunge on with our familiar battle, arguing until I no longer know what I'm saying or whose argument I'm following or who did what to whom.

Then Richard does something he has never done before. He pulls over to the side of the road. "Get out," he says. "Out of the car." It's pouring.

"Are you crazy? *You* get out."

"Fine, and back to Boston tomorrow. I can't take it anymore." Richard jumps from the Jeep into the night and slams the door shut.

Alone in the Jeep under the downpour, I choke on sobs. Eventually, I crawl into the driver's seat and head home slowly, my vision blurred with tears and rain. Richard has finally unleashed the desperate anger bottled up inside him.

When I get home, I make a mad dash to let the dogs out

and run around like a crazy woman, locking doors. I turn on the outside lights and on a whim decide to lock the guest cottage, too. I fall on the slippery brick path and cut my knees. The rain drenches my hair and a dress that Richard loves and that I vow never to wear again.

In the main house, I let Bentley and Bella back in, not caring about the prints they make or that I'm dripping rain and blood on the hardwood floor.

Click, click, click. I turn off all the outside lights. No stars to brighten the sky, no streetlights to illuminate the road. Rain-drenched, I crash on the sofa.

At two, I hear Richard turn the spare key that we keep under a conch shell in the driveway. He ignores the dogs and me on the sofa and goes upstairs. The rain has stopped, and I'm awake, so I fix a cup of tea and have it on the deck, watching the full moon waver on the ocean.

Sometimes I think Richard and Jake are too much alike, that my sister and I caused the problem ourselves for marrying strong, unyielding men. But it's becoming harder and harder to ignore the mistakes I have made in my marriage. Confiding to Elizabeth and Jill about my troubles with Richard all these years—I really should have kept my marital issues private. The problem is that my conflicts with Richard have affected my relationships.

The sky awakens with shades of pink and turquoise, another island day for all to enjoy. Richard and I have finally managed to ruin Nantucket.

At seven, I wake him. "I'm going back to Wellesley," I say.

I brace myself for a grumpy response, for Richard to roll over and pull the covers over his head, or to protest. But, to my surprise, he sits, awake.

"Samantha, I have something to tell you. A few weeks ago,

I rented an apartment in Boston. I planned to move there after the summer—I've given it a lot of thought. I think it's best that we live apart for now. You know what?" He smiles. "I almost canceled it the night you got here. I'm glad I didn't. It hurts, but your family is still in the way."

I stare at him, trying to process. "You rented an apartment?" *He's* leaving *me?*

"A loft in the South End."

Seeing something in my face, Richard raises his hands appeasingly.

"Let's view it as a trial separation. Maybe it can still work out between us. We'll both have a lot of time to think," he says.

I move closer to my husband, looking into his deep-set emerald eyes. I bury my head in his chest, speechless, reaching for comfort from the man who is hurting me. Richard puts his arms around me and kisses me like a child.

"Let's keep the house intact," he says. I can see that he has it all figured out, months of planning and rumination. "I'll just take my clothes. I'll buy furniture for the apartment."

I imagine him clearing out his suits, leaving a hole in our shared closet, hangers rattling, just as I did with my summer tops, pants, and skirts this morning in Nantucket before he woke. All of this premeditation, and I find myself on the receiving end of one of Richard A. Freeman's venture capital deals.

"I'll drive you and the dogs to the airport now," Richard says, pulling on the same khaki shorts and T-shirt, still damp from the night before.

Richard carries my bags and tosses them in the back of the Jeep. He flings open the driver's side door and slides in. I climb onto the passenger seat and put Bentley and Bella on my lap. We drive to the airport in silence.

"It's time for you to start choosing us first," Richard says when he hands me my suitcases at the curb. "Figure out a way to do that *and* still be there for your sister, and we can stay married. Safe flight." He pecks me on the cheek.

Choking on emotion, I wave goodbye with Bentley and Bella's leashes. It feels awful to be the person put on probation. I suddenly regret having taken Richard for granted.

Now that I've gotten what I asked for, it's time to figure out whether it's what I really want.

From my car on the mainland, I call Jonathan Mann. Not quite believing my own words, I tell him that Richard and I have separated. I've had Jonathan on retainer since Brooke's bat mitzvah. It feels safer that he knows.

"I advise you to file for divorce immediately," he says, to my surprise. "Now that you're separated, you need to protect yourself."

Thinking about divorce, I get dizzy—I hang up the hands-free and pull over to think. Thank God Alexandra's at camp. We'll wait until she gets home to break the news. No need to upset the rest of her summer. I pull back onto the road.

Thoughts of Richard living alone in his South End loft cloud my mind. My car creeps into the next lane; another driver leans on his horn and gives me the finger. I swerve back and glance at the speedometer. I'm going seventy, fifteen over the limit. I check my rearview mirror—thankfully, no police. I slow down, and now other cars zoom by, drivers craning their necks to see who could possibly be driving so poorly.

Separating from Richard is what I thought I wanted. Now that it's happening, I feel like a failure. Not because I'm getting dumped—because we couldn't make our marriage work. It speaks to the inadequacy of our love, how we let all these hurtful events eat away at us, an emotional erosion, until we were no longer *us*.

In my driveway, I stare up with new eyes at my home, ticking off what Richard will claim as his. Pieces from our crystal Lalique collection and some of his favorite, signed sports memorabilia for sure. I unlock the front door and urge myself to be rational, walking through the empty house, past photos of Richard, Alexandra, Harrison, and our extended families. Richard will also certainly want some of these. I wonder if he'll take a picture of me to his new apartment. I put my face in my hands. What have I done? I unpack my clothing and place my jewelry in the small safe in my closet.

Later, I call my parents, sister, and brother with the news. "Richard's moving out," I say. It is not unexpected.

Chapter Seventeen

──────

*T*he next week, I drive to Elizabeth's summer home in New Seabury, and she does her best to distract me. We take a yoga class on the beach, swim in the bay side of the ocean, eat raw food, and make Reiki appointments.

Over lunch Elizabeth says, "Richard could never take you away from me."

"Of course not. Don't ever worry about that," I say. "Whether we stay married or not, he'll never come between us."

For the rest of the summer, I spend Monday through Wednesday with Elizabeth on the Cape, the days Jake commutes to Boston to work. He feels safer when I'm there. Elizabeth is beginning to act like her old self, but we don't discuss Richard. After all these years, she has finally reached her limit.

When I'm home alone in Wellesley, I have too much time to think, vacillating between relief and despair. Are in-laws essentially interlopers to Richard, people who cannot be trusted? Was it wrong for my parents to list me as the sole trustee on the Israel bond they purchased for Alexandra, instead of listing us jointly? I begin to appreciate the deep wounds of trust on both sides. I can't divorce my family for Richard, but should I divorce Richard for them?

In August, my brother invites me to spend a weekend in

Sag Harbor, where they have a house. It's the part of the Hamptons that reminds me most of Nantucket. Early Saturday morning, I load my bags and the two dogs. It's an hour-and-a-half car ride to New London, three ferries, and, once I'm on Shelter Island, still a fifteen-minute drive.

"Auntie!" Little Brittany shouts when I pull up. Her brother, Justin, is behind her.

"Where are the dogs?" he asks.

I open the door, and Bentley and Bella jump out, turning excited circles.

David and Jill walk down the drive.

"I would ask about the trip," my brother says, "but all I want to know is how you're doing."

"Careful what you wish for," I say, and shrug.

David gives me a hug. "Come, give me your bag. Let's talk." We settle into crisp white sofas in the living room, and Jill hands me a bottle of Fiji water.

"Maybe I should have treated Richard better," I say, sighing.

"You've been unhappy for so long," David says. "Now you both have time to weigh your options."

"You never know," Jill says.

"I'm so happy to be here, to get away," I say. "I've been looking forward to it."

That afternoon, while David and Jill run errands, I stroll along the boat basin and walk the docks. People are relaxing on yachts, sipping wine in the sun.

I recognize a boat from Nantucket harbor last summer, *The Perfect Prescription*, so named because its owner made his money in pharmaceuticals. Richard and I have viewed this pristine yacht many times, admiring the captain and his white-uniformed crew. The nostalgia makes me wince. At this moment, my husband could be reading a newspaper in his beach chair, or out for oysters and drinks, while I'm here, watching our life slip through my fingers.

The next morning David, Jill, and I take a boot camp class on the beach with a New York City trainer, ten of us doing squats, burpees, sprints, and light weights at the ocean's edge. We get back to the house, and I walk the dogs in my workout clothes with Brittany and Justin.

"Auntie, I wish Alexandra came with you," Brittany says.

"She's still at camp," I say, and bite my lip, missing her.

"We got a letter," Justin says. "She loves waterskiing."

"I know! One ski!"

"When will we see her again?" Brittany asks.

"Soon. Rosh Hashanah."

We turn left, circling the block. The kids fill me in on tennis and swim lessons, how they can't wait to go to sleepaway camp in Maine like Alexandra in a few years. I notice my easy smile, how much I adore this time, how often I feel at ease outside Richard's interference. I think about mentioning our separation to my niece and nephew, but something tells me they already know.

After a shower, David takes the kids to the beach and Jill and I walk into Sag Harbor for lunch. A collegiate, tanned hostess seats us on the waterside patio, a wall of windows inviting the outdoors in, and with enough noise to discuss things privately.

"Tell me everything," Jill says, my confidante and voice of reason. I relate the comedy of the beet incident in hindsight, and how it ruined things between Richard and me.

"Bottom line, he said I'd do anything for Elizabeth but not for him." I skip the Jeep ride and Richard's dramatic jump. "I told him I was going back to Boston, but he one-upped me. He'd already rented an apartment. He almost canceled the lease, but the beets were his last straw."

Jill takes my hand. The breeze tousles her dirty-blond hair.

"I feel terrible," she says. "David and I could have gone, but Jake insisted that we stay with the kids."

"I used to think Jake really cared about me," I say, flagging the server for two iced teas.

The restaurant is packed. Two women with cobalt and denim blue Birkin bags walk in, scan the crowd, and sit at the table next to us. There's a nice buzz, still noisy enough that no one can overhear our conversation.

"I'm sick of being used," I say. "Just because Elizabeth is ill doesn't mean I should forfeit my respect."

"He knows how to push your buttons."

"But Elizabeth?"

"She sticks up for you. She's not entirely against Richard. His love for you redeems him for her."

"I know."

"There must be *something* good about your marriage for you to stay in it."

I twirl the straw in my iced tea.

"This is a trial separation," I say. "Let's see how it goes."

"I'm glad you came to visit," Jill says, sensing an avenue closed, but I continue.

"It's like I'm living two lives. One with my family and one with Richard. I used to blame him for everything. I'm not so sure anymore."

Jill squeezes my hand.

"Don't be so tough on yourself. I'm not telling you to get divorced or not get divorced. It all depends on how you want to live your life."

I lean back and stare into the restaurant. This conflict has not been handled well.

Our mixed greens with grilled chicken arrive, and we

spend the rest of lunch people-watching. I enjoy the weekend with David and Jill's family, taking walks on the beach and reading Elin Hilderbrand's novel, *Summer People*, with a glass of rosé. As much as I love them both and love being there, I can't join their marriage.

From the car, I call Richard to check in, realizing that I miss him.

"Hey. How are you?" I ask.

"Great," he says, not elaborating. His tone is curt. "Where are you?"

"The Hamptons," I say.

"Of course you are."

My heart skips, and I try to remain calm. "What's that supposed to mean?"

"Always running to your family," he says. "Trying to reassure them. Meanwhile, this is the first time you've reached out to me."

His accusations hurt me, but I will myself not to cry. I don't want to fight anymore. "What are you up to?" I ask.

"Andrew is here," he says. "I have to go; we're on our way out."

"Who's Andrew?" I ask.

"A guy I met a few months ago. He's divorced."

WEEKS LATER, RICHARD returns from Nantucket to Wellesley for his clothes. He enters the house when I'm standing at the door with Bentley and Bella, about to go out. At the sight of me, his lips purse.

"I'm much more relaxed without you," Richard announces. I realize that he has felt the same way I have all along—tense.

I cross my arms and take a deep breath. It doesn't look like we're going to work things out. "What have you been doing all summer?" I ask, trying to be polite.

"Exactly what I want, when I want to."

It seems as if our separation has only inflamed Richard's anger. I look over his shoulder out the window. He has parked his Range Rover so close that it nuzzles mine. Always too close, not close enough. Now he's here to take custody of his suits, pants, and shirts, to make a hole in the closet and finalize the hole in my life.

Despite Richard's anger and rudeness, I try to show compassion, putting my hand on his arm. He shrugs me off and heads upstairs.

"Please," I call after him.

In the bedroom, I tug at his shirt to distract him, but he's focused, placing one item after another inside boxes that he hauled here in the Range Rover, methodical. Then he stops for a second and meets my eyes. No matter what he says or does, I know in my heart that he doesn't want a second divorce.

I persist, lean into his chest. I have always fit perfectly into his arms. He gives in, hugs me closer and kisses me. His lips are warm and soft. A chill traces my spine. I could make love to him right now—but will it do any good? For years I have wished to leave Richard, and now he's leaving me. Same same, but different. If he stays, our fights are guaranteed to continue. We haven't done the work.

"Think positively," he says, grasping at his mantra. "Who knows? If we come to an understanding, my apartment could be our pied-à-terre."

Richard takes his first box to the car. Eventually I am standing in the driveway, dazed, while he loads box after box into the Rover's backseat with a dismissive toss. It's windy.

Richard's sleeves flap on his toned and tanned upper arms. I open my mouth but can't seem to find any words.

He gives me one last look—a last chance—and speeds off.

I pull my cell out of my jeans and call—who else?—Elizabeth.

"He took all his stuff," I say.

Elizabeth sighs with relief. Without Richard, her life is less complicated, and I understand. Most important, her children could one day join my family without interference.

⟞⟨⟨⟨⟨⟞

AT THE END of August, when Alexandra comes home, Richard and I have seen each other only once, for the sake of planning how to tell our daughter. We collect her at the bus stop in Waltham on Route 128. A swarm of emotional parents stand by their cars. Alexandra runs toward us, thinner and taller, and my eyes brim with joy and sadness. "Mommy! Daddy!" she says, almost one word.

In the car, our bubbly daughter regales us with the names of girls in her bunkhouse and stories of how her group won the color war. She sings rendition after rendition of campfire songs and says that next summer they'll climb Mt. Washington.

Richard carries Alexandra's duffels into her bedroom and turns on the Red Sox game. We're winning eight to three, bottom of the eighth. As I begin to unpack, Alexandra blurts out, "As much as I love camp, I love being home more." She smiles, scanning her walls, the pile of stuffed animals, and her full-length mirror.

To my dismay, Richard is glued to the game. "Home run," he says over his shoulder. "Nine–three."

Alexandra places herself between Richard and the TV,

raising her hand for a high five. When the Sox make three consecutive outs, I interject.

"Daddy and I have something to tell you, sweetie pie," I say. As much as I would love to put off our announcement, as Richard appears to be doing, there's no good time.

"What?" she asks, sensing something. Her smile fades. Alexandra feels behind her for the bed and sits down.

"This summer while you were away, Daddy and I had a long talk. We decided it would be better for our family if he and I try living in separate places."

"I've moved to an apartment in Boston for now," Richard says, "but Mom and I love you very much. And we still love each other," he adds, giving me hope.

"When? When did you talk?" Alexandra asks. "You don't live here anymore?" she asks Richard, lowering her head. She starts to cry, but I sense she understands. For most of her childhood, she's lived in this stressful environment—her father's smug body language, my cries and quick retorts. She has been the closest witness of our unhappiness and the most affected.

"We'll still see each other all the time," Richard says. "You'll have sleepovers at my apartment. We'll go to Fenway Park."

Alexandra wipes her tears. "Okay," she says.

The three of us sit, listening to the recap of the Sox game, nothing more to say.

"Okay, I'll call you later, sweetie," Richard says gently. "I'm going now. Love you." He embraces Alexandra and leaves the room.

I lie down with my daughter on her bed. Her hair smells like sunscreen and forest air. I'm relieved that, even with Richard gone, I can still feel at home with her.

"Mom, are you okay?" she asks, so mature and kind.

"I am," I say. "The situation was too stressful."

"How's Auntie Elizabeth?" she asks.

"Not bad," I say. "She had a good summer. We spent a lot of time together."

⁓⁓⁓

FROM HERE ON out, Richard lives in his loft full-time but visits whenever he wants to see Alexandra. He takes her out to dinner and to ballgames, and once in a while she sleeps at his place. On occasion, he and I go still go to social events, a sporadic dinner with friends. Sometimes he stays for the weekend if we have a party or fund-raiser nearby to attend. "I thought you were separated," friends whisper to me when they see us together.

"We are," I say. I don't really know how to describe our situation, so I don't.

I discover that I prefer this way of being married to Richard: a lighter life with fewer fights. We actually get to enjoy ourselves. Once upon a time, I would have scoffed at running a marriage this way. When I was in my twenties, I never could have imagined "dating" my husband, if that's what I want to call it. But life is full of compromises.

Chapter Eighteen

***

*T*he Gordons are relieved about my separation, but we barely speak about it. Elizabeth focuses on her miracle—Iressa—weekly acupuncture with Tom Tam, and monthly blood tests with Dr. Varghas.

Richard and I don't wear our wedding bands anymore, but I know Jake feels betrayed that I haven't pulled the trigger and gotten a divorce. As coparents, Richard and I have occasion to speak on the phone almost every day. I revel in my freedom, but I can't help but feel it's a false truce. All it takes is a friend saying, "I saw Richard at Davio's last night at the bar" to inspire embarrassment and jealousy. For my part, I'm pouring any energy I might have had for dating into supporting my sister through her partial remission.

In early October, Elizabeth and I are in her bedroom. "I need to focus on the positive," she says, slipping on a pair of heels. "Positive affirmations."

Elizabeth's birthday is coming up, and I decide on the spot to throw her a party. But it would need to be announced and planned; she is not a fan of surprises.

"How about I throw you a forty-fifth at my house?"

"I'm not sure I want a party," Elizabeth says. "What's there to celebrate? I still have cancer. On the other hand, I can't believe I'm still here."

"It will be something to look forward to," I say. "Focus on the positive?"

Despite Elizabeth's stubbornness, I sense an inkling of excitement.

I hire MAX, my usual caterer, and find a piano player to entertain us with show tunes and ease us with classical. I choose an invitation bordered with pale tulips and roses in an elegant script that reminds me of Elizabeth. I want the afternoon to be perfect.

The day of the party, Elizabeth and my mother arrive early. Seeing the two of them standing in the doorway makes me thank God for Iressa. My mother is wearing a loosely draped beige pantsuit; her dark-blond hair is coiffed and shining. Elizabeth's hair has grown back thick, with a new wave. She wears it short. She looks elegant in suede chocolate pants, a signature cashmere turtleneck, brown lizard boots, and matching bag.

"What a vision," I say. "You're stunning." I squeeze their shoulders and invite them inside. I, too, have a new outfit for the occasion: beige leather pants, calfskin ankle boots, and a white silk necktie blouse.

I check my watch. It's exactly noon.

"Everyone will be here," I say, my voice frenzied.

I scurry around to place the orchids in tall vases. The house is full of flowers. Perfumey lilies, colorful tulips, and yellow sprays take up residence in the foyer and the dining room, so different from those arrangements that last year took over the Gordons', blooms marking celebration and hope.

Taking requests from our favorite Broadway shows, the pianist practices before the guests arrive. The caterers hoist silver trays crowded with champagne flutes and take their stations at the door.

Jill has flown in from New York. She, Jane, and Robin,

Elizabeth's best friends, are the first to ring the bell. Their eyes widen when they enter, smiles on their perfectly made-up faces, glowing like teenagers who've just arrived at the prom.

"Such a treat to see you," Jill says to Elizabeth. Her devotion to our family humbles me.

"Elizabeth, you look wonderful," Jane says.

"Short hair flatters you. Makes you look young," Robin adds.

They've all seen Elizabeth in her wigs, scarves, and baseball caps; now they revel in her new hair. Elizabeth blushes and grins at her friends' compliments, wrapping a curl behind her ear, but I can tell she's holding back. To look so good and still have cancer in your bones and your lungs are hard truths to reconcile.

Soon we're greeting Auntie Gloria, who looks stunning in her tweed Chanel pantsuit and chunky gold necklace. She was devastated upon hearing the news of Elizabeth's cancer and calls her every day to try and cheer her spirits. Auntie Gloria is like a second mother to us. Over the next fifteen minutes, nearly fifty of Elizabeth's friends and relatives pour in, so many of whom brought dinners, sent flowers, left challah on the Gordons' doorstep, or drove Brooke and Lauren home from school. Today, they enter with spirited eyes, ready to celebrate a life extended.

"What a terrific day," Auntie Gloria remarks. My mother, too, seems joyful, though later she will tell me she felt like an ostrich with her head in the sand.

I watch Elizabeth work the crowd and hope she's enjoying the moment. I run upstairs one last time to reapply lipstick, then slip the tube into my pocket. As I run down, out of the corner of my eye, I spot my mother standing alone on the deck. She's facing away from the house, and her shoulders are slumped. I join her through the French doors.

"Mom?" I say, closing the door for privacy.

"Oh! Sorry!" she says, dabbing the corner of her eye with a cocktail napkin. "I just needed a minute."

"I thought you were having a good time."

"I am," she says, and laughs at the contradiction. Though I've seen my mother cry a lot more recently than I ever have in my life, this moment seems different. I'm stunned.

"These are happy tears," she insists, but I'm not convinced.

My mother surveys the backyard, the trees and bushes crisp with the oranges and yellows of early autumn, soon to welcome deep reds.

"She has so much to live for. . . ." She trails off.

"I know, Mom. I hope so, too."

My mother reaches over and rubs my arm, unable to say anything else, but the moment feels unresolved. There's something deep that she wants to express but can't. I know the feeling—it must run in the family.

"Let's get back in," I say. I don't want Elizabeth to see anything upsetting.

Hooking elbows, my mother and I join the party just as the caterers serve lunch. Bubbe's antique China flowered cups and saucers shine next to my sterling silver and fine Baccarat glasses. Silver candelabras are lit on the dining room table, and by evening their tapers create waterfall sculptures of wax.

Women chat and fill their plates with mesclun, grilled salmon, and crispy baguettes. I have always thrilled at having a sizable dining room that fits, comfortably, twenty-five. How I've looked forward to gathering my whole family at this table for holiday meals, delighting in the details of a floral centerpiece, pressed linen napkins, and the heirloom butter dish. Now my family is split and has no need for this room.

But today the warmth of everyone's faces and the easy

laughter reassure me of a future for us and Elizabeth. We sing "Happy Birthday," followed by enthusiastic applause. I serve cake baked and decorated at a favorite local bakery, with frosting whipped into designer bags and shoes. Elizabeth bends to blow out the candles, then clinks a fork against her glass.

"Attention, please. First of all, I am completely overwhelmed. Thank you." She tosses me an extra big smile. "Thanks, as always, to my sister, Samantha, for throwing this party. Ever since we were kids, she has been by my side. It is not an exaggeration to say that she saved my life." The room's chatter quiets into trembling lips and liquid eyes. Elizabeth goes on to thank everyone for their friendship and support, how lucky she is to have them.

Jane and Robin present Elizabeth with a beautifully packaged gift. She unwraps the navy paper and opens the box to reveal a turquoise-and-gold Van Cleef bracelet.

"We thought this looked like you," Jane says. "Everyone contributed."

"Oh my God!" Elizabeth says, slipping it on her petite wrist, to oohs and aahs.

I close my eyes to summon the few words I want to say and raise my glass.

"Elizabeth, I am blessed to have you. Happy, *happy* birthday."

I draw her in for a warm embrace and live the moment with my sister, celebrating life in all its fragility.

Chapter Nineteen

———

*L*ife alone with Alexandra is unexpectedly satisfying. I drive her to middle school every morning and to dance lessons in the afternoons. Richard and I continue to see each other on some weekends and occasionally go out for dinner. Sometimes I miss our ordinary life, hanging out on the couch, watching TV, grocery shopping, and how Richard announces the headlines every morning as he reads the *Globe*. When we're together, he never mentions my family, except to ask how Elizabeth is doing, which I appreciate. Just the asking satisfies me. He doesn't need to hear the details. "She's better," I say.

Richard continues to deposit money monthly into my accounts, and I continue to pay the household bills. Even though I have filed for divorce with Jonathan Mann, my attorney, I don't push it. I see my therapist once a week.

Catherine and I discuss how marriages are made strong through the resolution of conflicts, the compromising of differences. Richard and I haven't been able to do that. When I recount events in which I thought Richard was rude or in the wrong, I try to look at them now through a new lens. Richard is not a villain, and I do not have a halo on my head.

❖

IT'S BEEN TEN months since Elizabeth's forty-fifth birthday. Just afterward, she set a new priority in her life: to spend quality time away from doctors and chemo. We entertained ourselves in New York, shopping for spring fashions and checking out trendy downtown restaurants. Auntie Gloria treated us to a show on Broadway. I never could have estimated how satisfied I'd be to see Elizabeth engrossed in *Jersey Boys*.

Five months ago, our beloved Dr. Varghas left Beth Israel for a position at the Cleveland Clinic in Ohio. But he left us his cell number and specifically said we could call him anytime for a second opinion or advice.

We met a colleague of Dr. Varghas's at Beth Israel but didn't feel comfortable working with him as our new oncologist. We decided to interview the highly recommended Dr. Foley, chief of thoracic oncology at Mass General Hospital, the largest teaching hospital of Harvard Medical School. Although Dr. Foley isn't nearly as warm as Dr. Varghas, he's professional and has a brilliant reputation.

Elizabeth's blood counts and scans were stable for seven months. The Iressa kept her feeling healthy and strong. Then her cancer markers started to rise and Dr. Foley switched Elizabeth to Iressa's stronger cousin, Tarceva—exactly what Dr. Varghas said he would do if the cancer woke up.

Initially, I wasn't alarmed. But the markers continued to rise. Elizabeth broke out in a prickly rash resembling severe acne across her forehead, one of Tarceva's known side effects. That was supposed to indicate that the drug was working, at least.

Disappointed in her progress, Dr. Foley recommended that Elizabeth seek a clinical trial, one that would include another novel drug, Avastin. The drawback was that Avastin was already known for harsh side effects, like dry mouth, loss of appetite, mouth sores, hair loss, loss of taste, jaw pain, and gum infections. Worst of all, it would have to be administered in conjunction with chemotherapy. Chemo again.

In addition to the acne, Elizabeth has lost her energy. She's been lethargic, complaining of throbbing occipital headaches so terrible she can't lift her head from the pillow. Yesterday she went for an MRI of her brain. We called Dr. Varghas in Cleveland to discuss the pros and cons of the clinical trial. He was optimistic, though he did dwell on the side effects because he was concerned, as always, about how they would impact Elizabeth's quality of life, the time she has left with her children.

To have Varghas's endorsement is motivating because it means there are options. That's what the doctors have been promising all along: when one treatment stops working, they'll pull another drug from their arsenal, even from among those still in development. Of course, we can imagine that there is a limited supply of drugs, and of course Dr. Varghas did warn us that, at some point, all drugs could fail. There's another catch: in order for Elizabeth to begin a trial, she has to be off all medications for three weeks. That's when her worst headaches begin.

In a bleak mood, I force myself to celebrate my friend Debbie's fiftieth birthday, joining our friends at the Taj Boston hotel. White-gloved waiters dispense champagne and lobster salad on tiny crackers, and the sleek flatware reflects elegant flower arrangements. Visible through the windows are the Public Garden and the magnolia trees in bloom. Swan boats ferry vacationers around the hourglass pond.

Midway through this lovely party, I am distracted by an urge to check my phone, wondering whether I have received the results of Elizabeth's MRI. Discreetly, I open my bag and notice I have eight missed calls and two messages.

I excuse myself as the waiters are clearing entrées and exit to the hall. All eight missed calls are from Jake. "Where the hell are you?" he says on my voice mail, as if he's hyperventilating. "The MRI is bad. It's so bad. Don't call my house. I'm at the office. I haven't told Elizabeth. Call me ASAP."

With a hand on my heart, I dial.

"It's in her brain," Jake blurts when he picks up. "But not one spot—all over. It's all over. . . ." He stumbles on. "I'm leaving my office. Foley wants to give the results in person. I can't tell her myself. Can you be there? Meet us at the hospital in half an hour?"

"I'll be there." The fact that I can answer surprises me, so deep is my shock.

I end the call, and my phone becomes a brick in my hand. A woman passes me in the hall, ushering her child to the bathroom. Two friends from the luncheon gracefully walk to the ladies' room in their high heels. How odd to be surrounded by such beauty and elegance in this moment, as my world has just changed again.

I place the phone to my ear, but I don't know whom to call. I'm not at this party anymore. I can hear my own breathing, as if enclosed in a tunnel. Servers pass, wheeling a birthday cake and dishes, and I remember Debbie. I don't want to interrupt her party or add any type of distress. I decide to let her know that I must leave, but not why.

"I'm sorry," I whisper when I find her. "I have to pick Alexandra up at school."

"Everything okay?" Debbie asks, surprised that I'm leaving early.

"Yes. Please don't get up," I say, as I lean over to kiss her cheek. "Happy birthday."

I remain composed as I make my way quickly out of the room, following all the social rules even in an emergency. But when I reach the corridor, I run as fast as I can in my kitten heels. I give my ticket to the valet and pace back and forth in the hotel lobby, punching the black marble floor with my feet. The car comes quickly, thank God. Within minutes I am on Storrow Drive and exit for Mass General.

I arrive right behind Elizabeth and Jake. I leap out of my car at the valet stand to join my sister's side. I already know more than she does, and I can't look her in the eye. She's pale and frightened, similar to the way she looked the night she received the original fax with the Stage IV diagnosis. How I would trade that night for this moment now.

"My hand was shaking," Elizabeth says. "My eye twitched. My speech."

"When did all that happen?" I ask. My mouth is sandpaper dry.

"Just on the way here," Jake says.

Now I decide that I will look into my sister's eyes. Her pupils are dilated.

This is it, I think. *The death sentence.* We enter the lobby through heavy glass doors. Jake and I each hold one of Elizabeth's hands, afraid to let go, to let her float away. A young, slim woman at the main desk directs us to the eighth floor. The elevator door opens onto a sign that says NEURO-ON-COLOGY.

I scan the waiting room and see a thirtysomething-year-old woman with a partially shaved head, a somber teenager in a wheelchair, flanked by parents. It feels strange to be dressed in party attire and surrounded by white coats. My attention lingers on a gentleman around my age, with a shaved, stapled head. He can't be more than forty-five, fifty. His wife holds his hand. Everyone here is at the end. No one speaks.

Before we have a chance to sit, Elizabeth's name is called.

We're ushered into an office with a large picture window overlooking the Charles, today dotted with sailboats. We can see Storrow Drive, which carries a steady line of cars moving from one place to another. It's an attractive view for a place dealing in sickness and death.

Dr. Foley enters the room. "What are your symptoms?" he asks.

"I think I had a seizure in the car," Elizabeth squeaks.

Dr. Foley stares at us before responding, and it hits me: the chief of oncology at MGH doesn't want to tell us what he knows.

"Elizabeth, the disease has taken off," Dr. Foley says. "There's really no other way to put it. The MRI shows that cancer has spread to the meninges, the fluid surrounding your brain and spinal cord. This is very serious."

"I had a feeling it had spread," Elizabeth says, as if she had solved a mystery, strangely calm. I take her hand. Jake shakes his head.

"Can this be treated?" Elizabeth asks.

"Yes—but I have to tell you, it's not a great spot to be in."

I process Dr. Foley's words. This is the frankest any doctor has ever been with us. Maybe because the disease has progressed, he has no choice. Dr. Foley's face is pinched. It seems like he has lost hope for my sister. I want to vomit into the trash can. I cross one leg over the other and rub my forehead with my fingertips.

The door opens, and a short, round-faced, thirty-ish man walks in and stands beside wiry, thin-nosed Dr. Foley. "I'd like to introduce you to Dr. Hamilton," Dr. Foley says. "He's a neuro-oncologist. A good match for you, Elizabeth. Brain matters are not my expertise."

"Nice to meet you," Dr. Hamilton says, shaking our hands.

"First I'm going to explain what has happened, and then I'll answer any questions."

He turns on a computer and brings up the scan of Elizabeth's brain.

"It's as if the cancer is a thin layer of peanut butter spread over the brain. It's called leptomeningeal disease," he says.

I am listening, but it's hard for me to focus, knowing this is my sister's brain he's talking about. Peanut butter?

"Our best option is whole-brain radiation and chemotherapy to the spinal fluid," Dr. Hamilton says, and pauses for this to register. "I recommend radiation for three weeks, five days a week." When that's finished, he recommends surgically implanting an Ommaya reservoir in Elizabeth's head as a port for chemotherapy.

"I will still fight," Elizabeth says, but she sounds exhausted.

We didn't see this coming, and I can't help but wish that anyone—Dr. Varghas?—had prepared us for the possibility that Elizabeth's cancer would metastasize to her brain.

"Is this treatment the usual course?" I ask.

"Not usual, but promising," Dr. Hamilton says. "There are significant side effects from whole-head radiation, but it's the best option you have. We'll use a scalp block so that the hair loss will not be permanent."

In the midst of all this bad news, Dr. Hamilton's mention of my sister's hair makes my heart lift. Does this mean he thinks she'll be alive long enough for her hair to grow back?

Before now, Elizabeth has not been outwardly sick. Aside from some tiredness and a bit of nausea, the cancer appeared less physically taxing than it actually was. Now we're in an entirely differently league, the horrible cancer-patient stuff we've been afraid of and in denial about. This is going to require more than a wig and wheatgrass.

I feel flush; heat creeps up my neck. Deep down, I was hoping for divine intervention, that Elizabeth would have a miracle recovery featured in medical journals.

Leaving the office, I catch a glimpse of myself in the mirror and notice a profound weariness in my face. I wish I had Richard to hold me as I wallow in my grief.

Soon after the appointment, I sit him down and tell him everything. He sees and hears the anguish, the shakiness, in my voice. I understand that I am breaking my promise to Jake, but I need Richard to know. It's also time to tell Brooke and Lauren the true extent of their mother's disease.

⸎

WITHIN A WEEK, Elizabeth begins her new round of treatments. They're much worse than the routine radiation she got before. This time it's not just her body that's taking a beating; it's her brain.

I spend even more time with her than I did in the beginning, because she is slowly losing her independence. Her gait has become unsteady. I've been driving her to the grocery store and even helping her walk around the house. Her children are perceptive. Jake hasn't wanted to give the kids too much information, but Elizabeth's condition speaks for itself. In the hallway off her bedroom, Brooke whispers, "Auntie, why can't Mom drive? Did the cancer spread more? Will she have to have chemo again?" Dr. Foley has recommended that Brooke and Lauren start seeing a therapist at the hospital to help them understand their feelings. Jake makes separate appointments with a Dr. Singleton, the hospital's family psychiatrist.

I hesitate in the moment, but seeing Brooke's concern for her mother makes the words tumble out of my mouth. "Yes, sweetie. The cancer spread to your mom's brain. Yes, she'll need more chemotherapy."

"I knew it," Brooke says, her voice laced with anger. "This sucks. That's why we have *that* appointment."

"I understand you're upset. I am, too. It's not fair. Come with me into your mom's room. Let's watch TV with her," I say.

Reluctantly, Brooke follows.

Elizabeth and I lie on her bed, watching *Oprah*, with Brooke snuggled between us. We watch for the full hour with our arms and legs entwined. Even though we aren't talking deeply or openly about our feelings, this is the easy intimacy we share, even in the hardest times.

When the show ends, Elizabeth is half-asleep. Brooke props herself on her elbow and asks, "Auntie, can you take me to the tailor so I can get my pants shortened?" She has just bought new clothes for spring.

I smile at her, nodding. "Of course."

"Come in my room so I can show you," she says perkily, her voice now devoid of anger. I can see she craves the routine things her mother did for her, the everyday errands.

"Okay, sweetie pie." I turn to Elizabeth and gently squeeze her arm. "We'll be right back, okay?" She nods.

My hand on her shoulder, Brooke leads me across the hall to her bedroom.

"Look," she says, pulling out new jeans and sweaters and a pair of corduroy pants. "I have five pairs I need to get hemmed. Can we go now? Please?" She is like her father, Jake, always wanting things done.

My back is to the door, but I feel a presence. I turn to see Elizabeth holding onto the wall. She manages a few steps to plop herself down onto Brooke's bed.

"Hi, girls," she says, with a childish grin on her face, proud of herself for having snuck over here. But I can tell she's exhausted just from the trip across the hall.

"Hey! We thought you were sleeping," I say. "You didn't have to wake up for this." It takes me only a few seconds to realize that she did this to hold on to her place as Brooke's mother, captain of her ship. I feel selfish that I didn't think to bring Elizabeth into Brooke's room with us. How awful she must have felt, left behind while I walked out of the room with my arm around her daughter. I can imagine how much she wants to be the one to drive Brooke to the tailor. I imagine that she looks at me with health envy. I think I would if our roles were reversed.

Life goes on, though. Clothes have to be washed, meals have to be made, spring pants have to be hemmed. Elizabeth would do anything to be able to perform these tasks, all of which used to be simple and mundane. If it were Elizabeth taking Alexandra on errands while I had to stay home sick in bed, it would be tough to bear.

"Okay, we're all going to the tailor," I say. "Let's get our coats."

Brooke runs downstairs, and Elizabeth holds the banister. We go to the car.

When we get to Mario the tailor, Brooke changes in the dressing room and Elizabeth positions herself across from the mirror. I stand near her, watching with admiration as she takes control. When the tailor pins up each pair of pants, Brooke says, "Mom, is this the right length?"

"A little longer," Elizabeth says. When the tailor lengthens the pants a bit, she says, "A little shorter." He brings them up slightly. "Perfect," she says. She hasn't lost her eye.

I think about all the things, small and large, that Brooke

and Lauren will miss by losing their mother. Brooke's only sixteen, and Lauren just turned thirteen. I never thought my family would have to endure such devastation. But why not us? Who are we to escape suffering?

I grasp for the lesson in this challenge but feel only desperate for my nieces' future happiness. I have considered them less throughout this entire ordeal, perhaps because to watch Brooke and Lauren struggle will be more unbearable than my own grief.

Chapter Twenty

———

*A*nother summer, and Alexandra is away at camp in Maine. Richard is on Nantucket. I wouldn't want to be anywhere but with my sister.

Most mornings now when I pick up Elizabeth for radiation, I rush from the car into her house, fearing the worst. Then I'll collide with my sister behind the door: she's ready, wearing shorts and holding a Prada satchel. On the drive, we talk about her kids. Elizabeth says Lauren prays to God every night before she goes to bed. Brooke spends evenings lurking in her own room. When Elizabeth enters, half the time her older daughter is withdrawn and sad, and the other half she's worried.

"She just asked me about colleges," Elizabeth says, as we circle and climb levels of the MGH parking garage. "Jill said she'd help her with applications if I'm not up to it."

"Brooke likes talking to Jill," I say.

"I'll help as much as I can," Elizabeth says, as if wondering how much that will be.

The technicians accept us on time, and the treatment takes fifteen minutes. The session itself is uneventful, just as the earlier therapy was.

Back at the Gordons', Elizabeth can barely climb the stairs. I support her from behind. When she leans back, I'm afraid we might both topple backward. Elizabeth has always wanted to rip up the rug and restore her home's hardwood staircase, but now I thank God for carpeted stairs.

"I'm exhausted," she says when we reach her bedroom. She crawls into bed.

I tuck her in and give her a kiss, but just as I'm turning to leave, Elizabeth shouts, "Hurry—help me to the bathroom!" I rip back the covers, and Elizabeth barely makes it to the toilet. I hold on to her wig as she vomits again and again. So much for the anti-nausea drugs.

In July, Elizabeth has surgery to insert the Ommaya port into her brain. Her skull will be cut, the port placed just under her scalp, to access her spinal fluid. The surgeons call it a "simple" and "routine" procedure. It may be simple for the doctor, but not for the person whose head is incised. We have outgrown our cheerful selves, our upbeat thinking. Elizabeth no longer calls me for reassurances after I'm home. No more long hours of telling her she'll beat this. Even Jake's updates to the kids are blunt. It's in her brain. There is no cure. Treatment may buy her a few months.

After Ommaya surgery, Jake works from the hospital room. As Elizabeth has declined, he has become self-absorbed. He smells fresh—a new cologne—and is already tanned from his morning runs along the marathon route in Newton.

"Can you spend the night?" Jake asks. "I have a business dinner." He barely looks up from his BlackBerry.

I say that I can, reminding myself to ask the nurses for the overnight cot. "Mom and Dad will be here soon, too," I add.

"I can't stand seeing your mother so emotional," Jake says. "Don't let her cry in front of the kids."

"It is what it is," I say.

"Fine, but I'm leaving at five thirty." Jake ducks crucial

moments like these as if he thinks Elizabeth won't know, or can't comprehend, the difference. Or perhaps he can't warch her like this. There she lies, with her head shaved and stapled, hooked to IVs. If it were Richard, I'd be livid if he left this room just because he didn't want to deal with my parents.

When Jake has cleared out, I rub Elizabeth's feet, as if I could massage away the terrible nightmare we're living. I begin one of our meditations. I'm not sure Elizabeth understands what I'm saying. She stares at me, eyes wide open.

"You okay?" I ask.

No response. She looks away and gazes out the window at the boats on the Charles River, as if in another place, and I can't blame her.

When my parents arrive, they bend and kiss their daughter's bloated face. Elizabeth opens her eyes and tries to lift herself off the bed. She motions to the bathroom, even though she has a catheter. She must need to vomit, but there's no receptacle. I silently curse the nurses, holding Elizabeth's hand and rolling the IV behind her as she shuffles to the toilet. She throws up. I rub her back. She coughs and vomits again. My mother cries.

After Elizabeth is settled back in bed, Dr. Foley arrives. "Good afternoon," he says from the foot of the bed. "You did great."

Elizabeth regards him with skeptical, unknowing eyes.

Dr. Foley motions for my parents and me to join him in the hallway. "I'm sorry to tell you this, but I think you should consider hospice. I can refer you myself."

I try to hold up under the blow. Hospice is for the dying. My mother drops her face into her hands, and my father supports her.

"We must face the truth," Dad says to my mother and me. "Give me the number," he says to Dr. Foley.

The next morning when I awake, Elizabeth is propped up in her hospital bed, eating a poached egg.

"Hi," she says, much brighter than I expected. "Where's Jake?"

"He's working out," I say, checking my watch, the hour of his morning run. "I'm sure he'll be here soon," I add. *Her husband should be seeing her like this,* I think, *connecting with her while he can, whenever he can. But maybe he just can't bear the sadness.* "How are you feeling?" I ask.

"Eh," she says.

What a difference from one day to the next! I think it's a breakthrough, but the nurses say they see this all the time. Yesterday Elizabeth was on morphine, which eased her pain but slowed her full awakening after surgery—hence the dull, unresponsive eyes.

At discharge, Dr. Hamilton prescribes steroids. After three nights in the hospital, Elizabeth convalesces at home, where my father and Jake have arranged for hospice care. Over the next few weeks, everything, even Elizabeth's personality, changes. She becomes almost childlike at times, developing a tic of touching the stapled scar on her head and reacting with surprise. She stares into the mirror, poking her water-weighted cheeks and making faces at someone other than herself. Due to cognitive changes, Elizabeth is restricted to the house, except for chemo and radiation, and can no longer be left alone.

A different way of posturing her mouth when she concentrates on chewing. A new nasalness in her voice. Leptomeningeal disease causes neurologic decline, I've read. Elizabeth no longer seems to comprehend the seriousness of her situation and rarely cries or expresses concern about Brooke and Lauren.

As strange as I find this new absence of alarm, at least Elizabeth seems to have lost her sense of dread. That old saying, "ignorance is bliss." While I don't think Elizabeth is fully ignorant of her condition, or blissful, she might be on her way to a more accepting state. As my sister's physical suffering intensifies, I'm simply relieved to see her worry less.

⸙

AFTER A MONTH of this—Elizabeth staying upstairs, watching long stretches of television, and eating nothing but soft foods and soup—my sister announces that she wants to have lunch with friends.

I consider the complications of this request. It will be difficult getting her downstairs, and I don't know if I want her friends to see her like this. But she insists. I call Jane.

We schedule lunch for the following week. I tip Jane off to Elizabeth's condition and her decline, worrying that it might all be too much for her.

The day of our lunch date, Elizabeth takes the steps on her own, one hand gripping the banister. She's wearing shoes with a small heel, and her smile is wide but wary. An aide has helped her dress, but her wig is crooked. She's gained twenty pounds, and her clothes don't flatter. Her pants bunch and pull, her shirt buttons strain, and a favorite salmon-colored sweater hugs her bosom like a sausage casing. My sister, the fashionista who used to line her eyes with perfect, liquid strokes, is now an entirely different woman.

I'm afraid of what will happen once we're out. People who know us might stare and whisper at the sight of her or, worse, pity her. Elizabeth is private, and I don't want her to feel any shame. But, given all of her cognitive changes, I realize that only *my* shame is the obstacle here standing between us and a new normal.

"I'm ready," Elizabeth says to me at the bottom of the stairs, with uncertain pride.

"You look wonderful," I say. "Just a little fix on your wig."

Elizabeth leans on the wall while I tug her wig into place. Looking up, she says to herself, "I made it."

"Shall we?" I say, offering my elbow.

In the car, Elizabeth struggles with her seat belt, so I lean over to help. Our nervous energy makes this feel like a special occasion, and it is, but I worry. All week my sister has been looking forward to this lunch, and now I'm anxious that I haven't sufficiently prepared Jane. As one of Elizabeth's oldest friends, she will surely be shocked.

We're meeting at Aquitaine. Elizabeth bobs and weaves behind the hostess, resembling a drunk, but no one seems to notice as we take our seats. It's quiet today, the kind of environment that Elizabeth needs. I begin thinking it might go off just fine.

I spot Jane at the door, stylishly thin in a tailored business suit, with impeccable makeup and hair, straight from her corner office at the nearby bank. Jane and Elizabeth met at Northeastern and had kids at the same time. When Elizabeth first got sick, Jane delivered her fair share of meals and celebrated Elizabeth's birthday. But since the cancer spread, we have stopped accepting her food and other generous offers, favoring privacy.

Jane comes toward us, beaming. I see her miss a step when she notices Elizabeth's face, the mouth that won't close and the cheeks that look stuffed with marbles. I immediately regret having planned the lunch. The last thing Elizabeth needs is a friend falling apart in front of her.

After a beat, Jane recovers her poise. "Hi, ladies," she says. I can almost feel her effort to remain casual.

She slides into the booth and sits next to Elizabeth, kissing her on the cheek. Jane can't seem to stop clenching her hands, but she smiles, determined to make small talk. "What beautiful earrings," Jane says.

"Thank you," Elizabeth says. "So happy to see you."

Elizabeth orders the salade Niçoise, an old favorite, and again I foresee disaster. At home she has been eating only soft foods. "Do you want to order the soup?" I say brightly.

"No, the salad," she insists, like a petulant child. Her voice is loud, and her inflection makes her sound tipsy. Jane watches me from behind her menu.

"Salad it is," I say. When the server comes, I order the soup for myself. I plan to switch plates with Elizabeth when our meals arrive, afraid that she'll be embarrassed about chewing.

"So, what are Brooke and Lauren doing this summer?" Jane asks Elizabeth, buttering a piece of bread.

Elizabeth smiles but doesn't answer. Jane leans forward and repeats the question a bit more loudly, remembering what I told her on the phone about hearing loss. Before Elizabeth can answer, the server arrives with lunch. Elizabeth digs into her salad, forks some lettuce into her mouth, and pockets it in her cheek.

"Good?" I ask.

She nods enthusiastically, waits a beat, and then spits into her napkin. Elizabeth takes another bite—rinse and repeat. So much for the soup! She gives me a look, and I can tell that she is annoyed about my being overprotective. The look makes no difference; I still intend to protect her.

When the coffee arrives, Elizabeth and Jane are chatting about their children, and it's almost like old times. To my great relief, Elizabeth has become animated while discussing Brooke's summer program at UPenn. Jane's kids are off to Europe, doing a service program in Spain. Elizabeth is coherent, asking all the right questions, completely enjoying herself with a dear friend.

After our success, Jane embraces Elizabeth in the parking lot, then sets off in the direction of the bank. After I've got Elizabeth ensconced safely in her seat belt, we drive away. But as we leave the parking lot, I notice Jane leaning on a planter, retching and crying. My own eyes remain dry, as if a switch has flipped.

I decide to plan a string of new pleasures for Elizabeth: a manicurist at her house every Tuesday, a massage therapist on Friday, and a bouquet of her favorite peach roses for the weekend. I also tell myself that it's time for her to dictate letters so that her children will have something to remember her by.

We arrive back at the Gordons', and I unbuckle Elizabeth's seat belt. We hold hands until the front door. "That was wonderful," she says. "God, I'm tired." We laugh.

I assist Elizabeth to her bedroom and help her change her clothes. She crawls under one of the afghans that Bubbe made for her, either as a child or as a new bride.

"Want to lie down with me?" she asks.

I slip in on the other side, and, once again, we hold hands. The bedside table is crowded with amber pill bottles, and I decide to find the ones for sleeping, but Elizabeth waves them away.

"I don't take those anymore," she says. It's true—she has become a champion sleeper. I'm the one who needs the pills. Her breathing slows.

Before I go, I notice a teardrop in the corner of her eye, that part of my sister that still understands what is happening.

Chapter Twenty-One

———

*A*nother week, another round of chemo. At the blood draw, Elizabeth rolls up a sleeve and makes a fist, filling three vials. I turn my head. Her veins are getting weak; her arms are a riverscape of blue rocks. When the phlebotomist releases the rubber band, she is faint.

We stand conjoined, as if someone with a needle and thread has sewn up our clothes, and meet Jake in the waiting room. He registers our presence with a quick nod, sips a coffee, and puts his BlackBerry face down on the table.

When it's time to meet with Dr. Hamilton, the three of us walk together down the hall, enter the exam room, and take our seats. Elizabeth sits closest to the doctor's desk, Jake beside her. I lean on the bed with my terrible notebook. Dr. Hamilton enters with a tender smile. I want to believe that he will do everything he can to help. It turns out that Dr. Hamilton and his wife belong to our synagogue. He is the doctor whom Richard, leveraging his contacts on the temple board, originally offered to call.

"How is your energy?" Dr. Hamilton asks Elizabeth.

"So-so," she says. "I'm tired."

"How would you rate your fatigue on a scale of one to ten?"

"Five." Elizabeth looks at Jake for verification. He pockets his BlackBerry.

"She's up at eight and has a soft-boiled egg," Jake says. "Sleeps for three hours like a baby. The family has dinner at six thirty, and then she goes back to bed."

"You mean, that's when you leave," Elizabeth says.

An awkward silence. Dr. Hamilton raises a brow. I watch Jake realize that Elizabeth understands the significance of his scheduling dinners at seven, and she doesn't care if it helps with business. Not now.

The doctor ignores our dirty laundry and presses on. He has Elizabeth stand to test her balance and strength. She performs the test, wobbly.

"How is your memory?" he asks.

"Last week I went out for lunch," Elizabeth says.

"That's lovely. What day?"

"I'm not sure—but it was nice to get out," she says, with a quick smile.

"She's disoriented," Jake says. "When she takes a nap, she wakes up thinking it's morning."

"What causes this?" I ask. I know it makes the kids anxious to see Elizabeth asking for her poached eggs at dinner.

"It could be a side effect of radiation, or the cancer itself," Dr. Hamilton says. "There's really no way to know. Jake, how long does it take for Elizabeth to get her bearings?"

"Half an hour, with coaching." He lets out a tired sigh.

The exam has shifted to an interview between Dr. Hamilton and Jake because Elizabeth can't answer these questions. She listens, scrutinizing Jake's responses. I find it unsettling for them to discuss Elizabeth as if she's not even in the room, already too far gone to be included in a conversation about her own life. Dr. Hamilton reports that the spinal fluid they extracted shows few malignant cells. The cancer hasn't gotten worse.

"That's wonderful," I say. Incredible what you'll learn to accept as good news.

"Ready for treatment?" Dr. Hamilton asks Elizabeth.

"Yup. Time to put the chemo in my head," she responds in a singsong. My sister yanks her wig and tosses it to me. She's trying to bring comedy to the situation, but her personality is a bit off, and so is the humor.

"Here we go," she says, trying to salvage the moment.

Thanks to the block used during radiation, Elizabeth's hair is growing back—salt and pepper, not chestnut brown—offering scant cover of her skull and new scar. Her diamond studs sparkle, huge against her naked head. Dr. Hamilton takes his finger and feels through the stubble to find the catheter, a tiny hole that connects to a quarter-size reservoir now under Elizabeth's scalp. He rubs antiseptic on her skull in this precise area, lowers the exam table to prone, and inserts a syringe to extract cerebrospinal fluid.

The doctor holds the syringe for us to see. "Pretty clear," he says.

Clear is good; cloudy is not.

Knowing the pain we feel for Elizabeth, Dr. Hamilton asks if Jake and I want to assist in administering her treatment. Out of love for my sister, I open a sterile plastic bag the size of my palm and hand Dr. Hamilton the DepoCyt. Jake, getting ready to be the timer, looks at his watch. The chemotherapy will be injected for three minutes. Dr. Hamilton instructs us to let him know when each minute has passed so that he can push the fluid into Elizabeth's brain evenly.

"My parents are here from New Orleans," Dr. Hamilton says. "They've had no electricity or heat since Katrina, but their home is intact. Better off than most."

"That's too bad," Elizabeth says from the table.

"How you doing down there?" the doctor asks.

"Fine. As long as it's working."

"We'll know soon," Dr. Hamilton says. "Plans for the weekend?" he asks, for either Jake or me to answer, but I stay quiet. I don't tell anyone that I've begun dating again. They wouldn't like the guy. It's Richard.

"How's the marathon training?" Dr. Hamilton asks, now looking at Jake. He has decided to run with a bib number from MGH and plans to donate the proceeds.

"I'm up to ten or twelve miles, a few days a week."

Elizabeth groans. She's disappointed in Jake for spending so much time training and wishes he would be with her. Jake has confided that in order to survive, he needs to keep his mind focused on something other than what's happening with Elizabeth twenty-four-seven. He clearly assumed that Elizabeth doesn't notice when he also goes off at night, and certainly not for a run. He leaves Brooke and Lauren doing homework on their laptops, supervised by Elizabeth's nurses. On at least one occasion, however, this arrangement has backfired.

I flashback to when my cell phone rang recently after midnight, jolting me from a shallow sleep.

"Where is my dad?" It was Brooke, her voice filled with worry. "He won't answer his phone."

"Try to calm down," I said. "I'll find him. I'm sure there's an explanation. Go back to bed, sweetie. He'll be there when you wake up."

Furious, I hung up with Brooke and called Jake. He answered on the third ring, but I could barely hear him over the roar of a bar.

"Jake, go home," I said, imagining him in his Sox cap, holding a Grey Goose on the rocks, telling some stranger his tale of woe.

"Two minutes," Jake says to Dr. Hamilton. "David is running the race with me. He did the New York City Marathon a few years ago."

My sister closes her eyes and frowns. "Why run a marathon now?" she asks.

Jake trains his eyes on his watch. "To raise money, my dear. For cancer research. To help people like you—like us."

"Research won't help me."

"Time's up," Jake says.

Dr. Hamilton withdraws the syringe, and a nurse—one of our favorites—knocks on the door. She's here to swab the top of Elizabeth's head with a sterile solution.

"Thanks," Elizabeth says, as the kind nurse helps her to sit. "Whoops, little dizzy."

I jump up to hold Elizabeth steady, and she thanks me.

As we leave, Dr. Hamilton touches my shoulder compassionately, congratulating a member of the team. One of us to hold the wig, one to time, one to inject the poison. Last week, over a glass of wine, Jake told me he would never take his own treatment this far.

IN THE MIDDLE of December, I'm snuggling with Elizabeth on a cold winter night. I announce that I'm hosting family and friends for Hanukkah and invite her to come. She's propped on pillows, buried under a down comforter, holding but not drinking a bottle of Poland Spring. I haven't entertained on a holiday in over two years, not since her diagnosis. I know it might be difficult to persuade my sister to come to a party in her condition; on the other hand, it might be her last Hanukkah.

Elizabeth's eyes widen. "Richard loves Hanukkah. Will he be there?"

"Yes, actually." Feeling a twinge of guilt, I add, "He's Alexandra's father," as if his being my husband isn't enough.

My sister scrunches her face like she's sucking on a lemon. She scratches at her Ommaya reservoir, covered with new hair. I've come around to seeing her cognitive decline as a blessing, lessening her emotional pain, so that she appears sweet and innocent, not bitter and knowing. On rare occasions, she still has a surge of reality that something is dreadfully wrong, but mostly she appears content, lying in bed and watching *Oprah*.

"I'll come," Elizabeth says, and smiles demurely. "Who else will be there?"

"Debbie, Lynne, Nancy, Leslee, you know. Their husbands and kids."

Elizabeth nods. "I like them. They're always nice to me."

"If it's too cold, you don't have to come. You won't hurt my feelings," I say.

"I'm coming," she says, and I recognize my sister, her pure and basic loyalty.

My main reason to entertain is Alexandra. I have encouraged her to invite her closest friends and their families. For two years now, we have been at the Gordons' house almost every day, using their computers, eating at their kitchen counter, hanging out with their friends. I sense my daughter's need to be at the center of her own universe again. Hanukkah is the perfect occasion. Richard and I both embrace tradition. That's the example we want to set.

"Mom, give me a job. I'll arrange the dreidels and gelt," Alexandra says when we decorate the house. She dashes into the kitchen, where I keep our collection.

"Thanks, sweetie," I say, as she runs back with her arms full. "Spread it all out on the table first. See what you have."

"I'll make it look pretty, I promise," Alexandra says, and starts sorting.

My laptop chimes with a new message. It's from Jake. No greeting, just a tirade.

"The fuck are you thinking? A Hanukkah party for *Richard*? Shoot me now."

"It's not for Richard, it's for Alexandra," I type.

"Elizabeth insists on coming," he types. "Are you nuts? Won't set foot in your house if your husband is there. Neither will my kids."

"It could be healing for everyone," I respond, guilty of hope.

"You should have discussed this with me first. Why put such an idea in Elizabeth's head? Selfish." At Rosh Hashanah last year, Elizabeth invited my family to dinner, including Richard. Jake went ballistic beforehand, and at the meal he barely acknowledged Richard's presence. If Richard sat in the living room, Jake went into the kitchen—a sad but familiar scenario.

"You know what?" Jake writes before I can defend myself. "I'll call your parents. They can bring Elizabeth themselves."

Observing such hollowness in my own family stuns me. I turn away from my computer as if it were an enemy. My mother calls within minutes. In my family, word spreads fast.

"Jake asked Daddy and me to pick up Elizabeth. What's going on?"

"Good plan," I say, ignoring her question, savoring the irony that Elizabeth now defies her husband to be with *me*. The circumstances may be vastly different, but at least one thing is clear: no partner will ever come between my sister and me—not Richard and not Jake.

"Do you honestly think Elizabeth can make it?" I ask my mom. "Her balance isn't good." I watch an icicle hanging from the eave. A gust of heavy wind combined with a slight thaw, and it will shatter.

"Sure, she can be there a little while," my mother says. "She wants to please you."

"I know, Mom. See you tomorrow."

The night of the party, I place a silver menorah on the dining room table with a single candle. The rich smell of caramelized onion fills the house as I fry my signature latkes. Brisket and roast potatoes finish in the oven. Earlier I called Elizabeth to check in, and she sounded excited.

"But the kids can't come," she said. "Something big tomorrow at school."

I know it's a lie, and Elizabeth knows that I know, but she says it anyway. One thing my sister's illness has revealed: my family—excluding Jake, Mr. Blunt—doesn't know how to communicate directly. Rather than resent my sister's half-truth, I begin to resent myself for blaming everything on Richard all these years. Clearly, Richard is not entirely at fault.

A few hours later, my parents open the door and usher in Elizabeth. Wearing her wig, her face swollen from steroids, unsteady on her feet, she plops down on a chair in the living room, where she will stay for the evening. "Phew," she says. "Made it." Her eyes radiate quiet pain.

My mother takes me aside. When she and my father went to pick up Elizabeth, Jake looked like he wanted to stop them. But Elizabeth was ready in her hat, coat, scarf, and gloves. My mother tells me that Jake said they'd better have her back in an hour—and closed the door.

My parents don't deserve to be treated like this, certainly not when their daughter is dying.

"Where's Richard?" my mother asks, shifting focus to a different troublesome son-in-law. She takes a seat protectively nearby.

I perch on the arm of Elizabeth's chair. My friends gather.

"Do you want something to eat? A drink?" Leslee, one of my best friends, asks. I have made a big pot of matzo ball soup and took care to make the balls extra fluffy for Elizabeth to swallow.

I scan the room and see Richard in black jeans and a crisp shirt at the entrance. As he approaches us, I hold my breath.

"Hi," Richard says to Elizabeth. He hasn't laid eyes on her in months, not since the cancer spread to her brain. He crouches to see her eyes. "Good to see you."

"Happy Hanukkah," Elizabeth says, and smiles.

Richard kisses her on the cheek and pets her hand before standing and moving on to other conversations. With this moment of truth behind us, I sigh with relief.

"How are your kids?" Debbie asks.

"Brooke is checking out colleges. Her top choices are NYU, Syracuse, and BU. Communications major. Lauren might get recruited to play tennis for the Weston travel team." She beams with motherly pride.

Because of a hearing deficit, Elizabeth's voice is louder than normal. But we all ignore it.

It's the last time Richard sees my sister alive.

Chapter Twenty-Two

———

$\mathcal{F}$or Christmas, Richard wants to treat Alexandra and me to a vacation in St. Barts. I'm flattered by the gesture, but I can't shake my concern about being that far away.

"You stayed home with Elizabeth last year," Richard says. "Alexandra and I missed you in Mexico. Come on. You and Elizabeth were together on Hanukkah."

St. Barts is my favorite island—my Caribbean Nantucket—and the thought of getting out of snowy Boston for a week is always tantalizing. Even though we're still separated, I'm happy that Richard insists I should go, hopeful that the trip will help us.

"On one condition," I tell him. "I'm going to call my sister every day."

"Deal," he says.

With mixed emotions, I board the plane and fly two thousand miles from my sister's sickbed. One big factor softens my regrets: Alexandra. I can tell that she needs a vacation as much as I do. Her schoolwork has been getting more difficult, and she's constantly busy with after-school sports and clubs. Her auntie's cancer has only added an extra layer of pressure.

On this trip, because my sister is steadily losing her hearing, I begin to have to talk to Elizabeth through Jake, which slows down the process. Jake reports that she is having more trouble chewing, and now swallowing, but they can't be sure whether it's a result of the radiation or from the cancer.

We check into Le Sereno, an elegant beachfront resort that combines luxury and simplicity in St. Bart's postcard-worthy Grand Cul-de-Sac. Our suite accentuates the island's sexy-cool factor with white walls and espresso-dark floors, sliding glass doors that overlook the beach and crystal-blue waters. Each day the weather is more perfect than the next. After the interminable grays and whites of a Northeast winter, my eyes are greedy for color. I feel myself relax watching water ebbing and flowing from the white beach. I inhale the lush green plants, especially the pink hibiscus, and indulge in the taste of mango on my breakfast plate.

We sleep in, lounge on the beach, and have lunch at my favorite restaurant, Isle de France, overlooking the ocean. At night we enjoy ceviche and grilled branzino at Maya's. Afterward, over a drink, we watch suntanned French girls dance on tables at Le Ti St-Barth, pounding glasses of Veuve Clicquot.

"Aren't you glad you came?" Richard asks over dinner, squeezing my hand.

"I could move here," I say, smiling at him and then at my daughter. Alexandra sips a virgin piña colada the size of her face, complete with an umbrella and a wedge of pineapple. After just a few days in the sun, her skin is glowing, her hair streaked with natural gold. But no matter where we are, my thoughts are on my sister. Here I am, on an island full of beauty and life, while she's home in bed, recently bald, again.

Days later, we're languid from the heat and spend a late afternoon resting in our room. Alexandra sits in the oversize armchair, uploading pictures to her laptop, and Richard is propped on three pillows, reading a novel by James Patterson.

"Think I'll take a walk," I say, after I listen to messages on my phone from Jake. "Elizabeth is crying. Elizabeth is eating scrambled eggs. Elizabeth had a hard night—she's incoherent." I want privacy to call him back. No matter how paradisiacal this island is, I begin to realize that I shouldn't have come. I can't let go; I know I should be with my sister, who seems to be fading quickly.

Two days before we leave, the three of us set up our lounge chairs around a blanket on the beach. We make a small picnic of fresh fruit and cheeses from the beachside restaurant, and Richard and I sip rosé. An elegant Middle Eastern family sets up their blankets next to us. The woman wears an exquisite gold bikini that shows off her bronzed skin. Her black hair shines in the sun. She's with her husband and three children. I introduce myself and Alexandra while Richard is taking a swim.

The woman's name is Yasmine, and they're originally from Saudi Arabia but live in London. She's forty-six, and I can hardly believe it—the same age as Elizabeth. I can't help comparing this radiant, healthy woman of Elizabeth's age with my sister in her condition. The contrast is painfully apparent.

"We're from Boston," I say. "Here for a week. We're leaving New Year's Day."

"This is the first time with the children," she says. "They are having quite a lovely time. Perfect place to practice their French," she says in a British accent.

"*J'adore parler le français aussi*," I say, and laugh.

"*Très bien!*" she says. Her phone rings.

"*Pardonnez-moi*," she says. "It's my sister."

I turn my head to give her some privacy as she speaks in Arabic for five or ten minutes. Her husband is on his laptop, and the kids are sunbathing. When she hangs up, she asks me if I have brothers or sisters.

"One of each," I say slowly. "My sister is dying." For a second, I regret sharing this with a stranger, but something about Yasmine allows me to trust her.

Yasmine stands and seats herself next to me on my lounge. She asks me if I want to talk about it. I do. I tell her I don't want to burden her, but she insists, so I tell her the entire awful story, from the pain in Elizabeth's hip to the cancer in her brain.

"I am anxious to get home," I admit, quietly, so that Alexandra can't hear. "I almost left last night."

"I can't blame you. I would feel the same way," she says. "You'll make it."

For the last two days of our trip, this beautiful stranger becomes my friend. She and I meet on the beach after breakfasting with our families. Each day she wears gorgeous gold bikinis and sheer white cover-ups, her dark hair pulled back in a tight ponytail that exaggerates her dark eyes. The men swim together, and Alexandra becomes friendly with the middle child, a girl one year younger. Yasmine and I stroll to the water's edge. I confide in her about the problems between Richard and my family, how disturbing the conflict has become now that Elizabeth is so sick. I explain how I used to blame Richard entirely for not rising to my personal and idiosyncratic expectations of marriage, for not participating in my family's private agenda. How I wish we could find harmony, I tell Yasmine, a marriage in which we both feel loved.

Yasmine listens and comforts me, praising my sisterly bond. I feel lucky to find such compassion in a stranger. One woman to another, she gives me some advice.

"Samantha, I have found that my husband needs to feel admired. Men want women to support them in their business and their struggles. They want a woman who is their biggest fan. Someone who makes them feel important."

"I don't blame Richard for all of the family feud, but he's no peacemaker," I say. "Then again, neither am I." I am on the edge of my chair this time, my feet in the sand.

"I respect my husband. You might need to ask yourself: Do you respect yours?"

"I appreciate how hard he works. I just wonder if he really has our best interests in mind. Or just his."

"Have *you* always had your family's best interests in mind?"

"I think so," I say, considering the word's many meanings, what each shade of *family* includes and excludes.

"I have learned to listen to my husband, really listen, without being distracted," Yasmine continues. "Maybe you can have a conversation with Richard in a different way than you've ever had before? Marriage is not about one person winning an argument over the other."

"Maybe. He has stuck with me through this whole mess. I credit him for that."

"Give your marriage one last attempt. You are a beautiful family," she says.

"You are wise," I say. "Thank you." We hug. "I'd better start packing." Yasmine and I exchange numbers and email addresses. As we say goodbye, tears prick my eyes.

I wait on the beach for Richard and Alexandra to join me after frolicking in the surf one last time. Then we'll go up to the room, fill our suitcases, and prepare to continue the rest of our lives. Watching Richard at play, I realize how similar we are, struggling with the same confusion. I'm surprised to connect with him this way now, awed at how much a stuck marriage can shift. Maybe I have subconsciously been trying to re-create my parents' or even Elizabeth's marriage, and anything that's come up short hasn't been good enough. But Richard and I have a different dynamic. It's not fair to compare.

The flights back to Boston take seven hours. I drop my bags and head straight to Elizabeth's. I find her alert, propped up in bed, in good spirits.

"What happened to you?" I ask, chuckling. "Jake buy you another car?"

"You're not going to believe who called me while you were gone," she says.

"Who?" I ask.

"Your old boyfriend. Stuart Price."

Chapter Twenty-Three

───────

*H*appy New Year," Stuart greets me the next morning when I call. It has always felt good to hear his relatively high-pitched voice; it still squeaks when he's excited.

I learn that his daughter is a freshman at Boston University and he's in town to bring her back after the semester break. Stuart and I lost touch after college but reconnected the first time twenty years ago; he called me when he was up in Boston on business. Then, five or six years ago, I ran into him at an event in Manhattan and congratulated him for making *Barron's* Forty Under Forty, an exclusive list of successful New Yorkers.

"I just heard about your sister. I called her yesterday to check in," Stuart says. "Couldn't happen to a nicer person—I'm devastated." He pauses. "How are you?"

"She was thrilled to get your call," I tell him. "Very kind. Thank you. I'm okay."

"Matt connected us. He lives in Weston, remember?" Matt was Stuart's closest friend in college.

"Of course. His wife is famous around here," I say. Matt's wife is one of Wellesley's most successful neighborhood realtors, even advertising in movie theaters. "I ran into her and Matt last year at a fund-raiser. I asked for you."

"Meet me for dinner," Stuart says. "There's something I want to ask you."

Of course I'm curious, and I make the date. We had an intense connection and an unresolved breakup.

"That's my girl," Stuart says when we settle on a night when Alexandra has a sleepover. Before we say goodbye, he tells me, "Sam, my wife and I are separated."

I guess I'm not the only one struggling with my marriage, even if I am still on a high from St. Bart's. But I don't feel like telling Stuart that Richard and I aren't living together, either. I'll wait until I see him.

Friday night I dress in a pair of gray jeans, a clingy black sweater, and my favorite Jimmy Choo silver sling-back pumps. I don't tell anyone where I'm going, except Elizabeth. When I step into Mistral, a high-end, dimly lit Boston restaurant, Stuart is at the bar. Upon seeing him, my body floods with emotion. He embraces me, and I breathe in his musky cologne. It's been twenty-five years since we broke up. The timing wasn't right. My family certainly loved Stuart, and he loved them. I honestly wonder if I could have avoided all of the conflict with my family in a marriage to Stuart, instead of to Richard. My college roommate later told me that he suffered our breakup intensely.

Stuart smiles and takes my hand, appraising. "Goddamn," he says. His hair has grayed, and he's gained a few pounds since I last saw him, but he's tan, still fit and muscular. When we broke up, he was just a boy, and now he's a rich, powerful man.

A model-thin hostess who teeters in stilettos seats us at a prime table. Without missing a beat, our server appears, holding two bottles of water. "Sparkling or still?" He has an accent that reminds me of Dr. Varghas.

"Sparkling," Stuart says, and flashes a coy smile. "Unless

you prefer Boston tap?" How worldly he appears now, so much more sophisticated than in college.

"You look wonderful," I say. On his wrist I notice a Cartier watch with a black alligator band. It suits him.

"You look exactly the same. You don't age," he says.

"Well, I don't know about that," I say, laughing, sitting taller in my chair. Although my hair is the same length, it used to be dark brown. Now it's layered, side-parted, and auburn. I'm still slim, but I don't weigh 110 pounds, like I did in college.

Stuart takes my hand from across the table, and his fingers travel. "I've always loved your arms," he says. He used to tell me that in college—I guess because they're toned but still feminine, and not overly muscular.

Anyone watching us might think Stuart is coming on strong, but to me our instant intimacy honors the strong bond we shared when we were young. Stuart has always been a natural salesman. What he's doing is the sell, and I'm buying. Who knows what Elizabeth has told him about the state of things between Richard and me? In college, Stuart and I were completely enamored with each other. Then again, we were young. But I'm already feeling torn between the possibility of our mutual attraction and a second chance to mend my marriage.

The server takes our order.

"You're having the sole," Stuart says, before I can open my mouth. "Always watching what you eat, like in college."

"You know me," I say, flattered.

"My girlfriend will have the Dover sole, and I will have the sea bass, please," Stuart says proudly, handing over our menus. His words transport me back twenty-five years, to when we had our innocence. Like a best friend whom you haven't seen in a while, Stuart feels like home to me. Then again, life is completely different now. I wonder if it would be foolish to sacrifice a real future with Richard for nostalgia. But do I really have a future with Richard?

"How are your parents?" Stuart asks. "They were good to me."

"My parents adored you."

"They must be heartsick about Elizabeth. I can't even imagine—how they are coping? And you? I know how close you two are."

My face flushes. I reach for my water glass and wish I had something stiffer. Stuart's eyes pierce mine. As if he has read my needs, he flags the server.

"This lovely lady and I would like to split a bottle of the Sancerre," he says.

"Elizabeth is really sick. The cancer's in her brain," I continue when the wine has been poured. "Some days she's coherent, some not. Today was a good day. She was excited that I was meeting you for dinner. She sends her love."

"She sounded different on the phone. But she recognized me," Stuart says, with that sincere voice that I remember—a voice filled with kindness.

"It's only a matter of time," I admit, ripping a piece of crust from the bread.

"I'm so sorry," Stuart says, and looks me in the eyes.

"Thank you. Me, too."

"Remember our dinners in Ithaca? Ragmann's?" he asks.

"We always ate in style," I say. "You always found a way. How's business?"

"An empire of fifteen nursing homes in greater New York!" he says, chuckling. "I guess I've known how to make money ever since I was a kid."

For the 1976 Olympics in Montreal, my parents entrusted me to Stuart. We drove up on a whim, no hotel, no tickets. But even after an eight-hour drive, Stuart was savvy enough to buy scalped tickets, then sell those at a profit to get better seats, and still have enough left over for a delicious French dinner and a decent motel room.

"What happened between you and your wife?" I ask.

Stuart's smile fades for a beat, then reappears.

"It's a long story." He explains that when they had financial difficulties with his business, she blamed him and spent money they didn't have, which he resented. "Now that I'm back on my feet, I'm having trouble forgiving her." I find myself wondering what really happened. There are three sides to every story: his, hers, and the truth.

"What happened with your business?" I ask.

"I don't know if you understand my type of business. I overleveraged," he pauses. "But I pulled through."

Stuart and I belonged to each other in our youth, but it's beginning to sink in that now he's a married man with two daughters and responsibilities, a life as complicated and emotionally potholed as mine.

"Are you planning to divorce?" I ask. "Do you *want* to get divorced?"

Stuart takes a sip of water and clears his throat. I think I might have overstepped—he couldn't know that I'm asking myself the same question. But then Stuart leans across the table and takes my hand. Our eyes lock.

"Do *you* want to get divorced?" I realize that Elizabeth has told him everything.

When I don't answer, Stuart looks at his plate and says, "I've had a tough marriage. Our time together in college, Sam—we cut it way too short."

"I feel the same way," I say, then scold myself a little for saying the truth out loud. Our relationship came so easily. We took care of each other. He took me to my first Broadway show, *The Divine Miss M.* Comforted me when I got a C in Biology. I learned to like basketball because he did. I consoled him when his grandfather died. Could we have sustained those early connections for a lifetime?

"We had a lot of fun," I say. "Life was a lot less complicated then—"

"Damn right it was! I admit I'm struggling with the idea of getting a divorce. Sure, it works for my wife and me, but does it work for my family? We have two beautiful daughters. They love their mother. They can't see that she's a real pain in the ass." Stuart laughs. "And we don't have good chemistry in bed."

When we broke up at twenty-one, it was because I wanted to experience dating. Then, when I heard Stuart was getting married, I was filled with jealousy and regret. He was my first love, the first guy I slept with. I never contacted him to tell him my feelings, and now I think I should have. On the other hand, had we stayed together—had I never had these other experiences—I might have lived with a different kind of regret.

"I worked twenty-four-seven to build my business. I'm never giving her half," Stuart rants.

"Husbands don't usually build a business alone," I say, a little ticked off at the men of my generation. As if Stuart's wife hasn't run his household and raised his kids, all while helping him to succeed. Divorce brings out the worst in people.

"What about you, Sam? Your husband is a legend in private equity."

"He's done well."

"Elizabeth tells me you're separated."

"You know a lot," I say. I love how easy our communication is, how direct we are. I'm not like this with Richard. Sometimes not even with Elizabeth.

"We've both hurt and disappointed each other," I confide

in Stuart. "There's been a lot of ugliness. Things are calmer now with us living apart. I'm not pressuring myself to decide what should happen between us. For the moment, I'm focusing on Elizabeth."

"I'm just sick about your sister," Stuart says. "I remember her when she first got her license."

Stuart's sincerity makes my eyes brim. He takes my hand, tangling our fingers.

"We should have gotten married," he insists. At this moment, in the dim restaurant, it feels that way. But it's twenty-five years after we ended our relationship, and we're sifting through a handful of "should haves" and "could haves." If our love was so strong and a partnership possible, why didn't we contact each other before this?

I extract my hand, reach for my wine, and finger the rim of my glass.

Dinner arrives. Between bites and sips, we catch each other up on the less intense aspects of the past two decades. College friends, our children, our favorite vacation spots. We bond over a love of Positano on Italy's Amalfi Coast. Richard and I swore we would return but never did. I find myself imagining what that vacation would have been like with Stuart.

Stuart says his mother has Alzheimer's, and I am quiet with remorse. "I have a qualified nursing staff," he says into his plate. "At least she'll get good care."

Once the meal is cleared and we're polishing off our wine, Stuart leans across the table and kisses me drily on the lips. "I'm staying at the Lenox," he says. "Come back with me." I want to think he's joking, but Stuart's eyes hold mine, completely serious. The aggressive and idealistic boy I knew has hardened into a man of authority, substantial and without self-doubt.

I hesitate. I honestly would love to follow Stuart to his hotel room, but I feel I shouldn't. We are both still married to other people. Through all these years of conflict and heartache with Richard, I remain loyal to my husband. The thought of sleeping with Stuart makes me feel guilty. Could the seed of that guilt be the new blossom of my love?

"Who loves you more than I do?" Stuart insists. "No one ever will—you were my first." But he isn't saying that he wants a divorce.

"I don't want my time with you to end," I say, limiting myself to what's true.

"Who says it has to?"

I have enjoyed our meal so much, and it feels nice to be understood. I decide that extending the evening doesn't have to mean ending up in bed.

Soon we are in a cab. The Lenox is only five minutes away on Boylston Street. As romantic as I felt sitting across from Stuart at Mistral is as anxious as I now feel seated next to him in this taxi. I cast around for the courage to call it off. I haven't kissed another man for almost twenty years—not since Richard and I had our second date. As we walk into the lobby, my head spins, both from the wine and from being in a hotel with my college boyfriend, who is now a man.

Stuart leads me into the elevator and presses 6. The doors close, and he kisses me softly. I kiss back, remembering these lips, these hands, struggling to compare what I'm experiencing now with Stuart's relative youth and inexperience. The doors open with a ding, and he leads me to his room. I follow him down the hall, needing to silence my phone but not wanting to see a missed call from Richard.

Before the door in Stuart's room even closes, he has his hands in my hair. Then, in one dizzying motion, I'm lying on the bed on my back and Stuart is removing my Jimmy Choos.

We kiss furiously, like we used to in his dorm room, rumpling the hotel linens. With Stuart's hands on me, I give in to the pleasure of feeling attractive and wanted.

Stuart moves his focus to my waist and hips—he fidgets with the button on my pants—and though part of me craves this and wants him to go further, a bigger part of me feels I can't.

"Stuart," I whisper, pushing his hands away.

"What's wrong?" he asks, looking up, confused. I can feel his heart beating on my thighs through the walls of his rib cage.

"I'm still married."

"So am I," he says, relieved, and goes back to the button. I can't help but think he looks sweaty and handsome, his mouth smeared slightly pink from my lipstick.

"I didn't mean to lead you on," I say, and sit up.

"Come on," he says, with noticeable frustration. "We're not doing anything wrong. For all you know, Richard is with another woman tonight."

These words hit me like a slap. The truth is, I don't know what Richard does when we aren't together, except when someone tells me they saw him at a bar. But being here doesn't feel right to me. It feels secretive and deceitful. I have too much respect for Richard, I realize, to sleep with Stuart, and too much hope that we might work it out.

"I'm not ready for this," I say, resenting Stuart's mention of Richard. Perhaps sensing that he crossed a line, he resumes being the gentleman I know. Stuart hands me my heels and puts on his own shoes, too.

"I'll come down and put you in a cab," he says.

"No, thanks," I say. I straighten my blouse and fix my hair in the mirror before I open the door.

"This isn't over yet, Sam," Stuart says, as he kisses my cheek. "Keep in touch. I want you."

On the cab ride home, I wonder if Stuart and I actually will keep in touch, if a relationship that's not sexual would even hold his interest. But I also can't help but wonder if Richard will end up deserving the loyalty I showed him tonight.

Chapter Twenty-Four

———

*H*ospice nurses don't wear uniforms. We do not mention death. We purchase a Craftmatic adjustable mattress but keep the same sumptuous bedding: eight-hundred-thread-count sheets, silky throws, and plush pillows. Everything as "normal" as it can possibly be.

My sister's hearing worsens. She's deaf in her left ear and mostly deaf in her right. Jake pours himself into his work. He jogs fifteen miles a day for the marathon and disappears to business dinners at night.

One afternoon when I enter the Gordons', I see dozens of men's pants, shirts, sweaters, belts, and shoes strewn in the living room, as if a men's clothing boutique has popped up in their home. Jake is standing in the middle of it all with a spiffy young man.

"Starting a business?" I ask.

"Saks brought me their spring line," Jake says, and the salesman smiles.

Although I've always been a fashion fanatic, I am horrified by this lavish display. Jake sifts through piles of stiff-collared designer shirts. Elizabeth is in bed upstairs without the energy to dress, and Jake is buying a new spring wardrobe.

"How would it look, me on a shopping spree?" Jake asks.

"Alberto brought me the store. There's a solution to every problem is what I say. See what they'll do for a good customer?" Jake says, trying on a lightweight cashmere jacket. "What do you think? Slimming?"

"It's ridiculous."

"What's wrong?" He laughs nervously. "I've been running a lot. It fits."

"Does Elizabeth know what you're doing?"

"It's no secret. I'm not keeping it from her."

"I hope you don't go up and model," I say.

"I have another business dinner tonight," he says. "I need to feel productive."

Alberto has grown solemn and quiet, like he no longer wants to be here and would be happy to abandon these expensive clothes.

"You and I should go out one night," Jake says. "It will do you good, Samantha."

"I can't," I say, and rush upstairs. I am frustrated with Jake for not hanging on until the end, which is clearly not far off, but I know how much he loves my sister.

Kathy, one of Elizabeth's nurses, finds me on the staircase. An attractive redhead around fifty, she has a comforting presence. Kathy is efficient and self-assured, the type of person I gravitate to. In another situation, she might have been a friend.

"I need to speak to you privately," Kathy says.

She takes me into the office Elizabeth used to use, next to her bedroom, where she still keeps her computer and household bills.

"What's up?" I ask.

"I know this is hard. But I think it would be beneficial for to you have an honest conversation with Elizabeth about dying. She may want to say goodbye," Kathy says. "I've been controlling her morphine, but she's in a lot of pain." We're seated on floor cushions. Kathy places her hand gently on my thigh.

I bow my head and rub my fingers through my hair as the nurse continues. I hear but don't listen, cycling my own obsessive thoughts about Elizabeth's dying, all of my neurotic fictions that will soon be fact. In this moment I remember a friend who purchases World Series tickets on the field, charters private jets, and can buy his way into any trendy restaurant. When his wife died of ovarian cancer a few years ago, he wailed about how he could do or buy anything except what would save her. Elizabeth, too, has had access to the best doctors at the world's best hospitals, and she will still die young. I panic, wondering how I will survive without her.

I know that speaking frankly to Elizabeth is the right thing to do, but I'm terrified. It makes me realize how even the conversations we have shared over the years, those interactions I consider the most authentic and meaningful in my life, have sometimes been conducted under a superficial veil.

"I'm going to summon my strength," I tell Kathy. I must find the right time to tell Elizabeth that I will miss her, to assure her what a wonderful wife, mother, sister, and daughter she is, and soon. To duck this responsibility, to indulge my own fear and comfort craving, would be nothing short of selfish.

"Elizabeth might be waiting for this," Kathy says.

I leave Kathy and sit on the edge of my sister's bed while she sleeps.

Later, Jane comes by with markers and several dry-erase boards to help us all communicate better. I wish I had thought of this.

"What are these?" Elizabeth asks when we install them.

"Like a blackboard," Jane says loudly. "Now we can write you messages."

"Watch," I say, as I write in glossy letters, "What did you eat?"

Elizabeth smiles. "Scrambled eggs."

"I love you," I write, which draws another sweet smile. Her face looks lately like it did when she was a baby—hair cropped, pink cheeks, and big blue eyes, open and naive. She watches television with closed captioning and flips through *People* magazine. I'm not sure if she understands words anymore when they are lumped together in long sentences. *People* is good: glossy, colorful pictures with big, readable headlines. The prognosis was three months when Elizabeth was diagnosed with leptomeningeal disease. Already we have doubled that time, but Elizabeth doesn't turn her head now when people enter the room.

The phone rings, accompanied by a red light blinking to notify Elizabeth, a special phone for the hearing-impaired. A pop-up screen shows the words typed by an operator. Elizabeth can read it and respond back verbally. When she's finished speaking, she's supposed to say, "GA," short for "go ahead," to indicate that the operator should speak. But this proves difficult for her. "Hello, GA," she says. "It's Elizabeth."

I smile. Although it's the wrong way to use "GA," it's cute. Elizabeth perks up whenever the phone rings, as if she has something important to do.

"It's Robin," the operator types.

"Hi, Robin, when are you coming over?" Elizabeth says loudly.

"Half an hour," the operator types.

"Hurry up. You have to see my new phone," my sister says.

Soon Robin arrives in workout pants with a selection of fuzzy socks and a strawberry smoothie from J.P. Licks, Elizabeth's favorite ice cream parlor. Robin takes a seat next to me on the bench by the window, across from the bed. We make small talk, and for a few moments the bedroom is full of laughter, including Elizabeth's.

Next, David arrives. My father sits on a stool by Elizabeth's bed, rubbing her feet with lavender oil. My mother delivers a small lunch. Yesterday it was her homemade chicken soup. Today it's *lukshen kugel*, a traditional family dish of noodles, cream cheese, cottage cheese, and sour cream. I serve myself a small portion, as if I could somehow summon childhood with my mother's comfort food.

That night when I get home, I put myself to work planning this important conversation with Elizabeth. I'm running out of time.

David returns to the Gordons' the next afternoon. The way my brother kisses Elizabeth on the forehead, I sense he needs to talk. We take a walk. It's early spring, so we grab our jackets.

"She's trying so hard to hang on," David says, wiping a tear.

"Kathy says someone needs to talk to her about dying so she can say goodbye."

"Knowing you, Samantha, you're trying to do it alone. I think Mom and Dad and I should all be there."

Relieved, I give David a hug.

Later, Jane and Robin visit again, this time with two four-foot cloth dolls.

"This one is called Jane," Jane says.

"And this one is Robin," Robin says.

Elizabeth laughs as they lean each doll against the wall so that she can always see them from her bed. "They look just like you guys," Elizabeth says.

As the week goes by, Elizabeth loses her appetite, and she wastes. She can barely get out of bed. Her limbs are stiff, and her joints don't move smoothly, as if they need oil.

On Sunday, it is my turn to take Alexandra for her ski competition at Wachusett, a local mountain, an hour away. It's a beautiful day for skiing, high forties and no wind. The snow glitters. Alexandra is psyched for the race.

"This one is for Auntie," she says, putting her goggles on.

"For the win!" I say. "Love you. Good luck."

I take a video of Alexandra all the way down as her teammates cheer.

While we are on the mountain, my mother takes Elizabeth for an MRI, one of the only medical appointments that I have missed. I think it's ridiculous for the doctor to put my sister through this test—her condition speaks for itself. Alexandra and I drive directly to Elizabeth's to check on her after the race. My mother phoned me to say it was awful.

I peek in on my sister, peaceful beside her air purifier. She looks beautiful, in a way, cheeks rosy with natural blush. No plastic tubing or IV bag, no antiseptic smells. White orchids on the night table and bouquets of lilies on the windowsill perfume the air. I remove my shoes and, according to habit, crawl under the blanket to lie beside her, sighing with relief because there's nowhere I'd rather be than here in this sanctuary.

Holding my sister's hand, I listen to her faint breathing until my heart stops pounding. We lie like this, drifting in and out of sleep, for what seems like a long time, until I feel her stir.

"You're here," she says, her eyes heavy-lidded and unfocused.

"Mom told me about the MRI."

She closes her eyes, and I can't tell whether she has fallen asleep again. When she answers, she seems distant. "It was painful. The technician turned my head, even though it hurt."

"What a bitch," I say, and Elizabeth manages a chuckle. How dare someone make things even harder. Sadly, she is one of those who see my sister as only half a person, one who needs assistance walking and understanding directions. She and the others who tend to my sister now know nothing of her as a once vital, beautiful, and independent woman.

"How was the skiing?" she asks, and I'm enthused that she remembers.

"First place. Alexandra dedicated her race to you." I want to elaborate but can't bear to tell my sister about the wonder of being out in the snow and watching Alexandra compete. I can't say any of it, not because she no longer has the strength to listen, but because I don't want to flaunt my life.

"She always thinks of me," Elizabeth says. "That's why Jake and I call her Sweetness."

She drifts off to sleep. I kiss her and go downstairs. In the den, Alexandra, Brooke, Lauren, and Jake are talking quietly, sprawled in various poses on the L-shaped couch. The television is on, but no one is watching. I sit down beside Brooke, fifteen, dark hair framing her snowy face. "Your mom's sleeping," I say, and she nods, snuggling her head on my shoulder.

I know that Jake can tell I've been crying, but I hope the children can't. From the very beginning, we have tried to keep their life as normal as possible. "For the kids," we say, but it's been as much for the grown-ups. Now it's time for all of us to face the truth we already know and fear.

The next day, Brooke sits cross-legged on her mother's bed with a family album spread on the quilt. She points to a spunky-looking toddler holding on to a chair.

"How old was I when I learned to walk, Mom? When did I get my first tooth?" Brooke asks. She then points to a photo of herself holding newborn Lauren. "Tell me about when Lauren came home. What was I like?"

She jots Elizabeth's responses in a small notebook, an exercise the children's therapist recommended. It's brilliant, really. Bonding time, but it's also a way of learning their family stories before Elizabeth can no longer tell them.

Brooke flips to a photo of the four Gordons on the beach, arms intertwined, hair to the wind. "Remember Martha's Vineyard?" she asks Elizabeth. "Look—a picture of us at Auntie Gloria's for Passover. Are we going this year? Hers might be my favorite brisket."

Elizabeth looks at Brooke suddenly with a strange expression. "I have some jewelry for you to remember me by," she chokes out, then begins sobbing.

I swoop in to hug them both, and the three of us huddle together, crying, clinging to our lives. We stay that way until it's Elizabeth who takes a deep breath and says, "Okay, don't worry. I'm going to get better."

Brooke shoots me a look. We all know she's not getting better.

"Mom," she says, "can I have your gold locket?"

"Here, sweetheart," Elizabeth says, taking it from her jewelry box and placing it in her daughter's hand.

"I'm going to put your picture inside. From when you were healthy," she says.

⠀⠀⠀⠀⠀⠀⠀⠀⠀⠀⠀⠀⠀—‹‹‹‹‹—

RICHARD CALLS AFTER I get home. I'm in the kitchen, making Alexandra dinner, feeding my own intense need for control and to enjoy my home with my daughter.

Richard tells me that he'd like to stop by and talk.

"What about?" I ask.

"I'd like to see a mediator," he says. "Try to get our marriage back on track."

"Richard . . ." I pause and speak with the most empathic tone I can muster. "Another time. I had a tough day with Elizabeth."

⋘

BY THE END of March, Elizabeth needs a wheelchair to get to chemo. Jake is stone-faced as we cross the lobby and take the elevator. Once inside, Elizabeth says, "I don't think I can come here anymore." The cancer has won.

"What do you mean?" I ask, as the elevator climbs. "You want to stop treatment? Do you still want to do today?" I figure since we're here, we might as well have one more shot. I'm not ready to let go of my sister, but I'm also not surprised that she has reached her threshold.

And, as if to comfort me, Elizabeth adds, "If I feel better, I'll come back."

When we tell Dr. Hamilton, he nods his head sagely. He has kept Elizabeth alive for ten months, seven months longer than average. I can fully appreciate now what makes him an excellent neuro-oncologist: his necessary mix of optimism and arrogance, confidence and compassion.

I call my mother after dropping off Elizabeth. "Mom, this is it," I say.

When she speaks, resignation filters through her voice. "I don't want Elizabeth to be alone in the cemetery," she says. "It's haunting me."

"What do you mean, alone in the cemetery?" I ask.

"Buried somewhere without family nearby. In a plot all alone, waiting for Jake one day. What if Jake remarries? Or lives another hundred years? I want her to be with family," my mother says.

I stare blankly at traffic. "I'll speak to Jake," I say.

"Tell him that Elizabeth can have Daddy's and my plots. That way she can be near Nana and Papa," my mother's parents, who died five and seven years ago, respectively. "I already called the cemetery and spoke to a man in the office. They'll sell the plots to Jake."

"Mom!" I say.

"Two empty plots close by. I just can't stand the thought of Elizabeth being alone for so many years—she's too young."

This is the first time anyone has said anything about a cemetery, but we can't dance around it anymore. I call Jake and relay my mother's conversation.

"I'm not buying two plots near your grandparents. I don't like that location," he says, a clichéd realtor come to life.

"It's not a Stars."

"Call Sharon Memorial Park and make an appointment for us to see what else is available," he says.

A week later, Jake and I meet with Ira at Sharon Memorial Park. The cemetery is widespread, with roads in the middle. There are no headstones that stick up out of the ground, just plaques on the manicured grass, so that it truly resembles a park more than a cemetery.

Jake and I follow Ira past rows of graves: Feinstein, Goldberg, Cantor. Finally we see Bloomberg, my grandparents. I bend down and find a stone to place, a Jewish custom that started when graves were merely mounds of stones. Visitors added stones to the mound to show that they'll never finish building a monument to the deceased. It also serves as a reminder to others of all the visits to the grave. I imagine myself in the coming years visiting my sister at this plot, bringing tulips, placing stone after stone.

I read Nana and Papa's plaques. Their names are in capital

letters, with their Hebrew names inscribed underneath, "Loving Husband, Father, Grandfather, Great-Grandfather." "Loving Wife, Mother, Grandmother, Great-Grandmother." Reading the dates they were born and died, I calculate that Elizabeth will live only half the time our grandparents did.

Jake looks around, unsatisfied. "I want something more private," he says. "Big enough for all the Gordons." Although the cemetery has the beauty of a country park, its bushes and trees are out in the open; they do not enclose the space where my grandparents lie. Anyone can walk among the graves.

"Follow me," says Ira, and leads us to a pond. "This is our estate section." Manicured shrubs and trees surround well-tended family plots. It's just the beginning of spring, and some of the azaleas are flowering. The estates are like small private rooms, some with benches bearing the family name. Ira shows us an available private plot with eight graves.

Jake nods. "This is more like it."

"It's lovely, but we don't want Elizabeth to be alone," I say. "That's the point."

"Why not just move your grandparents here?" Jake asks. "Ira?"

My jaw drops. I haven't thought of that.

"Absolutely," Ira says. This is what Jake wants to hear, and, apparently, money is no object.

If my parents and grandparents are now to be buried with Elizabeth, Jake, and the kids, there won't be room for me. While I am grateful to Jake for accommodating my mother's wishes, he never asks how I feel. I am too stunned to argue that these are *my* grandparents and parents, not, technically, his.

"Send the paperwork to my office. Let's move them right away," he says.

Elizabeth will have a water view, I tell myself. It will be a pleasant, private place for Brooke and Lauren to visit her. Beautiful and private, like she is. My parents will be with her when they die, and, most important, this arrangement gives the living a morsel of peace.

On the way home, I call my mother and explain to her about moving the graves.

"Oh my God, that's wonderful," she says.

"I'll take you and Daddy tomorrow so you can see the location. Location, location—that's what Jake wanted. There are some papers you have to sign."

"My hero," my mother says. "I can't thank him enough."

"What about me?" I ask. "This means my whole family is buried with Elizabeth and the Gordons."

"Sweetheart, let's get through this for now," my mother tries to assure me. "Nothing has to be etched in stone."

"I know. I'm just upset."

If I stay married to Richard, he would never agree to be buried in or even near a Gordon plot, and I can't say I blame him. Richard would want a different cemetery altogether. I nearly laugh to realize that Jake has extended my marital conflict into the afterlife.

Chapter Twenty-Five

———

*T*he next day, I visit Elizabeth to have the talk, which I
have decided to do alone after all. It's midmorning, and
quiet in her bedroom. I switch off the TV and position myself
on the bed so she can see my lips move.

"We have to talk about how things might not work out the
way we want," I say, and she understands that I'm trying to talk
about dying.

"I told Jake to marry someone who will be good to the
kids," she says.

"No one will ever replace you." I say.

I cringe to think how we believed, or pretended to believe,
that Elizabeth would beat the odds and be a miracle. How naive
that I once thought bad things happen to other people. And
now my family has been humbled in the most devastating way.

"That's all I want us to say," Elizabeth tells me. "I know
what you're trying to do, but I can't have this talk. From the
day I got that fax, it's all been one big worry, treatment to
treatment, test to test. It's been tough to live my life like that."

"You are beautiful and so brave. I love you," I say. I take
her hands in mine. Elizabeth no longer weeps about not seeing
her kids grow, no longer rails against the unfairness of her life
being cut short. The rest of us are still pained, but for Eliza-

beth, now there is only this quiet room, perfumed by flowers, and whatever comes next. Illness has taught her what she can and can't control.

The next afternoon, Rabbi Goldberg visits. He sits in the chair that has remained at Elizabeth's bedside for weeks, dressed in a suit, his beard neatly clipped, hands folded in his lap. I park myself at the edge of the bed like a chaperone and wonder how many house calls like this he makes in a week. Two or three?

Elizabeth lies regally under the covers. I am amazed at her grace in receiving this distinguished visitor at her bedside.

"Hi, Rabbi," she says, as if speaking over headphones. "How are your children?"

"My son is studying for his bar mitzvah."

"He's already that old?" she asks.

When he reciprocates with the same question, she tells him that Brooke and Lauren are doing well in school. She tells him how much she enjoys his services at the temple, especially his provocative sermons during the High Holy Days. The rabbi accepts the compliment politely. Then they discuss the weather and she thanks him for coming to see her. He senses that she doesn't want to talk about death, and he doesn't push her. But I want her to have the chance to ask him questions about death, afterlife, angels—anything. So I push.

"Elizabeth, do you want to ask the rabbi what the Jewish religion says about—"

"Nope," she says, straightening her posture.

Rabbi Goldberg stands and recites the ritual prayer of confession, Vidui, in Hebrew. He asks God to forgive my sister any sins she may have committed in her lifetime, a Jewish death rite. He blesses her and kisses her on the cheek.

I walk him to the door.

"I know Elizabeth appreciates your visit," I say, and we embrace.

"God bless you," he says, and walks to his car.

The next night, Jake asks to meet me at the bar at Aquitaine. We drink medicinally, the same way we take Ativan or Ambien every night to sleep. Jake leans in; he's here with a purpose.

"It's only a matter of days—or a week," Jake says.

"What have you said to the kids?" I ask.

"That she's dying," he says. He takes a swig of iced Grey Goose. "I don't want Richard sitting with the family at the funeral."

"I cannot respect that wish," I say, sitting taller on the leather barstool. "I deserve to have Richard with me."

"You're separated. Think of the message it sends to our guests," Jake says.

"We're still married. Is that the message you're worried about?"

"I won't speak to him. His presence will upset my kids. You'll cause a scene—"

"Of course he upsets your kids. You badmouth Richard to Brooke and Lauren all the time."

"Elizabeth doesn't want him there, and you know it."

"You have it all wrong, Jake. She's forgiven him. She loves me."

"He's not part of *us*," Jake persists. "He doesn't belong in this family."

I shake my head and take a gulp of wine. "He won't go near you, don't worry." It's as if Jake can be sure of his place in the family only if Richard is excluded.

Jake downs the rest of his drink. He pulls out his wallet and slaps down two $20 bills. He purses his lips tightly, as if to prevent himself from saying something he may later regret.

"I agree that Richard's behavior has been upsetting," I say. "He's hurt Elizabeth, he's offended you. But you have given it right back to him every time," I say.

"I can't listen to this," he says.

"You can't make me feel guilty just for being married to him."

"I have to go," Jake says. "Tell Richard to keep his distance."

⟨⟨⟨⟨

FOR THREE DAYS, Elizabeth drifts into and out of sleep. The fourth morning is the day that hospice has prepared us for, when Elizabeth no longer acknowledges me. The night nurse, Kathy, tells me to summon David in New York because it's time. They control her morphine drip. I stay at my sister's bed all day and at 6:00 p.m. tell Jake that I'll be back in an hour. I rush home to feed Alexandra and the dogs.

"Take your time," Jake says. "I need to be alone with Elizabeth. I promise I'll call you if anything seems imminent."

I prepare dinner but can't eat. I open my book but can't concentrate to read. I think about Elizabeth, barely conscious, her legs stiff like rails, her panting. I turn on the TV, but nothing distracts me. I want to be with my sister.

I check in with Jake at midnight. "Nothing's changed," he says.

"I want to come over," I say.

"I told you, I'll call you when it's time," he says.

Just two hours later, the phone rings. I grab it.

"Hello," I say, too loudly.

"I'm sorry, she's gone. Will you call your parents?" Jake asks.

Pain pierces my heart. "What? You waited?" I'm furious that he didn't call sooner. I wanted to be there, for us all to experience it together, to have closure.

I drag myself into Alexandra's room, sit on the side of her bed, and kiss her awake. She looks at me, and she knows. We embrace for what feels like three long minutes.

AS SOON AS I step into Elizabeth's darkened room, where I have spent so many of my days and nights, I feel the difference, the absence of life. Elizabeth's body is there, but not her presence. I turn on the lamp and see her gray-cast skin. Her arm is limp. Her forehead, when I kiss it, is already cold.

Alexandra, David, and I huddle.

"My poor baby," my mother says, sobbing.

"My Elizabeth," my father cries.

My parents bend down and kiss their daughter. They can't stop touching her, and my heart aches for them. My father speaks as if in a private language, his voice muffled and caressing, inaudible to the rest of us. Brooke and Lauren are stiff, wincing, following every movement with their eyes. When I hug them, they pull away and retreat to the bedrooms, quiet and stricken. Their biggest fears have become a brutal reality. Right now everything hurts, and they just want to be alone.

Jake paces the hallway, avoiding everyone. How dare he not allow us the opportunity to be with her when she died?

I confront him in the hallway. "How dare you not call me! You *promised*."

"I didn't think the kids could handle screaming or crying," he says. "She died peacefully, with us."

"Hurtful," I say, and walk back in the bedroom.

I remain with Elizabeth for an hour, until the undertaker arrives to transport her to the funeral home. In the Jewish religion, the belief is that the soul does not depart the body until it is buried, and that there should always be someone with the body until the funeral. This person, known as a Shomer, or honor guard, will remain with my sister and pray for her soul. I never appreciated the tradition until now. I can't imagine Elizabeth being alone all night in a strange, cold place.

When they carry my sister out, I make sure that she is placed in the hearse respectfully. We are all there, with nothing to say.

An hour later, Alexandra and I go home. I put my daughter back to bed, and at 8:00 a.m. I phone Richard.

"My sister died," I say. I can hear my own exhaustion.

"I'll be right there," he says.

Elizabeth's life is over. I am still alive.

Chapter Twenty-Six

———

When Richard arrives, I try to nap, dozing for an hour. The phone rings constantly, and Richard answers. I can't bear to speak to anyone.

Later, Richard goes in to the office and Alexandra and I meet my family and the rabbi at the Gordons', all stillness and silence in Elizabeth's house. I still can't believe this is happening. I sit alone at the kitchen counter with my laptop and compose Elizabeth's obituary for the *Boston Globe* and *Jewish Advocate*.

Nearby, Lauren paces, wearing her pink Red Sox cap low like her father, covering her swollen eyes. My father can't stop sighing. David is a pale ghost. Whenever Jake walks by, my stomach constricts with tension. Did he hold her hand when she took her last breath? Did he wake the kids or let them sleep? In the end, Jake excluded us, Elizabeth's family of origin, for a definition of family just like Richard's. This hypocrisy enrages me. I force myself to keep tapping the keys, knowing that I will never again be the same person.

Rabbi Goldberg helps us choreograph the funeral, to decide who will speak, in what order. He asks detailed questions about Elizabeth for his eulogy. I praise her inner strength and maternal fierceness. How she lobbied for nut-free tables at school lunches and nut-free cakes for birthday parties to protect Brooke and her classmates with peanut allergies. I describe a love of different cultures that Elizabeth was just beginning to cultivate. The year before she got sick, she and Jake traveled in Europe, and she couldn't stop raving about Italy, the Vatican, and Tuscan wine. In Paris it was the lure of the Eiffel Tower, the fashion, and eating the creamiest brie. "It's the only reliable way to know other people," Elizabeth had said, "to see them in their own environment." I had coached her in French before her trip. "*Répétez après moi,*" I said. "*Je voudrais un crossaint, s'il vous plaît.*" With Italian, she was on her own.

I tell Rabbi Goldberg that Elizabeth was a devoted wife, beyond loyal. That she and I wanted to share as much of our lives as we could. I wail that none of this was supposed to happen. Elizabeth was never supposed to die at forty-six.

He takes detailed notes before interviewing my parents, Jake, and my brother.

That evening, Alexandra and I are home when Richard returns, our eyes red from crying. "I brought dinner," he says, giving us each a hug. "So terrible." Terrible was when I found out the diagnosis, terrible was watching my sister suffer and decline. That she died isn't terrible—it's unthinkable.

"Brooke and Lauren . . . ," I say, trailing off. The children's loss is something that I know Richard can empathize with.

"Children should never have to lose their mother," he says. It's the first time he has ever expressed sympathy for Elizabeth's kids. He seems sincere. But he could just as well be speaking for himself. Alexandra wraps her arms around my waist.

"What else can I do?" Richard asks, plating grilled steaks and asparagus from Mastro's—a nice touch. I sit with Richard and Alexandra, but I can manage only a few bites. I pull the cork on a bottle of cabernet and pour.

"Will you handle calling Harrison and your sisters about the funeral?" I ask, and he does so right after dinner. I hear Richard dial his son, who will take the first shuttle up from New York. Then he calls each of his sisters to say that Elizabeth has passed away. I can't stand those words. Passed away? Passing what? Away where? I fume at Richard's language but concede that there's no easy way to say someone has died. What really angers me is not the words but the fact that she's not coming back. For the first of many times, I close my eyes and fix Elizabeth in my mind so that I'll never forget her. But instead of birthdays and celebrations, I remember only chemo and radiation, her hair falling out, her wide, childlike eyes.

When Richard asks to stay over, I say yes. We can travel to the funeral together. As a precaution, he arrived with his suit in the car.

After dinner, Richard tidies the kitchen, slots dishes in the dishwasher. He attempts to soothe me in bed, but I lie on my back, hollowed, trying to conjure up Elizabeth.

I travel through memories of her and me as young mothers, our walks around the reservoir, birthday celebrations, our daily conversations—what they say flashes before your eyes when you die. Instead, my sister's life flashes before my eyes when *she* dies. It's an aspect of her death that, even though I knew it was coming, I didn't fully face: that part of me would also have to die. The night lasts forever, but then morning, the rest of my life, comes too soon.

I open one eye on the chilly April sunlight, hearing the clicks and chirps of birds in the early dawn. I must get up to bury my sister, but I'm immobile with despair.

I gather strength, walk into the bathroom, and see the mirror. I summon Elizabeth's presence to fill the space around me. I tell her how much I miss her already, and that, although we never managed to talk about her funeral when she was sick, hundreds of people in our community today will mourn her. David's friends from New York are traveling as I speak, along with my parents' friends, and Richard's, and mine, many of these circles overlapping, their addresses stretching to Florida.

I wake Richard and Alexandra and make a cup of coffee downstairs. Alexandra eats Special K, and Richard downs a glass of orange juice. On autopilot, we put on our black suits and drive five minutes to the funeral at Congregation Shalom Alechem.

We are ushered into the private, gold-carpeted, walnut-paneled chapel in the temple. In attendance: Jake, Brooke, and Lauren; my parents; David, Jill, Justin, and Brittany; Richard, Harrison, Alexandra, and me. An uneasy silence pervades the chapel, broken by my mother's sudden sobs. My father's arm hangs limply on her shoulder, his face stricken with grief. We find our seats.

The Gordons are seated in front of us. Brooke and Lauren gaze at the floor. Jake turns and, to my disbelief, catches Richard's eye. "Happy?" he mouths.

Richard looks at me and whispers, "Do you see this?"

"Not now," I say.

Justin and Brittany sit on either side of David to our right, each hanging on to their dad. The children are old enough to act somber but young enough that they are still distracted by curiosity; their heads are on swivels. Jill sits next to Justin and directs his attention forward.

Aunts and uncles, too, file into the private chapel, as well as my cousins, whom I see about twice a year, and both of Jake's brothers and his parents. Twenty of us. We sit on wooden folding chairs, facing each other, waiting. Unlike other funerals, we take no visitors.

Richard reaches for my hand. I try to say with my eyes that I am grateful he is here. Despite what I told Jake, I struggled with whether I would dishonor Elizabeth by bringing Richard to her funeral, but I do not regret my decision.

Jake's reaction to Richard also bothers me less than I would have thought. Ten days ago, he ran twenty-six miles in less than three hours, a photo of his wife taped to his jersey, but Elizabeth only resented it.

Rabbi Goldberg enters the chapel fringed with a tallit. He's used to presiding over funerals and comforting families, but less often someone so young. Listening to the rabbi review the details of the service, I feel embraced to have him on our mourning path.

As the private service is about to begin, I obsess about Elizabeth's final moments. How I long to ask my sister about the manner in which Jake cared for her in her lonely time of need. I even go so far as to rehearse how I would ask about it, and then I gasp, realizing she isn't here.

Richard clears his throat. He motions that the rabbi needs my attention. Indeed, the rabbi is standing in front of me with black ribbons trickling from his fist. Rabbi Goldberg helps Jake, in front of me, fasten one to his blazer. Three-inch black ribbons symbolize the traditional rending of one's clothing to show bereavement. In Orthodox law, you are supposed to tear part of your clothing and wear that same garment for the next seven days. As suburban conservative Jews, however, we tear the black ribbons and wear them during the seven days we sit shiva.

Rabbi Goldberg calls the names of those of us seated behind the front rows. We are recognized because of our proximity to the deceased: we are her first-degree relatives. Elizabeth's husband, Elizabeth's daughters, Elizabeth's mother, father, brother, and sister. I receive a black ribbon. Richard does not. The ribbons identify those of us whose grief is the sharpest, who will remember the longest. Religion finally answers the question that I have been grappling with, honoring the distinctions of family that Elizabeth and I held most dear.

"Feel blessed that you had each other," the rabbi says when he fastens my ribbon. His gesture feels nothing short of holy. My mourning period has officially begun, and I doubt it will ever be over.

The rabbi chants a short prayer. I tear the ribbon.

Elizabeth's body lies in the next room. At the casket, I ask how it feels to be shut up in a wooden box. I ask when she's coming back, despite myself. As close as I was to my grandparents, when they died I was not compelled to comfort their cold bodies; they had lived full lives. It's obvious that my mind cannot yet make sense of my young sister being dead.

When it's time to proceed into the main sanctuary, where we will have the public memorial, I put on my sunglasses. Richard takes my hand, and Jake sneers as we stand there, waiting for our family to gather, as if we're some kind of affront. Maybe now that he's lost Elizabeth, Jake will begrudge us our marriage even more intensely, warts and all. With my free hand, I reach for Alexandra and pull her close.

To begin the funeral, the twenty of us linked by blood and marriage will process from the chapel into the main sanctuary. Behind the surviving Gordons and my parents, I will walk with Richard, Alexandra, and Harrison. The service will begin with Elizabeth's favorite Hebrew song. When the cantor takes his seat on the bimah, the rabbi will eulogize my sister. Then Brooke, David, and I will be called upon to speak.

The main sanctuary holds nine hundred people, and there isn't an empty seat. The surreality of my sister's death persists, and I go numb. I avoid eye contact with all of my extended family, friends, community, and business associates—until I see the dark frames and endearing jug-handle ears of Dr. Hamilton, the man Elizabeth spent so much of her time with.

We take our seats in the second row behind my parents, Jake, Brooke, and Lauren. I plaster myself between Richard and Alexandra, hip to hip. "I love you, Mommy," Alexandra whispers, and I kiss her on the forehead.

The cantor commences the service from the back of the sanctuary with the Hebrew "*L'dor V'dor,*" "Generation to Generation." His voice is rich, his chanting sure, but I already feel robbed. If this song about life passing peacefully from generation to generation were accurate, my parents wouldn't be burying their daughter and Elizabeth's children wouldn't still be children.

The rabbi stands, commanding attention with his silence. He includes a detail in his eulogy about the intimacy of Elizabeth's marriage to Jake. "It was as if when she breathed in, he breathed out."

When the rabbi finishes, David, Brooke, and I approach the bimah together. I walk deliberately in my black heels, aware of everyone's eyes. I climb three stairs to the pulpit and gather my strength. I stare into the audience, speaking in a steady, somber voice.

"Hello, everyone. Thank you all for coming. Your presence here today, your support throughout the past two and a half years, your cards, flowers, gifts, calls, lunches, dinners, and, most important, your heartfelt compassion for our family during this most sorrowful time, have been invaluable. My sister, Elizabeth, and I had a special bond. I loved her deeply from the day she was born to the day she died." I pause, and bring a tissue to my eye.

"We each had only one sister." I go on to describe our childhood, Elizabeth's education, her love of family, our symbiosis, and our lack of sibling rivalry.

Before this vast audience, I then address my parents, risking that I will cry: "Mom and Dad, I'm so sorry you have lost Elizabeth. She was my sister, but she was your baby. She had so much more than half a life to give. In our hearts, she lives forever."

I sit on the bimah. Next, David gives his remarks. He describes Caribbean vacations with Elizabeth, how she hammered him for every detail about his children, how he will miss her terribly. "Because of Elizabeth and Samantha, I have three mothers," David says, and sits.

My niece, Brooke, who just turned seventeen, now stands. In her black suit and stilettos, she's suddenly a young adult, so different from the ninth-grade adolescent whose mother was diagnosed. Brooke's shiny black hair blends with her suit; I recognize for the first time her womanly build. Lauren resembles Elizabeth much more, physically, than her sister does with her big blue eyes and light brown hair. But as Brooke delivers her eulogy, I recognize so much of Elizabeth's own sensitivity and loyalty.

I glance over at Lauren and see that she's hanging on to her sister's every word. She wonders who will help her pack for college, who will plan her wedding. Brooke begins to cry, but I don't, even though her speech is raw and painful.

On the bimah, facing everyone in the synagogue, I feel my skin stinging, like Tom Tam is putting pins in my arms. From my vantage, it's all tears and tissues. Mascara streaks Robin's and Jane's faces. The men cry into their handkerchiefs or simply stare off, looking grave and bewildered. Not even God will say why this happened.

When the funeral ends, I again hide behind my sunglasses.

We are ushered into three black limos for the trip to the cemetery. Richard, Alexandra, Harrison, and I ride with my aunt and uncle, my father's sister and her husband. There's a police escort and, following our limos, at least a hundred cars holding friends, family, locals, and business partners.

The weather is sunny and crisp, a beautiful day for anything but a funeral, with smells of freshly cut grass and new buds of spring. Elizabeth's grave has already been hollowed, and her casket fits, suspended, inside. My parents sit on folding chairs next to the mountain of dirt that will close her in.

A crowd of three hundred gathers. The rabbi leads us in the Mourner's Kaddish, the ritual prayer for the dead. My eyes close as the casket is lowered. When it's in place, family and friends shovel some of the dirt, a final ritual. Hearing clods of soil strike my sister's casket makes me cringe, but the tradition is a great sign of respect signaling that we haven't left our loved one's burial to strangers. I lower a shovelful of dirt onto the casket, already obscured from view. When it's Richard's turn, Jake scoffs—Brooke and Lauren flinch. I can see that they've got Richard all wrong this time; my husband derives no joy from throwing dirt on my sister's grave. I now regret having participated in my family's hardening against Richard.

When the casket is fully covered, we retreat to our limos.

My aunt and uncle try to make conversation on our ride to the Gordons' from the cemetery. My uncle tells me that my eulogy was beautiful; my aunt says all sisters should be envious of my bond with Elizabeth. I appreciate their kind words, but they don't console me. I am chilled to the bone.

At the Gordons', we will sit shiva for the next seven days and nights. We will receive visitors and mourn the loss of our daughter, mother, sister, and wife. The caterers are at work in the kitchen. Richard is by my side. Elizabeth is dead.

"Come," I say to Richard, taking his hand and weaving through the crowd. Richard stops short, spotting Jake by the bar in the den.

"What the hell? You want me to talk to him? You know he doesn't want that."

"Just offer your condolences," I say, and something in my eyes convinces Richard that it will be okay.

"I'm sorry about Elizabeth," Richard says, when we catch Jake by surprise. He extends his hand. Of course, it's the proper thing to do, to pay respect, but my face flushes, as I now think it might have been the wrong move.

To my relief, the men shake hands. Jake nods but doesn't speak. I rub their shoulders and stand in the space between my husband and my sister's husband.

The house fills with friends attached in different ways to all of us; Alexandra, Brooke, and Lauren receive twenty-five teenagers upstairs. When a young person dies, it is a different shiva than if the deceased was an older person. The latter can be a type of celebration, but for Elizabeth's shiva, there's nothing we can do to erase the sense of injustice.

I could sit with Jake in the den, but I don't because Richard is with me. I could receive guests on the living room sofa next to my parents, or beside my brother at the kitchen table. I realize that I feel uncomfortable sitting at all, staking my flag anywhere in this family dysfunction. Richard and I will need to carve out our own space. In the meantime, I stand in the kitchen, accepting food from visitors and arranging it on the buffet: corned beef, turkey, chopped liver, and other traditional dishes.

"There are no words, Samantha," my friend Lynne says with glassy eyes.

I can tell that Richard is uncomfortable by the way he fiddles with his watch, but I shelve his particular feelings for now. Harrison is here; I whisper to him that he should keep his dad company. My focus then shifts to Alexandra and how she's faring upstairs. I check in on her and see a lot of teenage hugging, giving way to nervous laughter.

Back downstairs, my friends lavish me with memories of Elizabeth and me moving through the community, spotted at the gym, the reservoir, the hair salon, walking through a parking lot, and Whole Foods. Their stories remind me how lucky we were to have each other. Despite the problems our relationship caused in my marriage, I wouldn't trade a second that I had with Elizabeth. She and I packed the memories of a long life into a short one. I just wish the rift with Richard had been repaired before she died.

I find my parents, put my hands on their shoulders, and listen to their friends' thoughtful condolences. "It should never be this way," our solemn, silver-haired second cousin tells my mother, and an old friend from Gloucester takes her hand. "Sorry, Rachel. I remember Elizabeth's sweetness whenever she came to play with my Gail." My mother weeps freshly at every comment, but my father sits with a revived strength, wearing his *chai*. "Cry now," he tells my mother. "Soon you will have to be strong."

For the next week, the Gordons' is filled with mourners and all their corned beef, brisket, and deli; Elizabeth's death impacts so many people, even acquaintances. Richard attends for several hours each day, preferring sundown, when the rabbi leads the shiva service. Just like at temple, the Hebrew prayers are more meaningful to Richard than to me, even when they're for my sister. In his own way, he pays respect to Elizabeth. At night he returns to his South End apartment when I want to be alone with Elizabeth's memory and not have any interference.

At the end of shiva on the seventh day, seven designated mourners—Jake, Brooke, Lauren, David, my mother, my father, and I—walk around the block with the rabbi to signify shiva's conclusion. I prepare myself for the Gordon house to transform again: where it used to be four loved ones, it will be three. I didn't realize how much space her cancer took up physically, in her body and in her home as well. Now that Elizabeth is gone, so, too, are the nurses, the medications, everything surrounding her illness, including my purpose.

Later, in bed, when I have finally released shiva's constant stream of mourners making appearances, tears wet my face. I move to the floor, lying in complete surrender on my back, letting go of everything and feeling the wood beams support me. I have no imagination for it, but if my old life has ended, what new one will begin?

⸻

A MONTH LATER, I sit at Elizabeth's kitchen counter to finish writing acknowledgments and thank-you notes. Hundreds of donations were made to Dana Farber, Mass General, and Beth Israel Deaconess hospitals in Elizabeth's memory. I intend to personalize each appreciation.

Each time, it feels unnatural to be in Elizabeth's home without her, but I'm there to absorb any part left of my sister. Her photos, her perfume, the clothes still hanging in her closet. I write and write.

When I need an address, I search through the invitation list Elizabeth made up for Brooke's bat mitzvah, but it's not alphabetical, and hunting for a particular address can be a chore. When I first found the list and was looking for Weinberg, my sister's loopy, legible handwriting stalled my heart.

My name is first on the page. "Mr. and Mrs. Richard Freeman." No matter how she and Jake felt, Elizabeth always had us at the top of her list.

Chapter Twenty-Seven

———

*R*ichard continues to live in Boston, and we date on the weekends. He brings me flowers, takes me to our favorite restaurants, and is respectful of the time I still spend at the Gordons'. I think often of Yasmine and the advice she gave me in St. Barts. I can see how Richard and I could reconcile, but somehow I am fearful to commit.

In June, the kids finish school and ready themselves for summer plans. Jake immerses himself in work. Kathy, the red-headed nurse, has stayed on at Jake's request and runs the household five days a week. I can't imagine what he's paying her, but it's money well spent. Now Brooke and Lauren have someone else to rely on when their father hides behind his job.

During the week, Alexandra and I spend our time at the house I'm still calling Elizabeth's, making dinners and entertaining my parents. We attend school events together, movies, dine out, all of us still grieving her, trying to restore life to Brooke's and Lauren's vacant faces. Whenever their friends visit, the teens loosen up—loud music behind a locked door—and it makes me worry less. A few of Elizabeth's friends continue stopping by for a while with the occasional tenderloin or roast chicken, but little by little they return to their own lives, putting something new in that space that once held us and Elizabeth.

Meanwhile, because what Richard and I have going on in secret looks like a stalemate to friends, others are constantly trying to fix me up on a date. I'm torn about whether to accept these offers, but I eventually relent in order to gain more clarity on my situation.

"Steve is a really good guy," Robin said to me. "He belongs to Shalom Alechem, so that's a good sign. You should at least meet."

Steve takes me to Stella, a new restaurant in the South End with all-white decor and a South Beach vibe. I worry about the proximity of the restaurant to Richard's loft—I'm not sure how I would explain the date, since Richard and I are on the mend, and whatever I said, there's no guarantee that Richard would believe me—but I relax by imagining Richard with his newspaper and Wayfarers on the shores of Nantucket.

At six feet, Steve is a four-handicap golfer with an athletic build, divorced. I try not to pay attention to how fast he drinks or the way he splits each martini olive with his teeth. He's not a big traveler and doesn't collect art. Turns out the only thing we have in common, besides being Jewish, are our teenage daughters.

By our third and last date, our daughters are still the only topic of conversation. His girls are only thirteen months apart, and while the similarity in age generally makes them close, the downside is that they fight a lot—viciously. Now that Steve and his wife have separated, though, the daughters are sweet to each other. They've sided with their mother in the breakup, and, according to Steve, he's the focus of their anger.

"I've always done right by them," he insists, rolling an olive between his teeth. "Been a good provider, remembered birthdays, all those soccer games."

"Even people in love can't always make it work," I say.

Steve seems genuinely mystified about why his wife wants a divorce. "Maybe it's more about her and what she wants for her life. Getting a divorce doesn't make you a bad guy," I tell him.

But I can already see he's not for me, either. In my head, I'm explaining it all to Elizabeth: he's too reserved, emotionally closed off, the kind of partner who numbs out when you need him. The facts that he's not that good-looking and obviously not over his wife are nails in the coffin. What the hell was Robin thinking?

The next time a friend tries to fix me up with a "hot divorced guy" with whom I "have a lot in common," I decline.

-≪≪≪-

AFTER LEAVING THE office one night that summer, Richard stops at our house in Wellesley. I'm upstairs and hear the dogs barking. I meet him in the hallway and find him wearing a boyish grin.

"You know what? I miss you in my bed," Richard says, and laughs. "Come to Nantucket. We can have sex every night."

"Every night?" I say, laughing back.

"It will help," he says.

"With my grief or with the marriage?" I ask.

"Both," he says, and pulls me into his arms.

I'm concerned about leaving Brooke and Lauren, of treating myself to any time on Nantucket, even though Jake has rented another house in New Seabury. I know I'd be welcome, but they are their own family now. When I decide to take Richard up on his offer, I feel unexpected excitement. Although Richard left me two seasons ago on Nantucket over the beets, I'm hoping the island might work its good magic on us once again.

Once, in a Japanese antique store on Charles Street, I came across a magnificent blue-and-white bowl that had been restored with a gold lacquer. When I asked the owner, she described the Japanese art of *kintsugi*, repairing broken pottery with fine metals: platinum, silver, or gold. As a philosophy, *kintsugi* doesn't reject breakage and repair but embraces those experiences as the history of the object. A *kintsugi* bowl can never be perfect but can possess great beauty. If only I had known about it when I broke a piece of my grandmother's china, I could have it repaired the dish, incorporating my mistake into the history and beauty of the piece, rather than feeling guilty and disappointed as I swept up the shards. Now, instead of perfection, *kintsugi* became the test for my marriage: Could Richard and I make repairs and live with the cracks?

The day we arrive on Nantucket, we plant ourselves on a Main Street bench to people-watch. Women stroll by, chatting and drinking lattes, some carrying Nantucket lightship baskets as purses. I've wanted one for years. The ones I like are not really baskets but handbags or pocketbooks specific to Nantucket. The baskets are handmade and firm, with a top made of whalebone or scrimshaw, and a handle. On-island, these bags can sell for thousands of dollars, depending on the weaver, the vintage, and the amount of ivory on the bag. I have begun to admire the style and workmanship of the craft, similar to the way one admires a coveted Hermès Kelly or Birkin bag.

For an hour, Richard and I stroll the brick sidewalks in town and eventually stop in at Main Street Real Estate. Richard loves to talk shop with Greg, the top real estate broker on Nantucket, always looking for places to bank some of our cash.

"Welcome back," Greg says. "Having the year of your lives?" He doesn't know about my sister. Greg and Richard shake hands.

"Any big fish?" Richard asks.

"Housing is so hot right now, everywhere. Prices are nuts," Greg says.

"When I think a property is overpriced one season, it looks like a deal the next," Richard says, and chuckles.

"If I see anything that would interest you, I'll give you a shout," Greg says.

Seeing my husband in his element, confident and flush with success, always makes me compare what I'm seeing with the twenty-one-year-old Richard has told me about, the young man who lost his father while struggling to finish and finance his last year of college. Richard had no choice but to earn money—no time to mourn. It helps me realize the luxury and privileges that marriage to Richard has afforded me, right down to my grief.

"I feel like walking the docks," Richard says. "You?"

"Mind if I wait for you here?" It's more Richard's thing to admire multimillion-dollar yachts. I stay in town, content to browse antique stores and clothing boutiques.

Just as I've noticed a new art gallery, a female passerby overpowers me with her perfume. I recognize the jasmine-apple fragrance as See By Chloé, Elizabeth's favorite. It stops me in my tracks.

Eventually a steady stream of people forces me along: parents pushing double-wide carriages, families eating ice cream, husbands and wives holding hands. I'm near the Hub, a revolving door for newspapers and coffee. On the message board outside, I scan notices offering babysitting and house painting. One particular flyer catches my eye: the Nantucket Writer's Workshop, "a safe place to write through dangerous feelings."

My friend Lynne, to whom I have not yet had a chance to say hello, interrupts my interest. "You're here!" she says, and gives me a hug. "Sorry, I'm sweaty. I just walked five miles." Perspiration beads on her chest. We find spaces on a bench and sit down.

"How are you doing?" she asks. "I haven't seen you since . . ."

"Not bad," I say.

Lynne squeezes my hand. "I'm meeting a friend for lunch. Want to join?"

"Thanks, another time. Richard's on the docks."

"Okay. You give me a call," Lynne says, then puts her earbuds back in, continuing her athletic walk.

For the Fourth of July, Richard and I are invited to the whaling museum for dinner and fireworks. I stand on the roof deck in my white jeans and a long, crocheted sweater from Gypsy, my favorite Nantucket boutique. I sip champagne overlooking town, watch teenagers eat pizza from Stubbys, and spy on families standing in line for artisanal ice cream. The streets are congested with red and yellow Wranglers, MINI Cooper convertibles, bicycles, and, as always, Stop & Shop grocery trucks lined up for the ferry. It's one of the first times since Elizabeth died that I don't feel guilty for being alive.

The sun sets, streaking the sky with red, orange, and magenta. Throngs of people crowd the roof, and I spot my friend Joyce. She approaches me on long, shapely legs, leading another woman I've never met.

"I didn't know you were here!" Joyce says. "This is my sister, Wendy." I like this shorter, plainer version of Joyce and smile against my tears. *My sister.* Another blast. I'll never introduce my sister again. She belongs to pictures, the past tense.

Wendy extends her hand and smiles, but I'm overcome and walk away abruptly. Poor Joyce. She's a summer friend and didn't know my sister. She couldn't have had any idea that she was ripping a scab off a wound.

274 | SONDRA HELENE

The next morning, Lynne calls.

"You need some cheering up. I can tell," she says. Of all my friends, Lynne is one of the few who have walked in my shoes. She lost a brother to colon cancer. When Elizabeth was diagnosed, she was the first person I called.

"I should keep my mind occupied," I say. "It's not healthy to be sad all day." I think of Richard and his work, my mother and her bridge. I even gain a flicker of understanding about Jake and his damn marathon.

Lynne tells me that lightship basket classes are starting next week and suggests that I might want to weave my own bag. "Do you want to take the class with me?" she asks. "Usually I go alone. You're the only friend I'd take. Frankly, I don't want the secret to get out," she says, and laughs.

"I'll make a cocktail purse," I say, excited to try something new.

Soon, five mornings a week, Lynne and I go to Tim Peterson's basket-weaving shop. Six women sit in Tim's basement every morning at a long wooden table, each working on her own project at her own pace. People chat while they weave, filling the air with families and activities, a who's who of Nantucket: last night's dining experience at the Pearl, whose children are working and where, and whether Surfside or Cisco Beach is best for guests. Once in a while, someone brings up a sister or a nephew or mentions that a mother is visiting, but the talk is mostly about nuclear family and friends. I don't join in the conversation or say much of anything. Before Elizabeth got sick, did I spend too many hours focusing on extended family and neglect my own husband?

In many ways, Lynne is the best person I could be with. She doesn't mention Elizabeth unless I do, and then she listens with sincere attention. She says little in response, but her manner soothes me. I've seen her cry when she mentions her brother's birthday or his children. They were close, and I know she misses his good nature and sense of humor. It saddens her that her daughters have no uncles. "I'm afraid you don't ever get rid of the pain," Lynne tells me. "You make it part of you." I know that the invitation to Tim's shop is Lynne's way of supporting me, and I am grateful.

Basket weaving, Nantucket-style, is a fairly rigorous activity. You work with a mold and manipulate cane strips. I learn that Nantucket Native Americans originally taught basket weaving to the colonial settlers. It took off with the whaling industry in the mid–nineteenth century, when the first lighthouse was built to warn ships of dangerous offshore shoals. Basket weaving was perfect for sailors, who had a lot of spare time on their hands. With Elizabeth gone, I am not exactly bored, but for the past two years my focus has been to take care of her, and now she no longer needs it. And, as much as I try, I'm too heartsick with grief to enjoy much of anything, until this.

Tim, a native Nantucketer, walks around and inspects our work. "There," he says, and points to a row about halfway up my purse. "See how the weave is crooked?" I look closely to see what he means. The cane doesn't lie correctly, and it's folded over in a funny way. It's not the kind of glaring mistake that you notice right away, but still, Tim sees it and rightfully points it out. He makes me rip out my hard-won stitches and do it over again. Backweaving, he calls it. I don't mind. It's worth the effort to produce something perfect.

In Tim's basement—surrounded by cane basket molds, and handles made of wood and precious ivory—we have become modern basket weavers. It feels like a dreamy underwater world, our own private Atlantis.

Tim takes pride in his students' work and treats us like

apprentices. We learn about reed staves and basket rims, bone knobs for handles.

"How did you get into basket weaving?" I ask.

"Weaving is part of Nantucket," Tim says. "Not to brag, but when I took it up twenty years ago, I was a natural. It relaxed me, and I could make a living at it."

"This has made my summer," I say.

"How did you decide to come?" he asks.

I will myself not to cry. I take a few steps from the table and motion that he should follow me.

"My sister died in April," I say privately to Tim. "I needed something to occupy my mind. My friend told me about this class."

"I'm very sorry," he says. "How old was she?"

"Forty-six. She had cancer."

"Can I give you a hug?" Tim puts his rugged arms around me. He smells fresh, like a clean bath towel.

"Just so you know, when things bother me or I have a problem to deal with, that's when I do my best work. Basket weaving is my escape," he says.

I take my purse as homework. My mind drifts as I weave, thinking over the decisions still in front of me. I do want the same thing Richard wants—to be a tight family, woven together like this basket. I have always wanted to include my family of origin in the weave, too. Just as every one of these strands is crucial to make my lightship basket whole, so, too, do I need every one of the people I've known and loved all my life.

But maybe the time has come to prioritize my own little family. Without the essential strands, my husband and my daughter, I am a leaky basket that loses its shape, no more connected to anyone than I was when I was born. As my fingers work, I remember some wonderful moments between Richard and me. The time we made love on an airplane to Montréal, how proud he was of me when we first went to Paris and I spoke fluent French. I remember his joy when our daughter was born, and how he held her at eye level, making sure she had all ten fingers and toes. Maybe I should have listened when Richard pushed back against attending every family and school event. I'm gripped by a desire to rip out all the twisted, misshapen parts of our marriage.

I take my basket to Tim in the morning for inspection. The tips of my fingers are sore, blistering, but I don't care. I am creating something lovely, watching it take shape from day to day, and that makes me proud and optimistic. I pull the stitching tight and weave it smooth. It takes many, many strands to complete my purse. Any less, and it would not be as strong, or watertight, or beautiful.

When I finish, at the end of July, I trim my evening bag with wooden handles and a whale carved from ivory. On the bottom, I etch my name and the date. Someday, I will hand this down to my daughter. Unlike even the costliest bags on Main Street, my basket is made and designed by me.

In August, I sign up for the writing program. Instead of relaxing at the beach or setting sail on a friend's boat, I wonder if, like my basket, I can weave words, too. The writers' studio is peaceful, located down a dirt path in Pocomo, a remote part of the island.

Sunlight streams into the cottage, and air circulates like a warm ocean breeze. Sarah, the instructor, in a denim blouse and painter's jeans, welcomes us with fresh-brewed coffee and madeleines. She's just finished her MFA and is in the midst of writing her first novel. Each morning I drive to her house in the woods and carry in my notebook and pen. Sarah leads us through meditations and writing exercises. She instructs us to write about a house—first as we see it when a young couple comes home, carrying their newborn baby. Next she tells us to write about the same house, but now someone has died in it.

I don't think there can be a more perfect writing exercise for me. Though it makes me think of Elizabeth, and how her house felt different during each stage of her illness, writing about it gives me a necessary distance. Describing how things look at these different stages of life helps me sort out my emotions. I recently saw a photo album that my mother made of Elizabeth's life in a hand-bound book covered with lace that I had given her for Hanukkah. Putting this together, I imagined, helped her process unspeakable grief. I flipped to the last photo, the "forbidden" portrait that the photographer took of Elizabeth and me at Alexandra's bat mitzvah. In class, I describe the uneasy feelings I have about some of the photos: those that catch me averting my eyes from my sister's swollen face and grinning a fake smile.

In the end, the summer's weaving and writing are the tools that unlock my grief. Nantucket does work its magic, just not in the way I expected.

Chapter Twenty-Eight

———

*O*n the island, Richard and I carry full hearts for each other all summer, but back in Boston we retreat to our separate residences. I get Alexandra ready to start school.

In September, Richard and I meet for dinner near his apartment at the Buttery, a local establishment known for delicious salads and comfort food.

"I want to make our marriage work," Richard begins.

"Outside the bubble," I say, referring to how relaxed we are on Nantucket, even how we felt in St. Barts. I don't want to have an island marriage.

"My cousin suggested we try a mediator," Richard says, wiping the corners of his mouth with his napkin. "Different than the therapists we've seen."

"A mediator?"

"He's a lawyer and a psychologist. His goal is to help people stay married."

I'm enthused to hear that the mediator is a man, because all of our therapists have been women. Maybe Richard will relate better to someone of his own sex—as the saying goes, man to man. I always thought that separating from Richard would bring me such relief that I would rush to divorce. I imagined myself dating new men, laughing, feeling sexy and free. But no one I've met interests me. To my surprise, I miss Richard. The thought of him with another woman feels tragic.

"I'll try anything," I say.

I see the relief in his face. "Even with all the shit we've been through, Samantha, I can't imagine my life without you."

As strange as this sounds, as a compliment or a declaration of love, I feel the same way. Richard isn't perfect, but he's mine. We have built a long life together. He has broadened my world through our shared hobbies and interests. We enjoy modern art, trendy restaurants, Broadway shows, sports, and travel. Before we separated, on his way home from work, he would call and ask me if I needed anything. He's a man who shows up in almost every way—just not for my family.

Richard motions to the server for the check.

We walk back to his apartment, where I parked my car. He kisses me goodbye, and his eyes flick back and forth with excitement. "I'll make the appointment," he says.

⋘

THE MEDIATOR'S NAME is Harry Broffman. The following week, Richard and I drive together to his downtown office. The office, on the third floor of a high-rise, is nothing like the swank office of my attorney, but neither is his hourly rate.

Broffman is a short, stocky white man in his fifties. "Welcome," he says, wearing a tan corduroy jacket with brown suede patches, professor-style, over a pair of jeans. His office reflects his personality: disheveled but comfortable.

"I have never stopped loving you," Richard assures me, as we sit next to each other on the worn leather sofa. I think that he means it sincerely in the moment, but a tiny part of me is also alert to his performance.

I smile in response, but now that we are actually here, I'm worried. I hope these sessions will be better and more productive than those in our past. I'm much different now than I was when we saw all the other therapists. Back then, my goal was to change Richard, uphold my values, and defend myself. Now I realize I am the only person I can change. I also understand Richard better and can see my own flaws.

"Thank you both for being here," Broffman says, sitting across from us, crossing his right leg over the left. Behind him are shelves of books about law and therapy, marriage and custody arrangements. "I've heard some of your story from Richard on the phone, so why don't you start, Samantha? Tell me why you're here."

I tell Broffman everything about us, my sister, the family issues. I talk about feelings of jealousy and resentment and the terrible grief I now have.

"I always thought my husband would accept my relationship with my family. I never examined the dynamics, how my family's behavior may have made Richard standoffish." When I look over at Richard, he seems open but anxious.

"To be honest, I'm jealous of couples who are close to each other's families, whose nieces and nephews from both sides run in and out of each other's homes. I have resented Richard for years for not having this, but I'm beginning to understand that it's not all his fault."

"Really?" Richard asks.

"How did you come to that understanding?" Broffman says.

"I do think I paid too much attention to my family, at Richard's expense," I say. "I thought he could take care of himself. I should have stood up for him, and I should have worked harder at our intimacy."

When I'm finished, Richard hugs me. It feels good to fall

on his familiar shoulder, but I don't want to fall back into the same type of marriage that made us both miserable, that I tried so desperately to leave. I don't want a marriage that is like the definition of insanity, repeating the same behavior over again but expecting a different result. Nor do I want my life to be like a depressing novel on the bargain-book shelf.

"We should come first to each other," Richard says.

"I agree," I say. I need normalcy and stability in my life right now. I need a partner who helps me become the best person I can be.

"I'm the black sheep in her family," Richard says.

"Why do you think that is?" Broffman says.

"I've been rude," Richard admits. "It felt safer to keep everyone at a distance."

"And I told my family way too much about our marriage," I say.

"Samantha, I don't want to lose you," Richard says, and chokes up.

"What do you want to gain from therapy, Richard?" Broffman asks.

"I'd like Samantha to make better boundaries with her family—"

"Wait a minute," I interrupt. "This sounds like the old Richard. This is what you said ten years ago."

"Samantha, what do you need?" Broffman asks.

"For Richard to stop treating my family like intruders. And for me to feel understood. I don't want to hide things. I want one full life, not one where I have a life with him, and a separate one with my family."

"I think it's best if I meet with you both individually at the beginning," Broffman says, to defuse the situation.

OVER TWO MONTHS, Richard and I meet with Broffman about fifteen times, together and individually. I like Broffman because he validates me, then pushes me to see Richard's perspective, and does the same with him. Richard begins to understand that asking me questions about my family can bring us closer together. He learns this is a way to support me emotionally. And Richard needs to believe that I¹m truly listening to him when he speaks, in order for him to feel valued and respected.

In the middle of mediation, Broffman writes us the following email:

> *Success will require giving up all hope of a better past. Focusing on your past (and your grievances against each other, based on past behavior) is toxic and will sabotage your efforts to have a better future.*
>
> *The part of you that wants to move forward, instead of looking back, serves your needs by seeking to heal with each other. Successful negotiations with others require empowering your Self to lead a successful negotiation within. I believe that each of you has the strength to succeed at both of these negotiations.*
>
> *When you are negotiating to find a workable, long-term compromise about your behavior—with a loved one, a business associate, or yourself—it's important to be conscious about the choices you make and to choose the stronger, more positive, healthier aspects of yourself: generosity, warmth, acceptance, courage. If you can, try to push away the other side that won't help anyone: selfishness, blind egotism, jealousy, envy, and greed. If you can do this, then hopefully your marriage can survive. But we have to focus on changing old patterns.*

As I read and reread the mediator's email, I discover lessons both simple and profound. We choose how we look at situations, and we choose how we behave.

We continue with our sessions, and Broffman tells us we have a chance at saving our marriage. But he believes that we must get my family involved for a discussion before we can rebuild our relationship.

"Honestly, I don't have the energy for that," I say, feeling exhausted.

"Then I'll do it without you," Richard says, determined.

"When you're ready, I think it will be best to contact each significant individual in Samantha's family and have a heart-to-heart," Broffman says.

"What would be the point of that?" I ask. "I can't take any more stress, and I'm not sure I want to put my parents through it."

"Relationship with boundaries," Broffman said. "I can mediate these meetings."

"I don't know if I trust what Richard will say or how he will speak to them."

"I certainly know how to talk to people," he says. "I run a business."

"Take some time to think about it. Because we want a positive result. No need to rush," Broffman says.

"My parents are in Florida anyway," I say.

In December, when Richard takes a golf trip to Cabo San Lauren, I decide to join my parents in Florida for a week with Alexandra. I think to call Jake, to invite Brooke and Lauren to come with me, and Jake says, "We'll all go. We could use the getaway." I have mixed emotions about having him along, but I think it will be good for the kids and my parents.

Jake never slowed his business dealings, not even during shiva. Stars relocations are more profitable than ever, and my brother-in-law spends money as if he has unlimited resources. I can't decide whether he's embracing false comforts or genuinely trying to make life easier for Brooke and Lauren. Jake's most recent purchase is fractional ownership in Wheels Up; the way he justified it to me is that it will make his and David's business travel faster and more exclusive. But when Jake insists on arranging for a private jet to take us to Florida, I can see that his days of flying commercial are over.

"Why not just take JetBlue?" I ask.

"This will be much cooler."

A private car waits for Alexandra and me outside on the morning of our flight, and we are driven to Hanscom Air Force Base, in nearby Bedford. Once buzzed through the gates, we meet Jake, Brooke, and Lauren at the private terminal and file onto the tarmac.

"See how much easier this is?" Jake asks, not expecting a response. I cross my arms as the wind whips my hair. It's just another splurge, his way of dealing with his grief—not unlike the way I treated myself recently to a new Chanel bag and a pair of imported gold earrings. I decide to keep my judgment in check. It's actually exciting. I know firsthand how retail therapy can help relieve loneliness. At least for a little while.

"No waiting in line, no taking your shoes off at security," Jake goes on. "We walk right onto the plane. Can you believe it, kids?"

The five of us pile in, and I have to admit that it is a beautiful plane. Beige leather seats and platters of bagels, yogurt, and fruit await us onboard.

When the pilot announces it's time for takeoff, we strap ourselves in. No flight attendants, no announcements. Just two handsome pilots in the cockpit, ready to fly us to West Palm Beach.

"Elizabeth would have enjoyed this," I admit to Jake. She loved exclusive vacations. "This would have been the perfect prelude to Vegas shows and spas."

The kids get absorbed in a movie. The older girls sit side by side, and Lauren, one seat back, slots her head between the leather seats.

Jake and I drink a second cup of coffee and remark how our teens have taken to speaking in low whispers so that we can't hear. I don't at all mind being excluded from their conversations as they get older; I'm simply grateful that they have each other.

Jake, misreading my mood, blurts something that he will never be able to take back. "Wouldn't this be nice?" he says. "Just look at the kids and us—already like family. Let's get married."

"Jake!" I laugh, and swat his arm. "You're funny."

"I'm serious. We get along so well. We've known each other since we were kids! It's actually a Jewish custom, you know, dating back to the shtetl. My grandfather, when my grandmother died, married his wife's sister. Samantha, will you marry me?"

"That would be crazy," I say. My stomach drops. "Are you serious?" Jake isn't even *that* Jewish. He rarely goes to temple, even on the High Holidays. Now he's talking to me about the shtetl? Then I remember how he took me to dinner when Elizabeth was dying, his angling to keep Richard from the funeral, and Elizabeth's insistence that Jake marry someone who's good to the kids. How am I going to enjoy my weekend now? No turning back; we're midair. I get up and pour myself another cup of coffee.

"It's not crazy; it's tradition," Jake says when I return. He grins like the kid I knew growing up on Atlantic Road, the one who always managed to come up with two cookies when he stuck his hand in the jar. But maybe Jake thinks he wants me because I remind him of Elizabeth—or, for all I know, his crazy proposal might be not even about me but about hurting Richard.

"You're not even religious!" I say, as Jake goes on and on about tribe.

"Well, forget tradition. Just think how it would make things easier."

"Make what easier?" Marrying Elizabeth's husband is not my idea of mourning.

"Look—I love Alexandra, you love Brooke and Lauren, I love your parents, and they love me," Jake says smugly.

"Number one, I'm still married to Richard. Number two, we just lost Elizabeth." I'm comfortable with Jake, yes, but more like he's a brother. It's so obvious to me that he's confusing familiarity with love.

"I know what I'm talking about," Jake says, beginning to look hurt. "Are you really signing up for more rides on Richard's bullshit merry-go-round? Sure, he's on his best behavior now, but I guarantee he's the same asshole he always was. You know what I'm beginning to think, Samantha? I hate to say this—"

"Then don't."

"But you're not nearly as savvy as I thought you were."

I'm not in love with Jake. Nor would I ever just step into my sister's life. Even if he doesn't realize it now, what he's actually proposing is a prison, a life of constant comparison and measuring up. I imagine the kids waking in the morning and seeing us in bed. No. No. No.

"I love you like a brother. But marriage?" I say.

"Think about it," he says.

"Are you still dating?" I ask, trying to change the subject. A couple of months ago, Jake was introduced to someone sweet and pretty from Providence, divorced, with two teenage boys.

"She's just someone to pass the time."

I wince. But I can't blame him. He's still a young, attractive man.

"The kids don't even know about her, do they?" I ask. "Do they even know where you go at night?"

Jake's eyes get fierce, not unlike they did the night at Aquitaine before Elizabeth died. "You have no idea what it's like. I have to get out. This is how I grieve."

"By going on dates?"

"All I talk about is Elizabeth," he says. "It works for me."

"Jake, you've really got to start being home at night. Think of the kids." It's something I've been meaning to address with him.

"They're practically in college," Jake says. "Kathy is there if they need anything. Trust me, they barely notice me gone." He changes the subject. "Have you filed for divorce?"

I pause. "Jake, I'm not getting divorced."

"What? When did Richard move back in?"

"He didn't—yet. We're seeing a mediator, someone to help us work things out."

"That's old news."

"A mediator is different," I say.

"Shit or get off the pot, Samantha. People get divorced all the time! I can name ten couples off the top of my head," he says.

"What if I don't want to?" I say softly, and close my eyes. Is Jake's scheme just some way to make everyone feel better about losing Elizabeth? Obviously, for all his business success, Jake has suffered a terrible lapse in judgment. I know that everyone in my family and community would find his proposal as strange as I do, not least our children. What's worse, the proposal's premise makes me shudder. I am a decent woman who would never disgrace my sister's memory.

-‹‹‹‹-

BOCA RATON. FLORIDA—where my parents winter in a gated, sixty-five-and-over condo park—is a thirty-minute drive from West Palm Beach, where we land.

"Give your grandma a hug," my mother says when we see her in the condo, making her teenage grandchildren squirm. My father waves from a leather club chair stationed by the window.

Elizabeth's death has aged my parents; grief gravels their voices and stoops their backs. My father hoists himself up on a creaky knee and crosses the carpet with his eyes down. Losing a sister is traumatic, but losing a child is catastrophic. Though my parents put on their best faces and kvell lovingly to show their joy, I can see them making the effort to do what used to come naturally.

"It's comfortable for us," my mother says, touring me around their spacious, two-bedroom condo. They leave Boston after Thanksgiving and return before Passover. If I manage to visit Florida once or twice during the winter, we don't have to go long without seeing each other.

There isn't enough room at my parents' for us all to have our own beds, so we decided Brooke and Alexandra would share the queen bed in the guest room, Lauren would take the sofa bed in the den because she likes to sleep alone, and Jake and I would stay at the Breakers Hotel in Palm Beach. But after all that happened on the plane, I'm now feeling nervous about the arrangement.

Jake checks his watch. "Samantha, we should check in, relax a little. Mom and Dad," he says to my parents, "I'll send a car to collect you and the kids for dinner. We have reservations at La Cucina, right near the hotel."

"Jake, how nice," my mother says. For the sake of her grandchildren, she has forgiven his harsh behavior during Elizabeth's decline.

"Well, there's going to be a lot of back-and-forth," Jake says. "I don't want Joseph driving at night." Gesturing to the ceiling, he adds, "Elizabeth's idea." He nods his head, luxuriating in his own good deed.

On our way to Breakers, Jake tells me I should book a massage. "Treat yourself," he says. "I'll take care of everything this weekend. Kick back and unwind."

I call the concierge from the car. I don't mention to Jake that the biggest bit of unwinding I need to do is from the bombshell he dropped on the plane. Thinking back to the pet names Jake had for Elizabeth and me as kids—Princess One and Princess Two—I shiver. Thankfully, the massage therapist has an opening.

I'm unpacking in my room and tense when I hear a knock at the door. Through the peephole, I'm relieved to see a young man with a folding table. The massage therapist's skin is bronzed, clearly that of someone who lives in Florida all year long. His white polo shirt and khaki shorts display muscular arms and legs with every bit of hair removed. As he sets up the table, I am still quite disturbed, but with warm lavender oil rubbed into my back, I surrender my anxieties and sleep.

Later, I meet everyone at La Cucina, a Southern Italian, red-sauce restaurant within walking distance of Breakers. We have reservations for a table outside, where we can still smell garlic from the kitchen.

As we take our seats, Jake pulls out my chair. "Here, next to me," he says in a voice that everyone can hear.

Uneasy, I say, "Mom, let me sit by you. I've decided I do want to learn bridge." Brooke plops herself down in the seat Jake intended for me.

The server takes our orders, and Jake asks the kids about their afternoon. "How do you like Grandma and Grandpa's new pad?"

"We saw the shuffleboard courts," Lauren says.

"And Grandma took us swimming," Alexandra says. "The water was so warm, like a bath."

My parents are the happiest I've seen them in a long time, since Elizabeth's diagnosis. "All my favorite people are here," my father says at one point. "We're just missing the New York Kaplans," my brother David and his family, "and, of course, my Elizabeth." I remember a moment after my sister was diagnosed: I told my father that I wished it were I. "Live for your husband and daughter. And don't *ever* say that again," he told me.

My mother updates us on her new bridge tournament, before going over some of the details of play. "Daddy saw my name on the board for coming in first," she says. "That was a treat."

Our teens talk among themselves, forking meatballs with one hand and holding their cell phones in the other, desperate not to miss a single text from a friend. They take pictures of their food, shoot selfies with the palm trees that canopy the patio, sticking out their tongues.

"Let's spend tomorrow here at the pool," Jake suggests. "I have an awesome cabana. The driver will pick you guys up at ten thirty. Okay?"

"Sounds good to us," my mother says, between bites of her eggplant parm, pleased that she'll have some to take home. It suddenly feels strange to be here without Elizabeth; she and my mother would have shared that dish before. I begin to realize that this trip to Florida, rather than assuaging my grief, is making me miss her even more.

"I want to let you all in on a little something," Jake says, and I can just tell by his expression that this announcement is going to be a doozy. Even before he's speaking, I'm saying no, but no sound is coming out.

"What's that?" my mother asks.

"Samantha and I are thinking about getting married," he says. He pulls a ring box from his blazer, and I gag on my osso bucco.

My parents' faces pale.

"That's gross," Lauren says.

"No, it's not," Jake says. "My grandfather married his wife's sister after she died. It's in the Bible."

"That was, like, a million years ago, Dad!" Brooke says.

"He's not serious," I say, and look sternly at Jake, then at my parents, who don't know what to make of this. Jake puts the ring box back in his pocket and frowns.

"What about my dad?" Alexandra whispers, as if she's about to weep.

"I'm still married to Dad, don't worry," I say.

After dinner, we put my parents and the kids back in a car to Boca Raton—I can tell my mother is nervous to leave—and Jake proposes a drink at the bar. It's already ten, and the music is revved up, singles meeting and grinding on the dance floor. A typical Palm Beach scene plays out: young men seek wealthy older women, widowed or divorced; young women with pumped-up breasts seek wealthy older men. The women wear Manolos, and the men wear Gucci shoes. I remember being here with Elizabeth on a trip in our early twenties—two older guys hit on us.

"No drink. This has been an emotional day. You have some nerve," I say.

"Marry me," he says, taking a knee. "It's the last time I'll ask, I promise. Marry me. Put an end to our grief."

"I will *never* stop grieving—do you hear me? I will miss Elizabeth for the rest of my life."

"We had a great love, but you were part of it."

"Bullshit," I say.

Jake swallows. "Stay with me. Just stay with me at the bar. Don't leave me here all alone," he whines.

"Good night," I say.

"The box was empty, no ring in it," Jake says, looking down. "I was joking around."

"I'm still going back," I say.

The rest of the weekend passes awkwardly. When it's time for us to return to Boston, my parents, the kids, and I share tearful goodbyes.

"So long. Stay well," my father says. He and my mother, according to family tradition, never mention what happened at La Cucina, and the kids, for better or for worse, follow their cue.

Chapter Twenty-Nine

———

*R*ichard beats me home from his golf trip in Cabo San Lucas. When I am back from Florida, he calls.

"Mind if I sleep over after the game?" he asks. He's on his way to see the Patriots at Gillette Stadium with a friend. It means that he will be coming in late, but I am touched that he has used the excuse.

"Sure," I say. "Come sleep at home."

Alexandra needs help with an English paper. We work together for several hours on a computer in my office while my phone charges upstairs.

I put Alexandra to bed and finish making a few edits that we discussed. Richard returns from the game at eleven and greets me in my office.

"Well, that game really stunk," he says.

"Oh, no," I say, even though my sport is really baseball.

"We got killed. I don't know what Belichick was thinking. I'm exhausted."

Richard trudges up the stairs. Before I know it, I hear his feet pound back down.

It turns out that Jake has been drunk-dialing and texting me for the past hour from Stella, where I had all of my boring dates with Steve. Upstairs, my phone has been buzzing and buzzing, and Richard picked it up. When he sees ten missed calls and five sloppy texts, he reads them.

"You're *marrying* him?" Richard screams.

My heart jumps into my throat. "No! What are you talking about?"

"Here." He shoves my BlackBerry in my face.

"Once we're married, you'll be rid of him," Jake wrote in his final text.

"FUCK YOU, it's Richard," Richard texted in response.

I scroll through the previous texts and gasp. They're about how bad Richard is and how I'm wasting my life by staying with him.

"How could you do this to me?" Richard says. "We've worked so hard to get on the right track." To my utter surprise, he begins to cry.

"Calm down. It's all a misunderstanding," I say, and put my arm around him.

"I don't believe you," Richard says.

"Jake's had too many drinks. Please," I say. All I want to do now is choke Jake.

"You would do that to Elizabeth?" Richard asks.

"No, you've got it all wrong. In Florida we spent time with my parents and the kids. I thought he was joking about marrying," I say.

Richard smacks his hand on the counter. "Don't lie to me! Only one of you thinks this is a joke."

Alexandra appears at the top of the stairs. In addition to having her English paper due, she has a math test tomorrow. "Why are you fighting?" she asks, her face scrunched in tears.

"I'm sorry," I say to Richard, a vein throbbing in his forehead. "I can imagine how this looks." I tell him to meet me upstairs. I tuck Alexandra back in and kiss her good night. "Don't worry, sweetie pie," I tell her.

When I come out of her bedroom, Richard is gone.

The next morning, I call Jake. "How *dare* you text me all that shit about Richard and marrying me last night?"

"I was out at a bar," he says, as if that explains everything.

"You are out of control. I get it—you feel like your life is ruined, so you have to ruin mine?" I consider that maybe Jake wasn't drunk at all and knew that Richard might see those texts. I realize that I have to keep my distance from Jake.

For the next week, Richard exiles himself to the office. He invents excuses for not getting on the phone, and we don't speak. I don't get a chance to explain myself. Richard is obviously angry and deeply hurt, and this time I can't blame him.

Friday evening, I dine at the bar at Aquitaine, where Elizabeth and I had many lunches. I order a glass of white wine and an appetizer, intending to be alone with my thoughts, but after a few sips I notice someone else at the bar. He's bald, wearing a sleek, stylish suit, flashing the bartender a charming smile. I can't help but notice that my bar companion is not wearing a wedding band.

We make eye contact, and he points at the stool next to me. "Anyone joining you?" he asks from down the bar.

I shake my head, suddenly glad for the company.

The man closes the distance between us. "Mind if . . ."

"Not at all," I say. The man takes the stool next to me. The bartender slides a rocks glass from his old seat to his new one.

I learn that he's visiting from San Francisco. He and his eleven-year-old daughter—whose photo he shows me on his phone, and who, he explains, is adopted from China—are visiting his parents in Newton, where he grew up, and where his parents still own a local bakery, whose bagels I happen to love.

"Where are you from?" he asks.

"Originally? Gloucester," I say, and my companion smiles instantly. He used to sail in Gloucester as a kid.

We chat a while longer, and I learn that he avoided the bagel business for a finance career in private equity. I wonder if he knows Richard.

"What are you doing at the bar alone?" he asks.

"You first," I say, and then relent. "My daughter is out with friends."

"My wife passed away two years ago," he says, drumming his fingers, then removes his glasses on the pretext of wiping a spot.

"I'm so sorry," I say, placing my hand on his arm—a member of my club. "How?"

"Breast cancer."

"Terrible. She must have been young."

He launches into the whole saga, and we order another round. He tells me how his wife discovered the lump, how they endured the chemo, the surgery, the radiation, this doctor and that specialist. How weak his wife became, how desperately they grasped for more time, how defiant she remained before death—to the end.

"My sister died last April," I tell him. "Lung cancer."

"Cancer sucks."

I tell him how Elizabeth survived chemo and radiation went to acupuncture and healers. "I attended every appointment for two and a half years—I think I only missed one that whole time."

"I'm so sorry," he says. "Closure is a fiction. That hole will always remain."

We continue to make small talk, and when he asks if I'm married, I tell him the truth: my husband and I are separated but trying to reconcile. I don't give the details.

Before he leaves, the man hands me a business card. "I hope things work out the way you want them to," he says. "If not, give me a call."

The attention feels good, even if the timing is wrong. I turn the card in my hand to read it. JEREMY CARLTON, it says. That whole time we spoke, I never even asked his name.

Over the weekend, I embrace my solitude, reflecting on the new and the disintegration of the old. I've expanded my activities to things that Elizabeth wouldn't do, places we never went, where no one knows that half of me was my sister. On a stroll down Newbury Street, I notice a flyer in a café and register for another writing class. This time in Boston.

Restaurants that Elizabeth never knew have opened. I dine and chat with maître d's who don't even know I had a sister. I buy a sweater at a chic boutique on the block between Clarendon and Dartmouth; Elizabeth will never see the sweater or the store. But these are the superficial things. It's Brooke's high school graduation, Lauren's prom, where my sister's absence will be felt most.

⋘

COMING OUT OF a café with my laptop—I've been working on an assignment from my teacher—I stumble upon a small white sign with bold blue print: SYNERGISTICS, PERSONAL TRAINING.

I check my watch. Plenty of time before I have to pick up Alexandra. Curious, I take the elevator to the fourth floor. The reception area is sparkling new, the gym floor springy and light. A handsome black man in his mid-thirties greets me. He's ripped, and he wears a tank top to prove it.

"I may be interested in joining," I say. If anyone can help me get definition in my arms, it's this guy. "What is this place?"

I scan the gym. Four trainers working one-on-one with clients, hip-hop beats loud, inspiring movement. I have a good feeling about this place. It solves a problem that I didn't even realize I had until I was standing here: if I work out here, I won't have to dodge everyone's sympathies in Wellesley. Not that I'm ungrateful, but I'm in the mood for anonymity.

"I'll give you a tour," the young man says. He extends his hand. "I'm Robbie."

We begin on Monday. I've belonged to a gym for twenty-five years, and although I'm fit, I want more definition and flat, sexy abs. To build strength, Robbie is all about form. Whether he's demonstrating a weight-assisted lunge or a bicep curl, I learn that I've been doing it all wrong.

"Arms tight," Robbie says. "It's not just repetition—it's deliberation. Straighten that elbow. Loose and flail, you'll never build muscle."

I close my eyes and concentrate.

"Better," Robbie says. He gently presses my shoulders back. "Shoulders down and back, but don't puff the chest—bring those lower ribs in, root lock." Robbie has me stop while he demonstrates what he's looking for. It's hard work, but I feel renewed, energetic. The workouts go quickly, and I always look forward to the next one.

"So, what do you do?" Robbie asks one day, as we're toweling off our faces.

"I'm a mother, and I've started writing."

"A writer?"

"Yes," I say, and pause. I write, but does that make me a writer? Should I tell Robbie about my writing? I don't think I can do it without mentioning my sister, so I hesitate, but I realize that censoring my past in this way will prevent Robbie from ever knowing me.

"My sister died recently," I say. "I've been writing about the two and a half years she lived with lung cancer."

"I'm so sorry," Robbie says, really taking it to heart.

"Thank you."

"I'd like to read some of your work sometime," he says kindly. Next time I come, I will bring him a short piece about Elizabeth.

·─◄◄◄◄·─

I'M THANKFUL RICHARD and I are still meeting with Broffman. When I meet with him individually, I broach the subject of Jake's text messages and then tell him about Richard's stepmother, the one who made Richard and his sisters feel like second-class citizens. It still hasn't come up in a couples' session. Once I'm settled on Broffman's well-worn leather sofa, I start in.

"Lately I've been thinking a lot about Richard's stepmother. I can see connections between Richard's childhood experiences with her and his behaviors as an adult," I say.

Broffman nods. "Can you explain?" he asks.

"He's talked to you about his stepmother, right?"

"I know that he had one. Not an especially loving woman. But I'm interested in your interpretation—please go on." I explain that the outsiderness Richard tends to feel in my family mirrors the outsiderness that his stepmother made him feel—at best, unimportant, but more like invisible. It could be the reason Richard won't settle for less than number one and wants to discard any group that he's not the center of.

Leaning forward, Broffman asks, "Have you shared your insights with Richard?"

"Whenever I mention it, he dismisses me," I say, but this is starting to sound like just an excuse, even to me. I sink in my seat.

"What have you discussed?" Broffman asks.

I tell Broffman that Richard's reflex is to see my family negatively.

"Say more," he says.

"I think my family dynamic brought back memories of his childhood that made him angry. I could see the anger and the blame. I didn't realize that it all stemmed from being deeply hurt," I say.

"This is a rich area. I will bring it up next time I'm with him," Broffman says.

When I tell him about Jake's text messages, Broffman says, "Those are a symptom of the problem. Not the problem itself." And I agree.

I tell Broffman how useful I found his email about understanding and evolving into better selves. Even if Richard and I do get divorced, I don't want to repeat old patterns with someone else. Even if we don't stay married, what I want sincerely in my heart is for Richard to break free of destructive patterns, too.

"You're a wise and compassionate young woman," Broffman says, and we laugh about the *young* part.

Later in the week, on a balmy, late Sunday in February, I'm enjoying a cup of coffee in a coat on my deck, having already taken the dogs out for a long walk in the neighborhood. The poodles snooze at my feet, contented and exhausted, twitching their ears at chirping birds. Having lived in the same house for over a decade, I am intimate with its sounds: the gentle clack of tree branches against the side of the house and the scurry of squirrels over the top of the fence. Then comes another familiar sound, but from a different time, and one I did not expect: the key in the door, the squeak and whine of hinges, and the tap of footsteps on my hardwood floor.

I turn, shielding my eyes in the sun, and see Richard standing in the kitchen.

"What are you doing here?" I ask, sliding open the glass door.

"I'm here to talk."

We move to the sunroom. Richard pats the seat on the sofa next to him.

"I had a session on Friday," he says. "Broffman brought up my stepmother."

"What about her?" I ask, grateful that the mediator followed through.

"He pointed out that her cruel actions might have scarred me more than I thought." Richard's eyes find the floor; he rubs the back of his neck, a rare posture of vulnerability. I have been working with Broffman on de-escalation and empathic listening. With an interested expression, I remain silent and hold the space for Richard to go on.

"When my mother died, my feelings had nowhere to go. I internalized them. Then, on top of that, my father married a woman with no concern for his kids. I have always blamed my stepmother for making us outsiders. What I never connected with is the anger I had when my dad died. When I married you, you were so close to your family, it was like I had chosen the same situation for myself, unconsciously. I blamed you and your family for making me the outsider, when really I was mad at myself."

"Have you always known that?" I ask, blown away.

"Are you kidding?" Richard laughs. "Knowing and saying this is a miracle."

"I did put my family's feelings over yours. I was defensive," I say. "I didn't think it was my responsibility to make a change, but there were certainly changes I could have made. I too repeated old patterns from my parents' marriage."

"I never wanted my own niece and nephew to hate me," he continues. "Now, seeing them without their mother reminds me of how I felt after my mother died. I cringe that I became such a villain in their lives. After all that I suffered, how could I do this to them?"

Richard trails off and starts to cry. I kiss the tears on his cheeks as they fall, and he embraces me. When he pulls away, he excuses himself and disappears into the bathroom. After splashing water on his face, he says he feels like a drink, but I'm concerned that it's not even noon. I'm still finishing my coffee.

"Let's go out to lunch," I suggest, "and keep the conversation going. There's a quiet place in Brookline I've been wanting to try."

In the car, Richard tells me that nothing he's said excuses Jake's behavior.

"Let's stay on track," I say, "probing what's behind our own actions, not speculating about others. But I have a different subject. Next Sunday is Elizabeth's unveiling. I think I want you to come."

"Let me think about it."

"It will be just the immediate family," I say. "Which means you're invited."

We park on Cypress Street in Brookline a block from the restaurant I had in mind, a little café with large storefront windows. The aroma of roast coffee and baked goods greets us. A hostess seats us at a cozy table near the back.

After we order, I again hold space for Richard to begin, but he falls silent. I look into his eyes and can see a softness revealed behind an old wall. We are both starting to see how we've hurt each other.

Chapter Thirty

———

$\mathcal{O}$n the Jewish tradition, it's customary that the unveiling of a permanent bronze plaque or other headstone takes place around the first anniversary of a loved one's death. Today is Elizabeth's unveiling, and we are gathered again at her gravesite.

The air is a chilly forty-eight degrees as Richard, Alexandra, and I drive the winding roads of Sharon Memorial Park. But, as with the year before, the spring flowers are popping through newly melted snow. At the gate, tulips overtake the crocuses.

Rabbi Goldberg arrives at the plot and greets us. The azaleas are again flowering in vibrant pink. A stately granite bench has been installed, bearing our three family names: Gordon, Kaplan, and Bloomberg. Elizabeth's grave is the slightly sunken earth next to my grandparents.

Today we are fourteen: my parents, Aunt and Uncle, David, Jill, Justin, and Brittany; Jake, Brooke, and Lauren; Richard, Alexandra, and me. Harrison is back in New York. When Richard decided to attend, everyone but Jake knew he was coming. Sensing this, Richard greets and shakes hands with everyone but the Gordons. They stay away from him as if he doesn't exist.

"Welcome," Rabbi Goldberg says. "We are here to honor

Elizabeth's memory." He chants prayers in Hebrew, and we join in English. Then my mother walks forward, pulls a piece of paper from her purse, and begins to read.

"Dear Elizabeth," my mother begins, then pauses to clear her throat. "We miss your big blue eyes. Life sure is different now. Brooke graduated high school this year and is a communications major at Syracuse, just like you advised her. Lauren is number one on the Weston tennis team. My baby, you should be so proud," she squeaks. My father joins her, leaning on a cane. His backaches from spinal stenosis have flared up around the unveiling.

"Elizabeth, my little girl," he says, speaking somewhere above our heads, "we will never forget you. We will honor you with our good deeds. Your memory will be blessed because it's all we have."

Alexandra, Brooke, Lauren and I visited Elizabeth at this site six months ago for her birthday. I threw a blanket over the fallen leaves, and we picnicked next to her grave. I packed tuna fish sandwiches, potato chips, and Elizabeth's favorite, chocolate cupcakes. Alexandra lit a candle, and Brooke and Lauren blew it out. When the girls scampered off to read old headstones, I dug a narrow hole near Elizabeth's shoulder and buried her birthday card rolled up like a scroll, then carefully replaced the grass.

After my parents speak, David, Jill, and the children find us and take our hands. "A year," David says, and shakes his head. Between my brother and me, we silently hold all the time we had Elizabeth and, increasingly, the lonely future years without her.

The rabbi removes the white cloth that covers the plaque, and my throat clenches. Seeing my sister's name in bronze still manages to shock me, her life and death now permanently etched: "Elizabeth Kaplan Gordon, November 1, 1959–April 30, 2006. Loving wife, mother, daughter, sister, aunt, and niece." Rabbi Goldberg leads us in Hebrew in the Mourner's Kaddish, which by now I know by heart: *Yit'gadal v'yit'kadash sh'mei raba . . .*

When we finish, Jake pulls his children toward him and erupts in sobs. Brooke and Lauren stare at the plaque, heads down, quiet tears dripping. The fourteen of us stand shoulder to shoulder, encircling Elizabeth's grave. My father blows his nose into his handkerchief with force, his cries sounding like harsh, dry coughs.

I feel the wind brush against my cheek as if it is a message from Elizabeth. "I miss you," I whisper, but she can't answer back.

Just before we leave, Brooke's face crumples and she kneels to kiss the earth where her mother lies. Alexandra, Richard, and I hold hands walking to the car. Jake did not acknowledge my husband's existence the entire service, which means he did not acknowledge me. I want to go home and hold my daughter tight.

The next day, I get a call from my lawyer, Jonathan Mann. He asks me what my timeline is for proceeding with the divorce.

"Richard asked me to try a mediator," I say, knowing that Broffman's goal is to help us stay married—and have a better marriage—and Mann's goal is to help me profit from a divorce.

"Is that what you want?" he asks. "You're certainly exhausting all options."

"I think it's working," I say. "There's been a shift."

"Shift how?"

"Richard is much less combative. We're both more understanding of the other." I explain how I've also taken responsibility for our conflict. "Maybe that's what it really means to be in love."

"Tread carefully, Samantha," Jonathan says. "I'm wary of your taking any responsibility. He might have an agenda. This has been going on for a long time. You said yourself it's taken a toll. Is he giving you enough money?"

"Whatever I need," I say. "Richard is initiating conversations with my mother and brother. He really wants to work things out."

"Let me know what you decide," Jonathan Mann says, and ends the call.

———

THE FOLLOWING WEEK, Richard calls my mother; they meet over coffee and cinnamon-raisin bagels. The situation with my mother is too painful for me to go along. Richard promises to keep the conversation productive and short.

My husband later tells me that he apologized for causing friction in our family, but not without placing a lot of the blame on Jake. He even told my mother about his stepmother, how left out she made him feel when he was a kid, and how my family's close-knit dynamic triggered emotions he wasn't aware he still had. He said my mother admitted that she had never thought too much about what it was like for him to join their family, all those long-standing relationships, but that when Elizabeth got sick, everyone had to focus on her. Richard told my mother that he and I wanted to give our marriage another try, and she gave him her blessing. She wanted peace in her family, my mother said, would love a second chance to love Richard like a son. They sealed their promises with a hug.

A few days later, Richard called David and then told me about their lengthy conversation. David's main concern was that he wanted to understand why Richard had disliked and disrespected Elizabeth. Richard said that Elizabeth and I were just too enmeshed, that he was wired to want more separation. But, in hindsight, he knew it wasn't fair to project his own discomfort onto my relationship with Elizabeth. If what he wanted was better intimacy with me, a stronger marriage, he hadn't gone about in the right way. Richard admitted that he had been rude and standoffish to Elizabeth; when the whole family turned against him, it was too painful for him to reverse on his own. David admitted that he and Jill often tried to avoid Richard when they came to town. Richard proposed that he and David move forward and not focus on the past, and David agreed.

Later that day, my brother calls me and says that he will try to renew his relationship with Richard if it makes me happy, that he loves me more than he dislikes Richard. Thankfully, my brother rarely holds grudges.

As for Jake, however, he has made it clear that he wants nothing to do Richard. And Richard wants nothing to do with him. I will never give up Brooke and Lauren and have made that crystal clear. Meanwhile, Jake has ended it with Julie from Providence and is ready to date someone new.

The following week, Richard and I go to dinner. He picks me up and hugs me in the kitchen, softer than the man I've been wary of all these years.

We park at one of his leased spaces, in the alley behind a brownstone, and walk down Boston's busiest shopping street to 29 Newbury. It's the restaurant where he and I had our first date. I am stunned. I was not expecting Richard to be so thoughtful.

The host seats us at the two-top in the window where we first dined twenty-three years ago. Glasses of chilled champagne await us, their bubbles setting off small fireworks against my upper lip.

We toast, and Richard declares proudly, "I did it—just like I said I would." He relays more details of his conversations and emails with my family, kindly. I don't detect a hint of sarcasm or malice.

"I really do want to make amends," Richard says. "I'm actually looking forward to better relationships." He laughs. "I know it will be a process." Then he takes my hand and we talk about *our* future. I am delighted, but, despite myself, my head fogs with the fallout of stressful holidays and birthday parties past. It's like I have marital PTSD and live in fear of it all repeating.

We finish our champagne, and I ask about menus, and Richard says, "Menus? This is just our first stop."

We stroll for a few blocks, hand in hand, before I realize that our next destination is Grill 23, where Richard and I had our second date. Richard's romantic side takes me completely by surprise. Where has this man been all my life? I can't help but be skeptical of whether it will last. My stomach gets queasy as we take our seats, and my smile tightens.

"Damn, I've missed you," Richard says, reaching for my hand over the white tablecloth. "No one could ever love you as much as I do right now."

"I really want to believe that," I say, carefully choosing the words to communicate my truth. "But how do you reconcile love with all of the tension churning in my family? My sister is dead," I say, grasping at a sudden anger I didn't know I had. "You don't get a second chance to have a relationship with Elizabeth. Neither do I."

"I only ever wanted us to be more of a unit—"

"You say you fell in love with me, but that's *who I was*."

Richard leans back in his chair.

"My intentions are good. I want things to work out. But I

need your help. Your loyalty. I can't be blamed for everything—"

"And you can't send all of the blame the other way," I say, remembering what Jonathan Mann warned me about Richard's having an agenda. "We are both responsible, Richard. From here on out, this marriage has to be a compromise."

"You have to make our family central from now on, Samantha. That's no compromise, just the terms of a good marriage. Broffman says so himself. You don't have to be the matriarch of your sister's and your brother's families. Can't you settle for being a good and caring aunt?"

I'm quiet. I haven't thought about this aspect of the issue, that I'm as guilty of reaching into my siblings' marriages as Elizabeth and Jake were of reaching into mine. Maybe Richard is right. But now Brooke and Lauren have lost their mother.

"I know I can't replace Elizabeth, but I will always play a central role in her children's lives," I say, tearing up.

"I love you, end of story. Let's be positive and focus on the good in each other," Richard says.

"Love alone isn't enough," I say. "I think we've learned that the hard way."

"Let's renew our wedding vows. Let me buy you a new diamond. A fresh beginning."

I stare into Richard's eyes, testing what I see there, and my true fear articulates itself: Can I commit to being the kind of partner that Richard deserves?

The sommelier interrupts us, pouring Perrier-Jouët Belle Epoque into flutes. Without our ordering a thing, two servers appear behind him with a small plate of tuna tartare, a whole-roasted striped bass, and beef tenderloin au jus.

"To us," Richard toasts. We clink glasses and dig into the food. Tartare melts on my tongue from a crisp cracker. Richard fillets the fish. "I want to move home," he says when he's completed the deboning.

I am unsure about taking this step and say nothing in response. We eat in silence. I look away from Richard several times, gazing into the restaurant, crowded with couples savoring the food and the romantic atmosphere. I miss my sister. She was my sustenance. I can see how it comes between me and the moment, my enjoyment of the life she no longer has. If I stay with Richard, I need to find a way to live in the present and not resent Richard for what is gone.

Richard stays over that night. We trade apologies on the pillow.

"I'm sorry for not being in touch with my anger," he says. "I could have shared my feelings, instead of mistreating you and your family. Too much time of not being able to find peace with each other has gone by."

I am deeply touched. After all these years of feeling wounded when Richard didn't validate my feelings, I don't intend to make the same mistake. I have gone through many struggles to hold on to my marriage.

"I'm sorry for not trying to understand you better," I say.

MY FIFTIETH BIRTHDAY approaches, and while I usually love to celebrate, fifty sounds old. It's also my first birthday without Elizabeth. Lynne and Nancy plan a special day but keep it a surprise. The three of us chat in Nancy's car, killing time, at the delicious mercy of their whims. "Where are you taking me?" I ask, as we enter the parking lot of Temple Shalom in Newton.

"It's a spiritual surprise," Lynne says. She has always been thoughtful. Scanning the building, I notice a tiny white sign with black letters: MAYYIM HAYYIM MIKVEH.

"A mikveh?" I ask, surprised. A ritual bath is the last thing I expected. "Don't you have to be Orthodox? Or converting?"

My friends smile conspiratorially.

We head into the small brick building, and the director of the mikveh greets us, explaining how nearly every religious tradition uses immersion to mark change and transformation. In Jewish tradition, water signifies the journey when the Hebrews left Egypt via the waters of the Red Sea, passing from slavery to freedom. She gives us a tour.

Walking the bright space, I learn that Mayyim Hayyim is more than just a mikveh. It's a resource for learning, spiritual discovery, and creativity, a place where people celebrate milestones like weddings and conversions. Where people like me can find solace in the midst of loss.

I try not to blanch as I read these lines in a pamphlet from the director: "The mikveh pool recalls the watery state that each of us knew before we were born. The ritual of entering and leaving *mayyim hayyim*, living waters, creates the time and space to acknowledge and embrace a new stage of life."

The director's hand on my shoulder interrupts my reading. "I know you lost your dear sister," she says quietly. "This is one way to embrace the future."

"I'll give anything a try," I say, touched that someone recognizes my deep suffering. It's all beginning to make sense.

I smile at Lynne and Nancy. They beam as if they invented the mikveh themselves.

The director shoos my friends into a waiting room, where they will pass the time while I partake in this ceremony.

The director closes the door and leads me alone into a cavernous room with private mikveh pools and showers. A silver railing and three stairs lead down to the pool where I will submerge myself to mark my fiftieth birthday and the end of my mourning. A year to mourn, and then we must move forward, tradition tells me. It's not fair to the living, who need our love and attention, to wallow, and it's not fair to ourselves. I am grateful to religion for setting boundaries that I never could have made myself.

I enter the changing room to shower and wet my hair. The waters beckon, offering great possibilities. As I lower myself into the mikveh, of course I think of Elizabeth. Without her, I have become a stranger to myself. A year ends my mourning but commences an even longer period that I'll need to heal.

The tepid water is soothing. I immerse myself completely, even my head, and surrender my final tears to the bath. Surfacing, I exhale and breathe in the sacred air, then submerge again.

Below the water, I begin to forgive. Forgiveness for Elizabeth dying, and for Richard's inability to love me in the way that I wanted. Self-forgiveness for being who I needed to be and not the wife Richard felt he deserved. Self-forgiveness for not being able to prevent everyone's pain.

Coming up for air, I recite the ancient words written by Rabbi Nachman of Breslov: "Strengthen my ailing body, soothe my aching heart, mend my shattered existence, make me whole."

A second chance.

Book Club Questions

1. Why do you think Elizabeth's husband Jake accepted her close relationship with Samantha and Samantha's husband Richard could not?

2. What was Samantha's part in the love triangle between her, Elizabeth and Richard?

3. Do you feel Richard's demands at the beginning were based on not wanting to lose Samantha? Did he want something from her that she and Elizabeth had?

4. Do you think Samantha felt in some way responsible for Elizabeth's illness?

5. What do you think of how Jake handled Elizabeth's illness?

6. What about Richard's reaction?

7. How do you think Samantha's and Elizabeth's parents were treated by their son-in-laws?

8. How could the family have managed their reactions to Elizabeth's illness differently? Do you think they had unrealistic hope?

9. Do you think Samantha is defined by her care taking role?

10. Do you think Samantha and Richard will end up staying married? What would you do in a similar situation?

11. What is the significance of the title *Appearances*?

12. Discuss the concept of having enough love in one's heart for a husband and a sister.

Acknowledgments

First, I would like to thank Eve Bridburg, founder and executive director of GrubStreet, which has become a second home for me and has been instrumental in my writing journey. When I began taking classes ten years ago, I was impressed with the rigorous teaching, encouragement, and empathy I received from my instructors and fellow students.

I owe deep gratitude to Pagan Kennedy (whom I met at the Muse and the Marketplace) and Karen Propp for their wisdom and editorial insights into my story, right at the beginning. They inspired me to keep writing.

I want to thank Katie Willis and Trish Ryan for their comprehensive and thoughtful manuscript consultations.

I want to thank Stuart Horwitz and his Book Architecture method (*Blueprint Your Bestseller*) for believing in my story and helping me with the structure of this novel.

I want to thank Grace Talusan for her undying support, instruction on craft, and exceptional feedback after reading my early and later drafts of this novel.

I want to thank Ethan Gilsdorf, whose insightful feedback on portions of my manuscript during his essay classes was immeasurable.

I want to thank Andrew Goldstein, from SixOneSeven Books, for caring and encouraging me to delve deeper.

I want to thank Kerry Cohen for her advice on many of my chapters when I took her online class at Gotham Writers Workshop.

Thank you to Kathryn Kay, from Nantucket Writers Studio and A Writer Within, who helped me hone my early work.

I am grateful to Dani Shapiro, Hannah Tinti, and Michael Maren for giving me the opportunity to attend their Sirenland Writers Conference with a group of talented writers and teachers.

Thank you to Judy Katz from Katz Creative for her constructive feedback.

Thank you to Brooke Warner and Lauren Wise from She Writes Press for their belief in my story.

Thank you to Annie Tucker from She Writes Press for her superb copyedit.

Many, many thanks for the enthusiasm from my friends and family members who read various drafts of this novel.

Thank you to my sister-in-law for her support and insight right from the beginning of this incredible journey.

Deep gratitude to my daughter and my mother for their love, wisdom, and undying faith in me.

A big thank you to my husband for his generous support during the years of me taking classes and writing endless hours a day to complete this novel.

Finally, I want to thank Dawn Dorland, my amazing editor, whose brilliant feedback on characterization, conflict, and plot was invaluable to the completion of this novel.

About the Author

SONDRA HELENE is a board member and writer at GrubStreet, Boston's Center for Literary Life. She is a graduate of Ithaca College and received her master's degree at Columbia University. She lives in Boston with her husband and two poodles. This is her first novel.

Twitter @SondraHelene
Facebook Sondra Helene
Instagram SondraHelene

SELECTED TITLES FROM SHE WRITES PRESS

She Writes Press is an independent publishing company
founded to serve women writers everywhere.
Visit us at www.shewritespress.com.

Shelter Us by Laura Diamond. $16.95, 978-1-63152-970-2. Lawyer-turned-stay-at-home-mom Sarah Shaw is still struggling to find a steady happiness after the death of her infant daughter when she meets a young homeless mother and toddler she can't get out of her mind—and becomes determined to rescue them.

Appetite by Sheila Grinell. $16.95, 978-1-63152-022-8. When twenty-five-year-old Jenn Adler brings home a guru fiancé from Bangalore, her parents must come to grips with the impending marriage—and its effect on their own relationship.

Play for Me by Céline Keating. $16.95, 978-1-63152-972-6. Middle-aged Lily impulsively joins a touring folk-rock band, leaving her job and marriage behind in an attempt to find a second chance at life, passion, and art.

American Family by Catherine Marshall-Smith. $16.95, 978-1631521638. Partners Richard and Michael, recovering alcoholics, struggle to gain custody of their Richard's biological daughter from her grandparents after her mother's death only to discover they —and she—are fundamentalist Christians.

The Geometry of Love by Jessica Levine. $16.95, 978-1-938314-62-9. Torn between her need for stability and her desire for independence, an aspiring poet grapples with questions of artistic inspiration, erotic love, and infidelity.

Peregrine Island by Diane B. Saxton. $16.95, 978-1-63152-151-5. The Peregrine family's lives are turned upside-down one summer when so-called "art experts" appear on the doorstep of their Connecticut island home to appraise a favorite heirloom painting—and incriminating papers are discovered behind the painting in question.